CW01207372

Charles Lamb, Coleridge and Wordsworth

Charles Lamb, Coleridge and Wordsworth

Reading Friendship in the 1790s

Felicity James

palgrave
macmillan

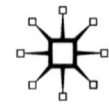

© Felicity James 2008

All rights reserved. No reproduction, copy or transmission of this publication may be made without written permission.

No portion of this publication may be reproduced, copied or transmitted save with written permission or in accordance with the provisions of the Copyright, Designs and Patents Act 1988, or under the terms of any licence permitting limited copying issued by the Copyright Licensing Agency, Saffron House, 6-10 Kirby Street, London EC1N 8TS.

Any person who does any unauthorized act in relation to this publication may be liable to criminal prosecution and civil claims for damages.

The author has asserted her right to be identified as the author of this work in accordance with the Copyright, Designs and Patents Act 1988.

First published 2008 by
PALGRAVE MACMILLAN

Palgrave Macmillan in the UK is an imprint of Macmillan Publishers Limited, registered in England, company number 785998, of Houndmills, Basingstoke, Hampshire RG21 6XS.

Palgrave Macmillan in the US is a division of St Martin's Press LLC, 175 Fifth Avenue, New York, NY 10010.

Palgrave Macmillan is the global academic imprint of the above companies and has companies and representatives throughout the world.

Palgrave® and Macmillan® are registered trademarks in the United States, the United Kingdom, Europe and other countries.

ISBN-13: 978–0–230–54524–3 hardback
ISBN-10: 0–230–54524–6 hardback

This book is printed on paper suitable for recycling and made from fully managed and sustained forest sources. Logging, pulping and manufacturing processes are expected to conform to the environmental regulations of the country of origin.

A catalogue record for this book is available from the British Library.

A catalog record for this book is available from the Library of Congress.

10 9 8 7 6 5 4 3 2 1
17 16 15 14 13 12 11 10 09 08

Transferred to digital printing in 2009.

Contents

List of Abbreviations	viii
Acknowledgements	xi
Permissions	xiii
Introduction: Placing Lamb	1

Part I Idealising Friendship

1 *Frendotatoi meta frendous*: Constructing Friendship
    in the 1790s — 13
    December 1794 — 13
    'Bowles, Priestley, Burke': The *Morning Chronicle* sonnets — 18
    New readings of familial and friendly affection — 24
    Pantisocracy and the 'family of soul' — 26
    Unitarian readings of friendship — 30
    Sensibility and benevolence — 34
    Reading David Hartley — 39
    Readings of feeling in Coleridge and Lamb — 43
    Lamb's sensibilities: two early sonnets — 47

2 Rewritings of Friendship, 1796–1797 — 55
    Spring 1796 — 55
    Coleridge's rewritings of Lamb — 56
    Trapped in the Bower: Coleridgean reflections in retirement — 62
    'Ears of Sympathy': Lamb's sympathetic response — 71
    Rewritings of Coleridge — 74

Part II Doubting Friendship

3 The 'Day of Horrors' — 83
    September 1796 — 83
    Aftermath — 85
    Reconstructing the poetry of familial affection — 91
    Nether Stowey: 'an Elysium upon earth'? — 96

4	**'Cold, Cold, Cold': Loneliness and Reproach**	**101**
	June 1797	101
	'Gloomy boughs' and sunny leaves: the Wordsworth-Coleridge conversation	103
	Visions of unity: *This Lime-tree Bower my Prison*	105
	The Overcoat and the Manchineel: Lamb's response	111
	The 'Reft House' of the 'Nehemiah Higginbottom' sonnets	114
5	***Blank Verse* and Fears in Solitude**	**120**
	February 1798	120
	Blank Verse and *Lyrical Ballads*	125
	Midnight reproach	130
	'Living without God in the World'	134
	Edmund Oliver: forging a 'common identity'	136
	Coleridge and the 'lying Angel'	139

Part III Reconstructing Friendship

6	**A Text of Friendship: *Rosamund Gray***	**145**
	Spring 1798	145
	Anxieties of friendship: letters to Robert Lloyd	146
	'Inscribed in friendship': the sensibility of *Rosamund Gray*	149
	The novel's family loyalties	152
	Rosamund Gray and *The Ruined Cottage*	155
	Communities of feeling in *Rosamund Gray*	163
7	**Sympathy, Allusion, and Experiment in *John Woodvil***	**167**
	Late 1798	167
	Redemptive family narratives	169
	Elian identifications	173
	Forgeries and medleys: Lamb's imitations of Burton	176
	'Friend Lamb': *John Woodvil* and its readers	177
	Reading and resistance: 'What is Jacobinism?'	180
8	**The Urban Romantic: Lamb's Landscapes of Affection**	**185**
	Early 1801	185
	Reading *Lyrical Ballads* (1800)	188
	Lamb's Wordsworthian attachments	195
	The voice of the 'Londoner'	200

'The greatest egotist of all': some Elian sympathies	203
Wordsworth's readings of Lamb	210
Lamb's afterlives	211
Notes	215
Bibliography	240
Index	251

List of Abbreviations

AA 1799	*Annual Anthology*, vol I, ed. Robert Southey (Bristol, 1799).
AA 1800	*Annual Anthology*, vol II, ed. Robert Southey (Bristol, 1800).
BiogLit	*Biographia Literaria, or, Biographical Sketches of My Literary Life and Opinions*, eds, Walter Jackson Bate and James Engell, Bollingen Collected Coleridge Series 7, 2 vols (London, 1983).
Borderers	William Wordsworth, *The Borderers*, ed. Robert Osborn (Ithaca, NY, 1982).
BV	Charles Lloyd and Charles Lamb *Blank verse, by Charles Lloyd and Charles Lamb* (London, 1798).
CLB	*Charles Lamb Bulletin*.
Curry	*New Letters of Robert Southey*, ed. Kenneth Curry, 2 vols (New York, 1965).
Early Poems	William Wordsworth, *Early Poems and Fragments, 1785–97*, eds, Carol Landon and Jared Curtis (Ithaca, NY, 1997).
EO	Charles Lloyd, *Edmund Oliver*, 2 vols (Bristol, 1798).
EY	*Letters of William and Dorothy Wordsworth: The Early Years, 1787–1805*, ed. Ernest de Selincourt; 2nd ed. rev. Chester L. Shaver (Oxford, 1967).
Friend	Samuel Taylor Coleridge, *The Friend*, ed. Barbara E. Rooke, Bollingen Collected Coleridge Series 4, 2 vols (London, 1969).
FS	Samuel Taylor Coleridge, *Fears in solitude, written in 1798, during the alarm of an invasion. To which are added, France, an ode; and Frost at midnight. By S.T. Coleridge.* (London, 1798).
Griggs	*Collected Letters of Samuel Taylor Coleridge*, ed. Earl Leslie Griggs, 6 vols (Oxford, 1956–71).
Howe	*The Complete Works of William Hazlitt*, ed. P. P. Howe, 21 vols (London, 1930–34).
JW	*John Woodvil: a Tragedy. By C. Lamb. To which are added Fragments of Burton, the author of the Anatomy of Melancholy* (London, 1802).

Lectures 1795	Samuel Taylor Coleridge, *Lectures 1795: On Politics and Religion*, eds, Peter Mann and Lewis Patton, Bollingen Collected Coleridge Series 1 (London, 1971).
Lucas	*The Works of Charles and Mary Lamb*, ed. E. V. Lucas, 8 vols (London, 1912).
Lucas, *Letters*	*The Letters of Charles Lamb, to which are added those of his sister, Mary Lamb*, ed. E. V. Lucas, 3 vols (London, 1935).
LY	*The Letters of William and Dorothy Wordsworth; Second Edition, Volume VII, The Later Years, Part IV, 1840–53*, rev. ed. Alan G. Hill (Oxford, 1988).
LyB	William Wordsworth, *Lyrical Ballads and Other Poems, 1797–1800*, eds, James Butler and Karen Green (Ithaca, NY, 1992).
Marrs	*The Letters of Charles and Mary Anne Lamb*, ed. Edwin W. Marrs, 3 vols (Ithaca, NY, 1975).
Mays	*Poetical Works of Samuel Taylor Coleridge*, ed. J. C. C. Mays, Bollingen Collected Coleridge Series 16, 3 (2 part) vols (Princeton, 2001).
MLN	*Modern Language Notes.*
MLQ	*Modern Language Quarterly.*
MM	*The Monthly Magazine.*
N&Q	*Notes and Queries.*
Notebooks	*The Notebooks of Samuel Taylor Coleridge*, eds, Kathleen Coburn, Merton Christensen and Anthony John Harding, 5 vols (Princeton, 1957–2002).
Poems 1796	Samuel Taylor Coleridge, *Poems on Various Subjects* (Bristol, 1796).
Poems 1797	Samuel Taylor Coleridge, Charles Lamb, Charles Lloyd, *Poems on Various Subjects* (Bristol, 1797).
Poems 1807	William Wordsworth, *Poems, in Two Volumes, and Other Poems, 1800–1807*, ed. Jared Curtis (Ithaca, NY, 1983).
PJ	William Godwin, *An Enquiry concerning Political Justice* (1793), vol. 3 in *Political and Philosophical Writings of William Godwin*, ed. Mark Philp, 5 vols (London, 1993).
Prelude 1799	William Wordsworth, *'The Prelude', 1798–1799*, ed. Stephen Parrish (Ithaca, NY, 1977).
Prelude 1805	William Wordsworth, *The Thirteen-Book Prelude*, ed. Mark L. Reed, 2 vols (Ithaca, NY, 1991).

PW	*The Prose Works of William Wordsworth*, eds, W. J. B. Owen and Jane Worthington Smyser, 3 vols (Oxford, 1974).
RC	William Wordsworth, *The Ruined Cottage and The Pedlar*, ed. James Butler (Ithaca, NY, 1979). Following Butler's identification of drafts, I use MS B to refer to the 528 line poem of January-March 1798, and MS D to refer to the 538 line copy of the poem made by Dorothy Wordsworth in a pocket notebook between February – December 1799.
RES	*Review of English Studies.*
RG	Charles Lamb, *A Tale of Rosamund Gray and old Blind Margaret* (London, 1798).
SEL	*Studies in English Literature.*
SiR	*Studies in Romanticism.*
Specimens	Charles Lamb, *Specimens of English Dramatic Poets, Who Lived about the Time of Shakspeare* (London, 1808).
Watchman	Samuel Taylor Coleridge, *The Watchman*, ed. by Lewis Patton, Bollingen Collected Coleridge Series 2 (London, 1970).
WC	*The Wordsworth Circle.*
Works 1818	*The Works of Charles Lamb*, 2 vols (London, 1818).
YCL	Winifred Courtney, *Young Charles Lamb, 1775–1802* (London: 1982).

I have given all references to plays in the format Act: scene: line, and all references to poems by line number (if available); title of edition, page number. Multipart volumes are in the format volume number: volume part: page number.

Acknowledgements

Appropriately enough, this book bears the traces of many friendly readings, much generous help, and plenty of sociable conversation. I enjoyed many fruitful discussions with Romanticists at Oxford throughout my graduate studies, especially at the Romantic Realignments seminar. Thanks to the Friends of Coleridge, including Seamus Perry, Paul Cheshire, Graham Davidson and Nicholas Roe, for their help, including thoughtful comments, grants to attend their conferences, and walks over the Quantocks. And, of course, the book owes an important debt to the Elian friendliness, good humour, and learning of all the members of the Charles Lamb Society, including (among many others) Mary Wedd, D. E. Wickham, Nicholas and Cecilia Powell, and Michel Jolibois who very kindly gave me his E. V. Lucas editions. The society has given me great encouragement, and also financial and practical help. Moreover, it was reading the splendid work of the Charles Lamb Bulletin as an undergraduate which first sparked my interest in Lamb.

I want to express my deep thanks also to the academics who not only first inspired me with their work but have also given me generous and friendly help and advice: Lucy Newlyn, David Fairer, Josephine McDonagh, and Duncan Wu. David Fairer's book, *Organising Poetry: The Coleridge Circle 1790–1798*, will appear too late for me to make use of it as I would have liked to do; however, I have been very grateful for his scholarship, as for his suggestions and conversation. Peter Conrad was an inspirational undergraduate tutor, and I owe a great deal to Angela Trueman's teaching. This book was completed during a British Academy Postdoctoral Fellowship, for which I am very grateful. I held this through the English Faculty at Oxford which also facilitated my research in various ways, and whose assistance I acknowledge with thanks. Thanks too to the staff of various libraries, including the Firestone Library, Princeton, the British Library, the Bodleian, and, especially, the staff of the English Faculty Library, Oxford, who were unfailingly helpful and cheerful. I owe a special debt to Christ Church which as well as academic help and support has provided me with a friendly second home.

I want to thank many friends for reading and commenting on various versions of chapters. Monika Class helped a great deal through seminar discussion and her very useful comments; so too did David

O'Shaughnessy, David Fallon, Karen Junod and Greg Leadbetter. Mina Gorji's helpful readings and sociable library presence helped the book along. David Higgins and Kelly Grovier also discussed their own work generously with me, and thanks too to Gurion Taussig, Tim Milnes, Simon Hull, and Anthony Harding. Stephen Bernard tirelessly read, proof-read, and advised. Any mistakes are entirely down to my negligence, or stubbornness.

Thanks too for the friendship and help of others, including Jim and Joyce Margison, Verity Platt, Beatrice Groves, Geno Maitland Hudson, Elizabeth O'Mahoney, Paul Wiley and Aideen Lee. And of course Aileen Collings for the literary sociability of Crown Street. Those in college also helped a great deal, including Thomas Karshan and Alex Harris, whose friendship was very important and whose suggestions were always helpful and enlivening – and of course the Christ Church custodians and porters, including Henry, Rab, Ferdie, Tony, Wilbert, and Philip Tootill, who all added a great deal to college life.

But the most important debts are to Peter Collings and my family: my parents, and my sisters, Penny and Haoli, who have all had to accept Charles Lamb as a permanent companion in their lives. They are behind this book's faith in the 'home-born Feeling'. Haoli's reassurance and Peter's great support helped get this written, and I could never have embarked on it at all without the help of my long-suffering parents, Margaret and Teddy James, to whom this book is lovingly dedicated.

Permissions

I am grateful to the *Coleridge Bulletin* for allowing me to reprint in Chapters 4 and 5 some material first used in two articles, 'The Many Conversations of "This Lime-Tree Bower"', *Coleridge Bulletin* 26 (Winter 2005), and 'Coleridge and the Fears of Friendship, 1798' *Coleridge Bulletin* 24 (Winter 2004). I am also grateful to the *Charles Lamb Bulletin* for allowing me to reprint material from the article, 'Sweet is thy sunny hair: an unpublished poem by Charles Lamb', *CLB* 127 (2004), 54–6.

Introduction: Placing Lamb

On 9 July 1798, the 36th and last issue of *The Anti-Jacobin* carried a long poem, *New Morality*, a lively, vehement condemnation of 'Jacobin' attitudes and associates, which targeted Whig politicians and radical writers alike. Parodying the 'Theo-Philanthropic sect' of revolutionary sympathisers, French and English, it attacked their 'mawkish' sensibilities and 'blasphemous' sedition, and was illustrated the following month by the ruthless cartoonist James Gillray.[1] To feature in one of his cartoons – albeit distorted and undignified – was to have arrived on the political scene, and his bestiary of revolutionaries, capering around a deconsecrated St. Paul's, clearly showed who were the main 'Jacobin' targets of the government in the late 1790s. The Duke of Bedford dominates the image, a monstrous whale whose inspiration, as the poem shows, comes from Edmund Burke's *Letter to a Noble Lord*.[2] Astride him are Charles James Fox and other Whig politicians, while William Godwin, a little donkey, and Thomas Holcroft, a snapping crocodile, scamper around. Before him, like Swift's image of the tub thrown to a whale, is a cornucopia of seditious literature. Pouring out come pamphlets and Whig newspapers – Mary Wollstonecraft's *Wrongs of Woman*, the *Enquirer*, the *Monthly Magazine* – pounced on by a donkey-eared Robert Southey, whilst Samuel Taylor Coleridge, also depicted as an ass, waves some *Dactylics* triumphantly. It is a reworking of Spenser's monster of Error, whose 'vomit full of bookes and papers was,/With loathly frogs and toades'.[3] And indeed, in the very middle of the cartoon, just at the foot of the cornucopia, sit a toad and a frog, croaking in glee as they clutch their own work, *Blank Verse* (1798). Charles Lloyd and Charles Lamb are right at the heart of this panorama of dangerous radicals.

Yet even as the other figures from the cartoon – Godwin, Holcroft, Southey – are restored to the narrative of 1790s Romanticism, Lamb and

Lloyd tend to be excluded. *Blank Verse* remains obscure, unread: we have now forgotten about this other collaborative volume of 1798, whose experimental poetics of radical simplicity pre-empted *Lyrical Ballads*, and whose authors were once regarded as a 'Jacobin' threat. Such overlooked works – which sometimes nestle in close proximity to much better known counterparts – form the central focus of this book, which makes the case for the reconsideration and replacing of Lamb in the literary, cultural, and historical life of the 1790s, one of the most productive periods of his early career.

Part of the reason Lamb has been largely overlooked is the difficulty of placing him in the period. His politics were never overt or easily categorised; even some of his contemporaries were baffled by his inclusion in the *Anti-Jacobin* cartoon. 'I know not what poor Lamb has done to be croaking there,' Southey commented, and his confusion has echoed through the nineteenth and twentieth centuries.[4] 'No one could be more innocent than Lamb of political heresy' asserted his Victorian editor and friend Thomas Noon Talfourd.[5] The great Elian E. V. Lucas – whose 1912 edition of the Lambs is still standard – agreed that the writings of Lamb and Lloyd 'were as far removed from Jacobinism as from bimetallism'.[6] For Talfourd and Lucas there is something comforting, even noble, about Lamb's apparent apolitical stance, a willed innocence which transcends worldly ties. For others, Lamb's evasiveness has been deeply frustrating. Apparently more interested in roast pig than Peterloo, Lamb's attention to the homely, the domestic and the familiar has been regarded with suspicion. Complacent, self-indulgent, interested in 'drink, gastronomy and smoking,' thundered Denys Thompson, while for Cyril Connolly, Lamb takes after Addison, an 'apologist for the New Bourgeoisie'.[7] For these critics of the 1930s, alert to the menace of war, Lamb is 'the bourgeois house-holder who lets the firebugs into his attic', who turns away from political threat to admire a tea-cup.[8]

Although this outcry soured Lamb's reputation through the mid-twentieth century, and probably triggered his gradual disappearance from school and university syllabuses, more recently this same evasiveness and resistance to categorisation has prompted some exciting criticism of both Charles and Mary Lamb.[9] The research of Burton Pollin and Winifred F. Courtney in the 1970s showed us how to read the *Anti-Jacobin* cartoon, demonstrating the ways in which Lamb was deeply – if idiosyncratically – involved with political thought of the period.[10] Jane Aaron's seminal monograph on the Lambs similarly showed the shaping importance of their historical and cultural context, while emphasising the complexity of their own attitudes, the way in which the 'swerves and slippages of their language' register 'a number of apparently contradictory possibilities'.[11] Recent work has furthered our sense of the ambiguities of the Lambs' place in social and literary history. Mary Lamb has begun to receive sustained critical and biographical attention, and Elia's complex political and stylistic negotiations with his *London Magazine* context have been freshly analysed in the last few years.[12] Karen Fang has argued for an imperialist Elia, whose essays offer 'an inclusive, consumer version of the romantic tradition'.[13] Denise Gigante has similarly emphasised Lamb's consumerist power: re-reading the gluttony of Edax and Lamb's own ready appetite for snipes, plum-cake and brawn, she sees his sensual gustatory pleasures as a knowing 'assertion of low-urban taste' which critiques and challenges Romantic ideals of 'pure aesthetic subjectivity'.[14] Gigante's stimulating readings mark a welcome rediscovery of Lamb's lesser-known work, also evident in Judith Plotz's analysis of the sometimes disturbing imagery of children – child-sweeps, boiled babies, Child-Angels – in his later poetry, essays, conversation and letters.[15] The neglected drama *John Woodvil* (1802) has similarly been discussed very usefully by Anya Taylor as a way into understanding the shifting identities of Lamb's drunken selves.[16] It is an unsettling, disconcerting, provocative Lamb who emerges from these new readings – a belated response to Mary Wedd's 1977 call for us to 'put the guts back into Charles Lamb', and an acknowledgement that the suspicions of the *Anti-Jacobin* might not have been misplaced.[17]

I want to continue and expand these exciting new readings of Lamb back into the 1790s: he needs to be fully replaced in the context of these rough politicised exchanges of the revolutionary decade. Not only do Lamb's early works merit rediscovery and re-reading – he is also crucially important as a friend and shrewd reader of others in the period.[18] Exploring the constant negotiations taking place within his 1790s friendships, I show how his complicated political allegiances are interwoven with personal attitudes and arguments. I argue that certain enduring principles and loyalties underpin Lamb's writing – such as his background in religious Dissent – creating what Joseph Nicholes has termed Lamb's 'politics by indirection'.[19] The *Anti-Jacobin* satirists were right to place Lamb in the midst of Unitarians such as Joseph Priestley, whom he deeply admired. Such Unitarian allegiances helped to inform the ideal of friendship and sympathetic feeling which lies at the very centre of Lamb's creative and social identity. Having understood the importance of this ideal, we can then see more clearly the deeper implications of his persistent focus on the homely and personal – and of his familiar, allusive style.

What looks at first glance like Burkean conservatism might very well be a beleaguered statement of Unitarian radical belief in home and family. A domestic quarrel amongst friends might have much larger ideological implications. An allusion to a friend's poem can open into a fierce political and literary dialogue, where attitudes to friendship, reading and writing, and society are simultaneously negotiated. I want to restore our sense of why that friendly pairing of Lamb and Lloyd – and their apparently innocuous verse of friendship – might have been viewed as dangerous by the *Anti-Jacobin*.

Although this book is about how friendship was read by (and in regard to) Lamb and his circle in the period, it is also about the importance of reading in these friendships. These were relationships forged through shared reading and mutual criticism, expressed through poems dedicated to one another and in dialogue with each other's work. Lamb is especially important as an intermediary, constantly reading and re-writing the works of his friends. Drawing both upon his Unitarian convictions and upon his eclectic and diverse explorations of literature, Lamb produces his own versions of Coleridge poems, and uses Wordsworthian techniques to describe his own urban experiences. In his diverse work of the period – letters, poetry, a novel, a drama and some playful forgeries – he responds on both a literary and an emotional level to his changing friendships with Wordsworth, Coleridge, and Lloyd. Phrases and ideas are transformed as they move from one context to another, from a letter by Lamb to a poem by Coleridge, from the private to the public sphere, and back again. While there is an enduring interest in the relationship between Wordsworth and Coleridge, Lamb remains the missing link. Reading his little-known works alongside, say, Coleridge's contributions to the *Monthly Magazine, Osorio, The Borderers,* or *Lyrical Ballads,* allows a much fuller insight into the creative dynamics of early Romanticism, and of Romantic friendship. Meshed together through allusion, quotation, echo, and personal reference, these works create a larger conversation of friendship: coded, deeply allusive, politically inflected.

Tuning into these multiple voices, or exploring the *Anti-Jacobin*'s rowdy bestial panorama of radicals, runs counter to a key myth of Romanticism: the concept of solitary inspiration in nature, the lone poet secure in his rural, bardic isolation. It is exemplified by Hazlitt's image of a Wordsworth who 'lives in the busy solitude of his own heart; in the deep silence of thought' (Howe, XIX: 11), or by Benjamin Robert Haydon's classic portrait of Wordsworth alone above the mists of Helvellyn, far removed from Gillray's raucous urban world.[20] The late-twentieth century saw a critical backlash against the emotional insulation of the solitary poet, and the perceived ideological shortcomings of the Romantic individualism he represented. More recently, there has been a recognition that his 'sociable other', in the words of Gillian Russell and Clara Tuite, has been within view all the time.[21] Recent criticism has explored the collaborations and networks – literary, social, political, religious, emotional – which characterised the period. Nicholas Roe's work, to take one example, has replaced Wordsworth and Coleridge not only in the context of radical history, but also among radical friends such as George Dyer, John Thelwall, and John Augustus Bonney.[22] Moreover, they were supremely conscious of how their own friendships and personal relationships could 'offer a compelling prospect of social renovation'.[23] For instance, the Hunt-Keats circle, sonnet-writing and tea-drinking together in Lisson Grove, conversing and picnicking on Hampstead Heath, carefully constructed a sense of a communal poetic and political identity. For these friends, as Jeffrey N. Cox has shown, sociability was nothing less than a 'first step in healing the fissures in the commonwealth [...] reclaiming society's ability to transform itself'.[24] I show in my first chapter the widespread nature of this belief in the power of friendship as a social ideal and model for reform, from the correspondence of Unitarian ministers such as Priestley and Theophilus Lindsey, to provincial groups of young friends such as Thomas Amyot and Henry Crabb Robinson. Lamb's friendships are rooted in this post-Revolutionary revaluation of social interactions: beleaguered from without and often contested from within, they nevertheless testify to a continuing faith in the reforming power of human affection.

The place of feeling is important in more ways than one to Lamb. Like Wordsworth, he attempts to define the landscape of affection, the power of the 'peculiar nook of earth' (MS D: 70; *RC*, 49), of emotional attachment to the 'local' (Marrs, I: 267). In Lamb's case, of course, these are located in London. His writing of the 1790s shows him forming his identity as a city writer, in response – and resistance – to the dominant narratives of rural inspiration put forward by Coleridge and Wordsworth. Constantly questioning the relationship between Romantic inspiration and environment, he has to negotiate the claims of town sociability and rural solitude in both personal and literary terms. Recent criticism is recognising that urban spaces – the bookshop, the theatre, the tavern – are as important to the landscape of the period as the Quantocks or the Lakes.[25] Lamb's gradual development of a city-based writing, formed in dialogue with Wordsworth and Coleridge, offers us an important insight into how such spaces were imagined, and how the Romantic writer might feel at home in the city.

If Lamb is thinking about new landscapes of emotion, he is also striving to define a new style which can incorporate the urban and the rural, the literary and the homely. Over the 1790s he develops a characteristically familiar, companionable voice, which attempts to bring these contrasting models into dialogue, and to create a sense of ongoing conversation. It is no coincidence that the germs of his essays are found in his private letters to friends: his style is formed in friendship, and he then attempts to create a similarly sociable relationship with the reader, through irony, puns, quotation and allusion – personal and literary.

Allusive writing creates a company of texts, breaking down authorial isolation by drawing previous authors and future readers into conversation. This form of sociability took on a special importance in the period, as social ideals changed direction and became channelled into reading and writing. As Russell and Tuite suggest: 'Romantic-period Britain is notable as the era in which imaginative literature assumes a fully-fledged cultural and political authority [...] sociability as both fact and value, reconfigured and realigned as a result of the repressed utopian moment of the 1790s, was a crucial element in the shaping of that authority'.[26]

This repositioning of authority also leads – as has been well documented recently – to a frenzy of authorial anxiety in the period.[27] Writers worried both about how to situate themselves in relation to their predecessors, and the way in which they themselves might be received by an increased and newly anonymous audience, amid a multiplication of texts and speakers. What part does the sociability created by allusion and quotation have to play in these vexed questions of literary influence and reception? How does reading and writing in friendship fit into our narratives of Romantic influence and inheritance?

Recent work on allusion has challenged Harold Bloom's gloomy Freudian family romance of literary influence and its focus on the aggressive 're-writing of the father' in favour of a more open model.[28] Lucy Newlyn has outlined a 'competitive/collaborative relationship', which might play out in terms of a relationship between siblings, or a married couple – or close friends.[29] Her analysis of the interweaving of the creative identities of Coleridge and Wordsworth shows how allusion, friendship, and rivalry might be intertwined, and how we might as readers work to understand 'the vocabulary and grammar of a literary dialogue'.[30] Thanks to the work of Newlyn and others, we are now familiar with the way in which Coleridge's writing 'interbraids' with that of Wordsworth: we have learnt to see their works 'as independent voicings of a mutual attitude developed in conversation', and dialogue as 'the essential generative condition of their poetry'.[31] Although my focus is slightly different, it is this work which underpins my readings of Lamb and his friends, as I explore their interlayered emotional and textual bonds. The allusive practice of the friendship group may swing between co-operation and rivalry, between love and envy, homage and parody. A text may act to enfold two authors, or a reader and an author, in a sociable space of understanding, but this is not always benign for all parties concerned. The joyous 'symbiosis' of Wordsworth and Coleridge in 1797 and 1798, for instance, is formed – as I show in Chapters 4 and 5 – against a backdrop of isolation, distrust and argument between Coleridge, Lloyd and Lamb.[32] The allusions of *Blank Verse* voice a poetics of reproach, swiftly crystallising into anger after Coleridge's allusive parodies in the 'Nehemiah Higginbottom' sonnets, which encourage the reader to join in a 'good-natured laugh' against the melancholy sensibilities of Lamb and Lloyd (*BiogLit* I: 26–7).

And yet, as I show in the final part of the book, allusion can carry an idealistic, restorative charge. Christopher Ricks, while acknowledging 'the possibility of envy and malignity', calls for allusion's more meliorative, generous function to be acknowledged.[33] He finds this allusive gratitude at its richest in Keats, and explains it in terms of Keats' 'sense of brotherhood with his peers. He declines the invitation to figure in the dark melodrama of *The Anxiety of Influence*'.[34]

The allusive happiness celebrated by Ricks connects with Cox's demonstration of Keats' belief in the 'key value' of sociability as a model for social reform. For Keats – as for Lamb – reading and writing are sociable, friendly practices, and their use of allusion expresses this sense of creative community. We can link Ricks' identification of a literary 'sense of brotherhood', moreover, with Russell and Tuite's assertion that the 'repressed utopian moment of the 1790s' lives again in the sociability of Romantic literature. As I explore in my first chapter, this sociably allusive practice counters and responds to another richly allusive, intertextual writer, Edmund Burke. Whereas Burke's use of allusion is intended to emphasise the crucial importance of tradition and continuity, these friends are self-consciously creating new textual communities. The sociable power of visions such as Coleridge's Pantisocratic scheme becomes invested – and to some extent, realised – in Lamb's allusive, inclusive style.

The first two chapters of my study show the importance of such ideals of affection and community in forming Lamb's concepts of friendship and affection. Delicately poised between conservative retreat and radical engagement, they find their first expression through an intense, religiously inflected idealisation of particular friends – especially Coleridge. But such ideals quickly collapse, partly under the pressure of Lamb's domestic situation, and partly because of the impossible burden of expectation laid upon friendship by all members of the group. The second part of my study therefore frames a narrative of disappointment, regret and desolation, as both Lamb's family life and his friendships fall apart. In Chapter 3, I deal with Lamb's re-evaluation of personal feeling in the aftermath of Mary's matricide in 1796, discussing his response to Coleridge's letters of consolation. Chapter 4 focuses closely on Lamb's interactions with Coleridge and Wordsworth during the genesis of *Lyrical Ballads* and examines his crucial role in the relationships of the 'annus mirabilis'. I take as my starting point Lamb's first visit to Nether Stowey in summer 1797, examining his contributions and reactions to the dialogue between 'This Lime-tree Bower my Prison' and 'Lines left upon a Seat in a Yew-tree', and between *Osorio* and *The Borderers*, replacing the poems and plays in the literary and personal context of the summer of 1797. Lamb's work now turns towards a darker exploration of religious vanity and personal failings, helping us to understand and to re-read the coded personal dramas of friendship and reproach at work in the plays and poetry of the whole group at this period. *Blank Verse*, for instance, which I discuss in detail in Chapter 5, is shaped both stylistically and thematically by the collapse of the friendship ideal.

However, as Lamb comes to terms with the destruction of his early friendship ideals, he begins to recreate them in textual form. The third and last part of my study argues that the subtle allusive strategies he begins to adopt in 1798 and 1799 are intricately connected to his developing concepts of reading and friendship. Through close readings of *Rosamund Gray*, *John Woodvil*, and his letters to Wordsworth, I show how his work comes eventually to enact the sociability he had once envisaged in company with Coleridge, bringing his many diverse allegiances – social, political and literary – into dialogue. This is not to suggest a post-Revolutionary shrinking from social engagement. Rather, Lamb is actively attempting to find a workable expression of personal attachment: throughout the 1790s, he is negotiating the place of sympathy and fellow-feeling, as writer, reader, and friend.

My argument recognises the ways in which readers of Lamb have always responded to his 'social sentiment'.[35] His contemporaries' appreciation of his writing is often bound up with descriptions of his own sociability, such as Haydon's recreation of the 'immortal dinner', for example, as 'an evening worthy of the Elizabethan age,' which 'will long flash upon "that inward eye which is the bliss of Solitude"', or Hazlitt's evocation of the 'many lively skirmishes' of the Lambs' Thursday evening parties: 'How often did we cut into the haunch of letters, while we discussed the haunch of mutton on the table! [...] "And, in our flowing cups, many a good name and true was freshly remembered"' (Howe, XII: 36).[36]

Both Haydon and Hazlitt create a narrative of sociability which brings the work of the group – Wordsworth's 'I wandered lonely as a Cloud' – into dialogue with forebears such as the Elizabethan poets and dramatists. Hazlitt's 'flowing cups', similarly, are a rewritten version of Henry the Fifth's reassurance to the 'band of brothers' that their exploits in battle will be remembered by future generations. Haydon and Hazlitt are continuing the work started by Lamb in his early letters to Coleridge, self-consciously creating a literary history of group Romanticism, a reconstruction of past friendship which is also a plea for future readership. The single-authored work – whether it is Haydon's diary, or Hazlitt's *London Magazine* essay, or Lamb's letters – has now to be representative of the sociable conversation, and the reader is called upon to supply an answering conviviality.

The aim of this study is to hear some of these sociable conversations of Romanticism more fully, and to appreciate the complexity of 'reading friendship' in the period. A close study of Lamb, I hope, will not only restore some of his little-known works to our discussion of the period, but also suggest some of the different ways in which friendship was 'read' in the period. He raises questions about how friends read one another, and attempt to befriend their reading audience – and also constantly challenges our own reading sympathies.

Part I
Idealising Friendship

1
Frendotatoi meta frendous: Constructing Friendship in the 1790s

December 1794

December 1794: a small dark back room in a London tavern, the 'Salutation and Cat'. A group of young men, all in their early twenties, are talking eagerly over steaming egg-nog, in a fug of Orinoco tobacco-smoke. This 'nice little smoky room' is a key space of 1790s Romanticism – a place of idealism, of shared creativity and mutual inspiration, where a group of friends gathers to read, write and talk of reform, both in poetry and politics (Marrs, I: 65). At the centre of this group is Coleridge, fresh from Cambridge. Through the winter of 1794, he had been active on the London literary scene, quarrelling with Holcroft, meeting Godwin, and publishing in the *Morning Chronicle*. He took the 'Salutation' as his base, and, since it was just opposite the gate of his old school, Christ's Hospital on Newgate Street, he was joined there by numerous school-friends: George Dyer, Robert Allen, Samuel Favell, the Le Grice brothers, Charles Valentine and Samuel – and Charles Lamb.

Lamb, born 1775, had been Coleridge's junior at Christ's Hospital, and had looked up to him, a 'Grecian', or senior scholar, destined for university and the Church. Lamb himself, partly because of his stammer, never became a Grecian, and in November 1789 left school to work. His background was modest, and his social position slightly ambiguous, since his father John worked as a waiter in the Inner Temple and a servant to Samuel Salt, one of the 'Old Benchers' celebrated by Elia. In 1792 Salt died, and the Lamb family had to leave his house in the Inner Temple; his parents were growing increasingly frail, and Lamb's wages were vitally necessary to help support his family. By 1794, Lamb had begun the job he was to hold for the rest of his life, working as a clerk in the vast East India House on Leadenhall Street. Eager for literary company, his evenings with Christ's Hospital friends Dyer, Allen, James White, and Coleridge were a focal point of his life in the mid-1790s. Once Coleridge had left London, 'the little smoky room' became the centre of Lamb's memories, and he wrote constantly to Coleridge recalling their meetings. The yearning letters form a counterpart to Coleridge's 1796 edition of *Poems on Various Subjects,* which included several poems by Lamb and one written with Favell. The letters and the volume of *Poems* are in dialogue, a conversation which has at its heart the memory of that small shared space of the 'Salutation' back-room, an emblem for their friendship.

These conversations are the important precursors of those much more famous discussions which take place when Coleridge meets Wordsworth: his early collaborations and experiments, however, have not attracted so much attention, despite being vital in the formation of the poetic relationships of 1797 and 1798. Indeed, the 'little smoky room' itself finds an incongruous rural parallel in a later space of friendship, Thomas Poole's bower at Nether Stowey. This 'lime-tree bower' is a frequent image of friendly, creative sociability among Coleridge's friends in the late 1790s. It is the 'Jasmine harbour' of the publisher Joseph Cottle's *Reminiscences,* supplied with bread and cheese and true Taunton ale, and it appears, also, in William Hazlitt's essay, 'My First Acquaintance with Poets':

> Thus I passed three weeks at Nether Stowey and in the neighbourhood, generally devoting the afternoons to a delightful chat in an arbour made of bark by the poet's friend Tom Poole, sitting under two fine elm-trees, and listening to the bees humming round us, while we quaffed our *flip.* (Howe, XVII: 119)[1]

This is a manly sort of pastoral, in which chat and poetry are roughened up by proximity to sociable male quaffing, a pattern which will be repeated as these writers try to defend and toughen notions of sensibility in retreat. It is also a very sensory experience, as tastes and sounds, such as those humming bees, are evoked to summon up a fully sympathetic experience.

This points to the wider meaning of the bower. It is a small spot, a 'narrow' scene, which, paradoxically, can hold a whole world within it:

> No scene so narrow, but may well employ
> Each faculty of sense, and keep the heart
> Awake to Love & Beauty[2]

Invested with imaginative and sensual power, it stands both as an emblem of sympathetic friendship, and of the ways in which the individual mind can be alerted to a wider sense of 'Love & Beauty' and 'promis'd good'.

Similarly, Lamb's 'little smoky room' contains a larger meaning. It not only functions as a reminder of Coleridge's friendship, it also acts metonymically to express a concept of friendship which, informed both by Hartleian philosophy and by Unitarianism, takes the individual relationship as the starting point for wider harmonious social relations. As we will see, throughout their letters and poems in the mid-1790s, Lamb and Coleridge argue that universal benevolence is premised on personal attachment: 'Some home-born Feeling is the *center* of the Ball,' Coleridge tells Southey in 1794, 'that, rolling on thro' Life collects and assimilates every congenial Affection' (Griggs, I: 86). This associationism is also evident in Lamb's comments on his collaborative sonnet with Coleridge on Mrs. Siddons, written in 1794 and published in the 1796 *Poems*:

> That Sonnet, Coleridge, brings afresh to my mind the time when you wrote those on Bowles, Priestly, Burke – 'twas 2 Christmas[e]s ago – & in that nice little smoky room at the Salutation [...] with all its associated train of pipes, tobacco, Egghot, welch Rabbits, metaphysics & **Poetry** – . Are we *never* to meet again? (Marrs, I: 65)[3]

Bowles, Priestley, Burke – this gives us a good idea of the conversations which might have been going on in that room and which might have helped to structure this concept of the 'home-born Feeling', and Lamb and Coleridge's ideas about their own friendship. There is a fourth figure, equally important, to whom a sonnet was also written in the 'Salutation', and who should be brought back into the conversation between Lamb and Coleridge: Godwin. Beginning with these major figures and then moving outward, I attempt in this chapter to reconstruct some of those discussions about politics, about Dissent, and about the mutual reading and writing of the literature of sensibility.

The intense emphasis placed on the importance of personal attachment by Coleridge and Lamb is partly prompted by a desire to engage with, and then to refute, Godwin. In *An Enquiry Concerning Political Justice* (1793), which Coleridge read 'with the greatest attention' in October 1794 (Griggs, I: 115), Godwin famously dismisses the hampering bonds of personal connection in the cause of 'general good':

> We are not connected with one or two percipient beings, but with a society, a nation, and in some sense with the whole family of mankind. (*PJ*, 50)

In brief, Coleridge turns around Godwin's argument and contends that it is precisely *through* our personal connection 'with one or two percipient beings' that we form our larger connection with 'the whole family of mankind'.

But Coleridge's insistence on the importance of 'home-born Feeling' is haunted by another writer who, similarly, keeps returning to the importance of domestic affection: Burke. His *Reflections on the Revolution in France* (1790) puts forward an equally compelling conservative reading of the personal connection, setting the power of personal attachment and love firmly against Revolutionary sympathies: 'To be attached to the subdivision, to love the little platoon we belong to in society, is the first principle (the germ as it were) of public affections. It is the first link in the series by which we proceed towards a love to our country and to mankind'.[4]

Coleridge strenuously asserts that private attachment 'collects and assimilates every congenial Affection' before allowing it to move out towards universal benevolence (Griggs, I: 86). But he is also troubled by the fear that this outward move might not be inevitable. Private affection might in fact represent a retreat or limitation, a move towards the insularity of a 'subdivision' or 'little platoon'.

Lamb and Coleridge construct their narrative of friendship against these two extremes: radical Godwinian reform, and Burkean conservatism. Their early relationship is shaped by their attempts to define – and to put into practice – a mode of friendship which picks its way between Godwin and Burke, and, more generally, between radical and conservative implications. It is their shared Unitarianism, symbolised by that sonnet on Priestley, and their mutual reading and writing – for instance, of Bowles – which helps Lamb and Coleridge negotiate an alternative language of private feeling. There is no easy middle ground, however, and often, as we will see, their concepts and expressions of friendship oscillate between the two poles, particularly strongly in the case of Coleridge.

There has been a great deal of excellent scholarship on the political allegiances of Coleridge and Wordsworth in the 1790s. A significant strand of criticism on Coleridge has been informed by Hazlitt's condemnation of his slippery politics: *'Once an Apostate and always an Apostate'* (Howe, VII: 135). Hazlitt's disenchantment is echoed by E. P. Thompson's brilliantly impassioned characterisation of Coleridge as a barely forgivable – and at times downright repulsive – renegade, and modified by critics such as Jerome Christensen and Charles Mahoney.[5] '"Once an apostate and *always already* an apostate"', runs Christensen's formulation, since 'at every point we examine him, even at the beginning, Coleridge is already falling away from every principled commitment.'[6] James Chandler has similarly suggested that Wordsworth falls away from radical principles very early in his writing life.[7] Tracing Wordsworth's Burkean allegiances through the 1790s, Chandler concludes that he adopted a conservative stance much earlier than has been recognised. Wordsworth's close early engagement with Burke, however, should not necessarily be taken as an attraction simply towards conservatism. Both Wordsworth and Coleridge grapple with Godwin and with Burke throughout the 1790s. They are both at first attracted to the radical possibilities opened up by Godwin, but then struggle to find a way to reconcile these with the aspects of Burke which they similarly found attractive – such as his emphasis on the local, the familial, the affectionate community.[8] In the words of Nigel Leask, Coleridge and his circle use 'the language of custom and affection against Paine and Godwin's interpretation of reason, but towards radical ends profoundly opposed to the Burke of *Reflections*'.[9]

Some of the best work in this context has shown the intense difficulty of defining the political commitments of Wordsworth and Coleridge in the 1790s. Their radicalism does not easily fit into any available categories – not the Whig Reform groups, nor the active plain-speaking popular societies such as the London Corresponding Society, nor yet the intellectualised reform offered by Godwin. Instead, their politics are intertwined with religious and familial allegiances, as critics such as Leask, Roe, and Kelvin Everest have shown.[10] Unitarian radicalism, like Coleridge's, was characterised by commitment both to a concept of revolutionary reform and to the importance of family affection, a 'conviction that enduring personal and social values sprang from, and were sustained in, the relationships of family and private friendship'.[11]

Coleridge's efforts to establish loving social relationships run alongside his quest for a sympathetic audience. His personal friendships were intimately connected both with political commitment and with a concept of an ideal readership. In this context, Lamb's friendship becomes important, and the idea of sympathetic response which Lamb continually explores may be politicised. As I suggested in the introduction, however, little attention – with some notable exceptions – has been directed towards the politics of Lamb in this era, and while his position within the Coleridge circle has been recognised, his active role there as reader and friend has not been fully explored. David Fairer, however, has drawn attention to the importance of works such as *Blank Verse*. Teasing out its intertwining of radical and conservative positions, he identifies 'the *organic* nature of a certain kind of radical sensibility' and shows that it may at once contain radical possibilities *and* the germ of conservatism.[12] Fairer's readings inform my approach in this study, which seeks not to identify clear political positions, but rather to explore the constant negotiations going on within these 1790s friendships, against a backdrop of wider political and cultural shifts in attitude towards affection and community in the late-eighteenth century. Friendship may be a fiery centre from which radical reform emanates, or an enclosing, limiting constraint; it may, sometimes simultaneously, be a nourishing, protective bower, or a place of betrayal and disenchantment. For Coleridge and Lamb, toasting their renewed friendship in the 'Salutation' in the winter of 1794, these debates were only just beginning.

'Bowles, Priestley, Burke': the *Morning Chronicle* sonnets

Coleridge's series of sonnets to 'Eminent Characters' in late 1794 and early 1795, including those mentioned by Lamb, offers a good early example of these complex negotiations. Published in James Perry's Whig journal, the *Morning Chronicle*, they appear embedded in a context of revolutionary excitement and fear at home in Britain.[13] On almost every page there were reports from Paris, commenting on the struggles within the republic post-Terror; these contended with reports of the aftermath of the Treason Trials in October 1794. Several members of the London Corresponding Society had been arrested the previous May, and three – John Thelwall, Thomas Hardy, and John Horne Tooke – were subsequently tried for high treason. Their acquittal, secured by Thomas Erskine, was marked by public celebration.[14] Coleridge joined in – his first sonnet praised the 'matchless eloquence' of Erskine himself; his second lamented Burke's betrayal of the cause, narrated by a dream vision of Freedom herself, who, hailing Burke as a 'Great son of Genius!', grieves over his 'alter'd voice'.[15] Unlike Pitt, who two weeks later, in the sixth sonnet of the series, appears as a thorough-going villain, a 'dark scowler' with an 'Iscariot mouth', Burke is essentially on the side of right, led astray by mixed motives and 'Error's mist' but never partaking of 'Corruption's bowl!'. Coleridge had long been fascinated by Burke: in his room in Cambridge, recalls C. V. Le Grice, there were gatherings to discuss each new Burke publication, when Coleridge would 'repeat whole pages verbatim'. Yet Coleridge was at the same time eagerly reading radical pamphlets: 'Coleridge had read them all, and in the evening with our negus,' Le Grice tells us, in a marvellous image of sociable politics, 'we had them *viva voce* gloriously.'[16] But by the time the Burke sonnet appeared in the 1796 *Poems*, it had a long note attached to the phrase 'Corruption's bowl!', calling attention to a 'paragraph in the *Cambridge Intelligencer*' which details Burke's generous pensions. Running alongside his appreciation of Burke's 'Genius', therefore, is Coleridge's desire to signal difference, in the shape of his own allegiance to Benjamin Flower's strongly Dissenting paper.

The mixed feelings of this sonnet are echoed by Coleridge's review of Burke's *Letter to a Noble Lord* (1796) in the first number of the *Watchman* (March 1796), which Lamb commended as the 'best prose' in the issue (Marrs, I: 10). Here Coleridge returns to the issue of Burke's pension and the *Cambridge Intelligencer* report. As with the sonnet, the tone is one of disappointment, rather than condemnation – Coleridge praises Burke's 'vigor of intellect, and ... almost prophetic keenness of penetration', defending his use of emotive, affective language, 'the aids of sympathy' (*Watchman*, 30). Similarly, he commends Burke's own powers of sympathy, singling out for especial praise the 'beautiful and pathetic tribute' to Burke's friend, Lord Keppel (*Watchman*, 31).[17] But Coleridge strongly dissociates this emphasis on personal attachment and on 'the consolation of friendship' from Burke's 'attacks' on 'Frenchmen and French principles' which he characterises almost as insanity, a recurrent paranoia (*Watchman*, 32). In separating Burke's capacity for sympathy from his anti-Revolutionary sentiment, Coleridge attempts to reclaim the language of personal attachment and emotive response for radical ends. The evocation of Burke's 'alter'd voice' in the *Morning Chronicle* sonnet is one of the first moves in Coleridge's long-running and sometimes fraught negotiation with Burke's legacy.

A month later, the same uncertainty marks Coleridge's ninth sonnet, to Godwin, written shortly after their first meeting in London on 21 December 1794:

O! form'd to illume a sunless world forlorn,
As o'er the chill and dusky brow of Night,
In Finland's wintry skies, the Mimic Morn
Electric pours a stream of rosy light
(ll. 1–4)[18]

This 'stream of rosy light' is itself illuminated by revolutionary imagery, such the 'beam of light' which Thomas Paine thought the American and French Revolutions would lend the world. As Roe has pointed out, it is also inspired by Thelwall's concept of 'electrical fluid' in his *Essay, on the Principles of Animal Vitality*.[19] The experiments of Thelwall and Godwin have a similar effect on society: shocking, or, in Roe's words, galvanising it into action. But behind the rosy glow of Coleridge's first excited reaction to Godwin is an ambiguity which is most clearly seen in the double negative of the final stanza:

Nor will I not thy holy guidance bless,
And hymn thee, GODWIN! with an ardent Lay.
(ll. 9–10)

The overt religiosity of the lines – 'holy guidance', 'hymn thee' – points to Coleridge's struggle to find a Christian answer to Godwin's atheism, a struggle which, as we will see, would continue well into the later 1790s, amongst the whole Coleridge circle.

Very soon Coleridge was regretting this 'ardent Lay', almost immediately expressing dissatisfaction with its *'most miserably magazinish'* opening lines (Griggs, I: 141), and writing to Thelwall in June 1796 that he regretted the 'precipitance in praise' which had led him into publishing 'my foolish verses to Godwin' (Griggs, I: 221). Later, he was to say that he had not even read Godwin when he wrote the sonnet, and that it had been written purely at Southey's instigation (Griggs, III: 315). He was clearly dissembling, since echoes of *Political Justice* sound throughout his writing, beginning with his 1795 Bristol lectures. 'Godwin was the real opponent in Coleridge's mind during the inception and preparation of the lectures,' argue the editors of his *Lectures on Revealed Religion* (1795), which are marked by a struggle to elucidate the radical *Christian* answer to Godwin's atheism.[20]

Coleridge's uncertainty about Godwin, and his disappointed opposition to Burke, was fuelled by his Unitarianism, something shared and encouraged by Lamb. The importance of their shared faith has been downplayed in accounts of their friendship, and of Lamb's early writing, but it was probably the reason for their renewed closeness. They worshipped together during the 1794–5 visit, since, when Southey came to retrieve Coleridge from the 'foul stye' of the 'Salutation', he found that he 'was gone with Lamb to the Unitarian chapel' (Curry, I: 91). This was the Essex Street Chapel established in 1774 by the pioneering preacher Theophilus Lindsey, a close friend of Priestley, who had seceded from the Church of England after the failure of an attempted repeal of the Test Acts, which continued to exclude Dissenters from public office.[21]

To be a Unitarian Dissenter was, however, not merely a question of religion, especially in the 1790s, as Coleridge's *Morning Chronicle* sonnet to Priestley (11 December 1794) makes clear. On the previous page, the newspaper had reported that 'Dr. PRIESTLEY is in good health and spirits,' and had been unanimously elected as a 'Professor of Chemistry in the College at Philadelphia.' Coleridge's sonnet picks up the idea of Priestley's success in America and makes its political inflection obvious:

> Tho' King-bred rage, with lawless uproar rude,
> Hath driv'n our PRIESTLEY o'er the ocean swell;
> Tho' Superstition and her wolfish brood
> Bay his mild radiance, impotent and fell;
> Calm, in his halls of brightness, he shall dwell[22]

The repeated condemnation of superstition and ritual, 'mitred State, and cumbrous Pomp', clearly signal Coleridge's allegiance to Priestleian Unitarianism. Moreover, this is 'our PRIESTLEY', a political and almost familial allegiance. But Unitarian figures such as Priestley and his friend Richard Price were dangerous figures to be claiming as allies. Their religious Dissent was intertwined with their revolutionary sympathies, as shown, famously, in Price's 1789 Old Jewry speech, *Discourse on the love of our country*, delivered both to mark the centenary of the Glorious Revolution and to rejoice at the events across the Channel. Such positions of double dissent attracted violent opposition, not only the brilliant verbal thrusts of Burke's *Reflections*, but also actual physical attack. The 'lawless uproar rude' of Coleridge's sonnet refers to the destruction of Priestley's house and laboratory by a Birmingham 'Church and King' mob in July 1791.[23]

The provocation for the riot had been a commemorative Revolutionary dinner held at the Birmingham Hotel, like the one at the Old Jewry in which Price had delivered his *Discourse*.[24] These dinners were not merely gatherings of friends – they were dangerously inflammatory radical acts, which show us how friendly sociability could be politicised in the 1790s. In a Gillray cartoon depicting the dinner which sparked the riots – 'A Birmingham Toast' (1791) – we see Priestley and Price, accompanied by the Whig leader Charles James Fox, Sheridan and Horne Tooke (none of whom had in fact been present), provocatively drinking a toast with a platter raised aloft. 'The – Head Here', Priestley is seditiously exclaiming, as the flushed men scramble to refill their glasses. The cartoon shows how the tavern, coffee-house, or public dining-room might become, in the words of James Epstein, an arena 'for testing the courage of men's political convictions'.[25] Drinking and dining and talking together about religion and politics might not merely be a private undertaking: it could carry a very public, political charge.

Trials such as those of Charles Pigott and William Hodgson, for instance, members of the London Corresponding Society, hinged on whether they had uttered seditious comments in public or in private whilst dining 'convivially together'.[26] Pigott and Hodgson were at a table in a coffee-house, talking between themselves about the 'bad private character' of the Duke of York, when they were accosted by a member of John Reeves' Association for Preserving Liberty and Property against Republicans and Levellers. Did talk 'between two friends in a public coffee-house, at a table where they were sitted together' constitute seditious activity? Apparently so. Although Pigott's indictment was discarded, Hodgson was sentenced to two years' imprisonment and a £200 fine. Small wonder that in this climate of repression John Thelwall never lost his paranoia: 'If he went into an oyster house, or an *à-la-mode* beef-shop, he would conceit that one-half of the boxes in the room had government spies in them, whose especial business was to watch and report, as far as possible, all he said and all he did'.[27]

It is against this backdrop that the 'Salutation' meetings, with their talk of Priestley and of radical politics, should be considered. Consciousness of the dangerous consequences of convivial meetings perhaps lies behind Coleridge's change to the first line of the Priestley sonnet when he published it in the 1796 *Poems*. The force behind the Birmingham riots becomes not the dangerously anti-Royal 'King-bred rage', as in the *Morning Chronicle*, but 'that dark Vizir', a reference, Mays suggests, to Reeves. In light of trials like those of Pigott and Hodgson, Coleridge was keenly aware of how his own radicalism might be viewed.

'Bowles, Priestley, Burke' – what, we might ask, is William Bowles the poet of sensibility doing in the company of these highly politicised contemporaries? In the series of *Morning Chronicle* sonnets, he stands out amid Erskine, Fayette and Kosciusko as not specifically politically engaged. Coleridge, perhaps aware of this, attaches a long note to the sonnet, making clear that Bowles' work is available from the Dilly brothers, the Whig publishers who had been known for their American sympathies and for their range of Dissenting publications. Whilst the sonnet itself is in the style of melting sensibility:

> My heart has thank'd thee, BOWLES! for those soft strains,
> That, on the still air floating, tremblingly
> Wak'd in me Fancy, Love, and Sympathy!
> For hence, not callous to a Brother's pains,
>   Thro' Youth's gay prime and thornless paths I went.

the note makes it clear that there is a radical edge to this softness. Bowles, says Coleridge, is admirable both for his 'tender simplicity' and for his 'manly Pathos'. That 'manly Pathos' shows that there is another aspect to this floating, trembling sensibility, since it awakes an active, engaged sympathy. Bowles' writing, while it employs the stock imagery of sensibility, is being claimed as a 'manly' mode, which runs alongside the homo-sociality of the 'Salutation' meetings. 'I shall half wish you unmarried (don't show this to Mrs. C.) for one evening only,' writes Lamb in June 1796, 'to have the pleasure of smoking with you, and drinking egg-hot in some little smoky room in a pot-house, for I know not yet how I shall like you in a decent room, and looking quite happy' (Marrs, I: 33). Theirs is a male sociability, a rough, pot-house affection, which seeks to evade charges of effeminacy or homosexuality through its emphasis on the stereotypically manly pleasures of public smoking and drinking.[28] However, as this letter suggests, there could be tension between fraternal and familial affection, between the manly public world and the domestic circle, which the friends persistently try to elide.

Another source of tension was the interplay between concepts of manliness and sensibility, which both radicals and conservatives attempted to exploit. Alongside a renewed defensiveness about the gendering and politicisation of sociability, sensibility was being toughened up for a fighting role in the political situation of the 1790s.[29] Aware of the ways in which 'manly Pathos' could be claimed for conservatism – by Burke's appeals to chivalric sensibility in the *Reflections*, for instance – Coleridge tries to put forward a concept of affective response which is inwardly strengthened by the 'manly' and the radical, which can participate alongside the public activity of Erskine or Fayette.[30] The response from a reader of Coleridge's *Morning Chronicle* sonnets, over the signature 'NOT TO BE MISTAKEN', demonstrates a recognition of how the link between masculinity and sensibility could be pressed into radical service:

> How the warm soul with indignation glows; –
> How VIRTUE mingles horror with delight,
> When thy nerv'd Lines seize on thy Country's Foes,
> And drag the lurking Felons into light!
>
> Scarce SYMPATHY restrains to read thy page,
> But, with a Godlike vengeance more than mann'd,
> Would wrest the fervid lightning from thy hand –
> And hurl it at the Monsters of the age.[31]

This is a 'more than mann'd' sympathy – a sensibility which is 'nerv'd' and strong, ready for the physical work of vengeance: seizing, dragging, wresting, hurling. Moreover, it revolves around the friendly act of reading and writing. 'Oh, my Friend!' declares this reader toward the close of the poem, 'thou know'st my secret soul: – '.

Those sonnets on Bowles, Priestley, Burke, composed within the space of the 'Salutation', give us a starting point for an understanding of how Coleridge and Lamb were formulating their concept of friendship in the mid-1790s. It was shaped by their mutual experiences of particular institutions and groups, beginning with their schooldays at Christ's Hospital, which gave them, as we will see, an education premised on benevolence. It was fostered in the midst of a group of radical, Dissenting male friends, whose sociability was inflected by idealism, whose drinking and talking sessions in London taverns opened new ways of relating to others, politically and socially. And, as the *Morning Chronicle* sonnets show, this political stance was inextricably linked to the rhythms and constructions of the literature of sensibility, their shared reading of authors such as Bowles and Mackenzie, who helped to form the language of their friendship. Looking at Lamb's letters and poems to Coleridge – the Coleridge side of the correspondence is, save for one letter, lost – and at the little-known poems of that era, I want to reconstruct a more general context for the language of friendship they might have been using around the fire-side in 'The Salutation'. Both their writings and their friendship, I argue, reflect, and help to shape, the wholesale revaluation of relationships – political, social, and familial – of the 1790s.

New readings of familial and friendly affection

The alternative domestic space of the pot-house offered by Lamb as an emblem of his friendship with Coleridge should be set against the backdrop of, in the words of Christopher Flint, 'widespread cultural reassessment of kinship and affective behaviour' in the eighteenth century.[32] It was a time when concepts of intimacy, domesticity, and kinship were being formulated and tested. From the hapless Tristram Shandy, constantly snagged by 'domestic misadventures' in his attempts to write his family history, to the spectres of incest and patriarchal violence which haunt and disrupt the Gothic novel, the family narrative of the eighteenth century keeps being re-written. The implications of this debate are still being discussed: on the one hand, Lawrence Stone has argued for the growing sentimentality of family life, partly due to the falling infant death rate and the promotion of marriage based on companionship.[33] On the other hand, historians such as Peter Laslett have shown that, under the economic and social pressures of the later eighteenth century, the whole concept of the family was an insecure and uncertain one.[34]

More recent work has developed both these ideas, showing that a new emphasis on affective relationship ran alongside an anxiety about how the family should be defined. Michael McKeon has argued more broadly for a full reconsideration of the shift between public and private experience across the seventeenth and eighteenth centuries. Showing in complex detail the 'self-consciousness with which English people were rethinking not only the state but also marriage and the family' he broadly agrees with Stone that 'what is truly innovative about this period is its extraordinary concentration upon the question of the marriage choice', and whether it should depend on affection or honour traditional economic ties – on love or money.[35] Related to this, work on kinship such as Ruth Perry's has shown that there was a movement, over the course of the eighteenth century, 'from an axis of kinship based on consanguineal ties or blood lineage to an axis based on conjugal and affinal ties of the married couple'.[36] Was 'kinship' a matter of blood-tie or social bond – could one, in other words, choose one's family?

This question had implications for friendship, and the term 'friend' was, in the eighteenth century, similarly contested. It could indicate, as Naomi Tadmor has examined, a familial or economic tie, and was used in a wide variety of contexts to refer to relatives, patrons, employers, and political allies.[37] By the later eighteenth century, however, there was a movement away from the concept of kin as friends, towards a more modern meaning of the individually chosen, voluntary affective relationship – friends as kin. This was a highly self-conscious formulation, almost amounting, in the words of Gurion Taussig, to a 'cultural preoccupation with friendship during the 1780s and 1790s', as quality and type of friendly affection was obsessively documented.[38]

These questions about familial and friendly affection took on a new importance in the 1790s. Radical societies named themselves the 'Friends of Liberty', since friendship, in the words of Mary Favret, 'denoted not just sympathy and understanding, but a political solidarity based on egalitarian principles and on correspondence itself'.[39] A good example of this self-consciously egalitarian construction of friendship may be found in the letters of a self-styled 'Triumvirate' of young men whose friendship and correspondence, like that of Coleridge and Lamb, also began in late 1794 and 1795. The Norwich-based William Pattison, Thomas Amyot, and Henry Crabb Robinson, all just the same age as Charles Lamb, exchanged, throughout the late 1790s, similarly self-conscious literary letters of poetry and friendship. This friendship, it is clear, is both an expression of mutual affection and a politically and socially informed formulation, despite the friends' difference in outlook. Pattison was a Democrat and an Independent Dissenter, Crabb Robinson a more radical Unitarian and admirer of 'the new-fang'd Doctrine of Godwin & Holcroft', and Amyot a sceptical conservative Anglican.[40] All three, however, shared a consciousness of the topical importance of friendship, a 'Science more worthy of being studied than Politics'.[41] Like the friendship of Coleridge and Lamb, their relationships were rooted in male sociability and expressed in the 'long lively and manly Letter'.[42] They attempted to articulate an ideal of such 'manly' friendship based on mutual esteem, sincerity, and open debate about contemporary issues such as Dissent from the Anglican Church, the theories of Godwin and Burke, the Treason Trials, and the French Revolution. 'I have a right to unlock your private Sentiments,' Amyot tells Pattison in November 1794, asking him to justify his position of Independent Dissent.[43] Again, Amyot, challenging Pattison's laments over 'the fall of Equality in France' and asking him to justify his views on the Revolution, backs up his comments with an appeal to their friendship: 'It is one of the highest privileges of Friendship to disclose Opinions without dissimulation and without fear of giving Offence'.[44]

Pantisocracy and the 'family of soul'

For these Norwich men, friendship was more than the relationship of individuals: it was an important step in 'the Cultivation of Social Benevolence'.[45] As such, it may be set alongside what Taussig has termed Coleridge's 'practical enactment of the latest theories of friendship', both in his intense emotional attachments, and in wider schemes such as the Pantisocratic plan.[46] The aims of Pantisocracy were religious and political: the 'small but liberalized party' of friends was to represent 'the Family of Soul' and provide a model of happy affective relationship (Griggs, I: 96; 102). It represented one way of bridging the gap between male fraternal friendship and familial domesticity. Coleridge hoped to put this into practice through the marriage of friends with sisters: he and Southey undertaking to marry two of the Fricker sisters, Edith and Sara, and a fellow Pantisocrat, Southey's poetic collaborator Robert Lovell, marrying a third, Mary. Another, George Burnett, proposed (unsuccessfully) to the youngest sister, Martha. 'America! Southey! Miss Fricker!,' exclaimed Coleridge in an access of linguistic and friendly exuberance in September 1794, 'Make Edith my Sister – Surely, Southey! we shall be frendotatoi meta frendous. Most friendly where all are friends. She must therefore be more emphatically my Sister' (Griggs, I: 103). In his desire for a sister who is chosen, who is *made*, rather than tied by blood, Coleridge shows his rejection of traditional social relations of the earlier eighteenth century. Ties of property, too, would be left behind as the friends sailed for the New World, since all goods were to be held in common.

Pantisocracy had clearly been the subject of much of the intoxicating discussion that was going on in the 'Salutation', as the friends gathered to 'drink Porter & *Punch* round a good Fire'. 'My motive for all this,' Coleridge told Southey, somewhat defensively,

> is that every night I meet a most intelligent young Man who has spent the last 5 years of his Life in America – and is lately come from thence as An Agent to sell Land. He was of our School – I had been kind to him – he remembers it – & comes regularly every Evening to 'benefit by conversation' he says. (Griggs, I: 99)

This school fellow – and it is deeply significant that the encounter should be traced directly to an act of kindness between Christ's Hospital members – enlarged on the beauties of the Susquehannah region, its relative security from 'Indians...Byson...Musquitos', and other such inconveniences. The talk pleased not only Coleridge, but also the other Christ's Hospital boys: friends Samuel Le Grice and Samuel Favell, still at school, entreated 'that they may be allowed to come over after us when they quit College'.

Although, as Courtney points out, Lamb, apprenticed to the East India Company, and sharing family responsibilities with Mary, 'was in no situation to join the Susquehannah scheme, even if he had wanted to', joking allusions in his letters to those who have money in common suggest his intimate knowledge of the Pantisocratic plan, with all its ideals of mutuality and friendship.[47] Writing to Coleridge, after the latter had been taken off by Southey to fulfil his duty to Sara Fricker, he told him, 'make yourself perfectly easy about May. I paid his bill, when I sent your clothes,' adding in a later letter: 'never mention Mr. May's affair in any sort, **much** less *think* of repaying. Are we not flocci-nauci-what d'ye call-em-ists?' (Marrs, I: 3, 9; emphasis, here and elsewhere, in original, unless stated). The term reappears in a later letter, directly linked to 'visions of Utopias in America' (Marrs, I: 98). As Marrs points out, Lamb's allusion to common finances may recall William Shenstone's expression, in his *Letters to Particular Friends*, 'the flocci-nauci-nihili-pili-fication of money' (Marrs, I: 13).[48] It is a playful shared textual reference which looks forward to Elian coinages, but which has its root in Coleridge's linguistic inventiveness of the 1790s. Mirroring Coleridge's gleeful invention of the terms Pantisocracy and Aspheterism, it reflects Lamb's intense desire to create a commonality of experience. Coleridge's terms, as Tim Fulford puts it, 'not only expressed the pantisocrats' equality, but also defined them *as a group* with its own private and self-identifying code words': here Lamb, too, through allusion and private reference, is participating in a collective identity.[49] He has been excluded from the actual Pantisocratic scheme, but not from the structures of friendship and shared discourse which it signifies, its emphasis on the restructuring of family around a relationship of choice. Like Pantisocracy, his friendship with Coleridge was an attempt to reformulate codes of social relationship along lines of mutual esteem and shared property – in Lamb's case literary and emotional, drawing on their shared reading and writing of sensibility. 'I am writing at random, and half-tipsy,' writes Lamb in June 1796, not for the first time, 'what you may not *equally* understand, as you will be sober when you read it; but *my* sober and *my* half-tipsy hours you are alike a sharer in' (Marrs, I: 32).

The poems of this era, such as Coleridge's 'Address to a Young Jack-Ass, And its *Tether'd* Mother, In Familiar Verse' published in the *Morning Chronicle* on 30 December 1795, and the revisions he made to 'Monody on Chatterton' around this time, extend this emphasis on sharing and sociability. The invitation to participate in the Pantisocratic scheme is cordially extended to all, from dead poets – in the revised 'Monody', Chatterton is invited to take his place in 'peaceful Freedom's UNDIVIDED dale' – to young asses:

> I hail thee *Brother*, 'spite of the Fool's scorn;
> And fain I'd take thee with me, in the dell
> Of Peace and mild Equality to dwell

The enthusiasm is picked up by other members of the group, such as Favell, who wrote his own sonnet idealising the 'Vale' of Pantisocracy as a place 'where bloom in Fadeless Youth/Love, Beauty, Friendship, Poesy and Truth'.[50]

This innocent ideal seems to fit with Coleridge's later description of the Pantisocratic scheme 'as harmless as it was extravagant'. Quoting the closing lines of the 'Monody' in *The Friend*, Coleridge dismisses it as a youthful dream, a Utopian vision of innocence and culture which, moreover, had spared him from 'the pitfalls of Sedition' (*Friend*, 146–7). This urgent disavowal is itself suggestive. Much as he might have wanted in 1809 to portray the Pantisocratic scheme as a 'tranquil nook or inland cove' out of the 'general current' of Jacobin enthusiasm, it was in the 1790s a highly politicised gesture, shaped by radicalism and by Dissent. As a Unitarian radical, Coleridge would have been considered by many in the period as very close to 'the pitfalls of Sedition'. Emigration to America was a move invested with radical significance, political and religious. Associated with Revolutionary sympathies, as Leask has argued, it seemed a way out of the 'ideological cul-de-sac' in which radical Dissenters found themselves after the collapse of Girondin republicanism.[51] Moreover, by April 1794 the persecuted Priestley had emigrated to Pennsylvania, settling on the Susquehannah – another factor in the Pantisocracy plan.[52] Indeed, after meeting Dyer in September 1794 and explaining the scheme, Coleridge enthusiastically reported to Southey that Dyer 'was enraptured – pronounced it impregnable – He is intimate with Dr Priestley – and doubts not, that the Doctor will join us' (Griggs, I: 98).

Coleridge would also have known directly about Priestley through his Cambridge tutor, William Frend. Frend had converted to Unitarianism in the late 1780s, and had met Priestley at the Essex Street Chapel, collaborating with him on a translation of the Scriptures – work which had been burnt in the Birmingham riots. Through the early 1790s the persecution of radicals and Dissenters intensified. Frend, who had been tolerated as a Unitarian at Cambridge and permitted to remain resident at Jesus College, was put on trial in May 1793 after the publication of his pamphlet *Peace and Union*.[53] This again linked radical politics – approval of French Revolutionary principles, and opposition to the war – with Unitarian Dissent; Frend was condemned by the Master and fellows of Jesus for discrediting the clergy and the Anglican Church, and 'disturbing the harmony of society'.[54] Everest and Roe have shown us just how important an influence Frend was in shaping Coleridge's early radicalism: as a witness to the trial, Coleridge was supposed to have clapped and cheered Frend from the public gallery, and after both had left Cambridge Frend continued to shape his thinking, and his Pantisocratic plans.[55] The intricate connections are shown by the pun on his name embedded in Coleridge's exclamation, 'Surely, Southey! we shall be frendotatoi meta frendous. Most friendly where all are friends' (Griggs, I: 103).

Unitarian readings of friendship

Pantisocracy, then, was not simply an undergraduate vision: it was a sign of radical political allegiance, invested with revolutionary and religious idealism. More generally, its emphasis on the relationship of choice, unregulated by family ties, gives a powerful example of the way in which the authority both of family and state was being interrogated in the 1790s. In Burke's *Reflections* one is irrevocably intertwined with the other, a consanguineal tie which cannot be disrupted:

> we have given to our frame of polity the image of a relation in blood; binding up the constitution of our country with our dearest domestic ties; adopting our fundamental laws into the bosom of our family affections; keeping inseparable, and cherishing with the warmth of all their combined and mutually reflected charities, our state, our hearts, our sepulchres, and our altars.[56]

Family and state hold one another together: the feudal order which transfers property from father to son is equivalent to the 'constitutional policy, working after the pattern of nature', with the monarch as head of the family.[57] The assault of the French Revolution on established social laws becomes, in Burke's rhetoric, an assault on the family: literally in the case of the attack on Marie Antoinette, Burke's 'Roman matron'.[58] Emphasising her identity as a mother of infants, part of a family, Burke famously pictures her hounded and persecuted by ruffians 'reeking with...blood', in a palace 'swimming in blood, polluted by massacre, and strewed with scattered limbs and mutilated carcases'.[59] The 'image of a relation in blood' has become horribly literal: once the 'natural' blood-tie – of family, and of state – has been severed, only bloodshed can follow.

These descriptions, countered Thomas Paine in his reply to Burke, his *Rights of Man* (1791), were no more than 'tragic paintings', 'theatrical representation'.[60] Burke's rhetoric is itself predicated on an unnatural view of family, the artificial construct of primogeniture: 'Aristocracy has never but *one* child. The rest are begotten to be devoured.'[61] Using Burke's own language of nature in counter-attack, Paine sets up aristocracy, 'root and branch', as a monster, 'kept up by family tyranny and injustice' which the French Revolution has destroyed in order to restore proper familial relations.[62] The state rests not on 'hereditary despotism', but on choice, on connection between individuals, who have *'entered into a compact with each another'*.[63] In Paine's reading, the ideal relationship is the one of conscious choice: a relationship of friendship or conjugality, rather than the tyranny of the consanguineal inheritance.

This is taken a step further by Godwin, whose *Political Justice* similarly attempts to counter Burke. Like Coleridge, Godwin had admired Burke, and the closing chapter of *Political Justice* contains a lament for his betrayal which perhaps inspired Coleridge's own writing: 'our hearts bleed to see such gallantry such talents and such virtue enslaved to prejudice' (*PJ*, 472). The whole book, as Marilyn Butler points out, was conceived as Godwin's 'ultimate answer' to Burke: 'the source of energy and the main determinant of its rhetoric' is the *Reflections*, and, in particular, Burke's powerful 'image of a relation in blood'.[64] Godwin argues against this hierarchical, traditional ordering. Social relations, he claims, should not depend on inherited bonds, but on an individual's exercise of reason. This argument leads him into what Lamb termed 'the famous **fire** cause!' (Marrs, I: 263), where Godwin notoriously attempts to argue that the philosopher François Fénelon should be rescued from a burning palace rather than the chambermaid, even if she were 'my wife, my mother, or my benefactor':

> What magic is there in the pronoun 'my,' to overturn the decisions of everlasting truth? My wife or my mother may be a fool or a prostitute, malicious, lying or dishonest. If they be, of what consequence is it that they are mine? (*PJ*, 50)

In Godwin's uncompromising revision of social relations, neither the consanguineal nor the conjugal tie is privileged. 'Esteem and affection' (*PJ*, 199) is still crucially important, but this must be based not on family bonds, tradition, or hierarchy, but on reason and justice, 'pure, unadulterated justice' (*PJ*, 50).

Pantisocracy sought to bring together this Godwinian emphasis on justice with a belief in the central power of familial or friendly love. In some senses, it picked up Godwin's emphasis on choice and reason, on affection determined by merit. As George Burnett explained in 1796, 'no man would gain applause or distinction from his fellow-men, unless by superiority of genius and virtue'.[65] But it also showed the traces of a quite different allegiance: Burke's insistence that 'we begin our public affections in our families. No cold relation is a zealous citizen'.[66] Pantisocracy is obviously no conservative undertaking, but its radical agenda is formed not solely in opposition to Burke, but in negotiation with it, just as it is in dialogue with Godwin. To reconcile these two very different approaches, Coleridge and Lamb turned to the language of family and affection in Unitarianism. Coleridge's enthusiastic Pantisocratizing went far beyond Godwinian bounds of strictly determined merit; it also gleefully overshot the Burkean mode of cultivated gentlemanly friendship. Hailing a jack-ass brother, or exclaiming, 'I call even my Cat Sister in the Fraternity of universal Nature', evaded both modes (Griggs, I: 121). The only way these affections could be contained at all was within the Unitarian 'vast family of Love' described in Coleridge's epic of December 1794, 'Religious Musings'.[67]

Lamb's comments in the letters of early 1796 afford us a valuable insight into the kind of Unitarianism which the friends shared in the 'Salutation' era. He was keenly enthusiastic about 'Religious Musings', for instance, with its emphasis on the sheer power of 'sacred sympathy' felt between individuals. And while astutely objecting to the ornate exaggeration of the piece, fearing that it would make it an easy target for its opponents – 'lions, tigers, and behemoths is carrying your resentment beyond bounds' (Marrs, I: 10) – he responded to it as a serious piece of Unitarian idealism and hero-worship:

Lo! Priestley there, Patriot, and Saint, and Sage,
Whom that my fleshly eye hath never seen
A childish pang of impotent regret
Hath thrill'd my heart.
(*Poems* 1796, 165)

Lamb was pleased to point out his advantage over Coleridge in having seen Priestley. Moreover, he was sufficiently an authority on Priestley's writings to be able to recommend them to Coleridge; two facts which suggest that far from his having 'adopted [Coleridge's] beliefs with fervour',[68] as has been suggested, those shared beliefs had first drawn them together. Indeed, Lamb may even have encouraged Coleridge's Unitarian readings:

> Coleridge, in reading your R. Musings I felt a transient superiority over you. I *have* seen **priestly**. I love to see his name repeated in your writings. I love & honor him **almost profanely**. You would be charmed with his sermons, if you never read em – You have doubtless read his books, illustrative of the doctrine of **Necessity**. (Marrs, I: 12)

Lamb had perhaps seen Priestley preaching at the Gravel Pit, Hackney, or, more likely, at the Essex Street Chapel, where Priestley had worshipped shortly before leaving for America in early 1794, and where, as has been noted, Lamb took Coleridge during his stay at the 'Salutation'.[69] Lindsey, backed financially by Joseph Johnson, had set up this chapel in an auction room in the Strand in 1774. By so doing, he 'first organized Unitarian Dissent as a working force in the religious life of England', some 39 years before Unitarian worship was legally recognised in Britain.[70] The Essex Street Chapel would have been a particularly appropriate place for the renewed friendship between Coleridge and Lamb to have been cemented, since a recurrent theme of the sermons preached at Essex Street and neighbouring Unitarian chapels was the importance of sociable worship and friendship. Lindsey's sermon on the opening of the Essex Street Chapel suggests that religious and social unity could only be maintained by 'brotherly affection, and friendly correspondence one with the other'.[71] A sermon preached there by John Disney in the early 1790s emphasised the central role of sociability in the practice of 'genuine spiritual benevolent religion',[72] and Unitarian divines such as Price and Joshua Toulmin emphasised the importance of 'love and friendship' built up through habitual, shared worship.[73]

Friendship was also a key part of Priestley's identity as a writer. As Lamb goes on to point out to Coleridge:

> Prefixed to a late work of [Priestley's], in answer to **Paine** there is a preface given an account of the **Man** & his services to **Men**, written by Lindsey, his dearest friend, – well worth your reading – . (Marrs, I: 12)

Lindsey's account gives encouraging reports of Priestley's settlement in Northumberland, Pennsylvania, on a branch of the Susquehannah not far from Coleridge's intended spot for the Pantisocratic scheme. Lamb's recommendation also has a deeper significance because of

Lindsey's emphasis on the power of Priestley's friendship. Lindsey dwells on their 'happy nights of cheerful pleasantry, and free discussion of all subjects.' Despite Priestley's departure to America, Lindsey tells us, 'all does not end here: for there is an assured hope of living again, and conversing with virtuous friends in a more durable and still happier state'.[74] This idea borrows from Priestley himself, and finds a plaintive echo in Lamb's own letters, when he tells Coleridge, in January 1797:

> **Priestly**, whom I sin in almost adoring, speaks of 'such a choice of company, as tends to keep up that right bent, & firmness of mind, which a nec[e]ssary intercourse with the world would otherwise warp & relax. Such fellowship is the true ba[lsam] of life, it[s] cement is infinitely more durable than that of the friendships of the world, & it looks for its proper fruit, & complete gratification, to the life beyond the Grave.' Is there a possible chance for such an one as me to realize in this world, such friendships? (Marrs, I: 88)[75]

Lamb is casting himself in a drama of friendship which sees Coleridge as a Priestleian figure, having realised that dream of emigration. He has, in fact, only got as far as the West Country, but Lamb, like Lindsey, persistently recalls the idealised days of their time in London with an intensity verging on the spiritual. 'O noctes coenoeque deum,' he exclaims in January 1797, remembering the 'Welch rabbits, punch, & poesy' of the 'Salutation' (Marrs, I: 93). His playful invocation of 'nights and feasts of the gods' does not conceal the powerful feeling, shared by other members of the circle, that friendship is, as Taussig persuasively puts it, 'a relation through which they might mediate a divine love, and improve their spiritual nature'.[76] As Coleridge reproachfully tells Southey in November 1795, shortly after the latter's loss of faith in the Pantisocratic scheme, 'FRIEND is a very sacred appellation' (Griggs, I: 166).

Sensibility and benevolence

We can now see that friendship, bounded not by familial ties, but by shared ideals, was, in the charged climate of the 1790s, more than a matter simply of individual affection. It carried a political, social, and religious charge; it also engaged with a century's worth of speculation – philosophical and literary – about man's social relations. The traces of this much wider eighteenth-century debate are visible in Coleridge's attempt, still in the flush of the Pantisocratic ideal in mid-1794, to justify 'particular Friendship' to Southey:

> Warmth of particular Friendship does not imply absorption. The nearer you approach the Sun, the more intense are his Rays – yet what distant corner of the System do they not cheer and vivify? The ardour of private Attachments makes Philanthropy a necessary *habit* of the Soul. I love my *Friend* – such as *he* is, all mankind *are* or *might be*! The deduction is evident – . Philanthropy (and indeed every other Virtue) is a thing of *Concretion* – Some home-born Feeling is the *center* of the Ball, that, rolling on thro' Life collects and assimilates every congenial Affection. (Griggs, I: 86)

What might this 'home-born Feeling' be? In essence, the interest in 'Feeling' goes back to Locke's exploration of 'the concept and definition of sensation' in his *Essay Concerning Human Understanding* (1690), and the connections it set up between body and mind, matter and spirit.[77] In this account of the way in which the perceptions of the individual are built up, firstly through sensation and then through reflection and association, where do morality, or friendship, or virtues such as philanthropy, fit in? Are they purely, as Locke's famous *tabula rasa* formulation implied, the product of association?

Later philosophers, such as Anthony Ashley Cooper, third earl of Shaftesbury, find this difficult to accept. In some ways, Shaftesbury suggests, despite Locke's emphasis on the importance of tolerance and reason and his view of man as a social animal, his rejection of innate principles could be dangerously harnessed to a Hobbesian view of man as essentially governed by self-interest, an idea which would have profound consequences for concepts of social behaviour. Rejecting the ethics of obedience and reward crucial to Locke's model, Shaftesbury instead seeks to ground his ethics in natural response. Just as Locke emphasises the importance of sensory perception, Shaftesbury argues for a faculty of *moral* perception.[78] Moreover, friendships, he claims, provide evidence of this innate morality, since 'almost all our Pleasures' stem from social interaction, from 'mutual Converse' and affection.[79] Benevolence helps us towards happiness, and it is so widespread that it *must* be instinctive. A similar argument is offered by Hutcheson, who borrows the concept of moral sense from Shaftesbury and who goes further in theorising its connections with benevolence, arguing for benevolence as a 'natural' affection.[80] On the other hand, what if this benevolence does not stem from virtue, but from self-interest?[81] A lively counter to Shaftesbury's argument is offered by Bernard Mandeville, who, like Thomas Hobbes, sees self-interest as the motivating force for human social relations. Whilst not denying the existence of 'Friendly Qualities and kind Affections', Mandeville famously suggests that 'what we call Evil in this World, Moral as well as Natural, is the grand Principle that makes us sociable Creatures.'[82]

The issue was further complicated by the inheritors of these debates in the mid-eighteenth century, particularly David Hume and Adam Smith.[83] Hume's *A Treatise of Human Nature* (1739–40) poses worrying questions about self-consciousness and the relationship between self and society, furthered by his *Enquiry Concerning Human Understanding* (1748) and *Enquiry Concerning the Principles of Morals* (1751). Hume's account of the self as an unstable entity – a 'bundle or collection of different perceptions', to which the individual constantly responds – sets up an anxiety which resonates through the latter half of the century.[84] One way through this new anxiety, and the fears of scepticism and solipsism it aroused, is the cultivation of sympathetic friendship. However, as John Mullan has suggested, Hume's own concept of the power of sympathy is 'uneven', perhaps shown most clearly in the contrast set up in the concluding chapter of Book I, Part IV of *A Treatise*, between the philosophy which leaves him feeling 'inviron'd with the deepest darkness' and the relief of social company:

> I dine, I play a game of back-gammon, I converse, and am merry with my friends; and when after three or four hour's amusement, I wou'd return to these speculations, they appear so cold, and strain'd, and ridiculous, that I cannot find in my heart to enter into them any farther.[85]

Although he then makes a cogent case for the usefulness of these speculations, this seems part of a repeated pattern of oscillation in Hume's writing between the anxiety of scepticism and his own 'open, social, and cheerful humour'.[86] Similarly, Smith's work worries at the nature of sympathy and its role in society, attempting in his *Theory of Moral Sentiments* (1759) to bring together morality and emotion, and arguing that sympathy is a mechanism for regulating social relations. In Smith's outline of subjectivity we are always both spectators who are sympathetic to the positions of others, and simultaneously aware of ourselves as observed, the possible recipients of such sympathy. Putting ourselves in the place of others may be a self-interested device, akin to a commercial transaction.[87]

These struggles with the nature of sense, of *feeling*, shape the literature of the eighteenth century, particularly its representations of sentiment and sensibility.[88] Indeed, James Chandler sees Smith's as perhaps the 'most influential account ever offered for what might be called the sentimental paradigm', a moral and epistemological shift which reflected commercial and literary changes over the eighteenth century.[89] The literature of sensibility asked what part the individual responses of the 'man of feeling' had to play in a wider social structure. On the one hand, the indulgence of sensibility might arouse a more general responsive sympathy towards others, in keeping with a Shaftesburian faith in benevolence and the connection between the individual and the social.[90] This informs, for instance, the 'purest and tenderest affection' of Tom and Sophy in *Tom Jones* (1749), in which Fielding sets 'the family of love' against, as G. J. Barker-Benfield notes, the Hobbesian world he had previously explored in *Jonathan Wild* (1743).[91] On the other hand, sensibility might be a more self-interested mode. *Tom Jones* has robustly enjoyed some less sentimental relationships before his 'conversion' to monogamous mutual esteem, and Fielding makes the point that sensibility does not get far without some self-interested 'Prudence' and 'Circumspection': 'Goodness of Heart, and Openness of Temper [...] will by no Means, alas! do their Business in the World'.[92]

Even in the classic of the genre, Henry Mackenzie's *The Man of Feeling* (1771), troublesome complications arise even as the extreme benevolence of our eponymous hero Harley is being celebrated. 'From what impulse he did this, we do not mean to inquire;' the narrator comments as we see him leading a dying prostitute to an inn, 'as it has ever been against our nature to search for motives where bad ones are to be found.'[93] Whether Harley is bursting into tears over madwomen and beggars, falling prey to card-sharpers, or extending charity to prostitutes, we are always invited, subtly, to question his motives. The scene always broadens to include the sceptical onlooker, the sniggering waiter, whispering 'Cully' in the background. The reader, too, must wonder whether his benevolence might not be, as others so often see it, absurdly excessive, a self-indulgent foolishness. Sensibility might also be a solipsistic turning away from real engagement with pressing issues – self-interestedly propping up a sense of benevolence, whilst actually acting as a retreat from active social responsibility.

These issues came sharply to the fore in the 1790s, as sensibility became a battle-ground for radical and conservative ideologies in post-Revolutionary writing. Each side accused the other of a fatally partial viewpoint, with conservative writers, while not willing to relinquish the power of affective language, branding sensibility as radical. For the *Anti-Jacobin*, the excessive and undirected emotionality of radical writers ran alongside a dry, dangerous lack of feeling in other ways; their 'Sweet Sensibility' is:

> False by degrees, and exquisitely wrong; –
> – For the crushed beetle *first*, – the widow'd dove,
> And all the warbled sorrows of the grove; –
> *Next* for poor suff'ring *guilt*; and *last* of all
> For Parents, Friends, a King and Country's fall.
> (ll. 135–9)[94]

The *Anti-Jacobin* makes clear who is responsible for this perverted sensibility:

> Sweet child of sickly Fancy! – her of yore
> From her lov'd France Rousseau to exile bore
> (ll. 125–6)[95]

The Shaftesburian tradition in England paved the way for a positive reception of Rousseau's emphasis on inner sentiment.[96] This is certainly visible in Lamb's comment to Coleridge that he loves the latter's sonnets, 'as I love the Confessions of Rousseau, and for the same reason: the same frankness, the same openness of heart, the same disclosure of all the most hidden and delicate affections of the mind' (Marrs, I: 59). But in Coleridge's later comments on 'the crazy ROUSSEAU' he draws attention to 'the strange influences of his bodily temperament on his understanding; his constitutional melancholy pampered into a morbid excess by solitude' in ways which recall conservative strategies of the 1790s (*Friend* I: 132, 134). This dangerously volatile excess subjectivity was the focus of Burke's fierce attack; Rousseau's individualism makes him a 'wild, ferocious, low-minded, hard-hearted father, of fine general feelings'.[97]

The fear about this French strain of sensibility is vividly shown in Gillray's 'New Morality' cartoon – alongside those gambolling beasts, just to the right of the toad and frog, stands the gaunt figure of Sensibility. She tenderly cradles a dead bird in one hand – her other holds a copy of Rousseau – whilst resting her foot on the king's head. This picks up Burke's vision of Rousseau as 'a lover of his kind, but a hater of his kindred', who 'melts with tenderness' for those with whom he is not connected, but who has no sustained power of sympathetic vision, and combines it with parody of writers such as Helen Maria Williams, who in her strongly pro-Revolutionary novel *Julia* (1790) included an 'Elegy' on finding a young thrush in the street.[98] But much the same argument about wrongly directed sensibility was deployed on the other side of the debate. A whole raft of radical pamphleteers attacked the emotive warmth of Burke's *Reflections* and what Mary Wollstonecraft styled his 'pretty flights' of chivalry. In her *Vindication of the Rights of Men* (1790), Burke's 'pampered sensibility' represents but another form of oppression.[99] Similarly, the luxuriant sentimentality of the descriptions of Marie Antoinette elicited Paine's comment that – just as the radicals of the *Anti-Jacobin* would be pictured weeping over the beetle – the misdirected Burke 'pitied the plumage but forgot the dying bird'.[100] Radicals and conservatives, then, overlap in their anxiety both to exploit and to denounce the response of sensibility.[101] Indeed, its very power lies in its instability, its malleability in the service of different political and ideological ends. To find a way to make it work for them, both Coleridge and Lamb employed an approach based on their concept of the 'home-born Feeling' and the Christian benevolism of David Hartley.

Reading David Hartley

Hartley usefully offered a model which seemed, in the mid-1790s, to bring together Coleridge's interest in the local and familial with commitment to a wider Unitarian radicalism. The letter to Southey evoking the 'home-born Feeling' is clearly informed by Coleridge's readings of Hartley, and he returns to the point in his lectures, such as his *Conciones ad Populum* (1795):

> Domestic affections depend on association. We love an object if, as often as we see or recollect it, an agreeable sensation arises in our minds [...] The searcher after Truth must love and be beloved; for general Benevolence is a necessary motive to constancy of pursuit; and this general Benevolence is begotten and rendered permanent by social and domestic affections. (*Lectures 1795*, 45-6)

In a direct echo of the letter to Southey, he adds that these intense private attachments work towards universal benevolence: 'the nearer we approach to the Sun, the more intense his heat: yet what corner of the system does he not cheer and vivify?' (*Lectures,* 46). The idea of 'private Attachments' accustoming the soul to philanthropy is a concept drawn almost directly from Hartley.[102] His theory of vibrations portrays the mind as a subtle mechanism programmed to lead, through an accretion of complex associations, to an ultimate losing of self in God. Similarly, through affection for those personally connected with the individual, the immediate and particular sensation may gradually expand and transform itself into a wider sympathy. In his *Observations on Man* (1749), published in a condensed version by Priestley, Hartley sets this idea out as a simple equation: 'acts of benevolence, proceeding from *A* to *B*' tend 'to excite correspondent ones reciprocally from *B* to *A*, and so on indefinitely', until, in time, '*A*' will perhaps consider 'every man as his friend, his son, his neighbour, his second self'.[103] In annihilating selfishness, it also helps the individual to create a new identity, sharing in '*the mystical body of Christ*'.[104] Friendship becomes imbued with philosophical and spiritual importance: personal affection can unlock universal benevolence.

In Lamb's letters of the period we see a similar emphasis on the vital importance of 'social and domestic affections' and on Hartleian patterns of association and their connection with friendship. It is an '*associated train* of pipes, tobacco, Egghot, welch rabbits, metaphysics, & **Poetry**', for example, which helps him towards his memories of 'Salutation' friendship, echoed by his assertion that,

> I have been drinking egg-hot and smoking Oronooko (*associated circumstances,* which ever forcibly recall to my mind our evenings and nights at the Salutation). (Marrs, I: 65; 32, my italics)

We know from a letter sent to Le Grice (but now lost), that Lamb had read Hartley's *Observations on Man,* and reported on it in terms, appropriately, drawn from his own associations:

> Hartley appears to me to have had as clear and insight into all the [secrets] of the human mind as I have into the items of a ledger – as an accountant has – a good counting-housical simile you'll say, and apropos from a clerk in the India House.[105]

These teasing allusions to associationism belie the group's serious engagement with Hartleian philosophy throughout 1795 and 1796. The small room of the 'Salutation' becomes itself a symbol of the 'home-born

Feeling' Coleridge described to Southey, the small spot which lies at the heart of a larger benevolence.

Another member of the 'Salutation' group, Dyer, was similarly working to express this belief in reform achieved through affection. As Nicholas Roe has discussed, his pamphlet of early 1795, *Dissertation on Benevolence*, specifically connects the spread of benevolence to the cultivation of small communities and societies.[106] Three years earlier, in his *Inquiry into the Nature of Subscription*, Dyer had put forward his Unitarian concept of equal, familial human relationship: 'by considering the relation, which all men bear to the common Parent, I immediately see the relation, which subsists among all mankind, as a family'.[107] His *Dissertation on Benevolence* attempts – rather like the Pantisocratic plan – to work out how this familial relationship might actually be structured in society. The pamphlet is prefaced with a quotation from Bowles:

> But 'tis not that Compassion should bestow
> An unavailing tear on want or woe:
> Lo! fairer order rises from thy plan,
> Befriending virtue, and adorning man.[108]

The poem is labelled by Dyer as 'On Benevolence'; it is actually entitled 'On Mr. Howard's Account of Lazarettos', which in itself points out the practical aspect of Dyer's concept of benevolence. Like Coleridge, Dyer is eager to show how sensibility can move outward, from the compassionate emotion to the practical, and politicised, action. The final section of Dyer's *Dissertation* deals with 'The cases of persons lately indicted for treason and sedition'; like the *Morning Chronicle*, it sympathetically reports the cases of Hardy, Horne Tooke, and Thelwall, quoting from the latter's *Poems Written in Close Confinement in the Tower* as an example of the horrors and uncertainties endured by Dissenters – religious or political. Social reform based on benevolence can combat this, argues Dyer, and he sets forward several plans for benevolent structures of education, including a 'plan of a charity school for poor Children, in large towns, to be supported by Subscriptions from the Children of the rich'.[109] This, he hoped, might encourage mutual esteem and friendship between children of different social levels. In the mean time, he gives examples of benevolence successfully at work in society, his first being his alma mater, Christ's Hospital.

The school fostered particular ideals of friendship, spirituality, and community. It had been founded by Edward VI in 1552 to provide for 'fatherless children and other poor men's children that were not able to keep them'.[110] This meant that the school took on the role of 'substituted paternity', as Lamb termed it, as the individual was absorbed into a familial, enclosed community.[111] This is not to suggest that the ideals of the school were always put into practice, since at times there seems to have been cruelty and harshness from masters and older boys.[112] But the way in which the boys became reliant upon the social patterns and hierarchies of the school fostered a particular friendly intimacy, expressed with spiritual intensity by Leigh Hunt in his autobiography: 'if ever I tasted a disembodied transport on earth, it was in those friendships which I entertained at school'.[113] Lamb's writing about the school in 1813 uses the language of close familial affection, yet at the same time is permeated with nostalgia for once having belonged to a larger 'body corporate'. While the essay centres around personal recollections, it continually returns to the theme of collective identity: 'The Christ's Hospital boy is a religious character'; the school has a 'pervading moral sense, of which every mind partakes'.[114] This oscillation perhaps explains why Lamb found the discourse of Unitarianism, with its use of the imagery of family affection to emphasise the importance of social worship, so appealing: why, also, he, Dyer, and other Christ's Hospital alumni, such as Allen, the Le Grices, and Favell, were so receptive to Coleridge's talk of Pantisocracy.[115]

Moreover, this emphasis on the connection between personal affection and benevolence as a way through the self-indulgent aspect of sensibility may clearly be seen in some of the poems of the 'Salutation' group, such as 'To an Old Man in the Snow', written by Coleridge and Favell in winter 1794, and published in the 1796 *Poems*. 'Sweet Mercy! how my very heart has bled', the poem begins, emphasising the benevolent sympathy of the young observer, who then offers the old man his own garment, inviting him into the family home, 'our fire side's recess'. The model for this benevolence is a strongly Unitarian, human figure of Jesus:

> the GALILEAN mild,
> Who met the Lazars turn'd from rich man's doors,
> And call'd them Friends, and heal'd their noisome Sores.
> *(Poems* 1796, 61)

A crucial part of the Unitarian tenet of Christ's full humanity was his capacity for friendship: 'Christ was the *suffering, dying friend;* a character which insinuates itself into the heart, and constrains affection'.[116] This idea is echoed in the political lectures of 1795, with their assertion that,

> Jesus knew our Nature – and that expands like the circles of a Lake – the love of our Friends, parents, and neighbours leads us to the love of our country to the love of all Mankind. The intensity of private attachment encourages, not prevents, universal philanthropy. (*Lectures 1795*, 163)

This is almost a direct echo of Pope's description in the fourth epistle of *Essay on Man*, where 'self-love', like a pebble in a lake, sends circles outward to embrace 'friend, parent, neighbour', country and humanity (ll. 363–8).[117] But crucially, Coleridge's rippling circle does not spread from 'self-love' but from 'the love of our Friends, parents, and neighbours': his invocation of Jesus shows how he was struggling to articulate a concept of benevolence based both on associationism and Unitarianism, incorporating the affective response of sensibility but defending it from the charge of solipsism.

Readings of feeling in Coleridge and Lamb

The struggle is perhaps best seen in the changes Coleridge made to his sonnet to Bowles between its publication in the *Morning Chronicle* and the 1796 edition of *Poems*. Coleridge's love of Bowles might not quite seem to fit with his condemnation in *The Watchman* (March 1796) of the reader of sensibility:

> She sips a beverage sweetened with human blood, even while she is weeping over the refined sorrows of Werter [sic] or of Clementina. Sensibility is not Benevolence. Nay, by making us tremblingly alive to trifling misfortunes, it frequently prevents it, and induces effeminate and cowardly selfishness (*Watchman*, 139).

The distinction, he suggests, is between 'Benevolence' and 'mere sensibility', since 'Benevolence impels to action'. In Coleridge's distinction, then, sensibility is an inward turn, while benevolence – or benevolent sensibility – moves outward. So Bowles, for instance, whilst clearly being a poet of sensibility, is acceptable because he encourages the reader to be, in the terms of that *Morning Chronicle* sonnet, 'not callous to a Brother's pains'.[118] The description of Bowles' verse as 'tremblingly' awakening Coleridge's sympathies is, in light of the *Watchman's* 'tremblingly alive', cut out. In its place comes a more outward-looking image which looks forward to the language of the Clevedon and Nether Stowey poems, since the first lines now read:

> My heart has thank'd thee, BOWLES! for those soft strains
> Whose sadness soothes me, like the murmuring
> Of wild-bees in the sunny showers of spring!
> (*Poems* 1796, 45)

The elision between Bowles' words and the sound of the wild bees suggests that the 'soft strains' of sensibility are something organic, natural, and productive. Moreover, Coleridge, casting himself as Bowles' heir and emphasising his literary gratitude, strengthens the idea of a specifically 'manly' mode of sensibility and friendship. The note on Bowles' 'manly Pathos' is actually incorporated into the 1796 version in the form of a description of his 'mild and manliest melancholy'. Coleridge followed this up in his *Biographia Literaria* reference to Bowles' sonnets, given to him by a Christ's Hospital friend, going on to 'inspire an actual friendship as of a man for a man' (*BiogLit*, II: 12). This is no shrinking effeminate self-indulgence, but an active generosity and mutuality between male poets and friends.

The ideal is undercut slightly by the fact that those wild bees had appeared before murmuring the praises of another friend, in Coleridge's *Morning Chronicle* sonnet to Southey in December 1795:

> SOUTHEY! thy melodies steal o'er mine ear,
> Like far off joyance, or the murmuring
> Of wild Bees in the sunny show'rs of Spring – [119]

Just a few days after the publication of this sonnet, however, Coleridge was accusing Southey of wrapping himself up 'in the Mantle of self-centering *Resolve*', and of turning away from the friendship, and the Pantisocratic scheme, through 'disgusted Pride' (Griggs, I: 150). By mid-1795, Pantisocracy had collapsed in a flurry of mutual recrimination, and by November, Coleridge was accusing Southey of outright 'Apostacy': 'You are *lost* to *me*, because you are lost to Virtue' (Griggs, I: 163). Coleridge's anger with Southey vividly shows the difficulty of putting friendly benevolence into practice. His transference of the phrases from the Southey to the Bowles sonnet suggests a new literary direction for the concept: if this ideal of the 'home-born Feeling' could not be put into practice on the banks of the Susquehannah, perhaps it could be realised in the pages of a volume like *Poems* 1796. But even this expression of feeling is hedged round with difficulty, as Coleridge's need to justify the difference between his concepts of sensibility and benevolence, and his references to the 'manliness' of Bowles, suggest.

Perhaps because of tricky negotiations like these, we too still experience difficulty in reading the feeling of Romantic writing. As Adela Pinch has pointed out, 'contemporary criticism still seems afraid of seeing romanticism as being in any way about emotion – as if to do so would involve believing that poetry really *was* the spontaneous overflow of powerful feelings'.[120] Jerome McGann has probed the possible reasons for this fear. Although we have long since managed to recuperate Romanticism from the strictures of institutional Modernism, his argument runs, its repressed sibling sensibility has for many years remained amid a 'nightwood of lost or forgotten writing', neglected, obscure.[121] Efforts to define and compartmentalise sensibility and Romanticism, perhaps first visible in Coleridge's separation of 'manly' feeling from female sensibility, have obscured our understanding of a wider 'cultural revolution' concerning ways of thinking about feeling in the period; in McGann's words, 'we have been taught for so long how to *un*read' the literature of sentiment and sensibility.[122] The need for a more sustained reading of feeling in the latter half of the eighteenth century has been taken up by Pinch, whose epistemological reading traces a 'long "era of sensibility" stretching from the end of the seventeenth century into the beginning of the nineteenth', placing Romanticism as the last phase of this much larger movement. Similarly, James Chandler, who traces the emergence of 'sentimental probability' from the commercial theories of Adam Smith through Sterne to Wordsworth, suggests that 'key aspects' of our concept of Romanticism will become to be seen as 'perhaps better understood in the context of a newly defined set of roles and rules for "sympathy" in human intercourse'.[123] Chandler's work, which stretches forward into the conventions of early twentieth century Hollywood, is part of a wider effort to think about the ongoing importance of sensibility and the affective response to our understanding of the processes of reading and criticism.[124] In a recent issue of *19*, Nicola Bown suggests that it is time for a reconsideration of the 'aesthetic power and moral value' of the sentimental response; she is echoed by Emma Mason who argues that the recovery of a 'sense-based reading' – reading with feeling – might have implications for our own critical practice, helping us to 'acknowledge our affective susceptibility'.[125]

Readings of Lamb have long been shaped by this very issue of 'affective susceptibility'. Nineteenth-century critics vied to read him with the proper sort of feeling, 'warmly and emotionally', a loving response which, in A. C. Swinburne's eyes, precluded any sort of criticism: 'nobody', he concluded, 'can do justice to his work who does not love it too well to feel himself capable of giving judgement on it.'[126] Victorian critics agreed that the reader comes 'to entertain a feeling towards him almost like personal affection, and such a circle of intimacy will always be small'.[127] In these affectionate readings, life and writing were often conflated, starting with Leigh Hunt's full-length review in the *Examiner* (1819) which, alongside astute criticism of Lamb's 'anti-critical' attitude, suggests that 'as a Christian himself in the truest sense of the word, he sympathises exceedingly with patience and gentleness and the forgiveness of wrongs'.[128] Hunt's comments paved the way for Lamb's near-sanctification by Victorian writers, exemplified by Edward FitzGerald's comments when planning a biography:

> I hesitated at expatiating so on the terrible year 1796, or even mentioning the Drink in 1804; but the first is necessary to show what a Saint and Hero the man was; and only a Noodle would fail to understand the Drink, etc., which never affected Lamb's conduct to those he loved. Bless him! 'Saint Charles!' said Thackeray one day taking up one of his Letters, and putting it to his Forehead.[129]

But making a special case for his weakness – 'only a Noodle would fail to understand the Drink' – is uncomfortably close to suggesting that there might be something *wrong* with Lamb, as in Carlyle's view of him as a staggering, half-crazed gin-drinker, an 'emblem of imbecility bodily and spiritual'.[130]

Something of Carlyle's vituperative exasperation informs those attacks of the New Critics in the 1930s, such as Denys Thompson's Leavisite condemnation of Lamb's 'regressive mind, shrinking from full consciousness'.[131] It is the sentimental response which enrages Thompson – both Lamb's own, and that of others to Lamb – and the terms he uses to characterise it seem similar to those levelled at sensibility in the eighteenth century: 'complacent'; 'self-indulgent'; giving 'no shock to self-satisfaction'. Lamb, for Thompson, represents unfocused feeling, rather than thinking or acting: a 'hypocritical' bourgeois irresponsibility something similar to the 'effeminate and cowardly selfishness' of Coleridge's tea-sipping reader of sensibility.[132] Thompson, in the words of Riehl, 'mixes classical canons (the desire for greater distance and clarity) with a left-wing objection to Lamb's identification with the middle-class and his lack of social purpose'. Thompson's attack on Lamb may be placed alongside the kind of repressive readings of sensibility noted by McGann, who suggests that the protocols of New Criticism such as the Intentional and the Affective Fallacies 'in effect forbade the critical deployment of the stylistic conventions of sensibility and sentimentality'.[133] Now that we are beginning to learn how, in Mason's words, to 'acknowledge our affective susceptibility', perhaps there is room to re-read Lamb with feeling.[134] While the recovery of the literature of sensibility has allowed some excellent work on women writers, similar attention has not yet been paid to Lamb's early work. Moreover, his constant thinking about patterns of friendliness and sympathetic response makes him an especially good case-study for this type of reading. Again and again, he returns to the image of response, and how to build his early thinking about the 'home-born Feeling' into his writing.

Lamb's sensibilities: two early sonnets

Perhaps the earliest surviving example of Lamb's experiments in sensibility is, appropriately enough, a collaboration with Coleridge, the sonnet to Siddons, composed in the 'Salutation' snug. It was published over Coleridge's initials as one of the 'Sonnets on Eminent Characters' in the *Morning Chronicle* (29 December 1794). Its subject, and much of its language, is firmly within the territory of sensibility, yet there is a difference in its treatment of the affective response which marks it out as rooted in the distinct atmosphere of the 'Salutation' era discussions.

The capacity of Siddons to arouse a sympathetic response was a recurrent subject for writers of the period. For Hugh Trevor, in Holcroft's eponymous novel, Siddons 'excited emotions in me the remembrance of ages could not obliterate!'.[135] A 1795 sonnet similarly describes Siddons' 'magic', 'the melting music of thy tongue' and the way in which she compels a response: 'Chilling the soul with sympathetic fear'.[136] Some sonneteers go still further, and present this sympathy as a post-Humean merging of identities, where the spectator loses all self-command, their emotions entirely under Siddons' sway, as in a sonnet by John Taylor which suggests that Siddons' 'plastic pow'r' shapes the heart of the observer, 'submitting all the passions at thy will'.[137]

Closer to home, another member of the 'Salutation' group, Le Grice, had published a sonnet, 'On Seeing Mrs Siddons the First Time, and then in the character of Isabella' in 1794, in a collection produced in

Cambridge by the Unitarian editor Benjamin Flower.[138] Le Grice similarly explores the idea that ecstatic response to Siddons' acting causes the viewer to lose his sense of self. Le Grice finds 'all my senses flown', and his mind and body become one, his soul hanging suspended in the act of looking at Siddons:

> My soul had fled it's nook, and in my eye
> Suspended hung in tearful extasy.

This *inability* to respond in the face of such emotion is also the subject of Helen Maria Williams' 1786 sonnet to Siddons, which more subtly suggests that it is almost impossible to pay proper homage to her acting, which can be felt but not described.

> who can trace
> The instant light, and catch the radiant grace!
> (ll. 13–14)[139]

Siddons' is an affective, emotional communication, which cannot be reproduced in any other form, exposing, as McGann comments of Williams' writing elsewhere, 'the necessary emptiness of the verbal response'.[140] Williams is pushing at the boundaries of sensibility, the problems of finding expression for this union of body and mind.

Despite her uncertainty, an effusive testimony to Williams' own success in creating a vital, emotive connection appeared the next year: Wordsworth's 'Sonnet on Seeing Miss Helen Maria Williams Weep at a Tale of Distress' (1787):

> She wept. – Life's purple tide began to flow
> In languid streams through every thrilling vein;
> Dim were my swimming eyes – my pulse beat slow,
> And my full heart was swell'd to dear delicious pain.
> (ll. 1–4)[141]

It is in reading Williams that Wordsworth has been moved, since he did not meet her for many years, but, perhaps with the Siddons poem in mind, it is the *sight* of Williams reading that prompts his tearful response. A cycle of spectating and responding is set up which is dependent on sensation, as Williams' weeping flows directly into Wordsworth's 'languid streams'. Moreover, although the sensation ripples outward from the centre of Williams' emotion, it seems to be spreading a kind of paralysis. Wordsworth's veins thrill, but paradoxically his pulse beats slow, like Le Grice watching Siddons with all his 'senses flown'.

Although Coleridge and Lamb adopt the same pose of homage as Le Grice, they offer a different description of the response prompted by Siddons:

> As when a Child, on some long Winter's night,
> Affrighted, clinging to its Grandame's knees
> With eager wond'ring and perturb'd delight
> Listens strange tales of fearful dark decrees
>
> Mutter'd to Wretch by necromantic spell
> Of Warlock Hags, that, at the 'witching time
> Of murky Midnight, ride the air sublime,
> Or mingle foul embrace with Fiends of Hell –
>
> Cold Horror drinks its blood! Anon the tear
> More gentle starts, to hear the Beldam tell
> Of pretty Babes, that lov'd each other dear –
> Murder'd by cruel Uncle's mandate fell:
>
> E'en such the shiv'ring joys thy tones impart; –
> E'en so thou, SIDDONS! meltest my sad heart! [142]

Some key words – 'shiv'ring'; 'meltest' – mark this sonnet as belonging to the trembling mode of sensibility. That 'shiv'ring joys', in fact, seems directly to echo Bowles' half-pleasurable 'shiv'ring sense of pain' in 'To the River Itchin'.[143] Yet in other ways it questions the nature of the response of sensibility. Williams asks how Siddons' performance can possibly be answered by the poetic muse; the answer, in this sonnet, is to evade all specific reference to it. Moreover, there is a strangely disorientating effect in comparing Siddons' acting to a grandmother telling stories. While it pays homage to Siddons' power to enthral, the analogy fiercely denies any personal attractiveness: more importantly, the emphasis is shifted from watching to listening. Whereas the young Wordsworth tried to express response to reading through the power of the spectacle – actually seeing Williams read – this sonnet expresses the power of the spectacle through the scene of reading and story-telling. We lose the experience of watching so vivid in other poems to Siddons, with their frequent emphasis on her facial expressions – Williams mentions her 'frantic look' and 'eye of softness', for instance.[144] Moreover, whereas for John Taylor or Le Grice, this watching produces a kind of paralysis, where the spectator's soul is 'suspended', here, with the focus turned away from Siddons' performance, a creative response to her words is emphasised, with the second stanza inspired by, but not directly citing, her famous portrayal of Lady Macbeth.

This might be set alongside Lamb's essay 'On [...] the Plays of Shakespeare, considered with reference to their fitness for Stage-Representation' (1811) in which he returns to Siddons' performance and speaks of the possible problems of response it engenders: 'We speak of Lady Macbeth, while we are in reality thinking of Mrs. S.' (Lucas, I: 114). Focussing too much on the specific traits of a successful actor, rather than on the words of Shakespeare, we find, according to Lamb, that we have 'materialized and brought down a fine vision to the standard of flesh and blood. We have let go a dream, in quest of an unattainable substance' (Lucas, I: 114). The essay is taken as the ultimate Romantic dismissal of the theatre, the snobbish expression of the 'armchair aesthete', as Roy Park puts it.[145] But of course, as Park notes, the Lambs were keenly interested in contemporary theatre, and Lamb is not 'arguing that Hamlet should not be acted, but how much Hamlet is made another thing by being acted' (Lucas, I: 117). Rather than simply making a lesser claim for acting, he is making a bigger claim for reading; the value of the affective response is not lessened, but brought to bear still more strongly on the scene of private reading and story-telling. The most famous response of the Lambs to Shakespeare's plays was, of course, to turn them into *Tales from Shakespear* (1807). Here, Shakespeare becomes part of a scene of family reading, as older brothers are asked to explain 'to their sisters such parts as are hardest for them to understand', and then to read aloud to them from the plays themselves, 'carefully selecting what is proper for a young sister's ear' (Lucas, III: 2). No mention is made of the staging of Shakespeare: affective response is, instead, channelled into the 'wild tale', just as the sonnet transfers the power of Siddons' performance onto the grandmother's 'strange tales'.

In some ways, this may be seen as a conservative movement, as the sociability of the theatre contracts into the fire-side family story. From the volatile space of public reaction and emotion, we are returned to the heart of Burke's 'little platoon'. But we need to remember the publication history of the sonnet, its appearance in the pages of the *Morning Chronicle* alongside talk of the Treason Trials and the Revolution, and its later publication in the 1796 *Poems*, sandwiched between sonnets celebrating Sheridan and Kosciusko. As we have seen, a claim is being made in the Coleridge circle in the mid-1790s for the radical power of the personal, emotional attachment, and we should read the poem's appeal to the scene of family reading and story-telling in this light. In removing

Constructing Friendship in the 1790s 51

the paralysing aspect of the emotive response to Siddons and transferring the power of feeling onto a different, creative scene, the poem may be read alongside the other writings of the group – Coleridge's sonnet to Bowles, or Dyer's *Dissertation* – as making a claim for a more active sensibility.

The sonnet's literary and personal allusions also help this outward move. Even as the scene of Siddons' performance narrows to the fire-side, it expands backwards into eighteenth-century poetry, since Coleridge and Lamb have borrowed their story-telling 'Beldam' from Beattie's *Minstrel*, to whom Edwin listens with 'wonder and joy', as she tells stories of midnight 'hags, that suckle an infernal brood', 'fiends and spectres':

> But when to horror his amazement rose,
> A gentler strain the Beldam would rehearse,
> A tale of rural life, a tale of woes,
> The orphan-babes, and guardian uncle fierce.[146]

Furthermore, the effect of the stories on the imagination of the child connects with Coleridge's comment to Thomas Poole:

> from my early reading of Faery Tales, & Genii &c &c – my mind had been habituated *to the Vast* [...] Should children be permitted to read Romances, & Relations of Giants & Magicians, & Genii? – I know all that has been said against it; but I have formed my faith in the affirmative. – I know no other way of giving the mind a love of 'the Great', & 'the Whole'. (Griggs, I: 354)

That the expansion of the mind through reading fairy tales had been a topic of conversation between Lamb and Coleridge is evident from Lamb's later comment:

> Think what you would have been now, if instead of being fed with Tales and old wives fables in childhood, you had been crammed with Geography and Natural History.? (Marrs, II: 82)[147]

These ideas may have been discussed as early as their schooldays: fairy tales and wonder-stories, perhaps obtained from chapmen or in Newbery's versions, were freely circulated at Christ's Hospital. Lamb recalled the 'peculiar avidity with which such books as the Arabian Night's Entertainments, and others of a still wilder cast' were sought after by the boys.[148] The image in this jointly written poem of the child listening avidly to the fantastic tale is, perhaps, a scene drawn from shared experience, an allusion to the wild stories of their school days, which is also prompted by their wider reading of eighteenth-century poetry, and by the writing of a school contemporary, Le Grice, and his sonnet to Siddons.

As we will see in *Rosamund Gray* and *John Woodvil*, the use of allusion is a key factor in Lamb's development of a sympathetic mode of reading and writing. Using quotations and references which have specific personal resonance within the group, he actively involves his friends as readers, writing them into the text. Those December evenings passed telling stories and reciting poems in the 'Salutation' find expression in the 'long winter's night' of this sonnet. This small flawed sonnet, like Wordsworth's sonnet to Williams, suggests new directions for creative response: both poems question the response of sensibility, attempting to map it on to a scene of private reading or story-telling, and, in so doing, to invest it with a new sort of power.[149]

This attention to reading with feeling is continued in another of Lamb's early sonnets, 'To My Sister', enclosed in a letter to Coleridge of May 1796:

>   to my sister
>   If from my lips some angry accents fell,
> Peevish complaint, or harsh reproof unkind,
>   Twas but the Error of a sickly mind,
>   And troubled thoughts, clouding the purer well,
> & waters clear, of Reason: & for **me**
>   Let this my verse the poor atonement be,
>   My verse, which thou to praise: wast ever inclined
>   Too highly, & with a partial eye to **see**
>   No Blemish: thou to me didst ever shew
> Fondest affection, & woudst oftimes lend
>   An ear to the desponding, love sick Lay,
>   Weeping my sorrows with me, who repay
>   But ill the mighty debt, of love I owe,
>   Mary, to thee, my sister & my friend –
> With these lines, & with that sisters kindest remembrances to C –
> I conclude –
>
> (Marrs, I: 4)

The poem is firmly within certain traditions of sensibility, in the interest it shows in the connection between mind and body, and in the social and emotional relations of the self, but it also continues the exploration of the mode of sympathetic response begun in the sonnet to Siddons. Again, this is a sonnet which situates sympathetic response within the family, as Mary is praised for the 'partial eye' of affection she brings to Lamb's verse, and her participation in Lamb's emotion – 'Weeping my sorrows with me'. Like poets such as Charlotte Smith, who emphasises the source of her *Elegiac Sonnets* in her own 'very melancholy moments', Lamb begins by drawing attention to his unfitness, his 'sickly mind,/ And troubled thoughts.' But here the 'desponding, love sick Lay' is less important than the affective response it evokes from his sister, which helps him move outward from imprisonment in his own 'sickly mind'. Through Mary's affectionate listening, the 'love sick Lay' escapes the charge of solipsism and becomes part of a social interaction, continued by Coleridge's reading of the poem.

The poem thus attempts to bring together male and female responsiveness – and the familial and friendly relationship. Mary is 'my sister & my friend'; Coleridge is the friend who Lamb thinks of 'as much almost' as his romantic interest. Mary's role in the sonnet, the female able to comfort and guide the peevish male, helps us think, too, about Lamb's response to Coleridge's concept of 'manly Pathos'. He addresses some problems arising from the transfer of the fraternal model of male friendship onto familial domesticity. While he takes on the active, benevolent aspect of Coleridge's sensibility, we see in this sonnet how he begins to dissociate this from masculinity and argues for a more inclusive model of reading. As Aaron has shown, Lamb's work persistently questions concepts of masculinity and gender hierarchy, partly, she argues, because his understanding of gender and rank prejudice, through his closeness to Mary and his ambiguous social position, help him formulate a resistance to all forms of dogmatism.[150]

So too does his experience of insanity. This sonnet was written, he tells Coleridge, when he was confined to Hoxton mad house for six weeks in the winter of 1795–6:

> I am got somewhat rational now, & **dont bite any one**. But **mad** I was – & many a vagary my imagination played with **me**, enough to make a **volume** if all **told** – [...] Coleridge it may convince you of my regards for you when I tell you my head ran on you in my madness as much almost as on another Person, who I am inclined to think was the more immediate cause of my temporary frenzy – .
> (Marrs, I: 4)

Little is known about Lamb's stay in the Hoxton asylum; the unnamed 'Person' is supposed to have been Ann Simmons, an unrequited adolescent love he had met in Hertfordshire, the shadowy 'Anna' who we will see featuring in his 'Effusions', and the Alice W—n of 'Dream Children'. Aaron locates one more likely cause of his breakdown in the sharp difference between his daily working existence as a clerk in the East India House and the kind of intellectual and literary life he now saw his Christ's Hospital peers pursuing.[151] Like John Clare adopting a Byronic alter-ego in the asylum, the form Lamb's 'frenzy' took was apparently the impersonation of a fictional character, Young Norval, from John Home's play *Douglas*, another, literal, instance of reading with feeling. Norval, like Ann Withers in the Lambs' 1808 collection *Mrs Leicester's School*, is a changeling, a royal reared as a shepherd, 'a stranger to myself'. Lamb, similarly, is caught between two worlds, questioning his role in society, and the incongruity of his place as a 'man of feeling' working as a clerk.[152] It is also a highly topical character with whom to identify. Norval is an important figure in Godwin's *Political Justice*, which quotes with approval his 'spirited reasoning' (*PJ*, 102) in rejecting the authority of the king, and again in his description of a poor labourer with 'a sense of injustice rankling at his heart' because he is unable to provide for his family: 'One whom distress has spited with the world' (*PJ*, 255). In the Hoxton episode, Lamb takes on the eighteenth-century character of sensibility: Norval embodies both the responsive, suffering aspect of sensibility, and its politicised element, its divided consciousness between worldly, practical considerations, and the pressures of feeling.

Both sonnet and letter suggest a way through this confusion: the 'home-born Feeling' of familial or friendly sympathy which was to prove central both to Lamb's identity as a writer and reader. His experimental writings of the 1790s, as we will see, show him striving to define this mode of reading and writing, shaped both by friendship and by the affective response in literature. But what happens when the response is *not* a sympathetic one? When a friend does not read with the same feelings? In the next chapter, I discuss differences of reading within the friendship, beginning with Coleridge's revisions of Lamb's sonnets, and moving on to Lamb's re-writings of Coleridge.

2
Rewritings of Friendship, 1796–1797

Spring 1796

Spring 1796. The 'Salutation' days are over. The group of friends has scattered. The Pantisocratic ideal has collapsed into mutual recrimination, and Coleridge, married to Sara Fricker in October 1795, is attempting to recreate the plan on a limited scale, cultivating philosophy amongst his potatoes in Nether Stowey. Lamb has been left alone in London. 'I go no where,' he writes miserably to Coleridge, '& have no acquaintance [...] no one seeks or cares for my society' (Marrs, I: 17). But if the religiously and politically inflected ideal of sharing and sociability discussed in 1794 and 1795 could not be realised in practice, perhaps it might find literary manifestation. In early 1796, Cottle published a little collaborative volume of *Poems on Various Subjects* which might have seemed, to Lamb, the natural successor to the warm sociable space of friendship idealised in the 'Salutation' days.

Indeed, the 'Preface' of *Poems* 1796 directly alludes 'to an intended emigration to America on the scheme of an abandonment of individual property', and Coleridge calls attention to the other poetic contributors – Lamb, Favell and Southey – as if the author has similarly ceded his intellectual property rights within the volume (*Poems* 1796, x). It was the first time Lamb had been in print, coming into the world of public authorship 'under cover' – to use his words from his collected *Works* of 1818 – of Coleridge's friendship and authorial identity. Like Leigh Hunt ushering Cowden Clarke and John Keats into print, Coleridge's inclusion of Lamb's contributions was a public statement of friendship and allegiance.

The poems themselves extend these ideas of communality, appearing to reinforce the radical and religious ideals of friendship discussed during the 'Salutation' evenings. The first poem, 'Monody on the Death of Chatterton', had, as we have seen in Chapter 1, gained a Pantisocratic allusion in 1795, extending a sympathetic response to Chatterton and inviting him to join the Susquehannah scheme. The second, 'To the Rev. W.J.H., While Teaching a Young Lady Some Song-tunes on his Flute', returns to these themes of mutual harmony, listening and response, again insistently placed within 'Freedom's UNDIVIDED dell' (*Poems 1796*, 13). All nine of the opening poems, addressed to authors and to friends, continue the 'Salutation' ethos by blending radical themes with the language of late eighteenth-century sensibility, as flattering allusions to Bowles run alongside denunciations of 'king-polluted LORDS' (*Poems 1796*, 26). Those *Morning Chronicle* sonnets discussed in Chapter 1, now entitled 'Effusions', occupy the central section of the volume – it is here that Lamb's four contributions are placed. The 'Effusions' blend the language of private, individual feeling with public statements of political intent; alongside the sonnets to Priestley, Erskine, Sheridan and Kosciusko come celebrations of domestic philanthropy and benevolence, such as 'Effusion XV: Pale Roamer thro' the Night!', which extends the hand of friendship to the outcast prostitute, or the collaborative poem with Favell: 'Effusion XVI: to an Old Man'.

The whole volume seems a manifestation of the 'home-born Feeling', with its movement between private affection and public, politicised benevolent action. But in many ways the poems themselves undermine and question the ideals which had originally prompted them. Their imagery of private spaces of affection often carries a troubling or threatening charge – never more so than in the changes Coleridge made to Lamb's poems. For when Lamb actually received his copy, he was startled to realise that his four contributions, despite appearing above the initials 'C. L.', had been heavily revised and, in two instances, substantially rewritten. In this chapter I examine the revisionary dialogue of Coleridge and Lamb, which reveals not only divergent creative viewpoints, but also different ways of reading friendship, and constructing the self. The re-writing of Lamb's 'Effusion XII', in particular, reveals tensions behind the benevolent ideal with which we optimistically began, by unconsciously providing an alternative narrative of creative imprisonment, anxiety, and enclosure.

Coleridge's rewritings of Lamb

The 1796 volume opens with a direct appeal to the reader's sympathy, by presenting itself, in the true tradition of sensibility, as an unmediated reflection of the poet's private feelings. Coleridge's 'Preface', a small masterpiece of defensive rhetoric, attempts to establish the importance of this type of poetic egotism. It allows direct communication, a beneficial process both for poet and reader:

> The communicativeness of our nature leads us to describe our own sorrows; in the endeavor to describe them intellectual activity is exerted; and by a benevolent law of our nature from intellectual activity a pleasure results which is gradually associated and mingles as a corrective with the painful subject of the description. [...]
>
> 'Holy be the Lay,
> Which mourning soothes the mourner on his way!'
> (*Poems* 1796, vii)

This image of gradual association, the movement outward from personal sorrows, looks back to Hartley, while the emphasis placed on communicativeness is reminiscent both of Unitarian discourse and readings of sensibility. The relationship between reader and writer is cast as one of friendship between 'featured individuals', allowing him to suggest that it provides another example of benevolence moving outward from a 'home-born' relationship. This is reinforced by references to Coleridge's own friendly patterns of reading, particularly of Bowles, from whom he had borrowed the idea of the poem communicating personal sorrows. Indeed, friendship, and, in particular, the image of the departed friend, is very important in Bowles' poetry. The whole collection of *Fourteen Sonnets* (1789) is shaped by a myth of loss, the wistful evocation of pleasures or landscapes that were once mutually enjoyed. Looking at the River Itchin, for instance, Bowles feels 'such solace at my heart,/As at the meeting of a long-lost friend', and the sonnet itself seems to afford a temporary restoration of this mutuality, as reader and writer communicate.[1] Responding sympathetically, Coleridge picks up the word 'solace' in his 'Preface', and applies it to the poetic process, suggesting that the friendly act of sharing and communicating can act both as reassurance and defence in the face of solipsism. Through the acts of reading and writing, the self is in fact valuably opened to the influence of others.

And yet there is a certain anxiety about this ideal, evident in Coleridge's frequent returns to the problem of reading with feeling. The 'Preface' begins with the difficulty of reading a whole set of poems 'at one time and under the influence of one set of feelings,' when those poems have been 'prompted by very different feelings'. The danger is constantly that the poems will be 'condemned for their querulous egotism'. Coleridge ingeniously concludes that authorial egotism is in fact unavoidable, and a sign of true poetic sincerity. For him, there is only one type of egotism 'which is truly disgusting': 'not that which leads us to communicate our feelings to others, but that which would reduce the feelings of others to an identity with our own'. (*Poems* 1796, viii)

Lamb, in his comments on the 'Preface', continues and expands this pattern of sympathetic response, setting himself up as the ideal reader:

> You came to Town, & I saw you at a time when your heart was yet bleeding with recent wounds. Like yourself, I was sore galled with disappointed **Hope**. You had 'many an holy lay, that mourning soothed the mourner on his way.' I had ears of sympathy to drink them in, & they yet vibrate pl[e]asant on the sense... (Marrs, I: 18)

Picking up and altering the quotation from the 'Preface', he testifies that Coleridge's own 'holy lay' *has* given him solace – its slight misquotation a testament to how thoroughly he has absorbed Coleridge's sentiment, so that it has become something personal, vibrating within the reader.

While in private the group freely misquoted, suggested changes, and even parodied one another's work, Coleridge's very public alterations of Lamb's works provoked a dismayed reaction. 'I charge you, Col.' exclaimed Lamb, **'spare my ewe lambs** [...] spare my **Ewe lambs!** [...] I say unto you again Col. spare my **Ewe lambs.'** (Marrs, I: 20–1). The repeated pun gains force from its biblical inflection, recalling the verses from Samuel in which David is rebuked for his ungrateful behaviour through the parable of the poor man, who 'had nothing, save one little ewe lamb', which 'was unto him as a daughter'.[2] The rich man, despite having many lambs of his own, takes away this cherished animal to feed a guest. Beneath its humour, the allusion figures Coleridge as a depredator, whose own rich poetic resources do not prevent him from stealing Lamb's poetic progeny – an ironic comment on the Pantisocratic ideals which lie behind the volume, and an early recognition of difference between the approaches of the two men to reading and writing.[3] Behind this letter lie larger cultural and literary divergences, significant not only in terms of the relationship between Lamb and Coleridge, but also for a wider understanding of structures of friendship and response in the 1790s. The revision history of Lamb's three poems – 'Effusion XI: Was it some sweet device of faery land', 'Effusion XII: Methinks, how dainty sweet it were, reclin'd', and 'Effusion XIII: Written at Midnight, by the Sea-Side, after a voyage' – provides a fascinating commentary on different attitudes towards friendship and mutual reading.[4] Having set up the concept of the reader/writer relationship as one of friendly sympathy, what then happens when the direct expressions of the writer are revised and countered by the reader, who, in Coleridge's case, is both a symbolic and a literal friend?

Lamb responded to Coleridge's revisions in terms deliberately drawn from the 'Preface':

> I love my sonnets because they are the reflected images of my own feelings at different times [...] & tho' a Gentleman may borrow six lines in an epic poem (I should have no objection to borrow 500 & without acknowledging) still in a Sonnet – **a personal poem I** do not 'ask my friend the aiding verse'. (Marrs, I: 20–1)

The 'aiding verse' is a reference to Coleridge's 'Effusion XXII: To a Friend together with an unfinished poem', an image of friendly dialogue at work, as Coleridge considers asking Lamb to complete a poem for him:

> Thus far my scanty brain hath built the rhyme
> Elaborate and swelling: yet the heart
> Not owns it. From thy spirit-breathing powers
> I ask not now, my friend! the aiding verse,
> Tedious to thee, and from thy anxious thought
> Of dissonant mood.
>   (*Poems* 1796, 68)

Lamb picks up and expands this idea of a distinction made between 'elaborate and swelling' verse and poetry of 'the heart', telling Coleridge that while some poems allow collaboration, in 'things that come from the heart [...] I would not suggest an Alteration' (Marrs, I: 21). Lamb's identification of two types of sympathetic response – one collaborative, friendly help, and the other an appreciative recognition of the power of original feeling – continues and expands the debate over the nature and limits of the expression of feeling begun with the sonnet to Siddons. Similarly, all three of Lamb's sonnets in *Poems* 1796 circle around the issue of how the poet's feeling can be structured and expressed – questions which come still more sharply into focus with Coleridge's unsympathetic revisions.

In 'Effusion XIII,' the poet gazes upon the rough sea:

> OH! I could laugh to hear the midnight wind
> That rushing on it's way with careless sweep
> Scatters the Ocean waves – and I could weep,
> Ev'n as a child! For now to my rapt mind
> On wings of winds comes wild-ey'd Phantasy,
> And her dread visions give a rude delight!
> O winged Bark! how swift along the night

> Pass'd thy proud keel! Nor shall I let go by
> Lightly of that drear hour the memory,
> When wet and chilly on thy deck I stood
> Unbonnetted, and gaz'd upon the flood,
> And almost wish'd it were no crime to die!
> (*Poems* 1796, 57–8)

This spontaneous movement of emotional response and release is comparable to the 'melting' effect of Siddons' performance in the earlier collaborative sonnet, 'As when a child', republished in *Poems* as 'Effusion VII'. Mirroring the child's experience of fearful joy in that sonnet, here the poet feels himself transformed, laughing and weeping 'ev'n as a child'. Indeed, this loss of self seems to have only one outcome, that of complete absorption into the landscape. Coleridge, however, concludes the sonnet in the 1796 edition with two lines which impose a more conventional ending:

> How Reason reel'd! What gloomy transports rose!
> Till the rude dashings rock'd them to repose.
> (*Poems* 1796, 58)

Although no drafts have emerged to indicate what Lamb's original ending might have been, Lamb's objection to the 'fiction' imposed by Coleridge's closing lines is shown by their pointed excision in the 1797 edition, where they are replaced by a row of asterisks.[5] The 1818 version probably gives us the clearest insight into Lamb's original intentions:

> Even till it seemed a pleasant thing to die, –
> To be resolv'd into th'elemental wave,
> Or take my portion with the winds that rave.
> (*Works* 1818, 67)

This turns the poem into a meditation on the sympathetic response. Resolution, and the ending of the poem, is achieved only through a complete union of the poet with the natural world, a total loss of self. It is not the artistic value of Coleridge's lines which Lamb disputes, but their emotional force, since the originals were 'the reflected images of [his] own feelings':

> To instance, in the 13th 'How reason reeld' &. – , are good lines but must spoil the whole **with me**, who know it is only a fiction of yours & that the rude dashings did in fact **not rock** me to **repose**.
> (Marrs, I: 20)

Coleridge's ending transforms the sonnet into a demonstration of egotism, where the environment is used by the poet to confirm and strengthen his sense of self, as the 'winds that rave' become transformed into a lullaby. The image can, metonymically, stand for Coleridge's revisions themselves, which enact not sympathetic absorption in another's feelings, but an egotistic transformation of them, the same reduction of 'the feelings of others to an identity with our own' condemned in the 'Preface'.

The question of how to express personal feeling similarly informs the revisions Coleridge made to the 1796 version of 'Effusion XI: Was it some sweet device of faery land'. Lamb's sonnet focuses on the wanderings of the solitary lover, who seems constantly in danger of losing the distinction between himself and the shadowy external world:

> Was it some sweet device of faery land
> That mock'd my steps with many a lonely glade,
> And fancied wand'rings with a fair-hair'd maid?
> Have these things been?
> (*Poems* 1796, 55)

Both the 1797 and the 1818 versions – now beginning 'Was it some sweet Delight of Faery' – suggest that this is, perhaps, imagined desire:

> Have these things been? or what rare witchery,
> Impregning with delights the charmed air,
> Enlighted up the semblance of a smile
> In those fine eyes?
> (*Works* 1818, 60)

Those feminine forms may perhaps be a mere projection of the poet's fancy, a manifestation of the power of feeling. Coleridge, however, in the 1796 edition, strives to make the events of the glade a little clearer by shifting the focus away from the purely emotional response and suggesting that this is a specifically magical 'device', overseen by particular spirits:

> Have these things been? Or did the wizard wand
> Of Merlin wave, impregning vacant air,
> And kindle up the vision of a smile
> (*Poems* 1796, 55)

Again, this limits the possibilities of the poem. The ambiguity of Lamb's 'rare witchery', with its connotations of imagination, femininity, or desire, is stopped short by the invocation of Merlin, wielding his wand. Shortly before the appearance of the second edition, Lamb pointed out that this might arouse unfortunate associations:

> In particular, I fear lest you should prefer printing my first sonnet, as you have done more than once, 'did the wand of Merlin wave?' it looks so like *Mr* **Merlin** the ingenius successor of the immortal Merlin, now living in good health & spirits, & flourishing in Magical Reputation, in Oxford Street & on my life, one half who read *it*, would understand it so. (Marrs, I: 86)

We have already touched in Chapter 1 on the way in which the emotional response of sensibility might leave itself open to charges of self-indulgence or self-interest, and Lamb's sharp contrast here between Oxford Street and the lonely glades of his sonnet emphasises the problems of presenting and marketing the literature of feeling to a possibly unsympathetic or parodic urban readership. Both Coleridge's revisions, and Lamb's responses, demonstrate their acute awareness of this potential reading audience, and the difficulties of arousing its sympathetic response. Lamb's joking fears about the Oxford Street Merlin show his recognition of the potential problems of reader response, but he nevertheless attempts to recall Coleridge to the sympathetic reading ideal put forward in the 1796 'Preface'. In substituting his own feelings for those of Lamb, Coleridge is breaching the compact of friendship between writer and reader based on 'the communicativeness of our nature' – a prefiguration of the defensiveness which will later characterise his concepts of reader response, and of the relationship between author and reader.[6] Lamb, on the other hand, despite his annoyance with Coleridge, continues to argue for a mode of reading based on the ideals of friendship and shared sympathy formulated both in the 'Salutation' days and in the 'Preface' of *Poems* 1796.

Trapped in the Bower: Coleridgean reflections in retirement

Coleridge's revisions to a scene of reading friendship in Lamb's 'Effusion XII: Methinks, how dainty sweet it were' bring this difference of approach sharply into focus – particularly when his rewritings of Lamb are placed alongside his better-known poems of the period, 'The Eolian Harp' and 'Reflections on Having Left a Place of Retirement'. All offer images of the poet within a bower – an image which carries a special literary charge, enclosing within its green space tropes drawn from the bucolic, the Christian *hortus conclusus*, and the romance epic. As Rachel Crawford has explored, it is a site of self-conscious, self-referential reflection which, she suggests, was used during the Romantic period especially 'to anatomize the process of poetic productivity'.[7] Coleridge's re-writing of Lamb's bower, then, in his revisions to 'Effusion XII', reveals strikingly different creative approaches.

A manuscript in Lamb's hand offers probably the earliest version of the sonnet, which may be placed alongside Coleridge's version as published in the 1796 *Poems*:[8]

Methinks, how dainty sweet it were, reclined Under the vast outstretching branches high Of some old wood, in careless sort, to lye, [Nor] of the busier scenes we left behind [Aug]ht envying; and, O ANNA, mild-eyed maid, Beloved, I were well content to play with thy free tresses all the summer day, Losing the hours beneath the cool green shade. Or we might sit and tell some tender tale Of faithful vows repaid by cruel scorn, A tale of true love, or of friend forgot; And I would teach thee, Lady, how to rail, In gentle sort, on those who [practise not Or love or pity, tho' of woman born]	METHINKS, how dainty sweet it were, reclin'd Beneath the vast o'er shadowing branches high Of some old wood, in careless sort to lie, Nor of the busier scenes, we left behind, Aught envying! And, O Anna! mild-eyed maid! BELOVED! I were well content to play With thy free tresses the long summer day Cheating the time beneath the green-wood shade. But ah! sweet scenes of fancied bliss, adieu! On rose-leaf beds amid your faery bowers I all too long have lost the dreamy hours! Beseems it now the sterner Muse to woo, If haply she her golden meed impart To realize the vision of the heart.
(MS, dated 1796. The Coleridge Collection, Part III: The Coleridge Circle, S MS F4.5. Victoria University Library, Toronto)	(ll. 1–14, Poems 1796, 56)

Lamb's gently eroticised bower fits in well with Crawford's identification of the enclosed space as feminine and sensual, drawing 'an association between containment and productivity'.[11] Coleridge's bower, on the other hand, associates this erotic enchantment with uncertainty and conflict. From that change in the second line, as the 'outstretching branches' become 'o'ershadowing', the sense of the poem is distinctly changed. Whereas the description of the branches as 'outstretching' – which returns in *Works* 1818 – conveys a slightly protective tone, reminiscent perhaps of outstretched, embracing arms, the recasting of them as 'o'ershadowing' implies a gloomier enclosure, carried forward into the 'green-wood shade' of line 8, the change from the 'cool green shade' of the MS version similarly heightening the sense of unease. Taking the Spenserian language of 'methinks', and 'dainty sweet' as his cue, Coleridge develops an allusion to Spenser's 'bower of bliss', the 'faery' bower with its embracing vines and hanging boughs, which is a place of erotic temptation and indulgence.[12] He is replacing Lamb's image of story-telling and loving companionship with the solitary, anxious, tempted poet. That time-wasting embowered dreamer, who will reappear in so many poems of this period, points to the way in which Coleridge's revisions to Lamb's 'Effusion' are bound up with his own anxieties concerning the move to Clevedon, and his own poetic vocation. Although the conflict evident in his revisions to 'Effusion XII' will go on, as we will see, to inform some of Coleridge's greatest work in this period, it is a hard-won and often painful productivity.

As he revised Lamb's work, Coleridge was struggling to complete *Poems Composed on Various Subjects,* and also to make the transition from the ideals of the Pantisocratic scheme to the practicalities of domestic life. By late 1795 he found himself not part of a radical community on the Susquehannah, but as a singularly unprepared husband, setting up home outside Bristol.[13] He transcribed the 'Effusion' for Cottle some time between August 1795 and late February 1796 (Mays, II: i, 315). In August Coleridge had found a cottage at Clevedon, to which he took Sara after their wedding on 4 October 1795; the early part of their marriage saw him rejoicing in finding a natural retreat which, he felt, would foster not only his creativity but also his desire for reform, a version of the Susquehannah community in microcosm.[14] But the extreme emphasis Coleridge places on the ideal of private attachment leads him into a corresponding anxiety over its dangers – political, and personal. He is acutely aware that the retreat to Clevedon might be seen as a Burkean, conservative escape into the domestic comfort of the 'little platoon'; it might also be seen as directed by an excess of self-indulgent sensibility, what Coleridge was later to characterise as a post-Revolutionary 'sinking into an almost epicurean selfishness, disguising the same under the soft titles of domestic attachment' (Griggs, I: 527).[15]

The way in which Lamb's poem becomes a nexus for these larger anxieties becomes clearer when we realise that the language of ambiguous embowerment imposed on 'Effusion XII' is picked up in two of Coleridge's major works of this period: 'Effusion XXXV, composed August 20th 1795, at Clevedon, Somersetshire', published in *Poems* 1796, which would later become 'The Eolian Harp', and 'Reflections on Having Left a Place of Retirement', published in *Poems* 1797. In both works, which show Coleridge at a personal and creative turning point, moving away from direct political intervention and towards poetic maturity, the bower represents a way of thinking about the importance of private attachment and affection. Although the small, smoky room of the 'Salutation' has been translated, in these poems, to the rural retreat, wreathed round with jasmine and myrtle, Coleridge is still working through the ideal of the 'home-born Feeling' which had informed his thinking in 1794 and 1795. The conversation poems articulate a recurrent theme in Coleridge's work, 'the retired, self-sufficient "dell" or "vale" or "nook" providing an intimately known home in nature,' a 'retired familial community' which is both an intellectual and political commitment and an expression of emotional insecurity.[16] It is always hedged round with anxieties, a retreat which is also a constraint.

'The Eolian Harp', singled out by Lamb for special approval as one of the 'things that come from the heart direct' (Marrs, I: 21), was one of the first fruits of the Clevedon experience. It began life as a 17-line draft, 'Effusion 35', which celebrates the sensual experience of the flowery cottage, the gathering dusk and the scent of the bean-field, and ends with an image of the harp 'by the desultory Breeze caress'd'.[17] Coleridge continued to work on the poem between October 1795 and February 1796, expanding the image of the harp into a symbol of perfect sympathy: mind and matter come together and the boundaries between the poet and the outside world is broken down.[18] But even as this ideal of 'trembling' sensibility is celebrated, it is also questioned. By the 1796 version, this is the suggestion of dangerous self-indulgence on the part of the poet, who yields to 'idle, flitting phantasies' and has to be rebuked by Sara:

> But thy more serious eye a mild reproof
> Darts, O beloved Woman!
> (*Poems* 1796, 99)

This introduction of Sara is a turning point which points the way towards Coleridge's development of the genre of the conversation poem. As we move from a personal 'effusion' of feeling toward a 'conversation' between Coleridge and Sara, the poem seems to turn and comment on itself, starting to voice a criticism of its own passive indulgence of sensibility, which is set at odds with a more active, responsible feeling, connected both to religion and to reform.[19] Sara is figured in Unitarian terms as 'Meek Daughter in the Family of Christ', and his mention of the 'Faith that inly *feels*' appeals to a footnote quotation from 'Appel a l'impartiale postérité, par la Citoyenne Roland,' the better to emphasise its Revolutionary credentials. It is all apparently in keeping with the active sort of sensibility discussed in Chapter 1 – and yet there remains an anxiety about the way in which this can be realised, which is expanded in 'Reflections on Having Left a Place of Retirement'.

Probably written in March or April of 1796, this was first published in the *Monthly Magazine* in October 1796, as 'Reflections on Entering into Active Life. A Poem, which affects not to be POETRY', and then, under the altered title, in *Poems* 1797. The poem continues and develops the movement of expansion and contraction seen in 'The Eolian Harp', as, enclosed in the 'blessed place', the poet becomes anxious over his solitary indolence, his 'vision-weaving' tendencies. He must leave the 'rose-leaf Beds' of his retreat and go out to join

>   head, heart, and hand,
> Active and firm, to fight the bloodless fight
> Of Science, Freedom, and the Truth in CHRIST.
> (*Poems* 1797, 103)

The image of this active work stemming from the 'dear Cot' seems to tie in with the ideal of the 'home-born Feeling' of the mid-1790s. The familial community enclosed within the 'VALLEY of SECLUSION' might be the starting point for a wider benevolence, as Coleridge goes back into the political arena of late 1795 and early 1796 and writes *Conciones ad Populum* and *The Watchman*. The strategies adopted by Coleridge during the move to Clevedon must be seen in the context of Dissenting beliefs in the power of intellectual reflection and retirement, which point back to social and political engagement.[20] Retirement should be seen as 'a complement, rather than an alternative, to political intervention in the 1790s'.[21] This draws on the rhetoric of the Coleridge and Southey circle during that time, such as Southey's assertion in a letter of July 1797 that 'It is for the sake of society that I would secede from it'.²² Southey's desire to 'secede', rather than escape or retreat, is mirrored by Coleridge, for example in his letter to Thelwall of December 1796, which will be discussed at greater length in Chapter 4: 'I am not fit for *public* Life; yet the Light shall stream to a far distance from the taper in my cottage window' (Griggs, I: 277). The optimism of that light, with all its connotations of radical enthusiasm, supports this argument for the positive aspects of retirement, and it is therefore possible to make a powerful argument for Coleridge's retirement as a step towards wider benevolence – as critics such as Leask, Everest, and, most recently, Daniel White, have suggested. 'Reflections,' White argues, must be seen as a 'social and political vision in Coleridge's idiosyncratic Unitarian terms, the same terms which inform Coleridge's thought as he writes and delivers his lectures, preaches his sermons, and composes his conversation poems, his *sermones*'.[23]

Yet the temptation of the 'rose-leaf beds', and the yearning towards the pleasure of the cottage, might seem to work against the presentation of social benevolence outside. There is an active critical argument for this reading too. Jon Mee, for instance, has recently contended that the 'delicious solitude' evoked in the closing stages of the poem exerts its own attraction, and that instead of pointing outward towards society the poem yearns, conservatively, to fold itself back into the comfort of the private attachment, a move he sees culminating in the contentment of 'Frost at Midnight' (1798). In this reading, even the change of title from 'Reflections on Entering into Active Life' signals this turn towards retirement, as the active benevolence of Howard seems to peter out into a generalised appeal to Christ. 'Some home-born Feeling is the *center* of the Ball,' argues Coleridge, but in Mee's estimation, 'the ball never really gets rolling in the conversation poems'.[24] Is this a case of Coleridge's poetry signalling a nervous conservatism which his sermons and political writings abjure?

An alternative, perhaps more complicated, narrative emerges when the two poems are read alongside the revisions which Coleridge was simultaneously making to Lamb's 'Effusion XII'. His re-writing of Lamb's poem reveals how closely radical and conservative possibilities may be bound together in the same work, intertwined with the fear of creative paralysis, and with anxieties over future readership. The revised 'Effusion XII' mimics the way in which the poet of 'The Eolian Harp' and 'Reflections' looks outward from his scene of dreamy embowerment towards a scene of active benevolence:

But ah! sweet scenes of fancied bliss, adieu!
On rose-leaf beds amid your faery bowers

> I all too long have lost the dreamy hours!
> Beseems it now the sterner Muse to woo,
> If haply she her golden meed impart
> To realize the vision of the heart.
>
> *(Poems* 1796, 56)

Indeed, the revisions of 'Effusion XII' seem to have been an early attempt at the scene evoked in 'Reflections':

> Ah quiet Dell! dear Cot! and Mount sublime!
> I was constrain'd to quit you. Was it right,
> While my unnumber'd Brethren toil'd and bled,
> That I should dream away the trusted Hours
> On rose-leaf Beds, pamp'ring the coward Heart
> With feelings all too delicate for use?
>
> *(Poems* 1797, 102–3)

The phrase combines a sense of plushy sensuality with the possibility of hidden thorns, unseen dangers, pointing to Coleridge's deeper anxiety about the scene of the private attachment, and the nature of the feeling which he is entertaining in the embowered retreat. In all three poems – the revised 'Effusion XII', 'The Eolian Harp', and 'Reflections' – there is a sense of continual oscillation, between solitary dreamy poetic musings, and active work in the wider 'Family of Christ', or amongst the 'unnumber'd Brethren', to which the poet has to be recalled, by 'the sterner Muse', or by the figure of Sara, or by his own guilt.

But looking back at Lamb's original 'Effusion XII' we see that this repeated trope of the embowered and anxious poet replaces an original scene of active, sympathetic exchange:

> Or we might sit and tell some tender tale
> Of faithful vows repaid by cruel scorn,
> A tale of true love, or of friend forgot;
> And I would teach thee, Lady, how to rail,
> In gentle sort, on those who [practise not
> Or love or pity, tho' of woman born].[25]

Lamb's bower is not a 'faery' enclosure, but a place of mutual creativity, where the lovers sit and tell stories to one another. As in the sonnet to Siddons, the response of sensibility is linked to an image of story-telling and education, as the poet exchanges stories with his lover, and 'teaches' her how to respond, and how to confront those who cannot empathise, do not feel 'love or pity'.

This aspect of mutual education is lent ironic significance by the fact that Coleridge, rather than encouraging response, overwrites his friend's lines without consulting him. After the revisions, the dominant image becomes that of the poet shunning his lover, and the bower, in order to 'realise the vision of the heart': his own poetic voice. But, as Lamb points out in his letter, the original words of his sonnet *were* the realisation of personal visions, the 'things that come from the heart':

> in my 12th Effusion I had rather have seen what I wrote myself, tho' they bear no comparison with your exquisite line, '**On** rose-leafd beds amid your faery bowers' &c. – I love my sonnets because they are the reflected images of my own feelings at different times (Marrs, I: 20).

He recognises the ways in which Coleridge's revisions reflect *his* own feelings: Coleridge's anxiety over the self-indulgence of sympathetic feeling and its paralysing effects on creativity actually blocks the process of exchange or response. Lamb's image of mutual reading is overwritten – literally, and conceptually – by Coleridge's creative anxiety.

At the heart, then, of the two major Coleridge poems, 'The Eolian Harp', and 'Reflections', a palimpsestically overwritten scene of reading friendship lies buried. Reading from Lamb's perspective, as he receives *Poems* 1796, and putting both versions of 'Effusion XII' back into dialogue with the Coleridge poems which share their language and tropes, a private narrative of reading anxiety emerges which should be set alongside the question of Coleridge's participation in public debates. This anxiety creates a stasis which prevents the emphasis on private feeling from being firmly identified as a contented retreat into conservatism, but also from fully realising its radical potential.

It is an uncertainty which haunts several other bowers in *Poems* 1796, reappearing, for instance, in 'Songs of the Pixies'. This presents the poet entering another 'faery' bower, a cave inhabited by the pixies (whose original belonged in Coleridge's Ottery St. Mary childhood). Like Lamb's bower in 'Effusion XII', the pixies' cell is associated with erotic assignation, but we find within it only a solitary young bard, who, instead of attending to his writing, is overcome by 'Indolence and Fancy', soothed to sleep by a 'murm'ring throng' of wild bees. We have met those 'murm'ring' wild bees before, in the 'Effusion' to Bowles in

Poems 1796 – but there, as we saw in Chapter 1, they are employed to bolster Coleridge's claim that the literature of sensibility *can* arouse an outward movement of benevolent sympathy. Their appearance here, as their 'drowsy song' conspires to lull the poet to sleep, suggests just how precarious that outward move might be. The dangers of the bower reappear in 'Lines on a Friend', which populates 'PLEASURE'S bower' by characterisations of 'FEAR', 'REMORSE' 'MIRTH' and 'FRENZY' which overcome those who are tempted in. Just as in 'Pixies', one of the chief dangers is 'INDOLENCE', and, musing on the friend's grave, the poet nervously fears he too may be overpowered by the same weakness, his reason, energy, and capacity for sympathy slipping away from him:

> Sloth-jaundic'd all! and from my graspless hand
> Drop Friendship's precious pearls, like hour glass sand.
> *(Poems* 1796, 35)

'Sloth-jaundic'd': that powerful physical image of indolence vividly conveys the way in which Coleridge's creative anxiety becomes a paralysing force. It is connected, also, with the need to ensure a proper readership for one's own work, since the full title of the poem is 'Lines on a Friend Who Died of a Frenzy Fever Induced by Calumnious Reports'. Those reports, we learn from a letter of November 1794, concerned – appropriately enough – rumours of 'literary plagiarism' (Griggs, I: 127).[26]

'In the Manner of Spenser' carries a similarly uneasy reflection on the dangers of embowered indolence. Again, the poem portrays the dangers of 'Fancy', who creates an erotic, entrancing form, as if from the 'Bowers of old Romance', in the shape of Sara herself. But this Sara is a false one, and while – yet again – lost in 'the sweet Trance' of sleep, the poet is led to forget the 'living Image of my Dream'. Rather than putting his reading in 'old Romance' to good use, the poet has become overwhelmed by it, lulled into a trance of vaguely erotic self-indulgence, as with those Bowlesian wild bees in the 'Pixies'. The bower may not be a source of benevolent social interaction, but of dangerous, irresistible temptation, associated with paralysing anxiety. As Coleridge hesitates on its brink, it also expresses his uncertainties about the reader – whether he should turn away from confrontation with his audience or engage openly with a possibly hostile readership.

One way to evade this is to gather a group of friendly readers around oneself. E. S. Shaffer has explored this in terms of an ideal 'hermeneutic community', arguing that Coleridge is constructing a new hermeneutic model which parallels that of Schleiermacher in its emphasis on the importance of 'the intimate conversation with a friend' as a mode of reading.[27] This intimacy reaches into the past, by incorporating the words of literary predecessors, and also into the future, by looking forward to an ideal community of friendly readers, the descendants of the original Pantisocrats. Far from being plagiaristic or unoriginal, Coleridge's intertextuality, his 'delicate art of quotation and reminiscence of quotation', may be seen as enacting this intimacy, this reading friendship.[28] This internalisation of dialogue also shapes the conversation poems, which actually bring the sympathetic response inside the verse – Sara's gentle remonstrance in 'The Eolian Harp', for instance, or the poet's self-rebuke in 'Reflections'.[29] This turn towards the conversational might seem to indicate a wish to involve the reader more closely in the poet's feelings. As we have seen, however, the 'conversations' of 'The Eolian Harp' and 'Reflections' are built on a scene of earlier, cancelled, exchange. Coleridge can often over-ride the responses of others, even of those who are a part of the sympathetic reading community. Yet the concept of the ideal hermeneutic community, descendant of the Pantisocratic commune, is kept alive by certain readers of Coleridge – pre-eminently, I think, by Lamb, who uses the concept of the 'home-born Feeling' to underpin a mode of reading which retains faith in the sustained power of sympathy between writer(s) and reader.

'Ears of Sympathy': Lamb's sympathetic response

Lamb's sympathy with Coleridge's anxieties – personal and literary – is a constant refrain of his letters in 1796, as he sets himself up as Coleridge's ideal reader. Recognising the ongoing, unsatisfactory nature of Coleridge's desire for union, he remarks that he grieves, 'from my very soul to observe you in your plans of life, veering about from this hope to the other, & settling no where' (Marrs, I: 51), and complains about Coleridge's constant, compulsive revisions (Marrs, I: 20). Lamb's shrewd comments suggest an awareness of the gap between the ideal of the 'home-born Feeling' and the unease of the embowered poet.[30] As friend and reader, he attempts to calm these anxieties. Anticipating Coleridge's own encouragement of Wordsworth, Lamb constantly reminds Coleridge of his own earlier ideals, and the force of Lamb's belief in his friend's powers:

> Coleridge, I want you to write an Epic poem. Nothing short of it can satisfy the vast capacity of true poetic genius. Having one great End

> to direct all your poetical faculties to, & on which to lay out your hopes, your ambition, will shew you to what you are equal [....] **Or do something, more ample, than the writing an occasional brief ode or sonnet; something 'to make yourself for ever known, – to make the age to come your own'** – (Marrs, I: 87)

Not only, in Lamb's view, does Coleridge have the capacity to 'write an Epic poem', he has the power to find an appreciative readership now and in the future. He urges Coleridge to believe in the continuing power of the sympathetic response – of reading, and writing, with feeling.

This emphasis, as we will see, shapes Lamb's later allusive style, which seems to enact the sympathetic absorption of another's feelings. As Hazlitt comments, Lamb is 'so thoroughly imbued with the spirit of his authors, that the idea of imitation is almost done away' (Howe, VIII: 245). Lamb's use of allusion and quotation works to create a fictional space which, far from being the threatening enclosure of Coleridge's reading, acts as a protective defence – what Mary Jacobus has termed 'an embowering refuge'.[31] Again and again, we come upon evocations of gardens in Lamb's work – the 'happy orchard' of the library in 'Oxford in the Vacation' (Lucas, II: 11); the 'classic green recesses' of 'The Old Benchers of the Inner Temple' (Lucas, II: 94) – Edenic visions which suggest that reading may restore pre-lapsarian possibilities. Within the *hortus conclusus* of the old book, the self can be remade, whereas in Coleridge's 'Bowers of old Romance' the self may be endangered, dangerously seduced.

In a sense, as we will see, Lamb and Coleridge spend the rest of their creative relationship working through the differences suggested by the revisions to 'Effusion XII', where Coleridge changes the image of Lamb's poem from a scene of seduction *through* reading to a scene of seduction *by* reading. *The Friend*, for instance, vividly returns to Coleridge's anxiety over the seductive power of the novel, whose hasty unconnected sentences exhaust the reader without satisfying:

> Like idle morning visitors, the brisk and breathless periods hurry in and hurry off in quick and profitless succession; each indeed for the moments of its stay prevents the pain of vacancy, while it indulges the love of sloth; but all together they leave the mistress of the house (the soul I mean) flat and exhausted, incapable of attending to her own concerns, and unfitted for the conversation of more rational guests. (*Friend*, I: 21)

The way in which the mistress, the seduced reader, lies exhausted and overcome by 'sloth' carries a reminder of the 'sloth-jaundic'd' poet narrator of 'Lines on a Friend', and the bard who is put to sleep by the pixies – the sense of compulsive guilt is strong. Compare this with the scene of seduction in the Elian essay 'Detached Thoughts on Books and Reading', where Lamb reworks the image of his much earlier poem. Here, the reading encounter is again linked with a scene of seduction:

> I do not remember a more whimsical surprise than having been once detected – by a familiar damsel – reclined at my ease upon the grass, on Primrose Hill (her Cythera), reading – *Pamela*. There was nothing in the book to make a man seriously ashamed at the exposure; but as she seated herself down by me, and seemed determined to read in company, I could have wished it had been – any other book. We read on very sociably for a few pages; and, not finding the author much to her taste, she got up, and – went away. Gentle casuist, I leave it to thee to conjecture, whether the blush (for there was one between us) was the property of the nymph or the swain in this dilemma. From me you shall never get the secret. (Lucas, II: 199–200)

This is a scene of complicity, rather than threat – those breathless pauses forced on the reader lend a Sternean dimension to this humorous interpretation of sexual tension. It strongly recalls Lamb's poems of the 1790s, with its evocation of pastoral romance through the words 'blush', 'nymph', and 'swain', and its picture of the reader/writer 'reclined at [...] ease on the grass' – a deliberate undercutting of the indolence enjoyed by Coleridgean bards. Lamb is mocking earlier, impassioned poses, but also, through the complicity of humour, suggesting reading as a naturally sociable activity. Moreover, playing with the idea of the gendered response, the feminine blush could be either 'the property of the nymph or the swain'. Both are reading with feeling, and the reader – 'gentle casuist' – is invited to join in.

The links between this novel-reading scene and 'Effusion XII' become more overt if the reader is aware of what the poet and Anna are actually reading in that earlier bower scene. An unknown poem, 'Sweet is thy sunny hair', which appears to be a version of 'Effusion XII', provides a clue.[32] This poem, which in its patterns of imagery seems to date from around 1796, uses the same scene as 'Effusion XII', the poet, sheltered by trees, who plays with his lover's hair 'all the live-long Summer's day':

> Yet not thy sunny hair,
> O Nymph, divinely fair,

Nor cheek of delicate hue,
Nor eye of loveliest blue,
Nor voice of melody,
O'er my fond heart could so prevail
As did the soul of sympathy,
That beam'd a meek and modest grace
Of pensive softness o'er thy face,
When thy heart bled to hear the tale
Of Julia, and the silent secret moan
The love-lorn maiden pour'd for Savillon.
(ll. 10–21)

The reference to 'the tale/Of Julia' is to Henry Mackenzie's popular novel *Julia de Roubigné* (1777), which will be echoed in Lamb's own small novel *Rosamund Gray* (1798), where Rosamund and Allan Clare fall in love over a copy of the book – reading, and appropriate response, may be seen as a way of determining friendship, or love. Through his effusive reference to Mackenzie, Lamb also makes his affiliations with the literature of sensibility clear. Like Mackenzie's earlier novel *The Man of Feeling*, where the text has been supposedly recovered from a fate as the wadding of a curate's gun, *Julia de Roubigné* has a fragmentary and disjointed narrative. It is made up of letters the narrator tells us he obtained by accident, and, since some letters have apparently been suppressed or gone astray, the reader is compelled to have a participatory role in deciding the exact development of the plot, and the true nature of the relationships described.[33] Lamb's overt reference to the novel suggests the ways in which he counters Coleridge's vision of reading as a threat. Rather, he understands the power of reading in arousing 'the soul of sympathy' in the reader, a sign of continuing faith in those earlier ideals of friendly exchange, mutual reading, and literary sociability.

Rewritings of Coleridge

If Coleridge overwrites Lamb's work with his own narrative of solitary anxiety, Lamb's own rewritings of Coleridge's poetry – at least in 1795 and early 1796 – attempt to put an alternative, sociable mode of reading and writing into practice. Faced with Coleridge's tormented self-presentation in 'Monody on Chatterton', for instance, Lamb proffers a lively alternative portrait in 'To Sara and her Samuel'. The

'Monody', begun at Christ's Hospital, was part of Coleridge's enthusiastic cultivation of the links between his own poetic identity and that of Thomas Chatterton, part of a larger Romantic mythology of impoverished, unappreciated youthful genius. 'Kindred woes,' Coleridge doomily mused, might 'persuade a kindred doom' – and more than one friend worried about the 'strong resemblance between Chatterton and S. T. Coleridge'. Lamb's poem, sent to Coleridge in the summer of 1796, deliberately plays upon and re-reads his friend's Chattertonian identification:

> For yet again, and lo! from Avon banks
> Another 'Minstrel' cometh! Youth beloved,
> God and good Angels guide thee on thy way,
> And gentler fortunes wait the friends I love.
> (Marrs, I: 39)

Coleridge, 'another "Minstrel"', shares Chatterton's inspiration but not his fate. He, a 'youth beloved' (or, in later versions, a 'youth endear'd'), *will* find a sympathetic, appreciative audience. The solitary monody has become part of a friendly conversation: Coleridge's image of the threatened creative imagination is included within a circle of sympathetic response.[34]

The sense of supportive reading friendship is reinforced by Lamb's eventual choice of publication for 'To Sara and her Samuel', John Aikin's *Monthly Magazine*, founded by Richard Phillips, and published by Joseph Johnson. In publishing here, Lamb was participating in a closely-knit network of radical Dissenters – mainly, like Aikin and Johnson, Unitarians – who supported reform through education, reading, and lectures.[35] The *Monthly Magazine*, with its lively debates on language, reform and Unitarian controversy, was an active voice in the Dissenting world, lending its support to 'radicals in religion and politics alike'.[36] It was astutely aimed at a particular liberal, intellectual readership, overlapping with Coleridge's own intentions in the shortlived *Watchman*.[37] Contributors included Aikin's sister Anna Barbauld, and numerous members of the Johnson circle such as Mary Hays and Mary Wollstonecraft. Their essays appeared in the context of 'original communications' from readers, participating in debates on topics such as female education, the treatment of animals, and the setting up of book-clubs.

Alongside these debates, one of the most interesting aspects of the *Monthly Magazine* was its assertion that it would attempt to set a standard of 'poetical merit' in its pages, actively challenging and questioning contemporary stereotypes of 'Magazine-poetry'. Regular contributors included William Shepherd, Gilbert Wakefield and Thelwall; Coleridge and Wordsworth conceived the 'Ancient Mariner' with a view to publishing it in the *Monthly Magazine* to raise funds for their German trip, and other members of the circle, including Southey and Lloyd, also published there. It would therefore have been a natural place for Lamb to embark on periodical publishing, and its literary and religious standpoint has distinct similarities with his outlook in the 1790s, connecting particularly with his Unitarian worship at the Essex Street Chapel.

As we saw in Chapter 1, it was Johnson who had helped Lindsey to finance the founding of the Essex Street Chapel; Aikin, too, had a deep personal and familial commitment to the Unitarian cause. His father had been a tutor at the Warrington Academy, and both Aikin and Barbauld fiercely campaigned for the Repeal of the Test and Corporation Acts in 1790. These links fostered a specific atmosphere in the pages of the *Monthly Magazine*, informed by key Unitarian tenets of, firstly, 'brotherly affection, and friendly correspondence one with the other', and, secondly, free enquiry of the sort encouraged within Dissenting Academies.[38] Within a framework of emphasis on sympathetic response, multiple topics are introduced, and brought into dialogue with one another. The idea of 'friendly correspondence' is also reflected and furthered by the poetry of sensibility published in the *Monthly Magazine* – there is a strong emphasis on friendship and sympathetic response, which becomes, as with Coleridge's 'Effusions' in *Poems* 1796, politicised through context.

Lamb's first contribution, in December 1796, was a sonnet 'To The Poet Cowper, on his recovery from an indisposition':

> COWPER, I thank my God, that thou art heal'd.
> Thine was the sorest malady of all;
> And I am sad to think that it should light
> Upon the worthy head: but thou art heal'd,
> And thou art yet, we trust, the destin'd man,
> Born to re-animate the lyre, whose chords
> Have slumber'd, and have idle lain so long;
> To th'immortal sounding of whose strings
> Did Milton frame the stately-paced verse;

Among whose wires with lighter finger playing
Our elder bard, Spencer, a gentler name,
The lady Muses' dearest darling child,
Enticed forth the deftest tunes yet heard
In hall or bower; taking the delicate ear
Of the brave Sidney, and the Maiden Queen.
Thou, then, take up the mighty epic strain,
Cowper, of England's bards the wisest and the best!
(*MM* December 1796, 889)

This had first appeared in the letter to Coleridge alongside 'To Sara and her Samuel': like that poem, this is no portrait of solitary inspiration, but a sympathetic celebration of a reading and writing community. Cowper is pitied for his mental illness (something which would have had added significance for Lamb by the time of the poem's publication), and reassured that he will again take part in an English writing tradition which stretches across centuries – a conversation which draws in Milton, Spenser and Sidney, all listening to one another. In the *Monthly Magazine*, it appeared in the midst of poems lamenting various forms of oppression: 'To a Wretch Shivering in the Street,' bemoaning the deserted homeless 'child of Wretchedness'; 'The Negro Boy', by Anti-Doulos, an anti-slavery poem which looks to Jesus to destroy 'Th'oppressors of the Negro Boy'; and an 'Elegy, Occasioned by the present frequent and pernicious custom of monopolising Farms,' which laments the gap between peasant and farmer which has opened up in the quest for profit: 'the social chain is broke – the link is gone' (*MM* December 1796, 890–1). In the pages of the *Monthly Magazine*, the poetry of sensibility is being used – not unproblematically – to engage with current socio-political problems and to raise questions of individual responsibility. This context lends force to Lamb's tribute to Cowper, who is urged to go forward and once again participate in the community: 'thou art yet, we trust, the destin'd man'.

When the poem to Coleridge is itself published in January 1797, under the title 'Lines Addressed, from London, to SARA and S.T.C. at Bristol, in the Summer of 1796,' it echoes this encouragement. Proudly demonstrating the allegiance between Lamb and Coleridge, a footnote refers the reader to the source of its quotation 'From vales where Avon winds, the Minstrel came' – Coleridge's 'Monody'. The poem exemplifies the ideal of 'friendly correspondence', since it not only springs from Lamb's personal correspondence with Coleridge, but also encourages the reader to find correspondences with Coleridge's poems, such as 'Reflections on Entering Into Active Life', published in the *Monthly Magazine* for July

1796. One poem answers the other; Lamb's 'Lines' acts as a public sign of his faith in Coleridge's ability to go forward and fulfil the active role over which he had hesitated in 'Reflections': 'Another Minstrel cometh!' (*MM*, January 1797, 55).

Both Lamb's rewritings of Coleridge, and his criticisms of Coleridge's revisionary practices, may be read alongside the responses of Barbauld, whose poem 'To Mr S. T. Coleridge', written in September 1797, was published in the *Monthly Magazine* in April 1799. Its use of the phrase 'fairy bowers entranced' and the emphasis it places on the dangers of 'indolence' make it a clear response to Coleridge's 'Reflections', and furthers the idea of the *Monthly Magazine* as a medium of conversation and exchange. It also seems to allude to the revisions of 'Effusion XII', and the conception of the dangerous bower which first appears there; Barbauld had received a copy of *Poems* in 1796 from Coleridge himself, so might well have known the poem. Barbauld's bower, half-way up the Hill of Science, is an arbour where the poet is overcome both by indolence and by the seductive power of metaphysics, which obscure and hamper his creativity:

> *Scruples* here
> With filmy net, most like th'autumnal webs
> Of floating Gossamer, arrest the foot
> Of generous enterprize; and palsy hope
> And fair ambition, with the chilling touch
> Of sickly hesitation and blank fear.[39]

Like Lamb, Barbauld is responding to Coleridge's insistence on his own blasted hopes in the 'Monody on Chatterton', and also, perhaps, to the obscurities of 'Religious Musings'. Picking up Coleridge's own use of Bunyan in that poem, Barbauld lends force to her warning with an allusion to the arbour in Bunyan's *Pilgrim's Progress*, where Christian, falling asleep, loses his scroll, in a scene which parallels Coleridge's own fears of creative paralysis within the bower. But, for both Bunyan and Barbauld, these moments of being overpowered or defeated are seen in a context of struggle towards spiritual understanding, and the arbour is a necessary, but temporary, refuge for those who will go on to climb the hill.[40] These fears and doubts can be transcended, and her vision at the end of the poem is a joyful reiteration of her confidence in Coleridge's powers:

> Active scenes
> Shall soon with healthful spirit brace thy mind;

And fair exertion, for bright fame sustained,
For friends, for country, chase each spleen-fed fog
That blots the wide creation –
Now Heaven conduct thee with a Parent's love!
                    (ll. 39–4)

Part II
Doubting Friendship

3
The 'Day of Horrors'

September 1796

September 1796: a cramped set of rooms on Little Queen Street, Holborn – dingy, crowded, down-at-heel. These were the Lambs' family lodgings in the mid-1790s, shared by Charles, Mary – who was working as a mantua-maker – their parents John and Elizabeth, and their Aunt Hetty, as well as Mary's young girl apprentice. Their brother, also John, was a frequent visitor: having sustained a serious leg injury earlier in the summer, he returned to the family home for nursing. It was a time of tension, financial worry and illness for the Lambs. After the death of Samuel Salt, the family circumstances had become steadily more straitened. John Lamb senior, mentally and physically feeble, was no longer fit for employment, and his wife had, by July 1796, grown 'entirely helpless' through paralysis (Marrs, I: 34). Although Charles had a steady job at the East India House, he had had to complete a three years' probationary period, and had brought home no salary until April 1795. His wages had to be supplemented by Mary's work in a profession beset by social and financial insecurities, and in which Mary's position was, in any case, tenuous.[1] Mary was also caring for her invalid parents, including 'daily and nightly attendance on her mother'.[2] She was rapidly becoming overwrought, and Charles, perceiving this, had attempted to find a doctor for her – without success.

Thursday 22 September: a thundery, oppressive afternoon.[3] Mary was trying to get the dinner ready, probably harassed by the complaints of the invalid parents and by the pressures of work, In a manic fit, she seized a knife from the dinner table and pursued the apprentice girl around the small room. Her mother shouted out in alarm – Mary turned on her and stabbed her to death. 'I was at hand,' wrote Lamb to Coleridge, 'only time enough to snatch the knife out of her grasp' (Marrs, I: 44). Their father, looking on helplessly, was weeping and 'bleeding at the forehead from the effects of a severe blow he received from one of the forks she had been madly hurling around the room'.[4] Mary's violence had bloodily destroyed the homely space; her knife-blow had struck at the heart of domestic affection, the 'home-born Feeling' idealised by Charles. The small spot of familial love had suddenly opened out – not into benevolence and social harmony as Lamb had once hoped, but into a scene of horror.

Newspaper reports, such as that in the *Morning Chronicle*, were sympathetic, emphasising the mitigating circumstances of the case, and Mary's affection for her mother:

> It seems the young Lady had been once before, in her earlier years, deranged, from the harassing fatigues of too much business. – As her carriage towards her mother was ever affectionate in the extreme, it is believed that to the increased attentiveness, which her parents' infirmities called for by day and night, is to be attributed the present insanity of this ill-fated young woman.
>
> It has been stated in some of the Morning Papers, that she has an insane brother, also in confinement – this is without foundation.
>
> The Jury of course brought in their Verdict, *Lunacy*.[5]

As Nigel Walker has shown, 'lunacy' was legally used specifically to denote a temporary period of madness – a 'visitation of God' – as opposed to 'phrenesis or madness', which denoted incurable mental illness.[6] This verdict meant that, after a short period of confinement, Mary could be cared for within the family, and Charles, despite his brother's apparent reluctance, pledged himself to look after her for the rest of her life. Mary went on this occasion to Fisher House, a private asylum in Islington. Throughout her life she would undergo periods of incarceration, usually in private asylums, but she was never confined, as she had initially feared, in 'Bethlem'.[7]

The mention made in the *Morning Chronicle* of 'an insane brother' probably points to the way in which Charles' confinement in Hoxton had been used by the defence. It also emphasises the way in which the destinies of brother and sister would thereafter be intertwined. Critics have pointed to the way in which Mary's later writing identity is predicated on her murderous act, showing how consciousness of the matricide is central to her works, such as *Mrs Leicester's School*, where mothers are eerily absent or dead.[8] As we will see in the following chapters, Charles' post-1796 writing also seems in many ways to take on Mary's guilt and sense of ostracism, from poems of desolation such as 'The Old Familiar Faces' (1798) to his play concerning familial destruction, loss and guilt, *John Woodvil*. The sense of the shared fate of brother and sister was to be reinforced in future years by knowing attacks such as those by Gifford, in the *Quarterly* of December 1811. In an allusion to Lamb's *Specimens of English Dramatic Poets, Who Lived about the Time of Shakspeare* (1808), Gifford termed the volume 'the blasphemies of a poor maniac': 'For this unfortunate creature every feeling mind will find an apology in his calamitous situation' (Lucas, I: 472).

A more sympathetic response was Coleridge's great consolatory poem of mid-1797, 'This Lime-tree Bower my Prison', with its coded allusions to the 'strange calamity' which had befallen the 'gentle-hearted Charles'. Nevertheless, this too, as we will see, projects its own version of Lamb as 'unfortunate', and suggests a particular, constraining role for him, which Lamb was later directly to complain about. In 1800 he begged Coleridge not to 'make me ridiculous any more by terming me gentle-hearted in print' (Marrs, I: 217) – 'please to blot out *gentle hearted*, and substitute drunken dog, ragged-head, seld-shaven, odd-ey'd, stuttering, or any other epithet which truly and properly belongs to the Gentleman in question' (Marrs, I: 224). Lamb's self-deprecating complaints point not only to Coleridge's persistent tendency to overwrite the experiences of others, but also to Lamb's own growing awareness of the problems and limitations of sympathetic identification and response, and the difficulties and responsibilities of claiming sympathy with others. Mary's actions had challenged the concept of the natural, spontaneous link between the 'home-born Feeling' and benevolence which he and Coleridge had formulated during the 'Salutation' days. In the face of Mary's violence, and of their brother John's refusal to care for Mary himself, assumptions about the natural sympathy of familial and friendly relations now had to be re-examined. The three short chapters in this section explore Lamb's difficult and ongoing negotiations with the concept of sympathy during this period, as he struggles to elucidate to his friends the difficulties of fully understanding the nature of one's own – or another's – feelings.

Aftermath

Bereaved and stunned, Lamb's immediate reaction after what he termed the 'day of horrors' (*BV*, 89) was to relinquish poetry, especially the poetry of sensibility he had previously published, and to turn towards

Coleridge to confirm and strengthen his Unitarian faith. 'Write, –' he begged Coleridge on 27 September 1796, 'as religious a letter as possible' (Marrs, I: 44). Although Coleridge had already asked him to contribute to the second edition of *Poems*, to be published in 1797, Lamb urged him to 'mention nothing of poetry. I have destroyed every vestige of past vanities of that kind' (Marrs, I: 45). That mention of 'vanities' points to Lamb's increasing struggles with concepts of vanity and hypocrisy throughout late 1796 and 1797, in part a legacy of his investment in the culture of sensibility and the importance of personal feeling, which, post-September 1796, he began to distrust. The chaos, madness and destruction of Mary's actions threw the dangers of reliance on the response of feeling sharply into focus. How much emphasis could safely be placed on one's own feelings? As we will see in Chapter 5, these doubts were to culminate, finally, in his dark explorations of religious and personal pride in *Blank Verse* and his *Annual Anthology* poem, 'Living without God in the World' (1798–9). Here, the preoccupation with vanity is picked up by Coleridge in his consolatory response:

> As to what regards yourself, I approve altogether of your abandoning what you justly call vanities. I look upon you as a man called by sorrow and anguish and a strange desolation of hopes into quietness, and a soul set apart and made peculiar to God! We cannot arrive at any portion of heavenly bliss without in some measure imitating Christ; and they arrive at the largest inheritance who imitate the most difficult parts of his character, and, bowed down and crushed underfoot, cry in fulness of faith, 'Father, thy will be done.'
> (Griggs, I: 239)

Coleridge's reply looks back to Unitarian discourse, not only in the emphasis upon Christ and his human suffering, but also in its Priestleian necessarianism – the idea that good must come from such suffering. Drawing, like Priestley's sermons, or like 'Religious Musings', upon the language of Revelation, the letter also recalls one of Lamb's favourite texts: Baxter's *The Saint's Everlasting Rest*. The language of this letter, confident and rhythmic, and elegiac in its evocation of a theological position Coleridge had already begun to abandon, feeds into the language of 'This Lime-tree Bower my Prison', which has its roots in this consolatory letter.[9] Foreshadowing the expansive movement of that poem, with its move outward from the darkness of the dell to the sunny Quantock landscape, Lamb is urged to imagine being roused 'from a frightful dream by the song of birds and the gladsome rays of the morning', and to imagine this as a precursor of the Resurrection: 'how infinitely more sweet to be awakened from the blackness and amazement of a sudden horror by the glories of God manifest and the hallelujahs of angels' (Griggs, I: 239). The imagery of the letter, from the figure 'imitating Christ...bowed down and crushed underfoot', to the sudden awakening into 'the glories of God manifest', similarly informs the structure of the poem, with its turn from the Christ-like suffering of Lamb:

> winning thy way,
> With sad yet bowed soul, thro' evil & pain
> And strange calamity.[10]

to the vision of the 'glorious Sun!' and its spiritual illumination. Reeve Parker has convincingly demonstrated the way in which Coleridge is drawing on Baxter's meditative prose, and borrowing, rhetorically and theologically, from *The Saint's Rest*.[11] Baxter's meditating subject is enabled to escape bodily and temporal imprisonment, projecting his spirits outward to access spiritual insight. Coleridge's letter is the literary equivalent of this meditative space, suggesting the ways in which Lamb's troubles may lead him to 'quietness', allowing him an apprehension of 'heavenly bliss'.

The letter proved, as Lamb told Coleridge in October 1796, 'an inestimable treasure' (Marrs, I: 47). This is not to say that he accepted it without qualification. Although he certainly responded to this idea of meditation on the nature of God and of necessarianism, he was more sceptical about Coleridge's personal interpretation of theological issues, in particular his closing sentiment: '[...] I charge you, my dearest friend, not to dare to encourage gloom or despair. You are a temporary sharer in human miseries that you may be a eternal partaker of the Divine nature' (Griggs, I: 239).

Lamb's response to this reveals a gradual emergence of doubts about Coleridge's friendship, closely bound up with concerns over his writing style. By the end of October he was expressing his doubts over Coleridge's 'certain freedom of expression, a certain air of mysticism, more consonant to the conceits of pagan philosophy, than consistent with the humility of genuine piety' (Marrs, I: 53).

Drawing attention to Coleridge's specific phrasing, in a way which recalls Coleridge's own attention to wording in his *Lectures on Revealed Religion* (1795), Lamb suggests that he is not keeping this humility in mind:

> in your first fine consolatory epistle you say, 'you are a temporary sharer in human misery, that you may be an eternal partaker of the

Divine Nature.' What more than this do those men say, who are for exalting the man Christ Jesus into the second person of an unknown Trinity, – men, whom you or I scruple not to call idolaters? (Marrs, I: 53–4)

Central to the Unitarian creed is the idea that, since there is no Trinity, Christ cannot be of 'Divine Nature', despite being, in Priestley's words, 'honoured and distinguished by God above all men'.[12] As Lamb frequently urges Coleridge, it is important that men consider themselves the 'brethren' of Christ, remembering their common humanity. To worship Christ is idolatry; so too is the suggestion that men might become divine on their ascent to heaven. This is the substance of Lamb's next complaint, as he warns that 'man, in the pride of speculation, forgetting his nature, and hailing in himself the future God, must make the angels laugh' (Marrs, I: 54).

The mention of speculative pride is of crucial importance here, as Lamb begins to question Coleridge's religious certainties. Aaron suggests that 'this passage marks a crucial change in their relation'. As she points out, Lamb is beginning to feel anxiety about Coleridge's 'easy assumption of their spiritual exaltation'.[13] Simultaneously, he begins to feel concerned about the way in which Coleridge projects these assumptions onto his friends. The two concerns run closely alongside one another: because so much emphasis has been placed upon the spiritual aspect of their friendship, a breach of it is both a personal and a religious matter. As Coleridge moves away from the closeness of his earlier friendship with Lamb, he also, in Lamb's view, loses the strength of his earlier religious convictions and becomes guilty of 'the pride of speculation'. As we will see in Chapter 5, these interconnected complaints finally come together in Lamb's satirical attack – the 'Theses' – on Coleridge's spiritual pride (Marrs, I: 128–9).

The letter Coleridge sent to Thelwall on 17 December 1796 continued this debate about what it constituted to be a 'partaker of the divine nature' – this conversation, too, feeds into 'This Lime-tree Bower'. As he was being criticised for moving away from Unitarian humility by Lamb, Coleridge defended himself all the more strongly to the non-believer Thelwall. Whereas he was trying to console Lamb, he is actively trying to convert Thelwall, yet the two letters use many of the same Biblical phrases and analogies, revealing Coleridge's underlying preoccupations, and the connections he was making between friendship and religious insight. The letter to Thelwall begins with a defence of Coleridge's retirement to the country: 'I am not *fit* for *public* Life; yet the Light shall stream to a far distance from the taper in my cottage window' (Griggs, I: 277).

The 'light' of this particular letter is the religious illumination he feels he can impart to Thelwall, as well as his particular friendship. This coupling of friendship and religion leads him into a defence of 'Brotherly kindness':

> I need not tell you, that Godliness is God*like*-ness, and is paraphrased by Peter – 'that ye may be partakers of the divine nature.' – i.e. act from a love of order, & happiness, & not from any self-respecting motive – from the *excellency*, into which you have exalted your *nature*, not from the *keenness* of *mere prudence*. – 'add to your faith fortitude, and to fortitude knowlege, and to knowlege purity, and to purity patience, and to patience Godliness, and to Godliness brotherly kindness, and to brotherly kindness universal Love.' (Griggs, I: 284)

To this description of Godliness he appends a description, translated from Voss' poem, 'Luise' (1795), in which a country clergyman describes how his affectionate feelings for his daughter are echoed by those of God, whose love *'swells with active impulse towards all his Children'*. The clergyman not only rejoices in this fellow-feeling, but sees it, in Baxterian terms, as a prefiguration of the day when all will *'fall asleep, and [...] wake in the common Morning of the Resurrection'*. This leads Coleridge into suggesting that Thelwall, though unconverted, might yet experience 'a progression in [his] *moral* character'. He ends with a vision of the two of them in the kingdom of Heaven together – 'and I with transport in my eye shall say – "I *told* you so, my *dear* fellow"'. Sara and Stella, meanwhile, are transformed into 'sister-seraphs in the heavenly Jerusalem' (Griggs, I: 285).

With those rather lovely 'sister-seraphs', however, we return to the kind of speculative vision which Lamb considered spiritually endangering. The letters of late 1796 to Lamb and Thelwall show that Coleridge, at this point, was placing a great deal of importance on the moral attributes of others, their ability to practise 'brotherly kindness'. Simultaneously, Lamb was suggesting that this might be undermined by Coleridge's own 'pride of speculation'. While 'brotherly kindness' is a central idea of Unitarian belief, over-reliance on human judgement can approach idolatry. Similarly, Lamb takes issue with a statement of Coleridge that 'it is by the press, that God hath given finite spirits both evil and good (I suppose you mean *simply* bad men and good men) a portion as it were of His Omnipresence!' (Marrs, I: 53). With phrases such as 'portion of

Omnipresence', suggests Lamb: 'You seem to me to have been straining your comparing faculties to bring together things infinitely distant and unlike; the feeble narrow-sphered operations of the human intellect and the everywhere diffused mind of Deity, the peerless wisdom of Jehovah' (Marrs, I: 56). Lamb is warning Coleridge about a general tendency not only in his religious philosophy, as Lamb saw it, but also in his friendship: the danger of placing too much emphasis on his own 'narrow-sphered' insight, and according his own views a 'God*like*-ness'.

Coleridge, in the mid-1790s, was strongly attracted by the speculative possibilities afforded by Unitarianism, such as Priestley's conception of matter as an energy or force. Indeed, looking at Coleridge's 'lifetime of experimental observation', Jane Stabler has identified 'a Priestleyan scientific pulse at the heart of Coleridgean poetics'.[14] But speculation is not, as she points out, given a free rein by Priestley, nor yet by Barbauld, and in some ways Lamb's letters run parallel to the attempt made by Barbauld in her poem 'To Mr. S. T. Coleridge', to warn Coleridge away from – in her words – 'the maze of metaphysic lore'.[15] Instead, Lamb emphasises the practical aspects of Unitarianism, and the value it places on familial and friendly affection.

This emphasis runs alongside Lamb's attempt to coax Coleridge towards simplicity. That phrase 'I suppose you mean *simply* bad men and good men' contains the seeds of his more famous criticism in the subsequent letter: 'Cultivate simplicity, Coleridge, or rather, I should say, banish elaborateness; for simplicity springs spontaneous from the heart, and carries into daylight its own modest buds and genuine, sweet, and clear flowers of expression' (Marrs, I: 60–1).

The advice is intimately connected to the warning that Coleridge is moving away from Unitarian humility in straining his 'comparing faculties to bring together things infinitely distant and unlike'. Lamb is struggling with the central Coleridgean desire to tap into the idea of 'Omnipresence', to perceive, as he tells Thelwall, 'something *one & indivisible*' (Griggs, I: 349). This not only leads him away from simplicity, it also prevents him from appreciating the very distance between or unlikeness of things – or people. This reproach, which functions on several levels – poetic, religious, and personal – seems to me to point to Lamb's actual experience of the Coleridgean dilemma noticed and explored by Thomas McFarland and Seamus Perry: his difficulty in negotiating between the external world and the poetic ego; his essential double-mindedness, which wants constantly to bring things together, even when – or perhaps especially when – those things are, in Lamb's words, 'distant and unlike'. Lamb's reproaches also run parallel to Thelwall's attacks of the same time on Coleridge's 'dreamy semblances'. In May 1796, Thelwall had written to Coleridge attacking the 'religious' aspect of 'Religious Musings', 'the very acme of abstruse, metaphysical, mistical rant'.[16] This attack runs alongside his criticism of Coleridge's poetic style: its strained comparisons, and its 'frequent accent upon adjectives and weak words – "Escap'd the *sore* wounds" – "Sunk to the *cold* earth"...', which, Thelwall maintained, with his characteristic bluntness, gave him 'the earache'.

Thelwall and Lamb, the atheist and the committed Unitarian, might seem to be arguing from completely different sides; there are, in fact, surprising similarities in the ways in which, as friends of Coleridge, they challenge and question him, and in the eventual fates of both friendships as Wordsworth enters the scene. Like Barbauld later urging Coleridge to avoid mazy self-referentiality, both Thelwall and Lamb attempt to lead him away from 'elaborateness' and speculation towards directed creative activity. For Thelwall, this meant putting his democratic principles into 'active exertions' in society – writing and speaking, using 'the energy of mind', as he comments in the *Tribune* in 1795.[17] For Lamb, thinking about the Unitarian emphasis on the affectionate bond, it meant a return to the simplicity of the known, the local, and the familial. This advice was also a form of self-reassurance on Lamb's part, since he himself was, at this point, attempting to justify his own writing.

Reconstructing the poetry of familial affection

As we have noted, Lamb was initially troubled by the 'vanities' of poetry writing in the aftermath of his mother's death, feeling that the egotism of poetic sensibility was inexcusable in the face of his family responsibilities. Yet he continued with his plan of contributing to Coleridge's *Poems* 1797, telling him in the same letter which urges simplicity: 'these questions about words, and debates about alterations, take me off, I am conscious, from the properer business of *my* life. Take my sonnets once for all, and do not propose any re-amendments, or mention them again in any shape to me, I charge you' (Marrs, I: 60).

But that very persistence that Coleridge should not continue to revise or amend the sonnets demonstrates Lamb's continued involvement with the poems. By his next letter, he had found a way to integrate this continued attachment to creative writing with his domestic responsibilities, asking for Coleridge's approval of his wish to dedicate his section of the volume to Mary (Marrs, I: 62). This dedication duly appeared in the edition, following a quotation from Massinger's play *A Very Woman* (1655), whose references to drunkenness and depression may have had personal significance for the Lambs. The poems, 'creatures of the fancy and the feeling', are 'with all a brother's fondness, inscribed to Mary Ann Lamb, the author's best friend and sister' (*Poems* 1797, 216) – a dedication which, in the light of Mary's having been named in some newspaper reports of the murder, functions as a public statement of defence and support.

By enclosing his poems within this frame of familial and friendly affection, Lamb also manages to negate his anxiety about their personal egotism or vanity, echoing his reassurance of Coleridge we saw in Chapter 2. As Lamb dedicated his poems to Mary, he also urged Coleridge himself to turn back to his own family, writing in the same letter: 'I rejoice to hear, by certain channels, that you, my friend, are reconciled with all your relations. 'Tis the most kindly and natural species of love, and we have all the associated train of early feelings to secure its strength and perpetuity' (Marrs, I: 64).

This is in keeping with the earlier ideals of the 'Salutation', but – like the dedication of Lamb's work in *Poems* 1797 – this re-assertion of familial affection as 'the most kindly and natural species of love' is in some ways a combative statement of Lamb's refusal to relinquish his belief in the 'home-born Feeling'.

This in turn strengthened Coleridge's own ideals. One of the practical effects of Lamb's encouragement was the dedication of *Poems* 1797: 'To the Rev. George Coleridge'. Written in May 1797, this poem was a product of Coleridge's new-found domestic content in Nether Stowey, which was, as Coleridge had hoped Clevedon would be, a successor to the Pantisocratic plan – a place not to withdraw from society, but to put into practice benevolent ideals of domestic attachment. His continued faith in those earlier associationist ideals of private affection and benevolence was embodied in the name he gave his son: David Hartley Coleridge, born in September 1796. By January 1797, the whole household, with the addition of his tutee Charles Lloyd, was installed at Nether Stowey. As Coleridge embarked on family life, he was led to think about his relationship with his own family, and his early childhood experiences, writing several autobiographical letters to Poole which dwell on the construction of the self. 'What I am,' he told Poole in the first of these letters, 'depends on what I have been', and this consideration perhaps pointed the way towards discussion of childhood experiences with Wordsworth and Lamb (Griggs, I: 302).

'To the Rev. George Coleridge' is a product of this renewed domestic focus. It draws together the various strands of Coleridge's creative imagination at the time and places them in the context of familial affection. As the dedicatory poem of *Poems* 1797, it works to frame the poems of Lamb and Lloyd within an encircling, natural domesticity, putting into practice the two ideas urged by Lamb, and, to some extent, Thelwall. Simplicity of style is echoed by a return to familial affection. While dedicated to his brother and his strong local family ties – 'fraternal Love/Hath drawn you to one centre' (*Poems*, 1797, viii) – it also celebrates his own fraternal friendship with Poole, who had been instrumental in obtaining the Nether Stowey house for him. As soon as he arrived, Coleridge was telling Cottle that 'a communication has been made from our Orchard into T. Poole's Garden', and within that garden was a further symbol of Poole's nurturing friendship: his bower (Griggs, I: 297). The bower is charged with the ideals of the 'home-born Feeling'; moreover, it is a place where nature and affection seemed to come together. With Poole as his mentor and support, 'assisting me in the acquirement of agricultural practice', Coleridge felt that he would be able not only to cultivate nature, but also to find a fresh way of perceiving it, as a stable source of friendly love (Griggs, I: 270).[18] Poole's friendship is invested with a mediating power, as in the words of dedication Coleridge wrote in Poole's copy of *Poems* 1796: 'I love to shut my eyes, and bring up before my imagination that Arbour, in which I have repeated so many of these compositions to you –. Dear Arbour! An Elysium to which I have often passed by your Cerberus, and Tartarean tan-pits'.[19]

Through the repetition of the poems within the arbour, again a reminder of the enchanting readings of the 'Salutation' days, Coleridge now brings Poole into the community of the volume. Indeed, Poole's friendship, identified with the 'imperious covert of one Oak' is seen as an over-arching, enclosing power, within which the volume is able to be written. The shelter of his friendship seems divinely conferred, 'all praise to Him', writes Coleridge, 'Who gives us all things' (*Poems* 1797, ix). And, in a movement reminiscent of the Unitarian emphasis on sociability, the poem offers some comforting images of embowered happiness, whether beside the 'cleanly hearth and social bowl', or outside, in the 'sweet sequester'd Orchard-plot' under 'an arborous roof' of blossom (*Poems* 1797, x–xi). This refiguration of 'Effusion XII' shows Coleridge surrounded by family members in an image of loving content and mutual communication. Instead of the dangerous 'rose-leaf beds' of his earlier poems, here we have 'loose blossoms' falling upon the family like a blessing, and nature bending to hold them within a protective, maternal embrace.

Within this small spot of domestic and creative content, Coleridge hoped finally to have reconciled his anxieties concerning retreat and social engagement. As he wrote to Lloyd's father, in fierce defence of the Nether Stowey plan,

> You think my scheme *monastic rather than Christian*. Can he be deemed monastic who is married, and employed in rearing his children? – who *personally* preaches the truth to his friends and neighbours, and who endeavours to instruct tho' Absent by the Press? In what line of Life could I be more *actively* employed? (Griggs, I: 255)

This ideal of activity in retreat is undermined, however, by the anxieties and tensions also present within the poem, 'To the Rev. George Coleridge'. The protective bower offered by Poole's friendship is contrasted with other, 'chance-started Friendships' and their hostile enclosure:

>   some most false,
> False and fair-foliag'd as the Manchineel,
> Have tempted me to slumber in their shade
> E'en mid the storm; then breathing subtlest damps,
> Mix'd their own venom with the rain from heaven,
> That I woke poison'd!
>   (*Poems* 1797, viii–ix)

The bitterness stems from his frustration with Southey over the failure of the Pantisocratic scheme, but it also points forward to the eventual collapse of the Nether Stowey household. The poisonous space offered by those Manchineel friends echoes the dangerous bowers encountered in 'Songs of the Pixies' and 'Reflections on Having Left a Place of Retirement'. The powerful idea of unconscious poisoning conveys earlier Coleridgean fears of indolence and paralysis, and also suggests problems with the friendship ideal, which may, similarly, become confining or paralysing.

The poem ends with a direct appeal to George:

>   These various songs,
> Which I have fram'd in many a various mood,
> Accept, my BROTHER!
>   (*Poems* 1797, xi)

The closing lines of the poem, with their desire to be witnessed and approved, alert the reader to a central preoccupation of the whole collection: the desire for an affectionate observer, who interprets Coleridge's errors with sympathy and understanding. Within the collection, this yearning towards the sympathetic reader is picked up by 'Reflections', reprinted from the *Monthly Magazine*. During 1797 and 1798, the theme would also re-emerge in 'This Lime-tree Bower my Prison' and 'Frost at Midnight', where the presence of the silent other is of great importance – release or inspiration only comes from picturing the responses of another. As Walter Jackson Bate notes, the conversation poems reveal the 'particular way in which he would wish – in fact needed – to be considered by others': 'He needed, for example, to show to others, and to reassure himself, that he was a benevolent man. And he *was* benevolent'.[20]

Bate picks up the rhythms of the phrase 'And we *were* blessed', Coleridge's reinforcement of the idea uttered by the Bristol citizen in 'Reflections'. A self-perpetuating cycle of gazing is going on, as Coleridge's conceptions of himself are mirrored by others.[21] Indeed, within 'Reflections' itself, there are two acts of gazing which point to the importance of being witnessed. The first takes place when the citizen, the 'wealthy son of Commerce' looks in at this place of retreat, and – like Milton's Satan peering in at Eden – gazes and muses on the '*blessed place*' (*Poems* 1797, 100–1).[22] This citizen remains an unspoken presence in the rest of the poem, a spectator or reader of the scene, who confers an extra dimension of blessedness. As Newlyn points out, his apprehension of the Edenic quality of the retreat seems to transform him from 'misreader to ideal reader' and thus 'performatively underwrites the poet's authority'.[23] This is reinforced by the way in which Coleridge similarly appeals for his brother's transformation from disapproving judge, finding the poems 'discordant', to ideal, loving reader.

The way in which this appeal was actually received by Coleridge's brother, however, was unfortunately symbolic. Coleridge added at the end of the poem in Southey's collection: 'N.B. If this volume should ever be delivered according to it's Direction, i.e. to Posterity, let it be known, that the Reverend George Coleridge was displeased and thought his character endangered by this Dedication!!' (Mays, I: i, 326).

As in the case of Coleridge's revisions to Lamb's work, the reader angrily answers back, rejecting the role projected upon him. Similar problems were in fact already undermining the friendly community presented in *Poems* 1797. The 'triumvirate' celebrated in the effusive Latin dedication by 'Groscollius' which Coleridge invented for this edition of the *Poems* was in fact already dissolving: 'We have a double bond: that of friendship and of our linked and kindred Muses: may neither death nor length of time dissolve it' (Griggs, I: 390).

This was in part due to Lamb's new-found spiritual doubts and uncertainties about pride, but also to the problems which were rapidly beginning to develop between Coleridge and the third contributor to *Poems* 1797: Lloyd.

Nether Stowey: 'an Elysium upon earth'?

On a financial level, Lloyd was in fact the chief contributor to the Nether Stowey scheme. A son of the wealthy bankers, Lloyd had rejected the family business in favour of intellectual enquiry. He had already published his own *Poems on Various Subjects* in 1795, and his letters of this time point to a preoccupation with many of the same issues Coleridge and Lamb were simultaneously discussing. Although the family were strict Quakers, Lloyd was, by November 1795, telling his brother:

> The pure ardour of universal benevolence does not abate at the sight of a Lutheran or a Quaker, a Catholic or an Unbeliever. No! it considers all the petty, paltry distinctions of parties and sects, which would separate man from man and brother from brother, as originating in the weaknesses and prejudices of mankind; it despises them all, and simply seeks by active usefulness, not by unintelligible dogmas, to diffuse good and enlarge the confin'd limit of human felicity.[24]

This was followed by a list of reading for the 16-year-old Robert, including Holcroft's *Anna St. Ives* (1792), Godwin's *Political Justice*, and works defending the Unitarian faith by Priestley and Lindsey. We can see that the course of reading Lloyd was pursuing paralleled that of the 'Salutation': similarly, his 1795 *Poems* correspond with many ideas addressed by Coleridge and Lamb in their namesake volume: the powers of 'fostering Friendship', for example, or the horror of war, when 'a *sword* is a passport to *Fame*'.[25] The attempt to distil 'the pure ardour of universal benevolence' through a gradual diffusion of good, a gradual movement outward from 'the confin'd limit of human felicity' demonstrates how Lloyd was, independently, considering the ways in which Hartleian philosophy might actively be applied.

Meeting Coleridge, when the latter had come to preach in Birmingham in early 1796, seemed to offer the opportunity to put these ideas into practice, and by September of that year, he was living with the Coleridges, paying £80 a year for board, lodging and tutoring.[26] That Lloyd's conception of the relationship went far beyond this practical arrangement is revealed by his sonnet, written soon after their first meeting:

> Coleridge, my soul is very sad to think
> We seperate so soon, for tho unfit
> To mould the prompt phrase with impetuous wit,
> truly
> I love thee, & my heart will sink
> Musing on the departed, nor the less
> Still it regret, because it never knew
> T'expose its feelings to the careless view
> Its simple store of wayward wretchedness.
> But I did fancy as mine eye met thine
> That there than erst e'er seen the social glow
> Intenslier dwelt – (I've wept in agony
> To think that glow the human face divine
> So scantily should radiate) if t'were so –
> If t'were a ray of soul, remember me!
>
> (ll. 1–14)[27]

Collected with several other poems in a notebook which appears to chronicle the months of Lloyd's stay in Nether Stowey, this sonnet emphasises the divine quality of friendly love. In its conception of Coleridge as a 'sun', whose social glow shines out over his acquaintances, Lloyd's poem is strongly reminiscent of Coleridge's own 1794 discussion of the 'warmth of particular Friendship', the sun whose 'intense [...] Rays' 'cheer and vivify' (Griggs, I: 86). This fosters the image of the 'bursting Sun' in 'Religious Musings' – to which Lloyd might well be alluding – sending forth 'new-born intermingling rays,/And wide around the landscape streams with glory!' (*Poems* 1796, 147), and Coleridge's assertion to Thelwall that the 'Light shall stream to a far distance' from his cottage window (Griggs, I: 277). This illuminating domestic ideal takes shape, for both Coleridge and Lloyd, as a reaction against their reading of Godwin. Both had been fascinated by the concepts of social enlightenment they had found in *Political Justice* whilst reacting against what they perceived as its dismissal of personal affection. As we can see from this poem, Lloyd structures his relationship with Coleridge as a refutation of Godwinian disinterest and atheism and an assertion, instead, of the spiritual and religious importance of domestic community: 'the human face divine'. The movement of affection 'as mine eye met thine' makes their fraternal interest common, breaking down barriers of self, and illuminating the reserves of Lloyd's own heart, its 'simple store' of emotion. The theme is continued in other poems in the notebook, as Lloyd sees Coleridge as an embodied figure 'of friendship and of sympathy', extending 'lavish promises' of mutual fraternal love.[28] Very soon, however, tensions emerged in the Nether Stowey cottage, which may simply have been physically too small, too cramped, to bear the burden of the Hartleian ideal the two men were attempting to impose upon it.[29]

To Lamb, however, on his own in London, Coleridge and Lloyd seemed 'to be about **realizing** an Elysium upon earth' (Marrs, I: 75). His isolation in November and December 1796 was acute, heightened by his awareness that Lloyd was enjoying the same kind of mutual conversational relationship he had once shared with Coleridge. 'Are we *never* to meet again?' he wrote to Coleridge in December, remembering the mutual creativity of the 'Salutation':

> How differently I am circumstanced **now** – . I have never met with any one, never shall meet with any **one**, who could or can compensate me for the top of your **Society** – I have no one to talk all these matters about too – I lack friends, I lack books to supply their absence – . (Marrs, I: 65–6)

His only consolation was Coleridge's letters, which he regarded as 'sacred things', and book packages, such as the 'poetical present' he acknowledges in a subsequent letter (Marrs, I: 73), containing Lloyd's *Poems on the Death of Priscilla Farmer* (1796), and the small collection of *Sonnets from Various Authors* Coleridge had put together in 1796.[30] David Fairer has shown how Coleridge's editing of this collection encloses the work of Lamb and Lloyd within a consolatory framework of other eighteenth-century sonnets, guiding both the younger men through times of trouble and loneliness.[31] The collection opens with Bowles' sonnet 'To a Friend'. In that poem, Bowles explores how 'the charm of song' can support the 'friendless', and the whole collection may be seen as Coleridge's attempt to put this into practice. His choice of sonnets dwells upon memory and sympathetic communion, whether that is with a scene of the past, as in 'To the River Otter', or with the 'poor old man' without a cloak in 'To An Old Man in the Snow', or with a writer who has moved him, as in 'To the Author of "The Robbers"'. Indeed, the collection itself mimics that movement of sheltering and enclosing seen in 'To An Old Man', which had previously appeared, as we have seen, in

Poems 1796. In a feat of sympathetic imagination, fuelled by the Unitarian sermons of the previous year, Coleridge again places himself in the position of 'the Galilaean mild', creating a friendly community of benevolence and religious sympathy. Just as Coleridge extends warmth and shelter to the old man, inviting him to 'talk, in our fire side's recess', this collection invites Lamb and Lloyd to enter into a sympathetic dialogue with other writers, a movement mirrored by his sending out of the sonnets to friends, including Thelwall and Lamb.

And yet this sympathetic dialogue is, again, partly a projection of Coleridge's own voice. Many of the sonnets have been altered or revised, including Bampfylde's 'To Evening', which has been substantially re-written, and appears over the name 'Bamfield'. Sonnet IX, 'When eddying Leaves begun in whirls to fly', is given as by 'Henry Brooks, the Author of the Fool of Quality' – in fact, under the title 'On Echo and Silence', it belongs to Egerton Brydges. Most importantly, this cheerfully casual approach to authorial intention also affected Lamb's sonnets, which appear with the very revisions to which he had formerly objected. Lamb was forced to tell Coleridge again, 'Do put 'em forth finally as I have, in various letters, settled it, – for first a man's self is to be pleased, & then his friends' (Marrs, I: 86). Although he continues that he longs to 'see our names together' it is significant that he urges Coleridge to recognise his separate identity, that he distinguishes 'man's self' as distinct from 'his friends'.

Lamb's demand to be defined as separate coincides with Lloyd's increasing separation from Coleridge at the same time, as Coleridge was forced to recognise him not just as a disciple, but a troubled man in need of actual physical care. By November, Coleridge was writing to tell Poole about Lloyd's disturbing fits, when he seemed to fall 'all at once into a kind of Night-mair: and all the Realities round him mingle with, and form a part of, the strange Dream [...] whatever he perceives & hears he perverts into the substance of his delirious Vision' (Griggs, I: 257). This goes beyond a description of Lloyd's illness to point to the ways in which the friend, trusted to perceive the truth, may 'pervert' what he sees to fit his own vision – a form of misreading which Coleridge, craving sympathetic understanding, may have found distinctly threatening. Certainly, the worsening of Lloyd's illness coincided with a withdrawal on the part of Coleridge from the idea of shared intellectual discovery. In December, he wrote to Charles Lloyd senior signalling the end of the tutorial scheme: 'If he [Charles Lloyd] be to stay with me, I can neither be his tutor or fellow-student, nor in any way impart a regular system of knowledge' (Griggs, I: 263).

He then told Poole, in marked contrast to the enclosing sympathy of *Sonnets*, that he had 'determined not to take the charge of Charles Lloyd's mind on me' (Griggs, I: 266).

This withdrawal possibly accounts for the growing closeness between Lamb and Lloyd. In January 1797 Lloyd visited Lamb, unannounced, and Lamb's poem celebrating the visit imagines his friendship in terms previously applied to Coleridge:

> I'll think less meanly of myself
> That Lloyd will sometimes think on me.
> (Marrs, I: 93)

This closeness was to prove important to both as Coleridge became steadily more preoccupied, retreating into a silence which Lamb complained of in April as 'so long, so unfriendlike' (Marrs, I: 105). Lloyd, too, was being sidelined, as his illness became more severe. In mid-March he was forced to leave Nether Stowey to be treated by Erasmus Darwin in Lichfield.[32] There was, of course, an underlying reason for Coleridge's silence, and his reluctance to continue the tutoring scheme after Lloyd's treatment. On a visit from Racedown to Bristol, Wordsworth had visited Nether Stowey for the first time, probably in early April 1797. Poole had met him, and, according to Coleridge, thought 'that he is the greatest Man, he ever knew – I coincide. – ' (Griggs, I: 325). A new community was about to take shape in Nether Stowey, in which Lamb and Lloyd were to be relegated to onlookers.

4
'Cold, Cold, Cold': Loneliness and Reproach

June 1797

Early June 1797: a cold wet summer illuminated by one famous meeting, crucial to our construction of Romanticism. A young man is running along a Dorset road. Suddenly, his end in view, he leaps 'over a gate' and, taking a short cut, he bounds 'down the pathless field'.[1] Coleridge has arrived at Racedown. The *annus mirabilis* has begun.

It's a story which has been told and re-told, firstly by Coleridge, the Wordsworth family, and their friends, and then by generations of critics, who have brought their own preoccupations and readings to bear on this 'symbiotic', 'dialogic' relationship, a company of two which naturally results in *Lyrical Ballads*. But, as I suggested in the introduction, this central Romantic narrative of the Wordsworth-Coleridge friendship has obscured the many voices involved in *Lyrical Ballads*, including dialogues and disagreements with lesser-known contemporaries, such as Thomas Beddoes, who, in an act of both parody and homage, actually inserted his own 'Domiciliary Verses' inside a copy of the volume.[2] Similarly, as I discuss in Chapter 5, that other collaborative volume published slightly earlier in 1798, *Blank Verse*, pre-empts many themes and phrases of its more famous counterpart.

In the next two chapters, then, I want to show how Lamb was participating, sometimes with prickly disagreement, in the conversations of 1797 and 1798, and I want to begin with an image of Lamb himself rushing with enthusiasm towards Nether Stowey:

> I long, I yearn, with all the longings of a child do I desire to see you, to come among you – to see the young philosopher to thank Sara for her last year's invitation in person – to read your tragedy – to read

over together our little book – to breathe fresh air – to revive in me vivid images of 'Salutation scenery'. (Marrs, I: 114)

Alongside that image of Coleridge running to meet Wordsworth we should place Lamb's yearning to join the Somerset community, if only for a long-awaited week's holiday – the postponement of which the year before had prompted Lamb's disappointed poem 'To Sara and her Samuel'. Like 'the young philosopher,' David Hartley Coleridge, now nine months old, Lamb humorously portrays himself as ready to have his mind moulded, his perceptions formed. That idea, too, of Lamb wanting 'to come among' the Coleridges carries a powerful charge, casting the family as a society: not merely to be visited but actually entered into, as into an enclosed community or religion. Somewhat more startling, perhaps, is that desire to 'revive [...] vivid images of "Salutation scenery"' in the midst of Somersetshire, bringing the urban into the heart of Coleridge's rural idyll, and reminding him of the ideals of mutual sympathy and Unitarian faith they had discussed there.

There had been a subtle shift in tone by the time of Lamb's subsequent letter, which marked his return from the cottage:

> Is the Patriot come yet? Are Wordsworth and his sister gone yet? I was looking out for John Thelwall all the way from Bridgewater, and had I met him, I think it would have moved almost me to tears. You will oblige me too by sending me my great-coat, which I left behind in the oblivious state the mind is thrown into at parting – is it not ridiculous that I sometimes envy that great-coat lingering so cunningly behind? – at present I have none – so send it me by a Stowey waggon, if there be such a thing, directing for C.L., No. 45, Chapel-Street, Pentonville, near London. But above all, *that Inscription!* – it will recall to me the tones of all your voices – and with them many a remembered kindness to one who could and can repay you all only by the silence of a grateful heart. I could not talk much, while I was with you, but my silence was not sullenness, nor I hope from any bad motive; but, in truth, disuse has made me awkward at it. I know I behaved myself, particularly at Tom Poole's and at Cruikshank's, most like a sulky child; but company and converse are strange to me. It was kind in you all to endure me as you did. (Marrs, I: 117–8)

This letter is a response to a friendship group in transition, offering an insight into the group which was gathering about Coleridge's cottage in the summer of 1797: the 'Patriot' Thelwall, Wordsworth and his sister, not quite yet installed at Alfoxden, Lloyd an unstable elusive presence off to the side of the scene. Thelwall himself was to offer a similar vision of 'the Enchanting retreat (the Academus of Stowey)' in a letter of a few days earlier to his wife Stella, describing how he, Wordsworth, and Coleridge, had been walking and philosophising together, 'a literary & political triumvirate'.[3] It is not only a sociable gathering, of course, but a highly productive literary one. Works discussed must have included *Poems* 1797 – the 'little book' to which Lamb refers in the previous letter – parts of *The Borderers* and *Osorio*, and a version of *The Ruined Cottage*.[4] The 'Inscription' to which Lamb refers is Wordsworth's 'Lines left upon a Seat in a Yew-tree', and his comment – 'it will recall to me the tones of all your voices' – gives us an image of the Nether Stowey household as a place of discussion and shared reading, a collaborative space of mutual creation.

This may not, however, have been an entirely harmonious reading community. Lamb was silent and awkward, not fully participating in the conversation. Again the image of Lamb as a child recurs, but here he is a 'sulky child', whose eager expectations have perhaps been disappointed. The first place in Coleridge's life was now occupied by the Wordsworths, and there was little room for others. That silence reflects both Lamb's inability to talk and Coleridge's inability to listen, as he began to separate himself from his older friends and collaborators. Commentators on the visit have emphasised Lamb's continuing state of shock about his family circumstances, or his resistance, his 'secret jealousy', concerning Wordsworth: 'It was only very gradually, and with difficulty,' suggests Emile Legouis, 'that he came to recognise Wordsworth's genius'.[5] Yet Lamb's immediate response to the power of the 'Inscription' gives the lie to this reading, which is influenced, as are most accounts of summer 1797, by Coleridge's own gloss on the situation, and his desire to cast Lamb, as in the visionary blessing of 'This Lime-tree Bower my Prison', as a follower in his footsteps.[6] Lamb's silence may not simply be that of an ousted, jealous confidant, but that of an observer who recognises a difficulty or conflict at the heart of the Nether Stowey community. Having had his own concepts of the 'home-born Feeling' so abruptly challenged in September 1796, perhaps Lamb was in a better position to perceive the faultlines of the sympathetic ideal being constructed in Somerset.

'Gloomy boughs' and sunny leaves: the Wordsworth-Coleridge conversation

'Lines left upon a Seat,' the 'Inscription' to which Lamb immediately responded, is a meditation on these very problems of sympathetic connection and response. Although written before the Wordsworths' arrival at Alfoxden, probably mostly at Racedown in the early part of 1797, it sets the tone for discussions with Coleridge later that year, and is placed as Wordsworth's first contribution to *Lyrical Ballads*. Opening with a sombre image of embowerment within 'the lonely yew-tree', the poem immediately questions conventional expressions of sensibility. 'What if,' Wordsworth asks the reader expecting a dreamy pastoral, 'these barren boughs the bee not loves'? What if, as the poem goes on to explore, the individual finds no sympathetic response, no answer for the feelings of his 'pure' heart? The poem shows Wordsworth, like Coleridge and Lamb in the mid-1790s, struggling to negotiate the questions of self and community posed by Burke and Godwin, further complicated by his own experience of revolutionary ideology. Indeed, it runs parallel to Lamb's attempts to respond to Coleridge's persistent anxiety over the place of the poet in society, since it seems directly to echo Coleridge's 'Reflections' – which Wordsworth might have encountered in the *Monthly Magazine*, part of the consignment of books sent over to Racedown by James Losh in March 1797.[7] But Wordsworth's poem begins where 'Reflections' ends. The man who sits within the yew-tree has already gone out into active life, 'big with lofty views', 'pure in his heart', only to find his idealism greeted with neglect:

> At once, with rash disdain he turned away,
> And with the food of pride sustained his soul
> In solitude.
> (ll. 19–21, *LyB*, 49)

Embowered by 'gloomy boughs' he sits and thinks of others 'warm from the labours of benevolence'. He himself is imprisoned by lack of sympathy – his own, and that of others – and by what Wordsworth characterises as the 'littleness' of his own pride.

This specific condemnation of pride parallels the recurrent anxiety of Lamb's letters to Coleridge of 1796. 'Lines left upon a Seat' seems to urge precisely the same kind of humility Lamb was, ineffectually, encouraging Coleridge to adopt at the time. Both Wordsworth and Lamb, sensitised by their own experiences of disappointment, were, by this stage, wary of placing too much emphasis on the sympathetic capacity. Lamb had already spoken about himself as being 'too selfish for sympathy', an idea which he must have heard echoed in Wordsworth's portrait of the misanthrope who cannot transcend his own narrow vision, for whom everything becomes 'an emblem of his own unfruitful life' (l. 29). For Lamb, in his grief and isolation, Wordsworth's poem must have had a poignant aptness, as both men explored the difficulties of putting the sympathetic ideal into practice in an unresponsive or hostile environment.

'Lines left upon a Seat' also demonstrates the same anxiety over the concept of retreat which had been exercising the 'Salutation' group in the 1790s, shaped, in both cases, by readings of Godwin and Burke. The closing moral of 'Lines left upon a Seat' appears to correspond, as Jacobus has argued, with Godwin's idea that 'the truly wise man will be actuated neither by interest nor ambition, the love of honour nor the love of fame,' but instead by comparing his achievements 'with the standard of right' (*PJ*, 195).[8] On the other hand, *The Borderers* shows how Godwinian participation can backfire, by demonstrating the difficulty in establishing a personal 'standard of right'. As Rivers' manipulation of Mortimer in the play demonstrates, attempts to determine one's own standard for behaviour in the wider community may be influenced by circumstances and the views of others. Active involvement, for Mortimer, is fatal; his attempts to reason 'of actions, and their ends and differences' are misguided.[9] By the time Wordsworth comes to write 'Lines left upon a Seat' he is not directly urging straightforward social involvement. Like Coleridge in 1794, he has come to question Godwinian certainties; Wordsworth has arrived, however, at a different conclusion, and is now suggesting that the value of the retreat must come from within. We might see this as a Burkean turn, away from political intervention and towards what James Chandler terms an explicit traditionalism, in which an image of natural culture – 'that is, of culture as a second nature' – becomes central.[10] But if this is an early formulation of conservative organicism it is somewhat gloomily envisaged. The bower is a place of constraint and darkness, a stony and 'unfruitful' space, and although the poem ends with an injunction – 'O, be wiser thou!' (l. 55) – no clear alternative vision is offered.

Visions of unity: *This Lime-tree Bower my Prison*

It was Coleridge who took it upon himself to provide this alternative. He responded both to 'Lines left upon a Seat' and to Lamb's calamity of 1796 with a powerful reformulation of the 'home-born Feeling' – his poem of summer 1797, 'This Lime-tree Bower my Prison'.[11] This looks again, with renewed clarity and intensity, at the small embowered space. It is part of a multiply-voiced conversation – in dialogue with the Wordsworths and the ideals of the Somerset community, and also with the preoccupations of an earlier friendship circle, the 'Salutation' group including Lamb. A bravura exercise in answering his own anxieties, the poem also echoes the way in which Lamb himself had tried to reassure Coleridge about the continuing power of 'home-born' friendly sympathy in, for instance, 'To Sara and her Samuel'.[12]

Within 'This Lime-tree Bower', the poet is shown escaping the consciousness of man's own 'littleness' which had haunted Wordsworth's solitary in his yew-tree. This escape comes, paradoxically, through a close focus on that 'littleness', on the particular and local, which the poem strives to bring into harmony with a wider prospect. We begin with the poet wounded, a Vulcan 'lam'd by the scathe of fire'. In fact, Sara had spilt hot milk on Coleridge's foot, but here the prosaic dangers of the cramped Nether Stowey domestic space expand into mythological dramatisation. From his imprisoning bower, the poet imagines his friends first looking down into a 'rifted Dell,' enclosing wild ashes and 'plumy ferns', and then walking out into the wide sunlit scene of the Quantock hills. At the turning point of the poem, the power of the poet's sympathetic imagination allows this expansive scene viewed by the friends to become projected back into the bower, lighting up its 'dark foliage' and allowing him to become conscious of the quieter sensual pleasures it affords: the sight of a 'rapid bat', the sound of 'the solitary humble-bee'. Unlike Wordsworth's solitary, brooding over the 'benevolent labours' of others, Coleridge's poet is allowed to contemplate 'with lively joy the joys, we cannot share'. The close of the poem unites him with the distant friends through the blessing he gives to a rook:

> deeming, it's black wing
> Cross'd, like a speck, the blaze of setting day,
> While ye stood gazing; or when all was still,
> Flew creaking o'er your heads, & had a charm
> For you, my Sister & my Friends! to whom
> No sound is dissonant, which tells of Life!
>
> (Griggs, I: 336)

The carefully detailed specifics of the landscape – its 'springy heath' and 'yellow Light' – find a place within an overarching idea of divine unity, a beautifully implicit statement of what he would later term 'the one life within us and abroad'.[13] The rook, for example – whose creaking is, in the published version of the poem, carefully footnoted – is at once real and, as it slowly wings homeward, part of a larger, illuminating vision. Moreover, in the revisions between 1797 and 1800, we can see how the poem is sharpened and improved by Coleridge's persistent return to these interconnected questions concerning the poet and his relationship to the external world, the real and the abstract, the particular and the speculative.

The 1797 version already demonstrates Coleridge's close thinking about how to express the actual qualities of things in words: the 'springy heath', for instance, of the fifth line, which in the first version of the poem comes with a footnote to Southey explaining the precision of the adjective, *'elastic*, I mean', so that an actual physical sensation is compressed into the verse. When Coleridge publishes the poem in 1800 in Southey's *Annual Anthology* his descriptions of the landscape become still more clearly and distinctly realised. Instead of being looked down on, the 'dell' is now entered into and closely observed by the friends; 'that same rifted Dell' (1797) has become, by 1800, 'that still roaring dell,' which nicely brings the sense of hearing into play, as well as conveying a subtle ambiguity through that word 'still'. As Everest has pointed out, 'the opposite connotations of the word, "fixed, unmoving", but also "ever, continually" underpin the development in Coleridge's mood' here, allowing him to hold two meanings in suspension, just as the lime-tree bower is at once a fixed 'prison' and a place of growth, movement, and creativity.[14] The 'home-born Feeling' and the sensual and emotional experiences of the small space, are – within the poem – united as part of a larger benevolent vision.

The 1797 description of the 'plumy ferns' carries a footnote which also reflects this movement between the real and the imagined, the poet and the world around him, as Coleridge earnestly points out the concrete observation underlying his use of the adjective: the ferns 'grow five or six together & form a complete "Prince of Wales's Feather" – i.e. plumy. –' (Griggs, I: 335). In 1800, the ferns have changed into weeds, and attention is specifically drawn to the way in which the friends observe them:

> And there my friends,
> Behold the dark-green file of long *lank weeds
> (*AA* 1800, 141)

That asterisk again fussily directs the reader towards the correct type of fern, the 'Asplenium scolopendrium, called in some countries the Adder's tongue', citing Withering's *An Arrangement of British Plants* as further confirmation. It is also a reference to Dorothy Wordsworth's journal, which would have been understood only by particular, intimate readers, binding them more closely to the text. She makes reference in her Alfoxden notebook for 10 February 1798 to 'the adder's tongue and the ferns green in the low damp dell', and the three subsequent entries (11–13 February) all mention walks with Coleridge 'near to Stowey'.[15] As Mays suggests, the fern may have been 'among the first near-private emblems shared by Coleridge and the Wordsworths'.[16] Those footnoted weeds therefore confirm and strengthen the poem's attachment to the real, the observable, the concrete – and also reassuringly confirm Coleridge's attachment to others.

Yet the verb 'Behold' also encodes an uncertainty about Coleridge's relationship to others. The reader is left unsure whether it is indicative, showing Coleridge sharing the viewing experience of the friends, or whether the verb is acting imperatively, as he actively directs their gaze, and instructs them to observe the weeds.[17] A similar ambiguity comes in the lines concerning Lamb's visionary moment on the hill-top, particularly in 1800:

> – So my Friend
> Struck with deep joy may stand, as I have stood,
> Silent with swimming sense; yea, gazing round
> On the wide landscape, gaze till all doth seem
> Less gross than bodily, a living thing
> Which *acts* upon the mind.
> (*AA* 1800, 142)

Here again the mood of 'gaze' is unclear – is the verb acting indicatively or imperatively?[18] So is the subject – is Lamb or Coleridge doing the gazing? The uncertainty is emphasised by the footnote Coleridge adds for Southey: 'You remember, I am a *Berkleian*' (Griggs, I: 335). But in many ways, as Perry puts it, 'the use to which Berkeley is being put is actually rather tentative', since the poem continues to assert the material presence of the landscape.[19]

The poem and its footnotes thus seem to act out Coleridge's own oscillation between the poles of the imagined and the real. Here he relies on the footnote to Southey to clarify an idealist position the poem itself does not seem to urge quite so strongly, since it is also tethered (by, for instance, those footnoted weeds) to the external world. He constantly strives to put the two together, to make these external details part of a much larger unified vision, but worries that this may only be his own projection. The note he adds to the version sent to Thelwall reinforces this idea:

My mind feels as if it ached to behold & know something *great* – something *one* & *indivisible* – and it is only in the faith of this that rocks or waterfalls, mountains or caverns give me the sense of sublimity or majesty! – But in this faith *all things* counterfeit infinity! –. (Griggs, I: 349)

This attempt to achieve something *'one* & *indivisible'* may be seen as running alongside Coleridge's desire, in poetry and in life, to bring the self into harmonious dialogue with others. His yearning towards something *'indivisible'* is constantly undercut by the fear that *'all things* counterfeit infinity! –'. He is also strongly conscious of the dilemmas and uncertainties of friendship, and the ways it, too, may be 'counterfeit' – a question which the poem itself poses.

On the one hand, the escape from the self-absorbed imprisonment of the early lines of 'This Lime-tree Bower' into the affirmative joy caused by identification with the imagined Charles is a powerful and absorbing transition. Friendship, that movement of empathetic connection, becomes a necessary confirmation and strengthening of the poet's sense of self, so that he is able to refocus on the bower and see its own 'deep radiance'. On the other hand, however, it is true that the changed status of the bower depends entirely upon Coleridge's perceptions: so too do the experiences of his friends. Lamb, on whom the empathetic movement of the poem depends, is of course defined mainly in relation to the poet himself. The 'Friend', who 'may stand, as I have stood', may simply be another, ventriloquist, self – just as the 'gentle-hearted Charles' suggests when he angrily answers back as a 'drunken dog, ragged-head, seld-shaven, odd-ey'd, stuttering' (Marrs, I: 224).

Lamb also disputes the substance of the vision he has been granted in the poem, the 'unintelligible abstraction-fit about the manner of the Deity's making Spirits perceive his presence' (Marrs, I: 224). This movement between the personal and the abstract might seem to connect with Lamb's warning, explored in Chapter 3, that Coleridge is moving away from Unitarian humility in straining his 'comparing faculties to bring together things infinitely distant and unlike' (Marrs, I: 56). Coleridge's desire to bring the particular details of the scene into harmony with the 'wide landscape' might be seen as another movement in that attempt to bring together, as Lamb notes, the 'feeble narrow-sphered operations of the human intellect and the everywhere diffused mind of Deity'. In terms of the poem itself, it is this time, I think, a successful move, delicately connecting the particular detail with the larger abstract thought to create a unified whole. In practice, however, it proved more of a struggle for Coleridge to bring the real experience into harmony with his larger ideals – behind the poem lurks the recurrent difficulty of putting the concept of the 'home-born Feeling' into practice.

Sending the poem to Southey, for instance, Coleridge framed it with a passionate declaration of affection for the Wordsworths: 'I brought him & his Sister back with me & here I have *settled them*' (Griggs, I: 334). Wordsworth has become a new mentor for Coleridge in the same way that he once looked up to Southey:

> Wordsworth is a very great man – the only man, to whom *at all times* & in *all modes of excellence* I feel myself inferior – the only one, I mean, whom I *have yet met with* – . (Griggs, I: 334)

Unmistakably, the letter and its poem, bound up with that triumphant expression of possession, 'here I have *settled them*', look back to that previous ideal of friendly community and mutual creativity, the Pantisocratic community. For Southey, then, the poem's celebration of friendship must have carried a particular, hurtful charge.

Similarly, when Coleridge sent Thelwall an extract from 'This Lime-tree Bower', alongside those comments on his desire to find something *'one & indivisible'*, it was in the context of his not having been able to find a cottage for Thelwall at Nether Stowey: 'alas! I have neither money or influence' (Griggs, I: 349). This was in sharp contrast to the enthusiasm of earlier letters, with their plans of retirement along Stowey lines, 'a little garden labor, & a pig stie' (Griggs, I: 305), and Thelwall's own joyful hopes of 'philosophic amity', such as his 'Lines, written at Bridgewater... on the 27 July 1797':

> Ah! Let me, far in some sequester'd dell,
> Build my low cot; most happy might it prove,
> My Samuel! near to thine, that I might oft
> Share thy sweet converse, best-belov'd of friends! –[20]

Coleridge's vision of friendly communication and identification with another might have thus seemed peculiarly painful to Thelwall at that moment. Roe argues that Coleridge and Poole, 'sacrificed Thelwall's residence in the neighbourhood for the company of Wordsworth and Dorothy', and Thelwall himself seems to register that sacrifice in his *Poems, Chiefly Written in Retirement* (1801), with its prefatory reference to a time when friendship 'shrunk from its own convictions, and left him in comparative insulation'.[21] As Walford Davies suggests, Thelwall responds with his own darker re-writings of Wordsworth and Coleridge, such as 'Effusion VII: on STELLA's leaving me, to Visit some Friends, at Hereford':

> WELL thou art gone – gone to the City's throng,
> My soul's sad partner![22]

Here, Thelwall, as if voicing Lamb's 'sad and patient' grief in the earlier poem, mourns his infant daughter Maria; he is also in mourning for his own ideals, grieving over his literal, and creative, isolation. The echo of 'This Lime-tree Bower' brings this loneliness into sharp focus: Thelwall's is a critical allusion, as he recalls lost, or neglected, visions of unity.

The Overcoat and the Manchineel: Lamb's response

Lamb, like Thelwall, was to use allusion and rewriting as a reproof, as in a letter of September 1797, as it became clear that Coleridge was distancing himself from his former relationships:

> You use Lloyd very ill – never writing to him. I tell you again that his is not a mind with which you should play tricks [...]

> If you dont write to me now, – as I told Lloyd, I shall get angry, & call you hard names, Manchineel, & I dont know what else – –. I wish you would send me my Great coat – the snow & the rain season is at hand & I have but a wretched old coat, once my fathers, to keep 'em off – – & that is transitory – –
>
> > When time drives flocks from field to fold,
> > When ways grow foul and blood gets cold –
>
> I shall remember where I left my coat – meek Emblem wilt thou be, old Winter, of a friend's neglect – Cold, cold, cold, –. (Marrs, I: 123)

Here, phrases from Coleridge's own works function as a subtly pointed reproach. When those literary borrowings are teased out, Lamb is shown to be accusing Coleridge of a breach of his own terms of friendship, that sacred ideal. He reproaches him most seriously on Lloyd's behalf, whom Coleridge had virtually cast off in the excitement of the Wordsworths' arrival. By September 1797 the tutoring plan had irretrievably broken down. Lloyd had, to Coleridge's annoyance, taken refuge in Southey's house, where he began to write the poems of *Blank Verse*, and conceived, perhaps at Southey's prompting, his novel *Edmund Oliver* (1798). The contrast between the idea of the 'Elysium' which they had had in mind and this neglect was striking, although Lamb does not directly draw attention to it. His letter, however, is full of allusions to false friendship, beginning with that 'hard name': Manchineel, the poison tree. It is borrowed from the dedication of *Poems* 1797, when, as we have seen, it appears as an indictment of the 'false and fair-foliag'd' friends whose shelter has poisoned Coleridge. Lamb's use of the image alludes both to the ideals of the Nether Stowey community, and to the collaborative effort of *Poems* 1797 – shared spaces which Coleridge seems, in his neglect of Lamb and Lloyd, to be betraying. The small space of the 'Lime-tree Bower' might itself be a Manchineel tree, a false embowering friendship.

Moreover, Coleridge has, on a very practical level, deprived Lamb of shelter – that forgotten great coat is a complex 'Emblem...of a friend's neglect'. We might recall Coleridge's 'To An Old Man', which had, as we have seen, been used as an expression of Coleridge's Christ-like benevolence in *Poems* 1796 and 1797 and the *Sonnets*. There, Coleridge offers the old man physical and spiritual shelter:

> My Father! throw away this tatter'd vest
> That mocks thy shiv'ring! take my garment – use
> A young man's arm!
> (Poems 1797, 81)

Lamb's letter picks up the idea of the 'tatter'd' garment; his 'wretched old coat, once my father's', sets up echoes with this earlier profession of sympathy, now coming into conflict with Coleridge's own actions. The symbolism is reinforced by the fact that Coleridge had himself received a coat from Poole a few months earlier, and had made it into a token of their mutually beneficial friendship:

> You shall be my Elijah – & I will most reverentially catch the
>   Mantle, which you have cast off. –
> Why should not a Bard go tight & have a few neat things on
>   his back? *Ey? – Eh! – Eh!*
> (Griggs, I: 338).

Through 'the Mantle', Elijah conferred his spiritual powers upon Elisha, who was then able to divide the sea and establish himself as prophet and king.

But if Coleridge is himself – as poet and friend – clothed in Poole's embracing mantle, he has, highly symbolically, left Lamb 'cold, cold, cold'. A Shakespearean weight of betrayal is compressed into that reproach, which summons up Lear's naked coldness on the heath, and Othello lamenting over Desdemona as 'cold, cold'. The link between physical cold and lack of empathy also foreshadows the theme of Wordsworth's poem of early 1798, 'Goody Blake and Harry Gill', where the cruelty of Harry, who stops the old woman gathering sticks for her fire, becomes physically translated into coldness. The poem is haunted by coldness – the cold ache of Goody Blake's old bones, the 'cold, cold moon' above her head – and coldness itself then becomes an instrument of remorse.

Lamb's quotation, however, does have a specific origin: the play *Osorio*, on which Coleridge was still working. *Osorio*, like *The Borderers*, is haunted by the theme of broken vows, brothers and friends betrayed or neglected. Led by pride and ambition, Osorio has arranged the murder of his older brother Albert in order to marry Albert's betrothed, Maria; spared by the assassin Ferdinand, Albert returns and confronts his brother, urging him towards remorse and reform. Cold becomes the physical emblem of emotional suffering in the play – 'fingers of Ice' clutch at Ferdinand, for example, as he learns the truth about Osorio's plans (IV: i, 14, Mays, III: i, 112), and Osorio himself, furnishing Lamb's quotation, suffers a pang of remorse as he thinks of Albert's 'murder':

> Oh! cold, cold, cold – shot thro' with icy cold! –
> (II: i, 107, Mays, III: i, 85)

Like 'Lines left upon a seat' and *The Borderers*, *Osorio* questions the nature of pride, and the fragility of the sympathetic bond. Like Rivers, Osorio is driven on by pride – 'He was a man, different from other Men,/ And he despised them, yet rever'd himself'. He is, as Albert tells us, a 'blind Self-worshipper' (V: ii, 81, Mays, III: i, 141), whose evil emphasises and bears witness to the Christ-like sufferings of Albert himself.

Lamb's reproach reflects his awareness of the complicated self-identification and self-contradiction at work in Coleridge's portrayal of Osorio and Albert. Coburn has suggested a mental connection for Coleridge between Osorio and Southey, and by extension, between himself and Albert.[23] Certainly, the play seems to have been bound up with Coleridge's relationship with Southey. When, for instance, *Osorio* was transformed into the successfully staged *Remorse* (1813), Coleridge went to some trouble to point out and explain the epigraph of the printed version to Southey. It was intended to emphasise the distinction between remorse and virtuous penitence: 'by REMORSE I mean the Anguish & Disquietude arising from the Self-Contradiction introduced into the Soul by Guilt' (Mays, III: ii, 1237).

When we turn to the epigraph itself, taken from the opening scene of the play, we are again confronted with the image of the poison-tree – the Manchineel already associated, through the poem 'To the Rev. George Coleridge', with Southey's betrayal. Remorse, it claims, 'is as the heart, in which it grows':

> [...] if proud and gloomy,
> It is a poison-tree, that pierced to the inmost
> Weeps only tears of poison!
> (*Remorse*, I. i, 20–3; Mays, III: ii, 1239–40)

The play is thus connected to an image of Southey's false friendship and the failure of the fraternal ideal; yet it also dramatises Coleridge's anxieties and guilty feelings. If Coleridge attacks Southey through the character of Osorio, he also accuses himself. Moreover, Osorio and Albert share many characteristics – double, dissembling selves, who take on aspects of one another.[24] What Parker has termed the 'twinship' or 'reversibility' of Albert and Osorio points to one of the most interesting aspects of the play: its central idea of intimate, reversible, connection between virtue and guilt. At its heart lies the notion of 'self-Contradiction', rather than the simple opposition of good and evil. The opposing, yet intertwined, brothers of *Osorio* symbolise the way in which Coleridge could easily direct his anger towards others while in fact turning against part of himself. In demonising Osorio, he was demonising some of his own characteristics, under the guise of attacking false friendship.

Lamb's sly comparison of Coleridge's neglect with Osorio's cruelty – 'Cold, cold, cold' – demonstrates his shrewd perception of this Coleridgean capacity for 'self-contradiction'. It would be further demonstrated by Coleridge's 'Nehemiah Higginbottom' sonnets, published under the title 'Sonnets Attempted in the Manner of Contemporary Writers' in the *Monthly Magazine* (November 1797) – poems which parodied the styles of Coleridge himself, as well as Lloyd, Southey, and Lamb.

The 'Reft House' of the 'Nehemiah Higginbottom' sonnets

Interpretation of the poems is skewed, in the first place, by Coleridge's own self-deprecating comments about them in *Biographia Literaria*: 'I myself was the first to expose *risu honesto* the three sins of poetry, one or the other of which is the most likely to beset a young writer'. His satires on *'doleful egotism,'* simplicity, and 'the indiscriminate use of elaborate and swelling language and imagery', were, he suggests, written only 'to excite a good-natured laugh', functioning as a self-aware commentary on his own youthful excesses (*BiogLit*, I: 26–7). His letter to Joseph Cottle, however, points to a more complicated attitude, as Coleridge patronisingly comments: 'I think they may do good to our young Bards' (Griggs, I: 358). By late 1797, Coleridge was outgrowing his early style of sensibility, just as he was beginning to find the friendship of Southey, Lloyd, and – to some extent – Lamb, frustrating and cloying. Moving towards a new friendship with Wordsworth, he was also moving towards a new style of writing, using parody of himself and others as a means of transition and distraction.

The reasons for this public declaration of his independence probably lie in the way in which the second edition of *Poems* was being interpreted by reviewers. The *Monthly Visitor* (August 1797) very closely identifies Coleridge, Lamb, and Lloyd as a 'Coleridgean school', speaking of 'a resemblance in the manner, and in the sentiments of this triumvirate':

> Mr. Coleridge, for instance, is very fond of the rhyme *ess* or *ness*; as distr*ess*, happi*ness*, &c. &c. and his friends have been very prodigal in this way. We meet with 'quietness' without end, in the poems before us, especially in those by Mr. Lloyd; and there is, sometimes, both in him and Mr. Lamb, a turgescence of style not very remote from affectation.[25]

These references to 'affectation' lie very close to Coleridge's letter to Cottle. Similarly, the 'turgescence of style' seems to find direct parodic expression in the 'inexplicable swell' of the 'Nehemiah Higginbottom' sonnets themselves.

These are – fatally – very funny. The lolloping assonance of 'Nehemiah Higginbottom' is comic in itself, reminding us of the earlier disguise adopted by Coleridge, when he joined the dragoons as the clumsy cumber-backed horseman Silas Tomkyn Comberbache. This bathos is reinforced by the gleeful parody of the sonnets, with their pedantic over-determination, hyperbolic exclamations, and gothic tropes of night-time, guilt and sorrow. The first portrays a tearfully excessive response to landscape:

> Pensive, at eve, on the hard world I mus'd,
> And my poor heart was sad: so at the moon
> I gaz'd – and sigh'd, and sigh'd! – for, ah! how soon
> Eve darkens into night. Mine eye perus'd
> With tearful vacancy, the *dampy* grass,
> Which wept and glitter'd in the *paly* ray
>   (*MM* November 1797, 374)

This image of distressed melancholy had a clear source in Lloyd's contributions to *Poems* 1797. Carrying a pensive epigraph from Bowles – 'I wrap me in the mantle of distress,/And tell my poor heart this is happiness' – Lloyd's section opens with a poem entitled 'The Melancholy Man', replete with the tears and sighs of 'unintelligible woe' beneath the 'paly eye' of 'eve's meek star'. Other Lloyd poems in the volume, such as 'Sonnet V' ('I had been sad'), contain similar images of the musing poet turning from the 'hard world'.[26] These were poems written within the shared space of Nether Stowey, overseen and corrected by Coleridge himself – these parodies thus break the circle of confidence, shattering the illusion of friendly mutual reading and writing.

They return, too, to the intense discussions about the language of sensibility taking place in the Coleridge circle at the time, and suggest that the response of feeling may indeed be nothing more than self-indulgence. Having paused and mused over the fate of the '*wretched ones*', our poet gets back to the obsessive indulgence of his own misery:

> But, alas!
> Most of MYSELF I thought: when it befell,
> That the sooth SPIRIT of the breezy wood
> Breath'd in mine ear – 'All this is very well;
> But much of *one* thing is for *no* thing good.'
> Ah! my poor heart's inexplicable swell!
> (*MM* November 1797, 374)

Earlier anxieties over the nature of sympathy may be nothing more than a form of self-love, a self-absorption in one's own 'poor heart'. In form and content, the parodies question the whole basis of sympathetic communion between friends, persistently revisiting and mocking the questions Coleridge had once seriously discussed with Lamb and Lloyd.

'Cultivate simplicity, Coleridge,' Lamb had urged Coleridge in November 1796 (Marrs, I: 60–1). Coleridge's response a year later in the second 'Nehemiah Higginbottom' sonnet is to attack the 'meek simplicity' of contemporary poets – and, still more pointedly, their obsession with sympathy and friendship:

> *So* sad I am! – but should a friend and I
> Grow cool and *miff*, O! I am *very* sad!
> And then with sonnets and with sympathy
> My dreamy bosom's mystic woes I pall;
> Now of my false friend plaining plaintively,

Now raving at mankind in general;
But whether sad or fierce, 'tis simple all,
All very simple, meek SIMPLICITY
             (*MM* November 1797, 374)

The parodies resonate with personal allusions, designed to be understood by those within the private circle. It is hard, for instance, not to read another attack on Lloyd, with his prosperous banking family background, into the sonnet's opening characterisation of 'Nehemiah Higginbottom' as ambling 'on Lady Fortune's gentlest pad', yet perplexed by 'each small distress' – never mind the fact that Coleridge himself had found the subsidies from the Lloyd family fortune very useful.[27] The line 'O! I am *very* sad', moreover, directly alludes to Lloyd's description of his own heart as 'very sad' in the manuscript poem of friendship, 'To Coleridge'.[28] The 'home-born Feeling' of their relationship had been created through friendly mutual allusion, shared reading and writing – similarly, allusion, employed as reproach and attack, would destroy it.

Parody and playfulness had always, admittedly, been a part of the group's humour. 'What shall I say to your Dactyls?' Lamb had asked Coleridge in June 1796, having just read his contributions to Southey's 'The Soldier's Wife'. The answer was a 'rough & **unlicked**' parody of the 'Dismal' dactyls, beginning 'Sorely your Dactyls do drag along limp-footed' (Marrs, I: 34–5). This seems dangerously close to the *Anti-Jacobin* parody of the very same poem, 'Sorely thy Dactylics lag on uneven feet.'[29] But the difference is that within a specific group friendly parody can be a strengthening force. 'Done well,' comments Graeme Stones, 'parodic prolepsis keeps the self ahead of its own failings,' and the same applies to writing within a friendship group or even a publication.[30] But Coleridge's sonnets breach the private bounds of the group, because his choice of publication, the *Monthly Magazine,* makes this a highly public attack. We have already seen the importance of the *Monthly Magazine* in fostering the culture of sympathetic response for the friendship group: in light of professions of sympathy such as Lamb's 'Lines Addressed to Sara and S.T.C.' previously published in its pages, the parodies become especially pointed.

In the months before the 'Nehemiah Higginbottom' poems appeared, both Lamb and Lloyd had published sonnets in the *Monthly Magazine* which appealed to the elusive ideal of sympathy. Two poems celebrating the joys of friendship by Lamb, 'Sonnet to a Friend' (to Lloyd), and 'To a Friend' (to his sister Mary), had been published in October 1797, celebrating the power of companionship. But these invocations of sympathy are, in the parodic sonnets, compromised by 'Nehemiah Higginbottom's' voice of reedy complaint, and undermined all the while by the incessant squeaking of the rats in the third sonnet, 'On a Ruined House in a Romantic Country':

> And this reft house is that, the which he built,
> Lamented Jack! And here his malt he pil'd
> Cautious in vain! These rats that squeak so wild,
> Squeak, not unconscious of their father's guilt.
> Did ye not see her gleaming thro' the glade?
> Belike, 'twas she, the maiden all forlorn.
> What tho' she milk no cow with crumpled horn,
> Yet, *aye*, she haunts the dale where *erst* she stray'd:
> And, *aye*, beside her stalks her amorous knight!
> Still on his thighs their wonted brogues are worn,
> And thro' those brogues, still tatter'd and betorn,
> His hindward charms gleam an unearthly white;
> As when thro' broken clouds at night's high noon
> Peeps in fair fragments forth the full-orb'd harvest-moon!
> (*MM* November 1797, 374)

The 'reft house' which Coleridge is parodically pulling apart is also a distorted image of the Nether Stowey plan of friendly, mutual, home-born creativity. The earlier ideal of friendly domestic affection so crucial to the friendship with Lamb and Lloyd is now, through the same medium in which it had been built up, being undermined by Coleridge. Again, private allusions are layered throughout the parody. Newlyn has convincingly argued that the 'glade' takes its cue from Lamb's first sonnet in *Poems* 1797, where the poet rather vaguely wanders through 'the lonely glade' seeking his Anna.[31] The torn trousers of Coleridge's knight humorously undermine this vision of chivalric quest, and suggest an altogether more ribald interpretation of the exercise of sympathy. The delicate reticence of those early poems and their attempts to puzzle out a response of feeling are roundly mocked. 'It never knew,' Lloyd writes of his heart in the manuscript poem 'To Coleridge', 'T'expose its feelings to the careless view'. The idea of the 'tatter'd' brogues plays on the idea of the anxiety of exposure – now those intimate feelings (as well as, possibly, intimate parts) are laid open to laughter.

The sonnet also, humorously, shows the extent of Coleridge's creative anxieties, worrying over ideas of property and authorial ownership, as Jack's 'malt', plundered from his house, is stolen away by the intruding 'rats'.[32] Those 'rats', intruders into the creative space, might symbolise false friends, or unsympathetic critics, who carry off ideas. Like ungrateful Bloomian literary inheritors, the 'rats' squeak wildly 'not unconscious of their father's guilt.' That persistent squeaking seems a cruel foreshadowing, too, of the croaking of the little frog and toad, Gillray's cartoon versions of Lamb and Lloyd which would appear the following August in the *Anti-Jacobin*. Lamb and Lloyd's attempts to appeal to sympathy through their poetry of distress become something ludicrous, verging on the sub-human.

Through 'a good-natured laugh', the reader has been drawn into a complicitous relationship with the parodist, setting up a pattern of allegiances working against the old dependencies from which Coleridge now wished to be free. Self-deprecatingly and evasively, Coleridge distanced himself from the ideal of creative sympathy fostered by his own early works, collaborations and relationships. Like his compulsive revisions to Lamb's earlier sonnets, these parodies over-write earlier narratives of friendship. They aggressively mark off Coleridge's later work as separate from that of his former collaborators – and ensure that the poetry of Lloyd, in particular, and, to a lesser extent, Lamb, would be denied serious critical appreciation – a lasting legacy. The myth of Coleridge's joyous creative domestication with the Wordsworths in 1797 and 1798 is built, we should remember, on the shaky foundations of an earlier 'reft house', previously shared with Lamb and Lloyd – now abandoned, neglected, desolate.

5
Blank Verse and Fears in Solitude

February 1798

February 1798: a small low-beamed room, sealed in by frost on a wintry Somerset night, the fire burnt low and fluttering in the grate, the baby asleep in its cradle. From this small space comes one of the great Romantic poems of meditative quietness: Coleridge's 'Frost at Midnight'. Published alongside 'Fears in Solitude', which lent its name to the collection, and 'France: An Ode' in autumn 1798, by Joseph Johnson, this celebration of an intensely private moment becomes something public. In the intervening months the political pressure on those perceived as 'Jacobin' had been turned up. In July, Johnson had been convicted for selling Wakefield's pamphlet replying to the Bishop of Llandaff, and the *Anti-Jacobin* poem 'New Morality' had appeared, followed by the Gillray cartoon, both featuring Coleridge prominently. Magnuson has deftly shown why this publication context matters, describing how 'Frost at Midnight' leaves the space of 'private consciousness' and becomes an important 'public defense of [Coleridge's] character drawn in the Tory press' – it thus participates, he claims, in a 'rhetoric of purposeful duplicity, distortion, and personal attack'.[1] This 'defensive duplicity' is, for Magnuson, a political matter, a coded voicing of dissent. As he suggests, Coleridge's allegiance to the domestic space – personal and national – seems in this pamphlet to leave itself open to interpretation as a Burkean patriotism, even as it looks back to his earlier formulations of universal benevolence: the collection deliberately leaves itself open both to radical and conservative implications. But 'duplicity [...] and personal attack' were not limited to anti-Jacobin political rhetoric. As we have seen in Chapter 4, they had already invaded the private homely space of the Coleridge-Lamb circle. 'Frost at Midnight' therefore not only represents

Coleridge's answer to the Tory press, but also his reformulation of the 'home-born Feeling' against a very personal backdrop of accusation, reproach and argument within his group of friends.

Against the image of homely warmth offered by 'Frost at Midnight', we should set the reft and desolate houses encountered in another volume of 1798, Lamb and Lloyd's *Blank Verse*, which pointedly declared their literary independence from Coleridge. In this volume, the warm glow of faith in universal benevolence has been replaced by a shivering fear of isolation. In 'Lines on passing a place of former residence', for instance, Lloyd remembers Coleridgean visions of familial fire-side bliss – 'the friendly taper, and the warm fire's glow' – only to find them gone, replaced by 'the unfeeling blast of night'. Instead of looking outside from a position of warmth and love as in 'Fears in Solitude', the poet is outside in the frosty night, hearing not the sounds of domestic companionship, but instead the rustling of 'the sere ice-glaz'd twig' (*BV*, 48–9). While Lloyd pays homage to the Coleridgean ideal of enlightened domestic benevolence spreading outward 'from the taper in my cottage window' (Griggs, I: 277) – it is here overwritten by a narrative of loss: 'I past my childhood's home, and, lo, 'twas dark! [...] No taper twinkled cheerily' (*BV*, 48). The same doubts inform Lamb's poems of loss and loneliness, culminating in the best-known poem from the collection, 'The Old Familiar Faces':

> Where are they gone, the old familiar faces?
> I had a mother, but she died, and left me,
> Died prematurely in a day of horrors –
> All, all are gone, the old familiar faces. [...]
> Ghost-like, I pac'd round the haunts of my childhood.
> Earth seem'd a desert I was bound to traverse,
> Seeking to find the old familiar faces.
>
> (*BV*, 89)

The 'home-born Feeling' has disappeared, although not the conviction of its importance, leaving the solitary poet constantly wandering in search of the vanished ideal. It is a narrative of loss which also, implicitly, accuses Coleridge, whose presence is constantly, although covertly, invoked in this volume by the two remaining members of the three once 'linked and kindred muses'.

Yet 'Frost at Midnight' continues to pose a powerful argument for the force of private sympathy. Like 'This Lime-tree Bower my Prison', the poem holds in delicate suspension the particular and the ideal, suggesting how and why the domestic space can connect with wider sympathy. Once again imaginative projection helps to illuminate the small space, as the poet identifies firstly with the 'companionable form' of the film fluttering on the grate, and then with the sleeping child, for whom the poet projects an expansive Wordsworthian childhood, schooled in the language of nature – 'But *thou*, my babe! Shalt wander, like a breeze,/By lakes and sandy shores'. In the 1798 version, Coleridge ends this tender address by imagining – as he had done for Lamb in the earlier poem – the future movements of the baby, who will

> shout,
> And stretch and flutter from thy mother's arms
> As thou would'st fly for very eagerness.
>
> *(FS, 23)*

The fluttering of the film on the grate is transposed onto the infant Hartley's 'stretch and flutter', bringing the experiences of the small space out into the bright morning light of the outside world, turning the 'silentness' encountered early in the poem into 'eagerness'. Activity comes from retreat, seeming to confirm Coleridge's earlier assertions that 'the intensity of private attachment encourages, not prevents, universal philanthropy' (*Lectures 1795*, 163). As its publication alongside 'Fears in Solitude' shows, this revaluation of the domestic is thrown into sharp focus by renewed national anxieties. 'Fears in Solitude' depicts 'A green and silent spot [...]/A small and silent dell' in loving particularity, down to the 'half-transparent stalks' of the unripe flax; here, once again, we discover a dreaming solitary poet lying 'wrapp'd/In a half-sleep' (*FS*, 1–2). But this sleepy retreat is suddenly shattered by

> Invasion, and the thunder and the shout,
> And all the crash of onset; fear and rage
> And undetermined conflict –
>
> *(FS, 3)*

Coleridge's anxieties over his social responsibilities have returned with a vengeance. The self-chastisement we encountered in his revisions of Lamb's 'Effusion XII' and in 'Reflections' over lost 'dreamy hours' in 'delicious solitude' is here translated into a more general lament over the 'deep delusion' of revolutionary sympathy and a feeling of alienation both from English behaviour and from recent events in

France. Within the poem, this frenzy of reproach and fear is somewhat uneasily quelled by the poet's return from the solitary dell to the society of 'Stowey', as he turns his footsteps towards Poole's house and his own family in their 'lowly cottage'. This return is emphasised in the published version by placing 'Frost at Midnight', the earlier poem chronologically, at the close of the pamphlet, so that a vision of domestic harmony is superimposed upon the conflict and anxiety of 'Fears in Solitude'. It is a move analogous to Lamb's attempts to subdue Coleridge's earlier fears in solitude through reminding him of the wider social and literary community. But setting it against Lloyd and Lamb's work we see the shortcomings and limitations of the ideal very vividly; the broken friendships and deserted homes of *Blank Verse* provide a forgotten commentary on the poems of *Fears in Solitude* – and, as we will see, *Lyrical Ballads*.

Blank Verse opens with a reminder of how, for Lloyd and Lamb, the small homely space had been fractured. Lloyd dedicated his poems to Southey, another person who had since been excluded from the Coleridgean friendship circle:

> In offering these Poems to you I am simply consulting my feelings. The greater part of them were written beneath your roof, and owe their existence to its quiet comforts. They [...] must certainly remain unclaimed, if not acknowledged by you. (*BV*, 6)

The dedication is heavy with the pressure of the unsaid – a pointed, if coded, reminder of the way in which Nether Stowey had failed to shelter Lloyd, failed to offer a space of 'quiet comforts'. The volume opens with an evocation of a similarly unsuccessful ideal, specifically footnoting the Pantisocratic scheme as 'a plan projected by S. T. Coleridge and Robert Southey [...] in which all individual property was to be abandoned' (*BV*, 9). The poem is crammed with Coleridgean references to Hartleian terms of 'disinterested loves' and 'high-soul'd fellowship' as the basis for wider benevolence, fervently asserting that the 'godlike scheme' shall live on. Individual relationship will pave the way for a future of 'equal man', watched over by a God related to the radical Jesus of Coleridge's *Conciones*:

> [...] who, with sympathies of holiest love,
> Shall teach best fellowship with kindred souls.
> (*BV*, 13)

The cumulative effect of these Coleridgean allusions was obviously enough to put the *Anti-Jacobin* on alert, creating a public image of a unified group dangerously advocating radicalism and equality.

Privately, quite a different narrative was emerging, of difference and dispute. The poem celebrating Pantisocracy, for instance, makes clear that Lloyd himself has found no 'brother heart', a coded reference to Coleridge's failure to fulfil the fraternal role. It is followed by 'Written at Burton in Hampshire,' of August 1797, bemoaning Lloyd's 'hollow friends' and asking, as Coleridge himself had asked in 'To the Rev. George Coleridge':

> Whom shall I trust? for I have trusted many,
> And they have been most false!
> (*BV*, 14)

The collection continually returns to the theme of loss, desertion and neglect, negotiating – as had the 'Nehemiah Higginbottom' sonnets – the limitations of sympathy.

While the poems all yearn towards the ideal of familial and friendly communion, without exception they find it frustrated, unattainable. Friends are absent, or – worse – treacherous; families are scattered. Lloyd's 'To A Sister', for instance, idealises sympathetic communion:

> I have listen'd to thee,
> And of thy innocent feelings have partook,
> E'en till I lived in thee, and melted down
> Years of past bitterness.
> (*BV*, 28–9)

But the poet is now alone, 'an alien from his kindred',

> now unblest
> By all the hallow'd charities of home,
> By all those nameless offices of love
> Which never pass its bounds.
> (*BV*, 29)

Those 'nameless offices of love' are echoed in 'Tintern Abbey', which similarly looks toward a sister's love, celebrating the power of

> little, nameless, unremembered acts
> Of kindness and of love.
> (ll, 35–6; *LyB*, 117)

Both poems call down a blessing on the sister, the poet's second self, and both end by looking towards 'holy confidence' (Lloyd), 'holier love!' (Wordsworth). For both men, the time of ardent idealism is past, but they retain a subdued, spiritualised hope in the familial. These echoes register the force of Coleridge's powerful arguments against *Political Justice* and demonstrate the way in which arguments about the place of friendly and familial love and the nature of sympathy were still being discussed by the whole group. But there is an important difference – the promise of Wordsworth's sisterly communion is realised; Lloyd's remains speculative, unfulfilled.

Blank Verse and *Lyrical Ballads*

As this suggests, there are numerous parallels between *Blank Verse* and *Lyrical Ballads*, and these two collaborative volumes of 1798 must be read alongside one another to bring out the full sense of ongoing conversation and response in the wider group in the late 1790s. *Blank Verse*, admittedly, does not have the same range and suppleness of tone and form as *Lyrical Ballads*. Its poems are private, Bowlesian meditations, couched in the language of personal feeling. It was this delicate tone which formed the focus of some acerbic comments on the volume, as in the *Analytical Review*:

> We may be very deficient in taste, but the whining monotonous melancholy of these pages is to us extremely tiresome. Mr Lloyd and Mr Lamb shed such a sepulchral gloom over every object, and their poetry is such an unvaried murmur, that, so far from sympathizing in their poetical sorrows, we feel a much stronger propensity to smile, than we do to weep.[2]

It is this 'propensity to smile', of course, which the 'Nehemiah Higginbottom' sonnets exploit, and which is probably responsible for a persistent critical reluctance to consider *Blank Verse* alongside its more famous counterparts. Thematically, however, in their exploration of subjectivity and sympathy, the two volumes are remarkably close. Fairer, one of the very few critics to address the book, has pointed out that Lloyd's 'The Dead Friend,' with its delicate attempts to explore the relationship between the 'shades of past existence', the 'former self' and the present day, must have been 'surely have been running through Wordsworth's head in July 1798' as he composed 'Tintern Abbey' – as must, I think, its companion piece in *Blank Verse*, 'To A Sister'.[3] As Fairer subtly shows, Lloyd's under-rated poems delicately probe the same questions as their better-known counterparts – exploring the nature of feeling for others, and suggestively raising issues of sympathetic identification. They are addressed to the lost and dispossessed: the 'dead friend', 'dishearten'd outcasts', 'despised ones'. While these outcasts are not rendered with so much particular detail as Wordsworth's female vagrant or convict, they reveal a similar interest in the poet's social responsibility towards the marginalised. Lloyd is also similarly interested in the effect of environment on the poet. The liveliness of Lloyd's descriptions in 'London, a poem,' show him half-fascinated, half-repulsed by the city, which appears to him when a child as a 'wondrous dream', smoky, crowded,

> it seem'd to me
> As though all living things were centred here.
> (BV, 57)

It is a phrase which shows the power of Lloyd's writing – not Wordsworthian, but pre-empting Wordsworth, calling to mind, for instance, the 'mighty heart' of the city in 'Composed upon Westminster Bridge'. Like that poem, discussed further in Chapter 8, 'London, a poem' is undoubtedly shaped by Lloyd's friendship with Lamb.[4] Rather than 'live a lonely uncompanion'd thing' in rural solitude, he chooses the 'numberless living and progressive beings', the 'infinite varieties' of the city.

Like Coleridge several years earlier expressing his desire to extract 'all that is good in Godwin', Lloyd's contributions to *Blank Verse* move between an excited fascination with Godwin and Wollstonecraft, to whom his last poem in the collection is dedicated, and a distrust, shading into conservative suspicion, of what he saw as their overthrow of familial affection. Lloyd's difficult negotiations with Godwin are revealed in his untitled portrait of a man who leaves society, 'Turn not thy dim eyes to the stormy sea', which struggles with issues of social retreat. It should be read alongside two poems in *Lyrical Ballads*: 'The Foster Mother's Tale', from *Osorio*, and 'Lines left upon a Seat in a Yew-Tree', both of which Lloyd heard during his stay at Stowey. 'Tis a sweet tale,' Maria tells us in the 'Foster-Mother's Tale', 'Such as would lull a listening child to sleep', and Lloyd similarly presents his story as a true tale, recounted in a family setting. The importance of the story or ballad form is emphasised, recollecting the way in which the 'Salutation' sonnet to Siddons (discussed in Chapter 1) transferred the power of her performance onto the grandmother's 'strange tales'. Like that poem, which channels the response of the spectator into the 'wild tale' recounted around the family fire-side, Lloyd's poem questions the nature of affective response.

The subject of Lloyd's poem has the capacity for 'warm benevolence', and a 'full soul'. But – like Wordsworth's solitary in 'Lines left upon a Seat' with his 'pure heart', or like Rivers from *The Borderers* – he has been bitterly disappointed by the neglect of society, and has had 'his prospects blasted, his fair name traduc'd'. He ends as a misanthrope – yet this misanthropy belies his yearning for human sympathy:

> I have e'en heard him, with most strange perversion,
> Brag that weak man was fashion'd by his Maker
> To live a lonely, uncompanion'd thing;
> That he was self-sufficient; that the smile
> Of sweet affection was a very cheat,
> And love's best energies impertinence:
> While ever on his favourite household dog
> He look'd such meanings of a hollow heart,
> His rebel eye express'd such sad misgivings,
> That all he spake fell flat upon the ear
> Self-contradicted.
>
> (*BV*, 44)

This is a clear refutation of what the Coleridge group perceived as Godwinian isolation, in favour of the need for 'love's best energies' and a yearning towards what the poem terms 'the expansive swell/Of warm benevolence'. But the poem is also informed by the impossibility of putting this benevolence into practice. The only resolution for Lloyd's 'self-contradicted' man is flight. Like the subject of the 'Foster-Mother's Tale', he sets sail for foreign lands and disappears: 'He went; nor human ear hath heard of him!'. In manuscript, the poem contains an additional few lines:

> I curse a world
> That moulds to guilt the energetic soul
> Of loftier promise, & for saintly worth
> Invents a discipline that ends in ruin!

Coleridge has added 'I should leave off at this hemistich, & leave my readers to deduce the moral –'.[5] It was clearly a lesson which Lloyd took to heart, since although some of his poems close with moralistic moments, such as 'Address to Wealth', which hopes

> to humanize the heart, t'expand
> The active soul, t'embrace, with one wide wish,
> The universe
>
> (*BV*, 54)

these wishes seem, in practice, to be frustrated, and the over-riding tone is one of uncertainty. While Lloyd's poems still firmly reject the rationalist strand of Godwin's writing, the emphasis on affection and benevolence has become much more tentative than in the days of his first joyous poems to Coleridge, or Coleridge's own visions of Pantisocracy.

A similar insecurity informs Lamb's contributions, beginning with a poem to Lloyd, previously published in the *Monthly Magazine*, which sets the tone of loss and loneliness:

> A stranger, and alone, I past those scenes
> We past so late together; and my heart
> Felt something like desertion.
>
> (*BV*, 75)

This feeling of desertion shapes the remaining poems, which, whilst they evoke the power of the 'home-born Feeling', persistently show the home disrupted, destroyed, desolate. Imbued with necessarianism and resignation to the divine will, they repeatedly return to the 'day of horrors', showing Lamb's acute self-examination through 1797 and 1798, in the aftermath of his mother's death.

As in Lloyd's poems, the power of domestic sociability is evoked, as in 'Written on the day of my aunt's funeral', where Lamb remembers his father's capacity to make 'life social' and to 'cheer/The little circle of domestic friends' (*BV*, 79). But his father is now a 'sad survivor [...] a palsy-smitten, childish, old, old man' (*BV*, 78), his aunt and mother are dead, and his friends have left him forlorn:

> A heavy lot hath he, most wretched man!
> Who lives the last of all his family.
>
> (*BV*, 85)

These explorations of difficult, lonely survival are echoed by several Wordsworth contributions to *Lyrical Ballads*: the 'woeful day' of 'The Last of the Flock', or 'The Female Vagrant' who has 'no earthly friend', where again the power of sociable community is invoked only nostalgically, and set against present loss and decline.

Indeed, Lamb's articulations of desolation and loneliness in *Blank Verse* resonate through later Romantic period literature. The mysterious lyrics of loss in the 'Lucy poems', for instance, may be informed by Wordsworth's knowledge of the Lambs' situation, and, in particular, his reading of the poem, 'Written on Christmas Day 1797'. Opening with a cry of loneliness and loss – 'I am a widow'd thing, now you art gone!' – the poem mourns Mary's illness, which has made her mind

> a fearful blank,
> Her senses lock'd up, and herself kept out
> From human sight or converse.
> (*BV*, 87)

Kelly Grovier has perceptively speculated that this may have shaped Wordsworth's quasi-epitaphic 'A slumber did my spirit seal' with its equally powerful images of locked-up senses – 'she seemed a thing that could not feel'; 'she neither hears nor sees' – perhaps similarly based on gloomy fears for his sister.[6] The grief and abandonment expressed in 'The Old Familiar Faces,' similarly sounds through Mary Shelley's own story of familial destruction: *Frankenstein* (1818): 'I loved my brothers, Elizabeth, and Clerval,' mourns Frankenstein when he leaves his home to study at Ingolstadt, 'these were "old familiar faces"'.[7] Indeed, David Higgins has drawn a suggestive parallel between the lonely wandering of Lamb's speaker – 'earth seem'd a desert I was bound to traverse' – and that of Frankenstein, who tells us he has 'traversed a vast portion of the earth'.[8]

As the *Frankenstein* echo shows, the poem articulates key Romantic questions of doubt and loss. It offers an alternative narrative of the 'home-born Feeling' – not the warm sociability of the 'Salutation', but a desperate plea for sympathy:

> Friend of my bosom, thou more than a brother!
> Why wert thou not born in my father's dwelling?
> So might we talk of the old familiar faces.
> For some they have died, and some they have left me,
> *And some are taken from me*; all are departed;
> All, all are gone, the old familiar faces.
> (*BV*, 90–1)

We seem to have come a long distance from the sociable early poems, with their emphasis on mutual reading, and from Lamb's own attempts to soothe Coleridge's anxieties with the assurance that he has a sympathetic circle of friendly readers. Now the kindness of friends merely serves to emphasise their distance, since they cannot help him to recapture the experiences of childhood. The yearning for readmittance into the language and response of childhood is, of course, a defining trope of Romantic writing: in 'Tintern Abbey', for instance, Wordsworth seeks to hear 'the language of my former heart'. But he has Dorothy as consolation, and the thought that her memory shall be a 'dwelling-place' for mutual recollections – a promise which is fulfilled as he starts to write *The Two-Part Prelude*. Mary's fragile mental state offers no such refuge, and, in this absence, Lamb's speaker is 'ghost-like', houseless, turned out into an endless lonely desert.

The importance of 'The Old Familiar Faces', however, comes not simply from the poignancy of Lamb's personal circumstances. It gains force, too, from his disappointed idealism, the frustration of the 'home-born Feeling' which had been such a powerful political and religious ideal a few years previously – and it tentatively begins to feel its way towards a new outlet for this feeling, in the shape of the reader. Real friends, such as Coleridge – the 'more than brother' – cannot supply any consolation, but perhaps the friendly reader will supply empathy and understanding, the familiarity he finds wanting in life. The poem is the seed for Lamb's novel, *Rosamund Gray*, where, as we will see in the next chapter, he begins to explore the active participation of the reader more fully. If the literal 'old familiar faces' have vanished, a literature based on a 'familiar' relationship between texts, and between reader and author, will, eventually, take their place.

Midnight reproach

The road towards this reconstruction, however, is a difficult and lonely one. The final poem of *Blank Verse* shows how Lamb is still mourning the loss of the ideal, and reproaching Coleridge for its failure. 'Composed at Midnight' – the negative, misanthropic counterpart of 'Frost at Midnight' – shows him angrily rejecting certain aspects of his relationship with Coleridge. Like 'Frost at Midnight', or like 'This Lime-tree Bower', we open with a solitary narrator. His isolation, however, is total. Unlike the Coleridge poems, there is no chance here to exercise 'each faculty of sense', and consequently, no blessing:

> From broken visions of perturbed rest
> I wake, and start, and fear to sleep again.

> How total a privation of all sounds,
> Sights, and familiar objects, man, bird, beast,
> Herb, tree, or flow'r, and prodigal light of heav'n!
> 'Twere some relief to catch the drowsy cry
> Of the mechanic watchman, or the noise
> Of revel, reeling home from midnight cups.
>
> (*BV*, 92)

Not even the 'light of heav'n' falls on this poet, cut off from nature and from God. 'This Lime-tree Bower' ends with the sound of the rook, possessing 'charm' for Charles, the man to whom 'No sound is dissonant, which tells of Life'. Lamb's own poet, by contrast, can hear only the dissonant sounds of the watchmen and of drunkards. That 'drowsy cry', in particular, has a specific resonance. It picks up the 'owlet's cry' at the opening of 'Frost at Midnight', and specifically alludes to another Coleridge poem, satirising the use of the nightingale in the poems of those who, like Lamb, are city-dwellers:

> Sister of love-lorn Poets, Philomel!
> How many Bards in city garret pent,
> While at their window they with downward eye
> Mark the faint Lamp-beam on the kennell'd mud,
> And listen to the drowsy cry of Watchmen,
> (Those hoarse unfeather'd Nightingales of TIME!)
> How many wretched Bards address *thy* name,
> And Her's, the full-orb'd Queen, that shines above.
>
> (*Poems* 1796, 71)

The description of Lamb in 'This Lime-tree Bower' as 'In the great City pent' unfortunately links him with these 'wretched Bards', composing their work 'in city garret pent'. By specifying the sounds of the watchman and the drunkards, Lamb is trying to counter Coleridge's city poets with their adulterated versions of the nightingale. Instead of yearning towards a poetic vision of nature, he deliberately uses the sounds of the city in his work – but unlike his later, lively city letters and essays, this is a dark unfriendly urban scene.

Mirroring his pointed, humorous use of *Osorio* in the letter discussed in Chapter 4, Lamb might also be figuring his disappointment in Coleridge's friendship by alluding to another poem, published immediately before 'To the Nightingale' in *Poems* 1796: 'Effusion XXII: to a friend, together with an unfinished poem'. This opens with a plea for collaborative friendship, a request for 'the aiding verse' which might complete Coleridge's work. In return, it promises Lamb fraternal love, and sympathises with him over Mary's illness, which, says Coleridge, he can understand because of the loss of his own sister:

> O! I have woke at midnight, and have wept,
> Because SHE WAS NOT! – Cheerily, dear CHARLES!
> Thou thy best friend shalt cherish many a year:
> Such warm presages feel I of high Hope.
> (*Poems* 1796, 69)

'Composed at Midnight', where the narrator himself wakes at midnight and remains unconsoled, uncherished, thus carries an allusive reproach.

In light of this, the poem takes on an added significance. While not directly allegorising Lamb's relationship with Coleridge, it certainly reflects some of the issues over religion and the afterlife with which the two had been struggling in 1796 and 1797. In a scene which recasts Coleridge's listening to the breathing of Hartley in the midnight cottage room, the narrator of 'Composed at Midnight' can only hear the 'moanings of the dying man' in the room above. Coleridge's scene opens out into a sunlit vision of Hartley's happy wanderings; Lamb's poet, listening to the 'cough/ Consumptive', is led into contemplation of death. The man,

> waits in anguish for the morning's light.
> What can that do for him, or what restore?
> (*BV*, 93)

This is a morning unlike the triumphal vision of Judgement Day offered in 'This Lime-tree Bower' or in Coleridge's letter of 1797. Instead, when death comes for the figure in the Lamb poem, 'Tis darkness and conjecture all beyond'. In a direct refutation of Coleridge's attempts to console Lamb there is no opening prospect, no spiritual consolation. Both are shown to be 'conjecture' and 'fancy', to be guarded against, just as Lamb had earlier instructed Coleridge to guard against the 'pride of speculation', of man 'hailing in himself the future God' (Marrs, I: 54). Lamb is ostensibly rejecting the Calvinist creed of the Elect separated from the damned to put forward a more humane, Unitarian vision of the afterlife. Yet his poem also carries a warning to those who over-value human judgement, and who place themselves above their own 'kindred or companions'.

> The man of parts,
> Poet, or prose declaimer, on his couch

> Lolling, like one indifferent, fabricates
> A heaven of gold, where he, and such as he,
> Their heads encompassed with crowns, their heels
> With fine wings garlanded, shall tread the stars
> Beneath their feet, heaven's pavement, far remov'd
> From damned spirits, and the torturing cries
> Of men, his brethren, fashion'd of the earth,
> As he was, nourish'd with the selfsame bread,
> Belike his kindred or companions once,
> Through everlasting ages now divorced,
> In chains, and savage torments, to repent
> Short years of folly on earth. Their groans unheard
> In heaven, the saint nor pity feels, nor care,
> For those thus sentenc'd – pity might disturb
> The delicate sense, and most divine repose,
> Of spirits angelical. Blessed be God,
> The measures of his judgements are not fix'd
> By man's erroneous standard.
>
> (*BV*, 94–5)

Lamb's attack here on narrow-minded religious bigotry or pride finds parallels in his letters. While maintaining a deep interest in the writings of the Quakers, for example, he condemns what he sees as a showy, 'fanatic' demonstration of their religion: 'I detest the vanity of a man thinking he speaks by the Spirit, when what he says an ordinary man might say without all that quaking and trembling' (Marrs, I: 103). The key word here is 'vanity', and the idea recurs in a condemnation of the leading Unitarian preacher: Thomas Belsham. Despite his own religious allegiances, Lamb despises the way Belsham 'glibly' speaks of 'the attributes of the **word God**, in a Pulpit, and will talk of infinity with a tongue that dangles from a scull that never reached in thought or thorough imagination **two** inches' (Marrs, III: 58). Coleridge, too, is not immune from this kind of attack, and Lamb's 'man of parts/Poet, or prose declaimer,' dreamily lolling on his couch, fabricating his own vision without genuine affection or empathy for 'kindred or companions', implicitly questions Coleridge's position.

The condemnation of the saint in 'Composed at Midnight' who 'nor pity feels, nor care' is reminiscent of the way in which the narrator of Lamb's 'Effusion XII' says he will teach his lover to 'rail [...] on those who practise not/Or love or pity'. Coleridge's heavy revisions of that poem had prompted Lamb's first doubts about his capacity for sympathetic identification. Now, seeing Coleridge deliberately distancing himself from his former friends, Lamb was forced to see the failure of 'love' and 'pity' at first hand. The over-riding anxiety of 'Composed at Midnight' is that sympathy, the move towards 'brotherly kindness' urged by the Unitarians, may be defeated by pride.

'Living without God in the World'

This fear of pride, a form of tyranny which hinders proper vision or self-worth, haunts the group in the 1790s, constantly threatening to undermine mutual reading and writing, and to destroy friendly relations. The pride of Osorio, for instance, fuels his fratricidal ambition: 'Pride,' in Albert's words, '[...] dup'd him into Guilt,' turning him into a 'self-created God' (III, i, 94–5; Mays, III: i, 100). In *The Borderers*, Rivers' pride, specifically identified as a Godwinian egotism, leads him to retreat from the world – like the misanthrope of 'Lines left upon a Seat', he sustains 'his soul in solitude' with 'the food of pride'. Lamb's participation in this debate, sharpened by his own experience within the friendship group, is visible in his poem 'Living without God in the World', which appeared in Southey's *Annual Anthology* (1799). As David Chandler points out, Lamb might have been working on the poem from the last months of 1797 – the inclusion of a passage in Lloyd's *Lines Suggested by the Fast* (1799) which differs from the *Annual Anthology* version implies that Lamb continued to revise the poem throughout 1798.[9]

'Living without God in the World' returns to the same questions debated in the days of Pantisocracy and 'Salutation' friendship, in particular the formation of the 'home-born Feeling', Coleridge's analogy between friendship and the 'intense [...] Rays' of the sun reaching into the distance (Griggs, I: 86). In 'Living without God in the World', Lamb supplies a bitter response:

> We consecrate our total hopes and fears
> To idols, flesh and blood, our love, (heaven's due)
> Our praise and admiration; praise bestowed
> By man on man, and acts of worship done
> To a kindred nature, certes do reflect
> Some portion of the glory and rays oblique
> Upon the politic worshipper, – so man
> Extracts a pride from his humility.
>
> (*AA* 1799, 90)

Lamb uses Coleridge's own terms to question his practice of 'particular friendship', which here falls far short of the radiating, vivifying, spiritually uplifting ideal they had once mutually imagined. It is instead a mutual contract, offering only a limited reflection of one's own self-worth.

Lamb does retain some aspects of his earlier outlook, continuing to reject the blindness of a particular Godwinian outlook:

> Some braver spirits of the modern stamp
> Affect a Godhead nearer: these talk loud
> Of mind, and independant [sic] intellect,
> Of energies omnipotent in man,
> And man of his own fate artificer
> (*AA* 1799, 91)

These lines have led Roe to read 'Living without God in the World' as a response to the *Anti-Jacobin*'s 'New Morality' attack, which particularly singles out Deists as 'the men without a God'.[10] The phrase is also, as Chandler has explored, a quotation from Priestley's *Letters to a Philosophical Unbeliever* (1780):

> A merely *nominal* believer in a God may be a *practical atheist*, and worse than a mere speculative one, living as *without God in the world*, intirely thoughtless of his being, perfections, and providence.[11]

By using it as the title for his poem, Lamb is strongly reinforcing his Unitarian allegiances, which are further reinforced by the poem's insistence on resignation to divine will: 'a mighty arm, by man unseen' (*AA* 1799, 90). Priestley's *'nominal* believer[s]' become, in the last stanza of the poem, Lamb's 'Deists only in the name' – those who are not fuelled by this deeper faith. Instead, like the mortals of *Samson Agonistes*, they 'wander "loose about," they nothing see,/Themselves except, and creatures like themselves' (*AA* 1799, 92).

This is partly an attack on Godwinian self-sufficiency and speculative atheism – indeed the references to 'life immortal' directly recall the question which appears in *Political Justice* with relation to population increase: 'why may not man one day be immortal?' (*PJ*, 460). It may be partly a response to the *Anti-Jacobin* cartoon, a reassertion of religious allegiance. It is also strongly signalling Lamb's continuing critical and creative engagement with his contemporaries, since the references to pride and short-sightedness also recall Wordsworth, and there is a direct quotation in 'Living without God in the World' from *The Borderers* – the reference to 'independant [sic] intellect'. Rivers tells Mortimer after his apparent murder of Herbert:

> You have obeyed the only law that wisdom
> Can ever recognize; the immediate law
> Flashed from the light of circumstances
> Upon an independent intellect.
> (III, v, 1493–96; *Borderers*, 210)

The way in which the law is flashed into the individual mind, sought by men 'diving [...] into their own bosoms', is another aspect of the same tendency Lamb notices in 'Living without God in the World': man's inability to escape the limited reflections of the self.

Rivers' pride has sprung up as a response to the neglect of others, and in Lamb's poem, we see a similar warning about putting too much of our faith in 'idols of flesh and blood', in affording too much importance to the 'praise bestowed by man on man'. This functions in two ways: firstly, to underline Lamb's own distress at the betrayal of Coleridge, and secondly to act as a warning as he sees Coleridge, in turn, investing Wordsworth with God-like qualities. In its startling ending, quoting from *Macbeth* and shadowed by personal experience of the 'day of horrors', 'Living without God' shows the devastation such misplaced faith can have:

> So on their dissolute spirits, soon or late,
> Destruction cometh 'like an armed man,'
> Or like a dream of murder in the night,
> Withering their mortal faculties, and breaking
> The bones of all their pride.
> (*AA* 1799, 92)

We might also recall the dreams of murder in *Osorio*, or the projected murder of *The Borderers* – betrayals which are the ultimate result of trusting in 'mortal faculties', of short-sighted self-worth. Instead of the glorious salvation of 'This Lime-tree Bower', or the breezy visions of 'Frost at Midnight', Lamb's poem promises only 'destruction'.

Edmund Oliver: forging a 'common identity'

In its double movement, questioning Coleridge yet continuing to voice his rejection of Godwin, 'Living without God in the World' is reminiscent of Lloyd's novel *Edmund Oliver*, written in late 1797 and published in April 1798, with a dedication to Charles Lamb. Politically and personally, this novel resists easy categorisation. Long held to be a brazen satire, it relates anecdotes about Coleridge's opium use and his brief spell in the dragoons which had been passed on within the friendship circle, either during Lloyd's stay in Nether Stowey or by Southey. The bounds of privacy, Coleridge felt, had been breached – 'calumny & ingratitude from men who have been fostered in the bosom of my confidence!' (Griggs, I: 407) – and critics have, until recently, largely agreed that Lloyd's is a 'merciless and faithless exposure', a 'work of blatant calumny'.[12] It is, however, as attentive readers such as Taussig, Fairer, and Philip Cox have noted, a subtle and richly ambiguous reflection of the political and literary conversations going on within the group.

Like 'Living without God in the World', it is on one level a Godwinian satire, which obsessively returns to the issue of investing too much faith in human relationships and too much pride in human judgement. It opens by refuting Godwin's 'indefinite benevolence...annihilating all the dear "charities of father, son, and brother"' (*EO*, I: vii–viii) and presenting an alternative vision in which 'domestic connections' lead to 'a rational and enlarged benevolence':

> The human mind never will be led to interest itself with regard to a *whole*, except it have been first excited by *palpable parts of that whole*.
> (*EO*, I: ix)

Clearly, to anyone who knew Coleridge's Hartleian principles at this period, this echoes his pronouncements on benevolence as a 'thing of *Concretion*', 'begotten and rendered permanent by social and domestic affections', as opposed to the *Political Justice* 'system of disinterested benevolence'.[13] The novel emphasises the failure of Godwinian rationalism using the same quotation Lamb had borrowed from *The Borderers*. 'We should be "governed by the light of circumstance flashed on an independent intellect"', argues the high-minded idealist Gertrude, justifying a relationship outside marriage – only to be made pregnant and abandoned by her lover (*EO*, I: 124).

Lloyd thus shows himself to be an enthusiastic participant in the Coleridgean group; he is also eager to mark himself out as an insider, quoting from a Wordsworth manuscript known only within the friendship circle, and presenting a vision of idealised fraternal friendship in the Coleridgean mode. His main narrator, Edmund Oliver, has a pseudo-filial relationship with the older Charles Maurice, who leads him towards 'the beauty of Christianity': 'You have formed me Charles; you have regenerated me!' (*EO*, I: 29).

This intensity points back to the early poetry Lloyd had addressed to Coleridge prior to the Nether Stowey scheme of domestication, and in fact *Edmund Oliver* is a textual model of what Lloyd had hoped to gain from life with Coleridge, a blend of philosophy and affection, which ends in a glorious realisation of Pantisocracy:

> Basil, Edmund, and I, have taken lands which lie contiguous to each other – we have banished the words *mine* and *thine* [...] we have abandoned the appearance, and have lost the sensations annexed to individual possessions. – We meet every evening at each other's house, and by means of reading or conversation endeavour to approximate to a common identity. (*EO*, II: 292)

The 'common identity' finds its textual equivalent in the characterisation of the narrator. Biographical details of Coleridge and Lloyd become merged, so that it is the Lloyd figure, the student Edmund, who relies on the Coleridge figure, Charles, for material support. Moreover, the anecdotes about Coleridge's experiences in the dragoons, and experiments with opium, are transferred to the Lloyd figure; Charles then rescues and redeems him.

Like Lamb in 'Living without God in the World', Lloyd voices ideas derived from Coleridge, but also desires simultaneously to criticise some aspects of his behaviour, in the shape of Edmund's volatility and unpredictability. Yet the use of intimate Coleridgean anecdotes is in fact in keeping with Coleridge's own repeated use of the private, domestic scene to make a larger statement about public principles, as in 'Frost at Midnight'. To read the novel purely as satire is to misread, in the words of Cox, its recent editor, 'the awkward alliance between the public and the private, the literary and the personal, that had characterized this particular group of writers from the start'.[14] Moreover, Lloyd's odd blend of criticism and homage finds a parallel in the political ambiguity of *Edmund Oliver*. Cox's edition places it in a series of anti-Jacobin novels – yet as he readily admits, it is at once a radical novel, and a satire on radicalism, since radical ends such as the Pantisocratic 'common identity' are achieved through the characters' conservative behaviour. In mid-1798, Lloyd responded to criticisms levelled at the novel by the *Anti-Jacobin* with a fierce disavowal of radical principles, retrospectively ironing out the ambiguities of his novel.[15] But Lloyd's retrospective struggles to define the pair's stance in mid-1798 only serve to reinforce the ambiguities of their earlier works. Just as the allusions of *Edmund Oliver* and *Blank Verse* tread a delicate line between private sympathy and public exposure, so too do these works hold the potential for both radical and conservative interpretation.

Coleridge and the 'lying angel'

The delicate, explosive mixture of criticism and homage tipped over into outright accusation in May 1798. Coleridge responded angrily to *Edmund Oliver*, breaking off his association with Lloyd: Lamb, in consequence, cut off contact with Coleridge. Coleridge's letter of response to Lamb is a masterly piece of self-justification and excuse, which he employed Dorothy to copy so as to vindicate himself with the Wordsworths. Himself accused of disloyalty, Coleridge turns the accusation against Lamb and Lloyd. Acknowledging the quasi-religious idealisation inherent in their relationship with him, he claims this has stemmed simply from their overblown, almost deranged, conceptions of friendship:

> I have been unfortunate in my connections. Both you & Lloyd became acquainted with me at a season when your minds were far from being in a composed or natural state & you clothed my image with a suit of notions & feelings which could belong to nothing human. *You* are restored to comparative saneness, & are merely wondering what is become of the Coleridge with whom you were so passionately in love. *Charles Lloyd's* mind has only changed its disease, & he is now arraying his ci-devant angel in a flaming Sanbenito – the whole ground of the garment a dark brimstone & plenty of little Devils flourished out in black. O me! Lamb, 'even in laughter the heart is sad' – (Griggs, I: 405)

The angelic vision Lloyd had previously entertained of Coleridge is set against his absurd appearance in 'a flaming Sanbenito'. Lloyd's devilish misconceptions are further refuted by a quotation from Proverbs 14: 'even in laughter the heart is sad'. Significantly, Proverbs 14 deals particularly with the nature of fools and false witnesses; the citation carries an implied rebuke.

The letter was answered by a list of satirical enquiries sent by Lloyd and Lamb to Coleridge in return, the 'Theses quaedam Theologicae'. The 'Theses' pick up this concept of the 'ci-devant angel' and use it in a sharp attack on Coleridge's religious discourse. Whilst Coleridge is in Germany, Lamb asks him to ascertain:

1. Whether God loves a lying Angel better than a true Man?
2. Whether the Archangel Uriel *could* affirm an untruth? & if he *could* whether he *would*?
3. Whether Honesty be an angelic virtue?

Particularly cutting is his seventh query:

7. Whether the Vision Beatific be anything more or less than a perpetual representation to each individual Angel of his own present attainments & future capabilities, somehow in the manner of mortal looking-glasses, reflecting a perpetual complacency, & self-satisfaction? (Marrs, I: 128)

Picking up on the idea of an 'echo or mirror' in 'Frost at Midnight', Lamb suggests that Coleridge's visions may be no more than a 'mortal looking-glass', the reflection of his own egotism, which turns all things – Lamb's sonnets; Lamb himself in 'This Lime-tree Bower' – into a projection of his own arrogance. Coleridge's attempts to 'christianize' a wider audience might, Lamb suggests, be fuelled by egotism and personal pride rather than divine inspiration.

This is reinforced by the deliberate echo in the 'Theses' of radical articles such as the January 1798 'Queries', reprinted in the *Morning Post* from *The Watchman* two years previously:

1. Whether the wealth of the higher classes does not ultimately depend on the labour of the lower classes?
2. Whether the man who has been accustomed to love beef and cleanly raiment, will not have stronger motives to labour than the man who has used himself to exist without either?[16]

Coleridge's political oscillations seem to find an equivalent in the patterns of recantation and self-justification in his friendships. In one movement, Lamb and Lloyd attack Coleridge's public discourse – religious and political – and simultaneously criticise his private discourse of domestic affection.

The 'Theses' marked a definitive breach of the friendships. After a two-year silence, Coleridge resumed his friendship with Lamb, but never forgave Lloyd. By the time *Fears in Solitude* was published, then, its strong argument for domestic sociability and friendliness had already been undermined from within. The scene of intimacy presented in 'Frost at Midnight' may now be seen as a public over-writing of an alternative private narrative of betrayal and reproach, which challenges the very basis of the 'home-born Feeling'. The 'defensive duplicity' noticed by Magnuson in the pamphlet as Coleridge shifts between radical and conservative positions also reflects ongoing negotiations over the friendship ideal – negotiations which are simultaneously personal and political, private and public. In the concluding chapters, I explore Lamb's attempts to reconcile his private disappointment in the failure of the friendship ideal with his continuing belief in affectionate sociability as a wider principle. If, like Pantisocracy, this belief could not be realised in practice, perhaps it could be reconstructed in print.

Part III
Reconstructing Friendship

6
A Text of Friendship: *Rosamund Gray*

Spring 1798

Spring 1798. Two deserted houses. Wordsworth's *The Ruined Cottage*, begun in spring 1797 and extensively revised in 1798, invites us to enter the 'four naked walls' of a house which is 'ruined', 'reft', offering the traveller only

> A cold bare wall whose earthy top is tricked
> With weeds and the rank spear-grass
> (MS D: 107–8, *RC*, 51)

Lamb's *A Tale of Rosamund Gray and Old Blind Margaret,* begun in early 1798 and published later the same year, similarly shows the pathos of the abandoned house, in which the narrator kneels, alone, contemplative, on the spot where his childhood bed had stood:

> I looked round involuntarily, expecting to see some face I knew – but all was naked and mute. The bed was gone. My little pane of painted window, through which I loved to look at the sun, when I awoke in a fine summer's morning, was taken out, and had been replaced by one of common glass. (*RG*, 109)

Wordsworth's ruin reflects the pressure of war and famine, which have split apart Margaret's family; more loosely, it reflects his 'imaginative reenactment' of family mourning and post-Revolutionary regret.[1] Lamb's abandoned house alludes to disaster closer to home – Mary's matricide and the collapse of his friendship group. Both start with the domestic space destroyed, the family scattered, and a sense of community fragmented. Margaret's 'houshold flowers', her 'rose and sweet-briar', have been replaced by weeds and rank grass; Lamb's painted window has been replaced by 'common glass' – both offer a narrative of decay and loss, where, as in 'Ode. Intimations of Immortality', the 'radiance which was once so bright' has disappeared.[2]

But crucially, both go on to offer a story of reconstruction and recovery. In *The Ruined Cottage* Wordsworth moves away from overtly socio-political comment – as in the 'Salisbury Plain' poems – into a more reflective, introspective mode. While the sorrow and despair caused by war are evoked, the poem ends by rejecting 'indignation and vengeance in the name of pity and love', a move which has been seen as 'a turn away from radical involvement towards self-involvement'.[3] Critics have called attention to the flaws and self-contradictions in this project of 'poetic renovation', questioning Wordsworth's attempt to 'conciliate literary recompense with political resolution'.[4] Indeed, Magnuson argues that this criticism began within the friendship circle, showing how Coleridge's 'Christabel' (begun April 1798), is in constant, unsettling dialogue with *The Ruined Cottage*. Lamb's *Rosamund Gray*, however, provides another, more sympathetic commentary on Wordsworth's meditative turn, showing how the introspection of *The Ruined Cottage* could be answered and actively used by others. The novel tackles the same themes of hope and despair as Wordsworth's poem, but offers an alternative vision of recovery and 'renovation'.

For at the same time as Lamb was lamenting the loss of friendship with Coleridge, he was also reconstructing a literary community – firstly, within *Rosamund Gray*, then through his play *John Woodvil*, his contributions to the *Albion* newspaper, his lively letters of London life, and his essays. These concluding chapters show how that community gradually took shape, beginning with *Rosamund Gray*, a profoundly self-involved, private story which nevertheless looks outward to appeal to others. While evading the problems posed by practical realisations of community feeling such as Pantisocracy, it works actively to create a friendly reading community. Employing allusions and phrases which would have had a specific meaning to particular readers, its narrative functions on multiple levels. It is a love story which is also a story about the love of reading, and about the love of friends, who will themselves be readers of the novel.

Anxieties of friendship: letters to Robert Lloyd

Two letters of mid-1798 to Robert Lloyd, brother of Charles, demonstrate how seriously Lamb was searching for a new reading of friendship, and for practical solutions to the anxieties posed by 'particular friendship', such as the over-idealisation and selfishness condemned in 'Living without God in the World'. The letters point towards a shift in Lamb's creative development as, instructing Robert in religious forbearance and Unitarian attitudes, he adopts a gently persuasive air of resignation and sufferance. Although Lamb is taking on the role of mentor and guide, his advice is tempered by his extreme sensitivity to the dangers of spiritual pride. As he rejects Robert's obviously flattering appeals for intimate friendship, his letter takes on a painfully self-critical tone: 'I know you have chosen to take up an high opinion of my moral worth, but I say it before God, and I do not lie, you are mistaken in me' (Marrs, I: 135).

Lamb's earnestness, and the way in which he continually underpins his argument with scriptural allusion, has obvious echoes with Coleridge's writing style, in those letters of consolation to Lamb in September 1796, or in his attempts to 'christianize' Thelwall. But Lamb is distancing himself from Coleridge's friendship, as demonstrated by his rejection of the poetry they had once enjoyed together – Bowles, and Charlotte Smith, 'sonnet writers & complainers,' who, he tells Robert Lloyd, 'can see no joys but what are past, and fill peoples' heads with notions of the **Unsatisfying** nature of Earthly comforts –' (Marrs, I: 144). Simultaneously, he pulls away from the belief that 'particular' affection may unlock wider benevolence. He now advises Robert that although friends may be a great consolation in times of hardship, 'the having a friend is not indispensably necessary to virtue or happiness' (Marrs, I: 134). In fact, he now actively discourages exclusive friendships:

> there is always, without very unusual care there must always be, something of **self** in friendship, we love our friend because he is like ourselves, can consequences altogether unmix'd and pure be reasonably expected from such a source. (Marrs, I: 134–5)

This is a close echo of 'Living without God in the World', and the lines condemning the way in which those who are spiritually blind see nothing: 'Themselves except, and creatures like themselves' (*AA* 1799, 92). This kind of self-reflexive friendship is undesirable not only because of its egotism, but also because it encourages Hobbesian self-interest, a failure of sympathy which can only be resolved by a return to religion:

> we love our friend, because he is *ours* – so we do our money, our wit, our knowledge, our virtue, and whereever this sense of **appropriation**

> **and property enters**, so much is to be subtracted from the value of that friendship or that virtue. [...] Robert, friends fall off, friends mistake us, they change, they grow unlike us, they go away, they die, but God is everlasting & uncapable of change, and to him we may look with chearful, unpresumptuous **hope**. (Marrs, I: 135)

The elegiac cadence of 'friends fall off, friends mistake us... they go away, they die' evokes Lamb's grief both for his family and for his lost ideals of friendship, as those insistent stresses and the assonance of 'friends fall off' culminate in the decisive iamb 'they die'. Immediately, however, this is picked up and answered by the next iambic phrase, 'but God'. There will be a way through the time of mourning.

We find an echo of that phrase 'friends fall off' in *The Two-Part Prelude* (1799). Here it comes to represent Wordsworth's own negotiations with the concept of domestic and friendly love, as he turns to nature for support and blessing during 'these times of fear':

> [...] 'mid indifference and apathy
> And wicked exultation, when good men
> On every side fall off we know not how
> To selfishness disguised in gentle names
> Of peace, and quiet, and domestic love,
> Yet mingled, not unwillingly, with sneers
> On visionary minds
>   (II: 478–85, *Prelude* 1799, 66)

Wordsworth had begun *The Two-Part Prelude* during the lonely winter he spent in Germany, at a point when he was becoming aware of the divergence between himself and Coleridge. It represents his negotiations with recollected grief, as he and Dorothy, isolated in freezing Goslar, remembered their childhood bereavements and talked over scenes of their past. Like Lamb in the summer of 1798, Wordsworth was by 1799 beginning to disassociate himself from his previous intimacies, and to move towards creative self-sufficiency. Lamb turns back to his Bible for support; Wordsworth, in *The Two-Part Prelude*, turns to a nourishing ideal of nature.

For both, this contemplative state results in a development in their thinking about loss and suffering. Whereas in the *Lyrical Ballads* suffering had appeared within a social context and framework, Wordsworth's poems written during the Goslar period, especially the tentative *Prelude* drafts, suggest 'loss as the constant of human existence', a part of his writing, woven into his meditations on the nature of childhood and memory.[5] Lamb's writings of 1798 and 1799 reveal a similar pattern of confronting grief, mourning, and gradual assimilation. Wordsworth overcomes isolation through the recreation of childhood associations in *The Prelude*; Lamb, similarly, uses the novel to recreate a friendly community.

'Inscribed in friendship': the sensibility of *Rosamund Gray*

From its very dedication, *Rosamund Gray* shows how it is rooted in affection: 'This tale is inscribed in friendship to Marmaduke Thompson'. 'Inscribed in friendship' – the novel is dedicated not only to a specific friend, but to the idea of friendship itself. Lamb had perhaps chosen Thompson, a Christ's Hospital school-friend, as the dedicatee because *Rosamund Gray* springs directly from 'The Old Familiar Faces', which he had sent Thompson in January 1798. The friendship recalls an older allegiance – predating his relationship with Lloyd, and unrelated to any recent collaborations, it represents enduring loyalty, a significant theme in the novel.

Thompson may be the named dedicatee, but the novel also pays homage to many other relationships – friendly and familial. Borrowing its title from a poem by Lloyd, and opening with an allusion to Wordsworth's *The Ruined Cottage*, *Rosamund Gray* is richly, and self-consciously, intertextual. Lamb describes it as a 'tale', possibly to connect with the ideals of *Lyrical Ballads* and their emphasis on 'low and rustic life', and Rosamund herself is a village maiden like those of Wordsworth's and Southey's poems, who stoically cares for her aged grandmother. Her name had first appeared in Lloyd's *Poems on Various Subjects* (1795), in a ballad of social protest celebrating 'the intuitive feelings of worth', '*Nature's Simplicity*', embodied in the poor Rosamund Gray. As well as these literary forebears, she also has parallels with Lamb's own youthful love Ann Simmons. The parallels with Lamb's own love-affair are reinforced by the setting of the novel – Widford, in Hertfordshire, where he had met Simmons. Rosamund is wooed by the young gentleman Allan Clare, who, with obvious parallels to Lamb himself, is devoted to his sister Elinor. Elinor's letters to her cousin Maria form part of the tale, allowing Lamb to introduce overtly literary elements into the narrative, and also to explore friendship bonds from a feminine perspective. The story of Allan's love for Rosamund ends abruptly, as Matravis, the Godwinian villain, is introduced. Matravis, 'cold and systematic in all his plans', is a proud and scornful figure, filled with jealousy at the intimacy between the Clares and Rosamund.

Constructing a 'scheme of delicate revenge,' he attacks and rapes Rosamund as she is wandering in the woods, which leads to her death. Her grandmother, too, dies from grief; Elinor's death from a 'phrensy fever' soon follows. At the heart of this love story is violence, loss, and death.

There is a strange coda to the tale, where the narrator actually enters the story, revealing himself as a lost friend of Allan. The narrator, haunted by 'the memory of old times' feels the urge to 'revisit the scenes of my native village'. Although he does revisit the scenes which witnessed the love affair of Rosamund and Allan, the true purpose of the visit is to recall his own lost childhood, and the passing of familiar landmarks. Grief over Allan and Rosamund becomes indistinguishable from the narrator's own sense of loss and abandonment. The intensity of his sorrow is only assuaged by a reunion with Allan himself, leading to the renewal of their friendship. The closing scene of the novel shows the narrator together with Allan, witnessing the death of the repentant Matravis, symbol of jealousy and envy, destroyer of friendships.

Significantly, Matravis is the only character in the novel who does not read, and, correspondingly, is unable to sustain any bonds of affection: 'He feared, he envied, he suspected; but he never loved' (*RG*, 97). He has thus never learned to exercise sympathy, as opposed to Rosamund, who from her early childhood has read Quarles, Wither, Baxter, and Bunyan, all authors with particular significance for Lamb, Mary, and their friends.

> Rosamund had not read many books beside these; or if any, they had been only occasional companions: these were to Rosamund as old friends, that she had long known. I know not, whether the peculiar cast of her mind might not be traced, in part, to a tincture she had received, early in life, from Walton, and Wither, from John Bunyan, and her Bible. (*RG*, 12)

Compare Rosamund's portrayal of her books as 'old friends' – the first mention of friendship in the novel – with Lamb's frequent assertion that his favourite authors are his acquaintances. 'Wither is like an old friend,' he exclaims to Southey in 1798 (Marrs, I: 142); 'books are to me instead of friends,' he tells Coleridge during one of Mary's illnesses (Marrs, I: 89). Indeed, Rosamund's imagination receiving a 'tincture' from her early reading is echoed by Lamb's explanation in the introduction to his 1818 *Works* that his writing has received a 'tinge' from his old reading (*Works* 1818, I: ix). It also looks forward to the descriptions of childhood literary exploration in the *London Magazine* Elia essays – appropriately, since it is in *Rosamund Gray* that he begins to move towards the elusive Elian voice of nostalgia and reflection. Again, like Wordsworth once the first intensity of his friendship with Coleridge is over, Lamb is returning to speculate on the sources of his own creativity, on scenes and affections which shaped his mind as a child.

This allows him to go back to his own derivative pastoral poetry with more confidence and insight, rewriting and intensifying its scenes – particularly those involving reading. For one of the central scenes in the love affair between Rosamund and Allan, Lamb returns to the earlier, unpublished poem, 'Sweet is thy sunny hair', where the two lovers are reading Mackenzie's sentimental novel *Julia de Roubigné*. We might remember how, observing his lover, the poet's emotions are aroused by

> the soul of sympathy
> That beam'd a meek and modest grace
> Of pensive softness o'er thy face,
> When thy heart bled to hear the tale
> Of Julia, and the silent secret moan
> The love-lorn maiden pour'd for Savillon.
> (ll. 16–21)

That scene then finds a direct echo in *Rosamund Gray*, as Rosamund, alone with Allan, reads aloud one of Julia's early letters telling her friend and confidante Maria that 'I have sometimes painted to myself a *husband*':

> The girl blushed as she read, and trembled – she had a sort of confused sensation, that Allan was noticing her – yet she durst not lift her eyes from the book, but continued reading, scarce knowing what she read.
>
> Allan guessed the cause of her confusion. Allan trembled too – his colour came and went – his feelings became impetuous – and, flinging both arms round her neck, he kissed his young favourite. (*RG*, 38–9)

Rosamund's blushes, and her trembling, suggest the same palpitating sensitivity to emotion which characterises the heroine of sensibility; Julia similarly displays faintness and tears. As Coleridge would have it, they are 'tremblingly alive to trifling misfortunes'.[6] Similarly, on an immediate narrative level, *Rosamund Gray* frequently borrows from the devices of the novel of sensibility; such features as the disrupted narrative, the frequent digressions, and the use of dashes, exclamation marks and apostrophes invite the reader to become sympathetically involved in the text. In the passage where Rosamund and Allan fall in love, the lengthy Mackenzie extract allows the reader to be present at the meeting of the lovers, and to read along with them. The breathless punctuation of the subsequent lines reflects the tentative nature of their love: 'Allan trembled too – his colour came and went – his feelings became impetuous –'.

As we saw in Chapters 1 and 2, however, sensibility is itself an unstable and suggestive mode, and Mackenzie's novel is fragmentary and disorientating, seeming to unsettle the conventions of the novel of sensibility from within. Probing the nature of emotional response, it constantly flirts with the danger of 'visionary indulgence'. Lamb similarly uses Mackenzie, in his turn, to question emotional reaction to reading or listening to stories of feeling, as he had done in his earlier sonnets. Unlike those poems, however, the novel is braced by humour, and while it narrates a tale of loss and despair, it invites a compensatory sociability. Gary Kelly notices the high incidence of 'specifically literary quotation and allusion' in the text, putting this down to the 'belletristic literariness' of the novel.[7] I think it has a more personal explanation: Lamb is using allusion in a way which would have specific meaning for certain readers. Like *Edmund Oliver*, *Rosamund Gray* is a meditation on the nature of friendship in the aftermath of a hurtful estrangement, but whereas Lloyd had used personal anecdotes to display his closeness to Coleridge, Lamb employs allusions to personal letters and previous collaborations to provide a testament to his enduring faith in his friendships – and the power of friendly reading. Beneath the love story of Rosamund and Allan is another, more complicated narrative, of Lamb's own friendly love, and its endurance through the tragedy of his mother's death, and his disappointed misunderstandings with Coleridge. Through allusion and quotation, Lamb's friendships are mapped onto the novel – a way of uniting the 'home-born Feeling' of the personal relationship with the literature of sensibility, and thus opening out the intimate scene of friendship.

The novel's family loyalties

The opening scene of the novel not only emphasises how family loyalties are confirmed and strengthened by reading, it also carries a subtle allusion to Lamb's own situation with his sister:

> It was noontide. The sun was very hot. An old Gentlewoman sat spinning in a little arbour at the door of her cottage. She was blind;

and her Grandaughter was reading the Bible to her. The old lady had just left her work, to attend to the story of Ruth.

'Orpah kissed her mother-in-law; but Ruth clave unto her.'

It was a passage she could not let pass without a *comment*. The moral she drew from it was not very *new*, to be sure. The girl had heard it a hundred times before – and a hundred times more she could have heard it, without suspecting it to be tedious. Rosamund loved her grandmother. (*RG*, 5–6)

The story of Ruth and Orpah represents the power of family sympathy in overcoming grief. The bereaved Ruth, despite being urged to leave her mother-in-law, refuses to abandon her, caring for her, and following her back to Israel. Hers is a Romantic narrative of alienation and loss, as in Keats' image of her 'in tears amid the alien corn', but it was her familial faithfulness which carried especial significance for Lamb, whose main concern since September 1796 had been caring for Mary, a task his brother had failed to understand.[8] 'I know John will make speeches about it, but she shall not go into an **hospital**,' he writes to Coleridge in the days following his mother's death:

[...] she was but the other morning saying, she knew she must go to **Bethlem** for life; that one of her brother's would have it so, but the other would wish it Not, but he obliged to go with the stream. (Marrs, I: 49)

Instead, like Ruth, Lamb remained loyal to Mary's wishes, and she was able to live mostly at home. *Rosamund Gray* is infused with praise of sisterly loyalty, and some obvious tributes to Mary, such as the close relationship between Allan and his sister Elinor: 'the kindest of sisters – I never knew but *one* like her' (*RG*, 66). These personal allusions draw Lamb's family into the narrative, creating a sociable form of writing, based around bonds of affection and shared emotion, which complements the scenes of shared reading within the text. Highly personal events are subtly alluded to within the text, coded messages for intimate readers. Elinor remembers her dead mother, for example, in words which irresistibly recall those of Lamb's letters to Coleridge in the aftermath of his own mother's death:

In the visions of last night her spirit seemed to stand at my bedside – a light, as of noon day, shone upon the room – she opened my curtains – she smiled upon me with the same placid smile as in her life-time. I felt no fear. 'Elinor,' she said, 'for my sake take care of young Allan,' – and I awoke with calm feelings. (*RG*, 69–70)

Compare the quotation from Mary's letter which Lamb sent to Coleridge in October 1796:

> I have no bad terrifying dreams. At midnight when I happen to awake, the nurse sleeping by the side of **me**, with the noise of the poor mad people around me, I have no fear. The spirit of my mother seems to descend, & smile upon me, & bid me **live** to enjoy the life & reason which the Almighty has given me –. (Marrs, I: 52)

Similarly, Elinor's assertion,

> Methinks something like an awakening from an ill dream shall the Resurrection from the Dead be. (*RG*, 81)

deliberately echoes the consolatory letter Coleridge sent after the death of Elizabeth Lamb, suggesting that, like being 'roused from a frightful dream', she would awake to 'the glories of God manifest' (Griggs, I: 238–9). In writing Mary's narrative into the novel, Lamb is demonstrating the way in which he will accept and care for her. *Rosamund Gray* becomes the extension of their loving bond, and the echoes of letters to and from friends reinforce the way in which Lamb places their relationship in the context of a wider community of feeling.

Thus the novel itself acts as a repudiation of what Lamb perceived as Godwin's disregard for affectionate bonds. Following Lamb's hostile reading of *Political Justice*, Matravis is an overtly Godwinian villain, very obviously unbound and unmoved by family affections, as Elinor exclaims:

> O ye *Matravises* of the age, ye know not what ye lose, in despising these petty topics of endeared remembrance, associated circumstances of past times; – ye know not the throbbings of the heart, tender yet affectionately familiar, which accompany the dear and honored names of *Father* or of *Mother*. (*RG*, 79)

In a novel which has opened with a celebration of the story of Ruth, this is damning; Matravis is not only unable to feel affection, he is insensible to the power of 'associated circumstances', the process of memory and connection. As the story progresses, we learn more about Matravis' inability to love:

> A young man with *gray* deliberation! cold and systematic in all his plans; and all his plans were evil. His very lust was systematic. (*RG*, 96–7)

In *Rosamund Gray*, Lamb repeatedly celebrates the power of 'association', the 'affectionately familiar', over the 'cold and systematic', leading some critics to see the novel as 'a deliberate refusal of the connectedness, the "philosophical" use of plot-as-argument in the novels of Godwin and the English Jacobins'.[9] Yet although Lamb's plot does not put forward a logical argument in the same way, for example, as Robert Bage or Elizabeth Inchbald, his text, in its allusive density, forms a 'connected' argument of its own, actually demonstrating the power of the personal bond and association. Systematic thinking is overturned through the fragmentary nature of the text, as well as through allusions and even puns. Matravis' '*gray* deliberation', for instance, as he contemplates violating Rosamund Gray, seems itself to be a type of violation, bringing the reader up short, startling them into an alert and active engagement with the text.

Rosamund Gray and *The Ruined Cottage*

This attack on 'systematic' thinking runs parallel to another attempt to answer Godwin: Wordsworth's *The Ruined Cottage*. Both Lamb and Wordsworth struggle to find a way to express the power of personal association and recollection, and to respond, too, to Coleridge – in political terms, as they echo his desire to find a workable alternative to Godwin, and in more personal terms, as they register the force of his anxieties about the poet's social responsibilities.

The version of *The Ruined Cottage* which Lamb heard is difficult to recreate, since the chronology is uncertain. In 1814, referring to *The Excursion*, Lamb wrote to Wordsworth telling him that he remembered some aspects of it, and had 'known the story of Margaret [...] even as long back as I saw you first at Stowey' (Marrs, III: 95). Lamb had, as we have seen, visited Stowey from 7 to 14 July 1797; Wordsworth had first read part of *The Ruined Cottage* to Coleridge on 5 June. He then added lines mainly concerning the Pedlar while living at Alfoxden in the spring of 1798, at the same time that Lamb was working on *Rosamund Gray*. Indeed, Dorothy told Mary Hutchinson on 5 March 1798 that Wordsworth had by then written 900 lines of *The Ruined Cottage* (*EY*, 199).

On 7 March 1798, Southey was to write to his brother Herbert telling him that 'Lamb has written a little tale, about a volume full – of which I only know that it is very dismal, and called *Rosamund Gray*' (Curry, I: 161–2). The similarities between *Rosamund Gray* and the version of *The Ruined Cottage* which Wordsworth was working on in early 1798, referred to in the Cornell edition as MS B, are striking.[10] They suggest that Lamb must have been aware of the ways in which Wordsworth was expanding the Pedlar's role in the poem, and his development of the theme of grief and sympathy as Margaret becomes a symbol not only of social injustice, but of universal human suffering.

From its very beginning, *Rosamund Gray* invites parallels with Wordsworth. Just as the mention of the story of Ruth and Orpah may have had particular significance for Mary, the whole opening scene sets up echoes with *The Ruined Cottage* – not apparent, of course, to the general reader at this stage, but highly significant to the group who had heard Wordsworth reading from the poem in summer 1797. The first two sentences, 'It was noontide. The sun was very hot', immediately suggest the opening of *The Ruined Cottage*: 'Twas Summer; and the sun was mounted high' (MS B: 1; *RC*, 42). Lamb's old blind Margaret has obvious kinship with her namesake; they are both humble cottagers, who work to support themselves by spinning. Both works thus engage with the theme of social responsibility and the position of the poor or dispossessed. Both, too, question the relationship of the author to such figures, notably through their intricate narrative structures. Although Wordsworth's poem is narrated by a solitary traveller, the main story is told through the words of the semi-autobiographical figure Armytage the Pedlar, so that the story of Margaret comes to us at several removes, framed by a succession of listeners and speakers. *Rosamund Gray* similarly deploys several voices, including the epistolary narratives of Elinor, before the narrator himself – previously detached and at times sardonic – enters the story and unsettles the reader by revealing himself to be a personal friend of the characters. These complicated narrative manoeuvres draw attention to the difficulty of relating tales of feeling – and they both also question the role of the story-teller within the community, a question which had been sharpened, for both Lamb and Wordsworth, by their contact with Coleridge.

The Ruined Cottage is in obvious dialogue with Coleridgean anxieties. Its opening scene, which sets the dreamer against the man of action, the toiling narrator, dramatises Wordsworth's repudiation of Coleridge's uneasy attitude towards the embowered poet. In 'Reflections', with its insistent contrast between the 'delicious solitude' of retirement and the 'bloodless fight' of active benevolence, the poet must leave the place of seclusion and 'toil' up the stony mount, where he makes the decision to go out into the world and participate 'head, heart and hand' in radical activity. *The Ruined Cottage* begins with an image of an embowered man, but the focus quickly shifts to the toiling poet, struggling across the 'slippery ground' of a 'bare wide Common', beset by insects and heat. Significantly, he toils not towards the outside world, but towards a scene of poetic communion in solitude, demonstrating the benevolent power of exercising sympathy in a 'place of retirement'. *The Ruined Cottage*, particularly in the expanded version of spring 1798, may thus be seen as a justification of Wordsworth's own rural retirement, a rhetorical 'defensiveness'.[11]

So in *The Ruined Cottage* he first of all summons up, and then dismisses, the image of the embowered, sleeping poet: his solitude is more strenuous and active. We have already seen how Lamb fiercely objected to Coleridge's projection of the anxieties of 'Reflections' – the 'rose-leaf beds' of dreaming indolence – onto his own poetry. Lamb's objections stemmed not merely from creative difference, but also because, on a deeper level, the revisions demonstrated Coleridge's different, more troubled approach to reading and dreaming. The rewriting represented by this opening scene of *The Ruined Cottage* suggests that Wordsworth is reacting in a similar way towards the anxieties expressed in Coleridge's 'Reflections' – a move with which Lamb would have sympathised.

He would also have understood the way in which Wordsworth goes on to vindicate the 'special, restricted sense' in which the poet *is* a dreamer.[12] For the toiling narrator then encounters another embowered, dreaming figure – the Pedlar, who sleeps not on 'rose-leaf beds', but on a bench which is, in the earliest versions, 'studded o'er with fungus flowers' (MS B: 38; *RC*, 48). But the Pedlar's dreaming and storytelling carries a positive charge, possessing deep consolatory powers:

> we have known that there is often found
> In mournful thoughts, and always might be found,
> A power to virtue friendly; were't not so,
> I am a dreamer among men – indeed
> An idle dreamer.
> (MS B: 286–90; *RC*, 58)

The act of meditation upon the dead transforms grief and brings acceptance. Wordsworth enlarges on the point in later versions of *The Ruined*

Cottage, beginning with MS D, written between February – November 1799. Here, after meditating on the tale of Margaret, the Pedlar is now able to perceive a vision of tranquillity. The 'rank spear-grass' of the opening lines is transmuted into the 'high spear-grass', silvered over with the rain; similarly, he is able to see his grief as something which may be transcended:

> an idle dream that could not live
> Where meditation was.
>   (MS D: 523–4; *RC*, 75)

This sets up parallels with *Rosamund Gray*, as the novel moves into its second half:

> It is now *ten years* since these events took place, and I sometimes think of them as unreal. Allan Clare was a dear friend to me – but there are times, when Allan and his Sister, Margaret and her Granddaughter, appear like personages of a dream – an idle dream. (*RG*, 106)

Like the Pedlar, Lamb shows the power of what might at first appear to be no more than an 'idle dream'. In writing the story and musing on the events, the narrator is impelled to return to Widford and to re-establish his bond with his lost friend Allan. Recollecting the dead, in particular, the act of writing their 'narrative', compels him to 'revisit the scenes of my native village', and renewed participation in its community becomes a way through mourning. For both Wordsworth and Lamb in 1798, meditation and reflection become a means of connection with others, answering Coleridge's fears about the 'delicious solitude' of retreat and simultaneously furthering his case against what he perceived as Godwin's argument against the power of the personal bond.

Both *Rosamund Gray* and *The Ruined Cottage* therefore repeatedly evoke the power of personal association. This serves a dual purpose, both refuting Godwin, and countering personal fears of loss and isolation in the late 1790s. Indeed, Allan repeats Lamb's phrases to Coleridge in the letters of that period. 'I am a wandering and unconnected thing on the earth,' Allan tells the narrator at the close of the novel, 'I have made no new friendships, that can compensate me for the loss of the old' (*RG*, 124), echoing Lamb's complaints that 'I have never met with any one, never shall meet with any **one**, who could or can compensate me for the top of your **Society**' (Marrs, I: 65–6). It also borrows from Mortimer's speech at the end of *The Borderers*:

> I will go forth a wanderer on the earth,
> A shadowy thing, and as I wander on
> No human ear shall ever hear my voice,
> No human dwelling ever give me food
> Or sleep or rest, and all the uncertain way
> Shall be as darkness to me, as a waste
> Unnamed by man! and I will wander on
> Living by mere intensity of thought,
> A thing by pain and thought compelled to live,
> Yet loathing life, till heaven in mercy strike me
> With blank forgetfulness – that I may die.
> <div align="right">(V, iii, 265–75; <i>Borderers</i>, 294)</div>

The echo is picked up and expanded at the end of *Rosamund Gray*, where Matravis is tormented by his memories. Like Mortimer, tortured by 'pain and thought', his 'intense pain had brought on a delirium' which forces him to make the associations he had once denied:

> One while he told us his dream. 'He had lost his way on a great heath, to which there seemed no end – it was cold, cold, cold – and dark, very dark – an old woman in leading-strings, *blind*, was groping about for a guide' – and then he frightened me, – for he seemed disposed to be *jocular*, and sang a song about an 'old woman clothed in gray,' and said 'he did not believe in a devil.' (*RG*, 133)

There is no resolution or forgiveness for Matravis, who, as a punishment for his former inability to appreciate the power of 'associated circumstances' and his 'systematic' lusts, is forced to undergo a process of uncontrollable, unconscious association. Matravis' dream is not only an image of his betrayal of Rosamund Gray and her grandmother – it also borrows from Mortimer's crime of abandoning the blind Herbert alone on the heath at night. Mortimer is similarly compelled to wander the earth after his abandonment of Matilda's father Herbert, perpetually atoning for the ruthlessly Godwinian approach to relationships adopted by Rivers. As we have seen, Rivers argues against the instinctive benevolence of family relationships. Rather, like Godwin putting forward the Fénelon argument, he suggests that morality must be 'flashed from the light of circumstances' (III, v, 33; *Borderers*, 210). Mortimer, in committing the murder under Rivers' instructions, severs his connections to humanity, and dooms himself to an endless torment of introspection, of 'darkness', 'waste' and constant solitary recollection, his quest for 'blank forgetfulness' an awful inversion of the search for a 'dwelling-place' for memory in 'Tintern Abbey'.

The image of the lonely wanderer resonates through the work of the group in the 1790s, from 'The Old Familiar Faces' to Coleridge's 'Wanderings of Cain' (1798) and Wordsworth's 'Song for the Wandering Jew', probably written in Goslar in the winter of 1798, and published in *Lyrical Ballads* 1800.[13] He reappears in the shape of the Ancient Mariner, described by Coleridge as 'the everlasting Wandering Jew', and finds his way into Coleridge's own letters, as he fears that without love, 'among objects for whom I had no affection', he should become like 'a man who should lose his companion in a desart of sand where his weary Halloos drop down in the air without an Echo' (Griggs, I: 471). What unites all these wanderers is their isolation, their inability to enter into sympathetic communication. Those 'weary Halloos' find no answer, no echo, just as the Ancient Mariner is compelled by a 'woful agony' endlessly to repeat his tale. These narratives express both authorial anxiety and the deep fear of personal isolation. Will their work ever reach a sympathetic audience? Will they themselves ever find friendly sympathy?

Both *Rosamund Gray* and *The Ruined Cottage* suggest that, though the wandering may not be over for their subjects, they *will* rediscover the connections of shared memories, and thus achieve a kind of resolution. Allan tells the narrator that when he appears 'over-thoughtful' this is a sign of his inward happiness:

> I am never more happy than at times, when by the cast of my countenance men judge me most miserable.
>
> My friend, the events, which have left this sadness behind them, are of no recent date. The melancholy, which comes over me with the recollection of them, is not hurtful, but only tends to soften and tranquillize my mind, to detach me from the restlessness of human pursuits.
>
> The stronger I feel this detachment, the more I feel myself drawn heavenward to the contemplation of spiritual objects. (*RG*, 123)

He has progressed through his mourning to a state comparable with that of the Pedlar: although he is a wanderer, he does not share the 'restlessness of human pursuits', he is sustained by his tranquillising memories. This is then echoed by the Pedlar's meditation, in the revised version of 1799, on the ruined house – 'So still an image of tranquillity,/ So calm and still' (MS D: 517; *RC*, 75) – a deep stillness which allows him freedom from his uneasy thoughts:

> I turned away
> And walked along my road in happiness.
> (MS D: 524–5; *RC*, 75)

Just as Allan's softened and tranquillised wanderings represent a distinct progression from the torment of 'The Old Familiar Faces', so too do we see a change in the revised version of *The Ruined Cottage*. It softens the bare last line of the earlier versions:

> and here she died,
> Last human tenant of these ruined walls.
> (MS B: 527–8; *RC*, 72)

The starkness of grief is transmuted into contemplation and the 'hurtful' immediacy of memories changed into a sustaining recollection. Like the 'spots of time' in *The Prelude*, these memories have 'fructifying' power. Wordsworth celebrates their nourishing virtue, the way in which the mind constantly returns to them to sustain and feed itself; in a similar way, the Pedlar's narration of Margaret's 'tale of silent suffering' may sustain the listener.

That meditation can lead outward into public communication is suggested by the way in which Wordsworth then uses *Rosamund Gray* to formulate his later thoughts about the epitaph. The scene in the novel where Allan meets the narrator again significantly takes place in a graveyard, where the narrator has been reading the tombstones:

> I read of nothing but careful parents, loving husbands, and dutiful children. I said jestingly, where be all the *bad* people buried? Bad parents, bad husbands, bad children – what cemeteries are appointed for these? do they not sleep in consecrated ground? or is it but a pious fiction, a generous oversight, in the survivors, which thus tricks out men's epitaphs when dead, who, in their life-time discharged the offices of life, perhaps, but lamely? – Their failings, with their reproaches, now sleep with them in the grave. *Man wars not with the dead.* It is a *trait* of human nature, for which I love it. (*RG*, 116–7)

How do we think about and commemorate the dead? What compels 'the survivors' to transform the dead into 'careful parents, loving husbands, and dutiful children'? The idea that failings and reproaches 'now sleep with them in the grave' recalls the Pedlar's description of Margaret:

> She sleeps in the calm earth, and peace is here.
> (MS D: 512; *RC*, 75)

It also finds an explicit echo in Wordsworth's second *Essay on Epitaphs*, of February 1810:

> When a Stranger has walked round a Country Church-yard and glanced his eye over so many brief Chronicles, as the tomb-stones usually contain, of faithful Wives, tender Husbands, dutiful Children, and good Men of all classes; he will be tempted to exclaim, in the language of one of the Characters of a modern Tale in a similar situation, 'Where are all the *bad* People buried?' (*PW*, II: 63)

Although this is a rueful, half-amused thought, Wordsworth uses it as a base for a consideration of the ways in which the mind heals itself through contemplation, through meditative story-telling. This is represented by the epitaph, a 'truth hallowed by love' (*PW*, II: 58), a kind of midway point between fact and ideal. As D. D. Devlin suggests in his excellent study of Wordsworth's epitaphic mode, it 'brings together the several publics which a poet might have or wish to have', it 'reconciles the general with the particular'.[14] Outside in the churchyard, 'a visible centre of a community of the living and the dead' (*PW* II: 56), it is not 'a proud writing shut up for the studious: it is exposed to all', 'open to the day' (*PW* II: 59). Strangers are drawn into communion with the dead through its words, introduced 'through its mediation to the company of a friend' (*PW* II: 59): 'It records a private grief, but with its traditional words 'Halt Traveller!', speaks publicly to all men'.[15]

The individual affectionate bond may thus come to have significance for a wider community of readers, through the power of sympathetic imagination. It also shows us a way to read *Rosamund Gray*, as a text of 'private grief' which is not only a commemoration of personal affections, but also a work of imagination which tries to bring together the particular, the 'narrow-sphered' personal preoccupation, and the universal. It revisits Coleridge's dilemmas of, for example, 'This Lime-tree Bower', and suggests its own way to resolve them.

For some critics, however, this represents an evasiveness: Wordsworthian 'meditation proves to be a region where natural and human history alike are debarred from entry'.[16] The narrative of loss and recompense articulated here may be viewed as epistemologically conservative, a private inward movement which backs away from radical public engagement and leads inexorably towards Wordsworth's later political standpoint. James Chandler sets Wordsworth's promotion of 'natural lore' against Hazlitt's assertion that 'books alone teach us to judge of truth and good in the abstract' (Howe, XIII: 40).[17] Hazlitt's stance, he argues, connects with a wider radical commitment to contentious literate debate and free inquiry, whereas *The Ruined Cottage*, like 'The Tables Turned', seems to rule out contention in favour of a programmatic, disciplinary prerogative. Lamb, as we will see in the last chapter, fiercely resists Wordsworth's prose attempts to coerce and direct the reader; in so doing, however, he seeks to expand a different strand of Wordsworth's thought. Reading *Rosamund Gray* alongside *The Ruined Cottage* allows us to see this different reading of Wordsworth at work, the profoundly literary response of an urban Dissenter with radical sympathies. It shows the interpretive possibilities of Wordsworth's work – the way in which the private moment can become public. It represents an opening out of the 'home-born Feeling', a continuation and expansion of ideas of the 1790s.

Communities of feeling in *Rosamund Gray*

Through his playful allusions to published poems, and more covert ones to personal letters, Lamb is creating a text which may summon up and sustain mutual memories. Prompted by his solitary recollections of the 'old familiar faces', he is attempting to create a reading and writing community of his own, as a way through the isolation of grief and also of what he perceived as 'systematic' thinking. Intertextuality is the central feature of *Rosamund Gray*; the way in which Lamb uses allusion works as a kind of coded inscription of friendship, offering a way of transcending the problem of solitary reading or dreaming, turning it into a mutual consolation.

It also represents a reconciliation of ideas which had been troubling him about his friendships. It is a commemoration of the dead, which also acts as a commemoration of a friendship and, perhaps, a move towards reconciliation. Wordsworth imagines the stranger being introduced to 'the company of a friend' through the mediation of an epitaph; Lamb was using *Rosamund Gray* as a mediative approach to a particular friend: Coleridge. Personal allusions are layered through the text, as in Matravis' speech as he lies dying – 'it was cold, cold, cold – and dark, very dark' (*RG*, 133). We have already traced this phrase through *The Borderers* and *Osorio* into Lamb's reproaches to Coleridge for his dereliction of duty towards both him and Lloyd (Marrs, I: 123). By the time it comes to be used in *Rosamund Gray*, however, it takes on a subtly different aspect, framed by a portrait of renewed friendship and pointing to the way in which allusion may be used as a reconciliatory tool.

Allan's approach to friendship at the close of the novel recalls Lamb's frustration with his former ideals in 1797 and 1798. In his resignation to the 'mighty arm' of divine will (*RG*, 125) Allan's attitude mirrors that of 'Living without God in the World', supported by his rejection of exclusive relationships. Instead, he spends his life tending to the sick and dying, an instance 'of a more disinterested virtue,' comments the narrator, 'than ariseth from what are called Friendships of Sentiment':

> Between two persons of liberal education, like opinions, and common feelings, oftentimes subsists a Vanity of Sentiment, which disposes each to look upon the other as the only being in the universe worthy of friendship, or capable of understanding it, – themselves they consider as the solitary receptacles of all that is delicate in feeling, or stable in attachment: – when the odds are, that under every green hill, and in every crowded street, people of equal worth are to be found, who do more good in their generation, and make less noise in the doing of it. (*RG*, 129–30)

That 'disinterested virtue' could recall Godwin's 'disinterested benevolence', but this rejection of sentimental friendship should be read in context, as Lamb celebrates the power of personal connection. Even as he outwardly rejects the idea of friendship's 'Vanity of Sentiment', he is drawing Coleridge back into his circle of intimate readers, with allusions to their past correspondence, and past events in their friendship.

The description of the way in which Allan's friend feels neglected in the face of his love for Rosamund, for instance, functions as a playful invocation of the 'Nehemiah Higginbottom' sonnets, alluding to and neutralising the whole affair:

> Allan's friend thought him much altered, and, after his departure, sat down to compose a doleful sonnet about a 'faithless friend'. – I do not find that he ever finished it – indignation, or a dearth of rhimes, causing him to break off in the middle. (*RG*, 50–1)

This is a knowing allusion to Lamb's own jealousies, and to Lloyd's poems about 'faithless friends' – its incompletion points to the absurdity of such reproaches. The writer of the 'doleful sonnet' is described as a friend from Widford, who had 'just quitted a public school in London' and was due to start at Edinburgh University the day after his meeting with Allan. Later, the narrator describes himself as having 'parted from Allan Clare on that disastrous night, and set out for Edinburgh the next morning': the attentive reader will realise that the narrator, the Lamb figure in the text, was in fact the annoyed friend, who misread Allan's distraction as 'coldness'. Lamb is humorously dismissing his own misreadings, and, instead, demonstrating his enduring faith in the ideals of friendly love and sympathy, formed and sustained through the power of sympathetic reading and response.

Like *Edmund Oliver*, *Rosamund Gray* offers textual visions of Pantisocracy. As in Lloyd's novel, Lamb's characters bring together aspects of himself and Coleridge, and twice in *Rosamund Gray* there are evocations of domestic fraternal communion. In words reminiscent of Lamb's description of Coleridge in 'The Old Familiar Faces' as 'Friend of my bosom, thou more than a brother!', Elinor tells her cousin that 'we have been more than Sisters, Maria!', and looks forward to the day when she may be 'inmate of the same dwelling', sharing 'mutual good offices', conversations and reading (*RG*, 81–2). However, since Maria has just been married, Elinor acknowledges that this vision of sequestered sisterhood is unlikely 'ever come to pass': we are reminded of Lamb vainly wishing that Coleridge might return to London and participate again in the smoky communion of the 'Salutation', well after his marriage to Sara. A parallel vision is imagined by the narrator after his reunion with Allan, and this time it is participated in by both:

> So we drank, and told old stories, – and repeated old poetry – and sung old songs – as if nothing had happened [...] Allan was my bed-fellow that night – and we lay awake, planning schemes of living together under the same roof, entering upon similar pursuits;– and praising GOD, that we had met. (*RG*, 121–2)

These 'schemes' are never actually brought to fruition in the novel: instead, we are left to imagine the realisation of sympathetic communion outside the text. It is again noticeable that ideas of reading and writing play an important part in these visions of community. Elinor imagines 'books read and commented on, together', and 'old stories' and 'old poetry' cement the renewed bond between the narrator and Allan. This points to the way in which this community will actually be realised – like Wordsworth's epitaphic community, it will be through the written word, rather than in reality. Lamb's is always, however, a tentative vision – behind this ideal lies a recognition of human potential for violence and an intimate understanding of despair.

The way in which Allan and the narrator are, finally, reunited seems to anticipate the renewal of friendship between Coleridge and Lamb, who met again in spring 1800, when Lamb wrote triumphantly, 'the more I see of him [...] the more cause I see to love him' (Marrs, I: 189). That love is, in fact, a constant undercurrent throughout Lamb's writing, despite the exasperation and bitterness of the 1797 period. The frustration and regret of poems such as 'The Old Familiar Faces' and 'Living without God in the World' are transcended in *Rosamund Gray*; phrases of earlier poems and letters are used in ways which show how grief and pain – of Mary's illness, of his mother's death, of his broken friendship – are slowly being absorbed into his writing identity.[18] The novel shows him attempting to integrate his idea of the importance of personal affection with his distrust of exclusive friendships; its allusive style shows him feeling his way towards a concept of reading, and of friendship, which might bridge these two ideas. Drawing together multiple texts and associations, it acts against the exclusivity of one particular bond, offering a way not only to transcend the problem of self-reflexive friendship, but also of solitary reading and dreaming. *Rosamund Gray* serves not only to reflect Lamb's thinking about sympathetic reading, as the characters are brought together over the prayer book, or over *Julia de Roubigné*, it actually puts it into practice, bringing together the text and its intended readers.

7
Sympathy, Allusion, and Experiment in *John Woodvil*

Late 1798

A scene of drunken merriment, laughter, singing. Lamb's play *John Woodvil*, begun in 1798 but not published until 1802, opens with a show of rowdy male humour which might seem to recall the 'Salutation' days. But this is no warm sociable Unitarian community – this is 'atheist riot and profane excess', the result of family disruption and fracture. The play opens with the servants drinking their mornings away in the wreckage of Woodvil Hall. The Woodvil family itself has been divided, physically and emotionally, by their different allegiances after the Restoration of 1660. The old knight, Sir Walter, a supporter of the old regime, has fled with his son Simon, and been concealed in Sherwood Forest. Meanwhile, under his other son John, his house is rotting from within. The old knight's orphan-ward, Margaret, is now harassed and affronted by John Woodvil's Cavalier companions, and Woodvil himself, although once her suitor, now seems to have forgotten her. Woodvil's thoughtlessness not only affects Margaret: the crisis of the play comes when, in a moment of drunkenness, he reveals the hiding-place of his father to a supposed friend.

The central theme of the play thus becomes the endurance of affection through betrayal and violence, showing how family loyalty and true friendship may be tested by pride. The old knight is hunted down and consequently dies; Woodvil himself is tormented by remorse and guilt, seeking comfort in the faithful affection of Margaret, and his own memories of childhood. He eventually achieves peace through the memory of infancy, the recollection of himself as a child kneeling down to pray by his father's side:

> It seem'd, the guilt of blood was passing from me
> Even in the act and agony of tears,
> And all my sins forgiven. –
>
> (*JW*, 104)[1]

In early versions of the play the emphasis on absolution through family reconciliation is heightened through the forgiveness of the other brother, Simon. The three then determine to 'seek some foreign land' where their story will be unknown, and they will be still more closely bound together.

John Woodvil dramatises the Lambs' own situation in an interestingly ambiguous way, showing a parental death specifically caused by a son's pride and repaired by the force of an almost sisterly affection. The play, like *Rosamund Gray*, is deeply marked by personal allusion. Yet it also represents an outward move. Whereas the novel directly echoes private letters and poems, the quotations and allusions of the play are far more wide ranging. Lamb's 1799 letters to Southey reveal a growing interest in the older playwrights, and *John Woodvil* is written in an 'antique' mode which reflects his reading of Shakespeare, Beaumont and Fletcher. The name John Woodvil, moreover, is borrowed from Colley Cibber's popular play *The Non-Juror* (1717). Lamb's textual community was expanding and ranging across time and genre, as he began to bring older, non-canonical texts into dialogue with his own preoccupations. This is a continuation and affirmation of his interest in the sociability of reading, and marks a progression in his allusive style. In *Rosamund Gray*, many of the references would only have been understood by particular readers who had access to his letters; *John Woodvil* shows him moving towards the distinctly Elian mode of dense literary allusiveness, with its composite voices, quotations and borrowings. Lamb's sociable reading circle is expanding, continuing the pattern we first noticed in Chapter 2 as he strove to reassure Coleridge. Furthermore, Lamb's use of the older writers was, in turn, to affect and influence younger authors; although *John Woodvil* was not fully appreciated by friends such as Southey, it had, as we shall see, a deep impact on Clare. Yet while I am emphasising the importance of its textual sociability, the scenes of 'drunken mirths' demonstrate Lamb's fearful awareness of another side to his sociability. His own drunken behaviour – like his humour – could have a cruel savagery, a wildness verging on the violent.² Again and again in his letters he refers to the problems caused by 'my cursed drinking' (Marrs, II: 169) and apologises for drunken outbursts, 'disgraceful circumstance[s]', 'shameful violation[s] of hospitality' (Lucas, *Letters*, III: 285; 405). His *Confessions of a Drunkard* (1813) dwells on the hidden price of social drinking, 'the wages of buffoonery and death' (Lucas, I: 157). The textual community created in *John Woodvil* is a fragile bulwark against this social suffering.

Redemptive family narratives

The play is thus intricately connected to Lamb's personal situation, a combination, as Symons notes, of 'personal quality with literary experiment', which functions both as an expression of Lamb's own fears and 'a sort of solace and defence for Mary'.³ Its connection with Mary's matricide is reinforced by manuscript changes. Lamb, for instance, cut out a speech by John Woodvil as 'bad':

> They hoot and spit upon me as I pass
> In the public streets: one shows me to his neighbour,
> Who shakes his head and turns away with horror –
>
>   (Lucas, IV: 390)

This bears distinct similarity to the fears which continued to torment him in the years after his mother's death, such as those expressed to Coleridge in 1800: '– nor is it the least of our Evils, that her case & all our story is so well known around us. We are in a manner *marked* –'. (Marrs, I: 202).⁴

The idea of being 'marked', implying a visible sign of guilt, like the mark of Cain, recurs in a letter to Manning the following week, 'poor Mary's disorder, so frequently recurring, has made us a sort of marked people. . We can be no where private except in the midst of London – ' (Marrs, I: 207). Lamb seems here to be participating equally in the guilt for his sister's crime, and the manner in which he takes her guilt upon himself here is echoed by the negotiations of the play. Guilt for the father's death rests solely upon John Woodvil. His neglect of his familial bonds, such as his affection for his sister-ward, Margaret, is linked with his craving for empty friendship, leading to the act of betrayal which kills Sir Walter. The sister figure, Margaret, is, on the other hand, seen as the regenerative source of family affection. Like Ruth, the figure who opens *Rosamund Gray*, her 'cleavings to the fates of sunken Woodvil' are described gratefully by John Woodvil himself:

> now in this
> My day of shame, when all the world forsake me,
> You only visit me, love, and forgive me.
> (*JW*, 93–4)

The reason for Lamb's own sense of guilt is connected both with drunkenness, and also with false friendship – both deceptive forms of sociability. Over-reliance on friends, and a concomitant drunken neglect of family relationships, leads directly to John Woodvil's crime. This recollects the anti-Godwinian message of *Rosamund Gray*, but whereas the systematic Matravis had no capacity for relationships, John's desire for sympathetic connection is fatally misplaced, causing him to disregard 'the ties of blood' and 'prejudice of kin' in favour of his own misguided choice of acquaintance (*JW*, 69). His proud reliance on his own judgement is condemned in ways which recall the fears expressed in the letters to Coleridge, or the bitterly satirical 'Theses'. Margaret's assertion, 'I am somewhat proud: and Woodvil taught me pride' (*JW*, 18), reminds the reader of the prolonged attack on the mutual pride of self-absorbed friendship in 'Living without God in the World'. As Lamb explains in his letters to Manning, the play was originally to be called 'Pride's Cure':

> Does not the betraying of his father's secret directly spring from pride? – from the pride of wine, and a full heart, and a proud overstepping of the ordinary rules of morality, and contempt of the prejudices of mankind [...] does not the pride of wine incite him to display some evidence of friendship, which its own *irregularity* shall make great? – (Marrs, I: 177)

John Woodvil refers to the ideal of friendship in terms which recall Lamb's references in his letters to Coleridge to the 'cement' of true fellowship (Marrs, I: 88):

> O for some friend now,
> To conceal nothing from, to have no secrets.
> How fine and noble a thing is confidence
> How reasonable too, and almost godlike!
> Fast cement of fast friends, band of society,

Old natural go-between in the world's business,
Where civil life and order, wanting this cement,
Would presently rush back
Into the pristine state of singularity,
And each man stand alone.
(JW, 64–5)

Here, the mention of 'godlike' immediately recalls those anxieties about idolatrous behaviour, which lead us into perceiving the double meaning of 'fast'. The 'fast friends' which John seeks are also swiftly made, and the betrayal he suffers at the hands of Lovel demonstrates the folly of temporary friendships. As F. V. Morley has astutely pointed out, the play demonstrates Lamb's desire to atone for his youthful anxieties concerning idolatry: *'Pride's Cure* is primarily the cure of pride in the Salutation kind of friendship'.[5]

This link is reinforced by the way in which the references to family affection in *John Woodvil* recollect Lamb's exhortations to Robert Lloyd at the same time. Instructing Robert not to place too much emphasis on personal friendships, he urges him to respect his 'not-ill-meaning parents' and obey their wishes in attending Quaker meetings: 'I know that if my parents were to live again, I would do more things to please them, than merely sitting still six hours in a week – ' (Marrs, I: 169).

The value of family and childhood affection is made clear to John only after betrayal and loss. Similarly, Margaret must be exiled from John's superficial 'flatteries and caresses', in order to regain his proper love and friendship. Her lament as she sets out, 'wandering', to join old Sir Walter in the forest carries a subtle echo of the expression of grief in 'The Old Familiar Faces':

All things seem chang'd, I think. I had a friend,
(I can't but weep to think him alter'd too)
(JW, 17)

That 'I had a friend' reminds us of the line, 'I have a friend, a kinder friend has no man', which signals the poet's move into the wilderness in the earlier poem. Similarly, Margaret's description of her earlier closeness to John is reminiscent of Lamb's description of Coleridge as a 'brother confessor' in the early fervour of their friendship:

His conscience, his religion, Margaret was,
His dear heart's confessor, a heart within that heart
(JW, 18)

Again, in a letter of early 1797 to Coleridge, Lamb apologises for not having written any poems specifically dedicated to him:

> So frequently, so habitually as I dwell on you in my thoughts, 'tis some wonder those thoughts came never yet in Contact with a poetical mood – . But you dwell in my heart of hearts, & I love you in all the naked honesty of **prose** –. (Marrs, I: 92)

Although this is an expression of mutual sympathy and confessional, 'naked' sincerity, the idea of Coleridge dwelling in Lamb's inner life, his 'heart of hearts' also carries a darker meaning, in its allusion to Hamlet's speech expressing his friendship for Horatio, his fellow sufferer, 'I will wear him/In my heart's core, ay, in my heart of heart' (III, ii, 62–3). Lamb's quotation points to the dynamics of suffering at work in that speech: unconsciously, perhaps, in the first instance, but, by the time of *John Woodvil*, openly alluding to betrayal and grief.[6]

Another link between the play and Lamb's relationship with Coleridge in the 1790s emerges when John learns of Margaret's flight, and attributes it to the way in which men's 'idolatry slackens, or grows less' (*JW*, 25). The word appears several times in Lamb's post September-1796 letters to Coleridge, as Lamb began to worry about the way in which friendly love might verge on 'idolatry', and recurs in the 'idols, flesh and blood' which appear in 'Living without God in the World'. Just as John is brought to realise the value of true affection through calamity and parental death, so too did Lamb feel he had to reconstruct his friendship with Coleridge, and draw closer to Mary, after the doubts and self-questioning of 1797 and 1798.

Subtle echoes of earlier work, deeply connected with Coleridge, resonate through the play to reinforce this sense of development and transition. Allusions have become more deeply embedded in Lamb's writing since *Rosamund Gray*, yet, read in context, they take on composite force. To take one example, John Woodvil's exclamation:

> Gone! gone! my girl? so hasty, Margaret!
> (*JW*, 25)

is a recollection of Othello's mournful:

> Cold, cold, my girl
> (V, ii, 273)

after Desdemona's death. Through that allusion, we are connected with the references to 'Cold, cold, cold', with its freight of literary and personal meaning, from *Osorio* to *Rosamund Gray*. The echo is slight, but read as part of Lamb's allusive idiom, it conveys deeper ideas of friendship, pride, and indifference: now the phrase, which had once conveyed reproach, becomes written into a larger story of repentance and forgiveness.

Elian identifications

This complicated personal and literary allusiveness looks forward to the playful, layered style of Elia. As John Woodvil sits in repentance, for example, he hears the church bells, recalling him to a sense of Christian community. These bells echo throughout late eighteenth-century literature, sounding along the shore for Bowles in his *Sonnets*, cheerfully recalling Cowper to scenes of his boyhood walk in *The Task*, and resounding with 'the joys of social life' for Lamb himself in the 1796 poem 'The Sabbath Bells' (*Poems* 1797, 232). But they are particular bells which Lamb has in mind for John – those of Coleridge's own birthplace:

Saint Mary Ottery, my native village
In the sweet shire of Devon.
Those are the bells.
       (*JW*, 100)

Lamb's adoption of Coleridge's 'native village' for his own character recalls similar sleights of hand in *Rosamund Gray*, where Allan is a composite figure of Coleridge and Lamb. It also looks forward to the playful slippage of identity in his essay 'Christ's Hospital Five and Thirty Years ago': 'How, in my dreams, would my native town (far in the west) come back, with its church, and trees, and faces! How I would wake weeping, and in the anguish of my heart exclaim upon sweet Calne in Wiltshire!' (Lucas, II: 15).

The mutuality of childhood friendship is acted out through the inter-changeability of memories, which, shared between Lamb and Coleridge, create a textual community. The narrator is simultaneously Coleridge – 'the poor friendless boy' – and Lamb, recalling with mingled love and shame the titbits brought into school by his aunt. But the narrator is also neither of these. Like the reader, he is an external observer, who can simultaneously see Lamb eating his aunt's veal, and hear 'Samuel Taylor Coleridge – Logician, Metaphysician, Bard!' (Lucas, II: 25) orating in the school cloisters. Moreover, a later allusion is incorporated with the mention of Calne. From late 1814 to April 1816 Coleridge had lived there with the Morgans, whom the Lambs had also visited, although shortly after Coleridge's stay there. Moreover, Bowles lived close by – Coleridge had visited him in 1815 – and the use of the Bowlesian word 'sweet' furthers the connection. The complex identification works on both a personal and literary level: for Coleridge, it would have echoed the preoccupations of younger days and reminded him of their later years of friendship. That allusion to Bowles, too, reminds the reader of earlier literature of sensibility, lying hidden behind the teasing Elian voice. It is an act of reading friendship, drawing friends – such as Coleridge – and readers alike into the familiar community of the text; different identities, along with fixed genres and periods, are held in suspension.

In *John Woodvil* we see Lamb moving towards this characteristic style, both through layered personal allusions and also through its multiple quotations and stylistic recollections of Elizabethan and Jacobean literature. He told Southey:

My Tragedy will be a medley (or I intend it to be a medley) of laughter & tears, prose & verse & in some places rhime, songs, wit, pathos, humour, & if possible sublimity, – at least, tis not a fault in my intention, if it does not comprehend most of these discordant atoms. (Marrs, I: 152)

The idea of a willed discordancy, a 'medley' which brings together all sorts of different allusions, periods, and styles, offers an early insight into Lamb's attraction towards the anachronistic. As Aaron has pointed out, this reflects Lamb's aversion to categorising tendencies, or fixed absolutes – an idea which will become of central importance in his descriptions of the urban. Aaron argues that this comprehensiveness may be seen as a 'deliberate antidote to the value systems of his own times': the emphasis on manliness and on authoritarianism, for instance.[7]

This rejection of fixed, conventional values is mirrored in his language itself. *John Woodvil* cannot readily be classified generically or stylistically. Just as *Rosamund Gray* plays with the genre of the sentimental novel, both exploiting and subverting the conventions of sensibility, so *John Woodvil* pushes at the boundaries of drama, allying the introspective sensibility of its characters with language and settings familiar from Shakespeare, Beaumont or Fletcher. Simon's description of his joys in the forest, for example, is a union of Shakespeare and Southey with a peculiarly Elian flavour:

To see the sun to bed, and to arise,
Like some hot amourist with glowing eyes,

> Bursting the lazy bands of sleep that bound him, [...]
> To view the graceful deer come tripping by,
> Then stop, and gaze, then turn, they know not why,
> Like bashful younkers in society:
> To mark the structure of a plant or tree;
> And all fair things of earth, how fair they be.
>
> *(JW,* 50–1)

This is the passage which, Hazlitt maintained, so affected Godwin that in later years, forgetting where he had first heard it, he searched for the phrase 'hot amourist' among the Elizabethan poets, until at length, 'after hunting in vain for it in Ben Jonson, Beaumont and Fletcher, and other not unlikely places, sent to Mr. Lamb to know if he could help him to the author!' (Howe XI: 183–4). These kinds of confusion unsettle not only chronological demarcations, but also the boundaries of intellectual property, which, as we have seen, had already been called into question in the Coleridge friendship. Lamb, in a letter to Southey, plays with such ideas of ownership and originality:

> I love to anticipate charges of unoriginality; the first line is
>   almost Shakespere's; –
> 'To have my love to bed & to arise'
>   midsummer nights dream
>
> I think there is a sweetness in the versification not unlike some rhymes in that Exquisite play – and the Last line but three is yours
>
>   an Eye
> 'That met the gaze, or turn'd it knew not why'.
>   Rosamunds Epistle
>   (Marrs, I: 160)[8]

This kind of free-ranging allusiveness, stretching across period and genre, and bringing the work of friends into dialogue with canonical texts, again foreshadows the style of the *Essays of Elia* (1823). In the essay 'The Old Margate Hoy,' for example, the phrase, 'I cry out for the water-brooks, and pant for fresh streams, and inland murmurs' (Lucas, II: 206), is a compound of the first line of Psalm 42, 'As the hart panteth after the water-brooks, so panteth my soul for thee, O God', and the 'sweet inland murmur' of the fourth line of 'Tintern Abbey'. Biblical and Wordsworthian phraseologies are amalgamated in the Elian voice, calling into question the very nature of original expression.

Forgeries and medleys: Lamb's imitations of Burton

A further clue to the way in which Lamb was beginning to create an allusive, dialogic community comes in the manner in which he finally published *John Woodvil* in 1802, alongside two small poems. One was a 'little Epigram': 'It is not my writing,' Lamb told Coleridge, 'nor had I any finger in it [...] I will just hint that it is almost *or* quite a first attempt' (Marrs, I: 233). This was Mary's first appearance in print – 'Helen', a poem which gently mocks a passionate lover, sparked by Charles' love of a particular picture at Blakesware.[9] The other is a 'Balad from the German', written for Coleridge's 1800 translation *The Piccolimini*, his version of the first part of Schiller's *Wallenstein*. Since Lamb did not know German, Coleridge had supplied him with a prose paraphrase. Both poems, therefore, emerge from affection, familial and friendly.

The final place in the volume is given to 'Curious Fragments, extracted from a commonplace-book, which belonged to Robert Burton, the famous Author of The Anatomy of Melancholy'. This collection of imitations are, as Charles suggests in the voice of Burton: *'a messe of opinions*, a vortex attracting indiscriminate, gold, pearls, hay, straw, wood, excrement, an exchange, tavern, marte, for foreigners to congregate, Danes, Swedes, Hollanders, Lombards, so many strange faces, dresses, salutations, languages, all which *Wolfius* behelde with great content on the Venetian Rialto' (*JW*, 112).

Like *John Woodvil*, this is a 'medley' which brings the words of *The Anatomy of Melancholy* into conversation with Lamb's own life. Lamb's Burton is required to help a man who has suffered from unrequited love for seven years, the object bearing some resemblance, in her 'gentle eyes' and 'smiling' hair, to the 'Anna' of Lamb's early poems. Sly allusions to 'his friends that were wont to tipple with him in alehouses' suggest the way in which Lamb has personalised this forgery. The second extract again reminds the reader of the jokes and satires he had levelled against Coleridge's pomposity, as he describes some 'disputacy-ons of fierce wits':

> [...] this man his cronies they cocker him up, they flatter him, he would fayne appear somebody, meanwhile the world thinks him no better than a dizzard, a ninny, a sophist. **
> ***Philosophy running mad, madness philosophizing, much idle-learned enquiries, what Truth is? and no issue, fruit, of all these noises, only huge books are written, and who is the wiser?*****
> (*JW*, 117)

These asides would have had an added piquancy, since 'Curious Fragments' came about in the first moments of his renewal of friendship with Coleridge, in 1800:

> Coleridge has been with me now for nigh threee weeks, and the more I see of him in the quotidian undress and relaxation of his mind, the more cause I see to love him and to believe him a *very good man*, and all those foolish impressions to the contrary fly off like morning slumbers – [...] He has lugg'd me to the brink of engaging to a Newspaper, & has suggested to me for a 1st plan the forgery of a supposed Manuscript of **Burton** the Anatomist of Melancholy. (Marrs, I: 189–90)

Prompted by Coleridge, and perhaps also gently parodying Coleridge's own notebooks, the forgeries are nevertheless distinctly recognisable as an expression of Lamb's own deeply allusive and personally symbolic style.

This style, with its varied, fragmentary qualities, also finds parallels in Lamb's comments about Mary's conversation when ill. In 1834 he described her talk as 'a medley between inspiration and possession', an amalgam of her reading and her memories. Yet, he claimed, 'her rambling chat is better to me than the sense and sanity of this world', largely because of the way it brings past associations so vividly to light: 'she fetches thousands of names and things that never would have dawned upon me again' (Lucas, *Letters*, III: 401). Thomas Noon Talfourd describes Mary's talk in ways distinctly reminiscent of Lamb's experiments with genre, identity, and language: 'her ramblings often sparkled with brilliant description and shattered beauty. She would fancy herself in the days of Queen Anne or George the First...the fragments were like the jewelled speeches of Congreve, only shaken from their setting'.[10] These antique fragments, comments Talfourd, had 'a vein of crazy logic running through them, associating things essentially most dissimilar, but connecting them by a verbal association in strange order.' This emphasis on the power of 'verbal association' – reminiscent of Lamb's urgent message about the wonders of Hartley before his own incarceration in Hoxton – suggests that Lamb's own later allusive, freely associative style perhaps carried a particular personal, and familial, significance.

'Friend Lamb': *John Woodvil* and its readers

Lamb's fragments and imitations bear strange similarities to the later forgeries of John Clare, whose own life, of course, was also profoundly shaped by mental illness and his asylum experiences. Clare, too, liked to create confusion between his own work and that of older poets, often claiming to have found poems on the fly-leaves of old books. His sonnet 'To Charles Lamb' is a direct response to his reading of *John Woodvil*, and reinforces the way in which poets may use borrowing, allusion, and imitations to create a context for their own work, a community within which it may be read:

> Friend Lamb thou chusest well to love the lore
> Of our old by gone bards whose racey page
> Rich mellowing Time made sweeter then before
> The blossom left for the long garnered store
> Of fruitage now right luscious in its age
> Although to fashions taste [austere] – what more
> Can be expected from the popular rage
> For tinsels gauds that are to gold preferred
> Me much it grieved as I did erst presage
> Vain fashions foils had every heart deterred
> From the warm homely phrase of other days
> Untill [sic] thy muses auncient [sic] voice I heard
> & now right fain yet fearing honest bard
> I pause to greet thee with so poor a praise
> (ll. 1–14)[11]

The Peterborough manuscript of the poem is subtitled, 'On reading "John Woodville", a Tragedy': a vivid demonstration of the way in which Lamb's style influenced others. Despite the failure of the play – it was rejected for Drury Lane by John Kemble in 1800, and Lamb claimed to have lost £25 in publishing it – it succeeded in gathering sympathetic readers. The address, 'Friend Lamb', immediately draws attention to the sociable aspect of Clare's reading, the shared appreciation of '*our* old by gone bards'. This sociability, as Mina Gorji has explored, became a driving force in Clare's creativity during the 1820s, as he attempted to participate in a wider poetic community through his contributions to the *London Magazine*.[12] Gorji shows how this was, in part, prompted by his growing loneliness and sense of isolation during these years: he was experiencing the same kind of desire for a sympathetic community that Lamb reveals in his letters of the late 1790s. Clare's sensual 'luscious', as he surrenders to the pleasure of reading these old bards, recalls Elia's descriptions of reading as a physical, tangible, almost sexual process: 'And you, my midnight darlings, my Folios! must I part with the intense delight of having you (huge armfuls) in my embraces? (Lucas, II: 34).

In his appreciation of the old bards, filtered through Lamb's 'auncient voice', Clare puts forward a similar kind of textual sociability which transcends period boundaries. His idea of the 'warm homely phrase' reinforces the sense of emotional refuge offered by the old poets, as opposed to the gaudy brashness of popular fashion. Clare's use of the word 'gauds' echoes Lamb's own Shakespearean characterisation of the 'new-born gauds' of modern literature in his first essay as Elia (Lucas, I: 7).[13] It also recalls Wordsworth's 1798 'Advertisement' to *Lyrical Ballads*: 'Readers accustomed to the gaudiness and inane phraseology of many modern writers, if they persist in reading this book to its conclusion, will perhaps frequently have to struggle with feelings of strangeness and aukwardness [sic]' (*LyB*, 738).

Clare, like Wordsworth here, is marking out a way in which his work must be read: he is emphasising the need for a sympathetic community of readers who will 'struggle' to achieve appreciation of the work.

The parallel also points out the radical implications of reading the 'old by gone bards'. This affection for the 'warm homely phrase' is not, as it might at first appear, a movement of retreat. On the contrary, Lamb uses the language of the old poets as a way of voicing dissent. As John Coates puts it, Lamb's use of the antique may be seen as a politically minded gesture, 'a sustained and deliberate corrective of his age's heavy-handedness'.[14] Despite its Elizabethan language, *John Woodvil* takes as its setting the charged atmosphere of post-Restoration England, satirising the Cavalier pretensions of the young John Woodvil, and evoking sympathy for the harried old Cromwellian, Sir Walter. This should be read in the context of Lamb's Dissenting sympathies, his affection for the persecuted Puritans, which fed into eighteenth-century conceptions of the Dissenting purpose.[15] Indeed, an unsympathetic review of *John Woodvil* in the Tory, government-funded *British Critic*, dismisses its ending as 'not a little puritanical'.[16] Perhaps the reviewer was also aware of the way in which the corrupt morals of John Woodvil's Cavalier household seem to function – as in Godwin's play *Faulkener* (1807) – as an analogy for liberal disapproval of Stuart politics. As Nicholes has pointed out, Lamb, in his portrayal of the harassed Sir Walter, may also have been thinking of his own pillorying by the *Anti-Jacobin*. His condemnation of Woodvil's political opportunism connects with his other political writing, such as the epigram, 'To Sir James Mackintosh', first published in *The Albion, and Evening Advertiser*, in 1801:

Though thou'rt like Judas, an apostate black,
In the resemblance one thing thou dost lack:

> When he had gotten his ill-purchased pelf,
> He went away, and wisely hanged himself.
> This thou may'st do at last; yet much I doubt,
> If thou hast any *bowels* to gush out!
>
> (Lucas, IV: 115)

This reveals the same sharp-eyed, dangerous observation noticed by the *Anti-Jacobin* in their 'New Morality' attack, and indeed the attention attracted by Lamb's dark epigram proved the death-blow for *The Albion*.[17] The savagery behind the humour here not only reminds us how closely Lamb's wit is allied to anger and frustration, but also points to deeply held opinions on the subject of betrayal and defection.[18]

The flight of Sir Walter to Sherwood Forest also links his trials to older ideals of English liberty; as his other son Simon points out, drawing analogies between their situation, 'Robin Hood, an outlaw bold [...] here did haunt' (*JW*, 40). Roe has analysed the way in which Keats, Hunt and Reynolds saw the story of Robin Hood, particularly when expressed in the language of older poets, as exemplifying a sociable, convivial ideal of poetic, and political, fellowship. Using old language, or imagery drawn from the old ballads, as Clare does in 'Robin Hood and the Gamekeepers', or Hunt and Keats do in their paired poems, 'Robin Hood: To a Friend', offers a way of voicing the 'spirit of Outlawry': 'opposition to the military, religious, and mercantile powers of imperial Britain'.[19] The language of 'old by gone bards' or the celebration of 'Old National Merrymakings', allows Hunt, Reynolds, Keats, and, later, Clare, to tap into this community of radical resistance; simultaneously, they are participating in Lamb's own textual circle, continuing the ideals of sociability and mutual reading he had been putting forward since the 1790s. The 'home-born Feeling' which had been so crucial in formulating Lamb's concepts of sociability therefore lives on into a second generation of radical writers, sympathetic to what Hazlitt termed his 'home-felt truth' (Howe, XII: 36).

Reading and resistance: 'What is Jacobinism?'

Lamb's article, 'What is Jacobinism?', again from *The Albion, and Evening Advertiser* (June 1801), overtly demonstrates the radical resistance of Lamb's early writing.[20] Just as *John Woodvil* and the 'Curious Fragments' had evaded categorisation, this article attacks the very need to categorise or name, and makes his political affinities, already evident from his association with the *Monthly Magazine*, strikingly clear. Lamb had only begun writing for the *Albion* that month, but he was soon supplying a good deal of its comment. In 1801, the paper was owned by John Fenwick, and Lamb describes its 'murky closet' of an office as if, as Courtney points out, Fenwick and Lamb himself might be the sum total of the staff. Lamb had been introduced to Fenwick by Godwin, with whom he had become friendly in February 1800, almost two years after they had featured alongside one another in the *Anti-Jacobin* cartoon.[21] Indeed, 'What is Jacobinism?' returns the attack, and shows that Lamb's radicalism had, if anything, become stronger in the intervening period.

The article begins with the description of a parrot calling out 'Jacobin' indiscriminately at passers by, an image of the gap between the word and actual political commitment. The parrot is no less discriminating than men who – like the *Anti-Jacobin* – brand others with the term Jacobinism: 'It is an easier occupation ... violently to force into *one class*, modes and actions, and principles *essentially various*, and to disgrace that *class* with one ugly name: for *names* are observed to cost the memory and application much less trouble than *things*' (YCL, 343).

By probing the disparity between the two, Lamb hopes to break down unreflective hostility, the spontaneous prejudice aroused by stereotypes.[22] He goes on to deplore the ways in which bodies such as the 'Anti-Jacobin Reviewers' launch 'malign attacks on persons and objects most *foreign* to politics', such as Methodist meetings, Sunday Schools, and – crucial to Lamb – Unitarian Christianity. Most indefensible are their attacks on the reading of Sunday newspapers,

> which disseminate among the lower orders of men some knowledge (not to be otherwise attained) of the state of public affairs, of the conduct of men in office, in which they are so deeply concerned; and, *what is more valuable*, by representing the daily occurrences of domestic events, births, and deaths, and marriages, and benefits, and calamities, and sad accidents of individuals or families, with all the multitudinous 'goings-on of life' teach their readers to be *men*, by the link of human interest, and human passion, to human affairs; transferring their rude and partial domestic feelings over a wide range of sympathy with *strangers* and persons *unknown*, which is reflected back with accumulated intenseness upon that charity which they are to manifest in relationships *which they do know*. (YCL, 345)

This is a foretaste of Elia's support of the newspaper, in, for example, 'Detached Thoughts on Books and Reading', where he evokes 'the pleasure of skimming over with his own eye a magazine, or a light pamphlet'

(Lucas, II: 199). Here, however, the emphasis is not on the pleasure of reading, but rather on its force as a social good. Reading the newspaper becomes a sociable mode of connection, a means of imaginative projection. Political and state information, moreover, is seen as secondary to news about the 'daily occurrences of domestic events'.

Lamb thus continued to promote the Unitarian ideals he had discussed with Coleridge in the late 1790s – specifically, the idea of domestic or friendly feelings unlocking wider benevolence, and then reflecting this warmth back with 'accumulated intenseness' upon the family circle. Lamb returns to the importance of domestic affection the group had been addressing in 1798 and 1799, in such poems as Lloyd's 'To a Sister', with its focus on the 'charities of home', and 'Tintern Abbey'. This emphasis on domestic affection now becomes more overtly linked with the act of reading, which functions alongside these human sympathies, actually 'teaching' the reader to disseminate affection, and to feel connection with the wider community. Similarly, Simon, in *John Woodvil*, comments on the way in which man should feel affection for 'all things that live,/From the crook'd worm to man's imperial form' (*JW*, 49). 'I am in some sort a *general* lover' (*JW*, 49) he explains to Margaret – one who makes no hierarchical or systematic distinctions. This not only chimes with Lamb's claim to Southey, 'I never judge system-wise of things' (Marrs, I: 163), it also finds a direct echo at the close of the article, 'What is Jacobinism?', where the mention of 'general lovers' also seems to prefigure 'Imperfect Sympathies': 'We have heard of *general lovers*, though we dislike the character: but these men are a sort of *general haters*, and discredit and cry down, at random, all that is *new*, and *good*, and *useful*' (*YCL*, 346).[23] This 'general hatred' stems from systematic thinking, judging on the basis of narrow prejudice. One way to counter this is through 'teaching' readers to respond by using their own experiences, their 'rude and partial domestic feelings' to relate to others.

This is an important point. Lamb is beginning to formulate a concept of reading which draws on, yet differs from, the theories of Wordsworth and Coleridge – a concept, moreover, which embraces his own urban allegiances. The allusions embedded within the article point to the ways in which he was subtly re-writing and re-interpreting Coleridge and Wordsworth. One striking example of this comes in the allusion to 'Frost at Midnight' in Lamb's evocation of 'the multitudinous "goings-on of life"' in his support of newspaper reporting. Lamb's newspaper-reader by his Sunday hearth is a version of Coleridge's narrator, enclosed within his warm domestic space, who projects his sympathies onto the outside world, the 'sea, hill, and wood' beyond: 'With all the numberless goings on of life,/Inaudible as dreams!' (*FS*, 19). But, as we saw in Chapter 5, Coleridge's poem is undercut by doubt and self-questioning, quelled only by the image of Hartley, who, raised in nature outside the world of men, will be free of such anxieties. Wandering the 'lakes and sandy shores' which Coleridge himself knew only through Wordsworth's description, Hartley will learn 'far other lore', the divine, eternal language of nature.

Lamb's article echoes the outward movement of the poem, describing the way in which domestic affection may open the way to a wider understanding. But Lamb, here, is stripping away the anxieties which accrete around Coleridge's idea of the reading and learning process in 'Frost at Midnight'. His is an affirmative view of the reader 'transferring their rude and partial domestic feelings over a wide range of sympathy with *strangers* and persons *unknown*'. These readers are taught 'to be *men*' by newspapers, rather than by the divine alphabet of the 'Great universal Teacher!' – furthermore, these newspapers are being read on Sunday, alongside 'the duties of prayer and attendance upon sermons'. The language of men and the practice of reading are thus supported by the divine, rather than being, as in 'Frost at Midnight', something separate. Lamb thus draws upon and expands the ideas of sympathy and domesticity explored in the Coleridge poem to put forward an alternative view of reading and learning as sociable, sympathetic forces, continuing and furthering the earlier shared 'Salutation' ideals.

Similarly, Lamb seems to be addressing Wordsworth's own preoccupations and fears about the nature of reading. Behind this article lies Lamb's reading of the 'Preface' to the second edition of *Lyrical Ballads*, and its anxiety about 'the great national events which are daily taking place, and the encreasing [sic] accumulation of men in cities, where the uniformity of their occupations produces a craving for extraordinary incident which the rapid communication of intelligence hourly gratifies' (*LyB*, 746).

That condemnation of the 'rapid communication of intelligence' provided by daily newspapers would have had especial relevance for Lamb. The prospectus of the *Albion* had exclaimed:

> The political aspect of Europe, the magnitude of the events that daily press upon us, and the desire of information which such a crisis naturally excites, render it unnecessary to make any apology for increasing the number of those vehicles which are so peculiarly adapted to the rapid communication of Intelligence.[24]

Wordsworth might therefore have been directly replying to a paper with which Lamb had a specific link. Lamb's article then becomes a vindication both of his creative independence from Wordsworth and Coleridge, and of a city-based language of men, the urban demotic of the newspaper. As an urban reader, Lamb is more resistant to the link between nature and sympathetic response promoted by Wordsworth and Coleridge, and the article makes clear that the 'real language of men' is not only found in poetry. Imaginative sympathy, he argues, may transcend genre or place, aroused by reading of 'births, and deaths, and marriages, and benefits, and calamities, and sad accidents of individuals and families' in a newspaper, or by reading the urban landscape. It is only killed off by systematic thinking, such as that of Matravis in *Rosamund Gray*, or the parrot-cries of anti-Jacobin reviewers – or even by the stereotypical condemnation of city-dwellers and daily newspapers in the 'Preface' to *Lyrical Ballads*, with which, as we will see in the following chapter, Lamb had a close engagement.

8
The Urban Romantic: Lamb's Landscapes of Affection

Early 1801

A little room up several flights of stairs, in the heart of the Inner Temple, cold, draughty, lacking much furniture – yet an embodiment of the 'home-born Feeling' for which Lamb had been searching through the troubled 1790s. Mary and Charles moved into 16 Mitre Court Buildings in March 1801, and would remain there for eight years. It was a homecoming in many ways, as brother and sister were reunited, making a home together in circumstances which had seemed impossible, and once again installed in the cloistered Inner Temple of their childhood. After the Lambs' father died in 1799, Charles and Mary had lived together in Pentonville, but she had had several recurrences of illness thereafter. However, in the summer of 1800, Mary had finally been well enough to leave the asylum and move into temporary accommodation in Southampton Buildings with Charles, before they found the Mitre Court rooms, selling the spare bed to pay for the move to these attic lodgings: 'mount up to the top of the stairs,' Charles instructed his friend Thomas Manning, 'and come in flannel, for it's pure airy up there' (Marrs, II: 3). From late 1800 onwards, as he contemplates the possibility of permanently settling down with Mary, his letters take on a new vibrancy, a lively fluency as he turns his attention to describing local scenes, his home within the city.

The Inner Temple room, a retreat in the heart of the urban – 'in a garden in the midst of enchanting more than Mahometan paradise **London**' (Marrs, I: 277) – represents a hard won refuge for the Lambs. It is the descendant of the idealised places of community of the 1790s, such as the 'Salutation' or the Nether Stowey bower, but it also registers the fragility of such constructions of friendly harmony and warmth.

As we will see, Lamb's attempts to establish his home in the city delicately negotiate the ways in which strong local and personal affections can be reconciled with wider sympathies, steering a course between the limiting conservative implications of Burke's emphasis on the 'small platoon' of one's own sympathetic links, and what Lamb viewed as the frightening impersonal abstraction of Godwinian disinterest. Mapping the 'home-born Feeling' of the earlier 1790s onto a wider urban landscape through his letters and his later essays, Lamb meditates on the *place* of the personal attachment, in several different senses. Related to this, he tackles questions of individual interpretation – how scenes, both of literature and of landscape, might be read differently.

His settling down in London coincides with the regrouping of the Nether Stowey group, slightly fractured, in the Lake District. The Wordsworths had settled in Grasmere in December 1799. Coleridge, who had lingered in Germany, had finally returned in July of that year. He spent some time in London, working briefly for Daniel Stuart at the *Morning Post,* and staying for five weeks with the Lambs in March and early April 1800 before succumbing to the pull of the Lakes and setting off 'on a visit to his God, Wordsworth' (Marrs, I: 191), moving his family to Keswick shortly afterwards. Lloyd and his wife, too, despite continuing frostiness with Coleridge, also decided to settle in Ambleside. Did Lamb, too, yearn to participate in this close-knit rural community, as he had once longed to visit Nether Stowey? A letter of late 1800 certainly suggests so. Seizing upon an invitation to spend a month with the Lloyds, he immediately wrote to tell Manning that he could no longer come to see him at Cambridge: 'I need not describe to you the expectations which such an one as myself, pent up all my life in a dirty city, have formed of a tour to the *Lakes.* Consider, Grassmere! Ambleside! Wordsworth! Coleridge! I hope you will' (Marrs, I: 247).

That playful evocation of the 'city pent' image from 'This Lime-tree Bower' nicely shows the ways in which the associations and loyalties of the Nether Stowey period were still shaping Lamb's response. But this is, in fact, a deliberate challenge. Just as Lamb had refuted Coleridge's failure to take account of his 'odd-ey'd, stuttering' reality in 'This Lime-tree Bower', so too does he challenge Manning's ability to read their friendship. The letter is a hoax, or as Lamb puts it, a 'bite'. Turning over the page, the reader finds:

Hills, woods, Lakes and mountains, to the Eternal Devil. I will eat snipes with thee, Thomas Manning. (Marrs, I: 248)

Lamb goes on to explain that he is 'not romance-bit about *Nature*. The earth, and sea, and sky (when all is said) is but as a house to dwell in'. This fires him to explore the power of his own local associations, rooted in the urban:

> Streets, streets, streets, markets, theatres, churches, Covent Gardens, Shops sparkling with pretty faces of industrious milliners, neat sempstresses, Ladies cheapening, Gentlemen behind counters lying, Authors in the streets with spectacles, George Dyers (you may know them by their gait) Lamps lit at night, Pastry cook & Silver smith shops, Beautiful Quakers of Pentonville, noise of coaches, drousy cry of mechanic watchmen at night, with Bucks reeling home drunk if you happen to wake at midnight, cries of fire & stop thief, Inns of court (with their learned air and halls and Butteries just like Cambridge colleges), old Book stalls, Jeremy Taylors, Burtons on melancholy, and Religio Medici's on every stall – . These are thy Pleasures O London with-the-many-sins – O City abounding in whores – for these may Keswick and her Giant Brood go hang. (Marrs, I: 248)

That lonely 'desert' in which he searched for specific 'familiar faces' is suddenly, boisterously, peopled. While he celebrates the power of private association – joking about George Dyer and hinting at his own romantic attachment to Hester Savory, a Quaker of Pentonville – this letter is also about very public experiences, celebrating affection felt for unnamed milliners, seamstresses, the very streets themselves. The urban scene is described in close, intimate detail, but is also more abstract and open to others, in what perhaps represents a more democratic – certainly a more demotic – interpretation of the ideals of the mid-1790s. Whilst Lamb retains his earlier emphasis on human connection and sociable affection, the intimate snuggery of the 'Salutation' has opened into a much larger, noisier scene. In a later letter to Manning Lamb explains that he has 'a mind that loves to be at home in **Crowds** – ' (Marrs, I: 277). That idea of being 'at home' in the crowd demonstrates how the concept of the 'home-born Feeling' has expanded and changed for Lamb over the course of the 1790s. Key ideas of the 'Salutation' period – association, sociability, and affection – modified through disappointment, doubt, and argument amongst the friendship group, now return in a different context, mapped onto the urban and explored through prose. Lamb's evocations of London allow a different narrative of Romantic creative development to emerge, separate from though intimately connected with Wordsworth, Coleridge, 'Keswick and her Giant Brood'.

This concluding chapter suggests possible directions for this different Romantic narrative, beginning with a letter written by Lamb to Wordsworth on 30 January 1801 which expands and deepens the preoccupations of the Manning letter. Although often quoted and excerpted, this key Romantic text deserves to be discussed as a whole. As subtle and intricate as 'This Lime-tree Bower' or 'Tintern Abbey' in its treatment of the power of personal association and memory and its reading of place, it also allows a special insight into Romantic reader response, since it is shaped by a close and absorbed reading of the 1800 edition of *Lyrical Ballads*. Yet it also profoundly differs from Wordsworth, since in arguing for the primacy of the individual reader, Lamb delicately exposes the contradiction between Wordsworthian theory and practice. His plea for the power of indeterminacy echoes and transforms some of the preoccupations of *Lyrical Ballads*; connected to his descriptions of the urban, it resonates through later explorations of the city, sounding as far as Charles Baudelaire and Virginia Woolf.

Reading *Lyrical Ballads* (1800)

From the start, the letter demonstrates the textual community of reading and exchange in which Lamb was situated, and shows the depth of his response to *Lyrical Ballads*. It opens by thanking Wordsworth for the present of the 1800 edition: '**Thanks** for your **Letter** and **Present**. – I had already borrowed your second volume – . What most please me are, the Song of Lucy...*Simon's sickly daughter* in the Sexton made me *cry*'. (Marrs, I: 265)

The extent of Lamb's interest in Wordsworth's work is evident from the fact that he had already, by 30 January 1801, managed to borrow a copy of *Lyrical Ballads*. The edition had only been published by Longman a few days before: indeed, Wordsworth himself had still not seen a copy by late February (*EY*, 319). Wordsworth's Longman accounts show that he ordered a copy to be sent to 'Mr Lambe' on 29 January – Lamb had pre-empted him by seeking it out beforehand, probably borrowing it, as Duncan Wu has shown, from John Stoddart, to whom it had been sent by Longman on 23 January, and by whom it was reviewed for *The British Critic* in February 1801.[1]

Insightfully, Stoddart's review picks up Wordsworth's own imagery – for instance in 'Tintern Abbey' – of memories *feeding* the mind:

> Even where the feeling intended to be called forth is of a rich and noble character, such as we may recur to, and feed upon, it may yet

be wrought up so gradually [...] that the subtle uniting thread will be lost, without a persevering effort toward attention on the part of the reader.[2]

He recognises that Wordsworth demands participation, 'persevering effort' from the reader, and singles out several instances of this, including 'the two Songs...[which] have a secret connection': 'Strange fits of passion have I known', and 'She dwelt among th'untrodden ways'. Both are 'Lucy poems' – the same which Lamb, too, singles out for praise at the beginning of his letter to Wordsworth, suggesting shared reading and discussion of the borrowed volume. Yet Lamb, save for those trailing dots, does not comment on the 'Song of Lucy' at all. Its effect on him is demonstrated, however, not only by the fact that he later copied it to Manning, as the 'best Piece' in the volume, 'choice and genuine' (Marrs, I: 274), but also by his comments in the later part of the letter to Wordsworth, which show him struggling to voice the ideas about reader response and interpretation it had raised. Like Stoddart, Lamb recognises the importance of readerly perseverance and involvement; he goes still further in trying to put it into practice in other situations. As will be shown, his letter offers a view of reading which anticipates and tackles many of the issues later raised in critical interpretations of the 'Lucy poems'.

Written at Goslar, in late 1798, the 'Lucy poems' were composed alongside early work on *The Two-Part Prelude*, at the same time Lamb was working on *John Woodvil*. Like that play, or like *Rosamund Gray*, the 'Lucy poems' show Wordsworth becoming preoccupied by processes of remembering and mourning, deeply associated with his thinking about familial and domestic affection. The 'Lucy poems' were first explicitly associated with the idea of the epitaph by Coleridge, writing to Poole in early 1799, shortly after the death of his baby son Berkeley. Wordsworth's 'sublime Epitaph' becomes linked to Coleridge's own feelings of grief and uncertainty, in a way which Lamb, similarly tormented by anxiety over his own sister's situation, must have echoed:

> But I cannot truly say that I grieve – I am perplexed – I am sad – and a little thing, a very trifle would make me weep; but for the death of the Baby I have *not* wept! – Oh! this strange, strange, strange Scene-shifter, Death! that giddies one with insecurity, & so unsubstantiates the living Things that one has grasped and handled! – /Some months ago Wordsworth transmitted to me a most sublime Epitaph/whether it had any reality, I cannot say. – Most probably, in some gloomier moment he had fancied the moment in which his Sister might die. (Griggs, I: 479)

Coleridge's inability to grieve 'truly' for Berkeley is echoed and given voice by the poem's uncertain 'reality'.

The uncertainty engendered by the 'strange, strange, strange' shiftings of death is echoed by the indeterminacy of the 'Lucy poems' themselves, which seem to invite readers to project their own narratives onto them. The attention paid to them by later readers and editors bears this out. Matthew Arnold's careful grouping of the poems in his influential 1879 anthology, for instance, turns them into a Victorian construction of mourning and commemoration, praised by editors such as Margaret Oliphant – herself still grieving for her husband and small daughter – who seeks a consolatory, ordered resolution to grief, and admires the way in which Arnold has 'permitted [the verses] at last to tell their own tale'.[3]

Their formation into a narrative is a point to which readers and critics repeatedly return – yet it is a highly cryptic one. The indeterminacy of the 'Lucy poems' simply won't allow them to 'tell their own tale', a source both of fascination and frustration for generations of readers. Walter Pater nicely displays this double movement when he comments that Wordsworth's ambiguities beget 'a habit of reading between the lines', a constant exercise in 'selecting [...] precious morsels for oneself', and yet in the same breath complains that this is an 'alien element', which obstructs 'purely literary' appreciation.[4] Mark Jones has used this great breadth of commentary about the 'Lucy poems' to argue for the 'political importance of anti-closural practices of reading, of the refusal to totalize' – what the best interpretations of these poems show 'lies partly in knowing what knowledge an interpreter must not claim'.[5] This, I think, is what Lamb himself is arguing throughout the 1801 letter. The difficulties of interpretation posed by the 'Lucy poems', their ambiguities and indeterminacies, are, as we will see, central to his own reading practice.

Yet although the 'Lucy poems' resist interpretative closure, the uncertainties of grief they present – the sense of giddiness and insecurity noticed by Coleridge – do find a response in the volume as a whole, which returns to the question – posed in *The Ruined Cottage* and *Rosamund Gray* – of how the dead might be remembered, and formulates its own epitaphic vision. As Lamb, too, would go on to do, Wordsworth explores the continuation of personal memories both within a wider sympathetic community and within a landscape of 'local attachment' itself. The second poem mentioned by Lamb in the 1801 letter, 'To A Sexton', vividly – and unsettlingly – evokes this continuation. Wordsworth's refusal to allow the Sexton to move the skeletons in the churchyard is a denial of the separate state of death, an insistence – like that of the child in 'We are

Seven' – that memories, and the narrative of these memories, can keep others present. 'Father, Sister, Friend, and Brother' are placed together, the family groupings of the village repeating themselves in the graveyard:

> Mark the spot to which I point!
> From this platform eight feet square
> Take not even a finger-joint:
> Andrew's whole fire-side is there.
> Here, alone, before thine eyes,
> Simon's sickly Daughter lies,
> From weakness, now, and pain defended,
> Whom he twenty winters tended.
> (ll. 9–16, *LyB*, 183)

Wordsworth presents himself as the upholder of family traditions and groupings, mapping the community onto the landscape of the graveyard. Unlike the Sexton, who, like the obtuse questioner of 'We are seven', sees only bones, Wordsworth draws no distinction between living and dead companions, creating a sociable, 'fire-side', continuation between the two. The same fascination with the way in which affectionate bonds break down the barrier between life and death is evident in Mary Lamb's later story, 'Elizabeth Villiers', or 'The Sailor Uncle', written for *Mrs. Leicester's School*. Here the small child Elizabeth remembers 'my father teaching me the alphabet from the letters on a tombstone that stood at the head of my mother's grave' (Lucas, III: 319). Like the girl of 'We are seven', she does not connect death with sadness, an element which is only brought into the story with the arrival of her grieving uncle: as in the Wordsworth poem, death does not destroy sociable reading or interchange.

The stories of the dead may be thus remembered and continued by the living, through oral tales, epitaphs, or poems. 'To a Sexton' and 'She dwelt among th'untrodden ways' both make a promise to remember and respect the dead, tending their memories within the landscape. Thus, Lucy is 'A Violet by a mossy Stone', and the Sexton is a gardener, who tends, 'Roses, lilies, side by side,/Violets in families'. Similarly, 'The Brothers', which Lamb also selected for particular praise, deals with the way in which the stories of the dead may be continued in landscape and memory, by individuals and by the wider community, as the Priest tells Leonard:

> To chronicle the time, we all have here
> A pair of diaries, one serving, Sir,
> For the whole dale, and one for each fire-side.
> (ll. 160–4, *LyB*, 148)

The Priest occupies the same position as the poet in 'To a Sexton': the chronicler and narrator of the stories of the dead. Behind the poem's insistence that the dalesmen do have 'an immortal part', that they 'in each other's thoughts/Possess a kind of second life' is Wordsworth's anxiety over the way in which the poet himself will be remembered, and his (successful) desire to fix his own memory to a specific landscape. It is this desire which shapes the closing poem of the 1798 *Lyrical Ballads*, 'Tintern Abbey', and its assertion that Dorothy's 'memory will be as a dwelling-place' for their shared experiences. Connected to this is the way in which the landscape may act as a mnemonic, a map of affection.

> these steep woods and lofty cliffs,
> And this green pastoral landscape, were to me
> More dear, both for themselves, and for thy sake.
> (ll. 158–60, *LyB*, 120)

Similarly, the landscape of the dales is intimately connected with the affection of the brothers, both shaping and commemorating it. Knowledge of the death of James is foreshadowed in the poem by Leonard's premonition that there has been 'strange alteration' in the landscape, 'that the rocks,/And the eternal hills, themselves were chang'd'. Although James does not have a written epitaph, emblems which recall him remain in the landscape and continue to be talked about, such as his staff:

> there for many years
> It hung – and moulder'd there.
> (ll. 401–2, *LyB*, 158)

The striking use of the term 'moulder'd', to which the pause draws attention, is reminiscent of the way in which Wordsworth emphasises the physical reality of the skeletons in 'To a Sexton'. This uncomfortable reminder of the presence of the bodies, down to their very finger joints, runs alongside his insistence that their stories are still living, remembered in the community and the environment. The mouldering staff, like the rotting wooden bowl of *The Ruined Cottage*, demonstrates the interpenetration of nature and individual, the way in which landscape may be read and used as a tool of recollection and narration.

For Wordsworth, the *type* of landscape is crucial; these emblems must exist in nature. Indeed, the affection of the brothers, he implies, could only have grown up in a rural setting, so closely is it allied to the unchanging rocks and hills. As he comments in the 'Preface', the poem celebrates 'the strength of fraternal, or to speak more philosophically, of moral attachment when early associated with the great and beautiful objects of nature'. (*LyB*, 745)

This is connected to the doubt in the Priest's mind as to whether Leonard is a proper reader of the scene. He assumes that he is a tourist, a 'moping son of Idleness', whose unobservant 'scribbling' demonstrates a lack of any deeper sense of the signification of the landscape. In contrast, for native inhabitants, in whom constant exposure to those 'great and beautiful objects of nature' has fostered an instinctive morality, story-telling, reading and writing take on a plainer, simpler aspect. The narrative of the Priest is imbued with moral force, tied to those 'permanent forms' of hills and mountains. Wordsworth is returning to the idea of the 'divine language' of nature put forward in poems such as 'Frost at Midnight' – a language that cannot be misinterpreted. This allows him to evade the anxieties caused by his awareness of the indeterminacy and subjectivity of language, but also imposes strictures on the nature of reading.

Lamb directly confronts these anxieties. While he admires the words given to the Priest, he subverts the viewpoint he represents, singling out for praise in the poem the character of the 'Happy Man' – the image the Priest uses to describe the kind of aimless tourist he despises. Lamb is at once a sympathetic participant in Wordsworth's reading community – '*Simon's sickly daughter* in the Sexton made me *cry*' – and an outsider, raised 'amid the smoke of cities' like Joanna, with whom he strongly identifies (*LyB*, 244). This double movement of sympathy and difference is at the heart of his approach to reading, which privileges the individual's capacity for response:

> An intelligent reader finds a sort of insult in being told, I will teach you how to think upon this subject. This fault, if I am right, is in a ten thousandth worse degree to be found in **Sterne** and many many novelists & modern poets, who continually put a sign post up to shew **where you are to feel**. They set out with assuming their readers to be stupid. Very different from Robinson Crusoe, the Vicar of Wakefie[l]d, Roderick Random, and other beautiful bare narratives. – There is implied an unwritten compact between Author and reader; I will tell you a story, and I suppose you will understand it. – Modern Novels 'St. Leons' and the like are full of such flowers as these 'Let not my reader suppose' – 'Imagine, **if you can**' – modest! – &c. (Marrs, I: 265–6)

Lamb, here, gets to the heart of Wordsworth's anxieties about controlling reader response, arguing forcefully for confidence in the reader's thoughts and feelings. His reference to the 'unwritten compact between Author and reader', for example, demonstrates his recognition of Wordsworth's fears about the reception of his work, and strives to allay them. The idea of a 'compact' – a mutual agreement – recalls the ways in which the community of *Lyrical Ballads* undertakes to remember and narrate the stories of its kinsfolk. It also anticipates Lamb's promotion of newspapers, which 'teach their readers to be *men*, by the link of human interest, and human passion'. The 'link of human interest', the provocation of sympathy, is all that is required for the stories to *teach* their readers. His own reactions to the 'Ancient Mariner' prove his point:

> I was never so affected with any human Tale. After first reading it, I was totally possessed with it for many days. – I dislike all the miraculous part of it, but the feelings of the man under the operation of such scenery dragged me along like Tom Piper's magic Whistle. – I totally differ from your idea that the Marinere should have had a character and profession. – This is a Beauty in Gulliver's Travels, where the mind is kept in a placid state of little wonderments; but the **Ancient Marinere** undergoes such **Trials**, as overwhelm and bury all individuality or memory of what he was. – Like the state of a man in a **Bad dream**, one terrible peculiarity of which is, that all consciousness of personality is **gone**. [...] You will excuse my remarks, because I am hurt and vexed that you should think it necessary, with a prose apology, to open they eyes of dead men that cannot see. (Marrs, I: 266)

Like Wordsworth, Lamb dislikes 'the miraculous part' of the poem, the supernatural events. But this does not preclude participation in the poem's deeper themes: it still provokes readerly enchantment and fascination, a physical compulsion – 'dragged [...] along' – which mirrors the unwilling involvement of the wedding guest. Lamb has sympathetically entered into the poem to such a degree that he has, like the Ancient Mariner himself, been overwhelmed, losing 'all individuality...all consciousness of personality'. For Lamb, as will be explored, this idea of losing identity is of central importance to the reading process, as reader and author become merged in the text – foreshadowing his declaration in 'Detached Thoughts on Books and Reading,' 'I love to lose myself in other men's minds.[...] Books think for me' (Lucas, II: 195).

This emphasis on imaginative involvement leads him to question Wordsworth's decision to add the Preface to the 1800 edition, suggesting that it would have been better if it had 'appeared in a separate treatise'. Whereas in the 1798 'Advertisement' Wordsworth had sought to disrupt 'pre-established codes of decision,' by 1800 he had grown absolute – seeking not only to overturn those 'codes', but to create new ones, his own directions as to how the work should be read, and understood as a unified whole. In a move typical of his complex critical strategies, Wordsworth prefaces his 'Preface' with a defence of his own behaviour:

> I was unwilling to undertake the task, because I knew that on this occasion the Reader would look coldly upon my arguments, since I might be suspected of having been principally influenced by the selfish and foolish hope of *reasoning* him into an approbation of these particular Poems. (*LyB*, 742)

Lamb, as 'the Reader', turns this anxiety back against Wordsworth – he finds it 'a sort of insult' to his readerly intelligence. The 'Preface', argues Lamb, has a *'diminishing'* effect on the poems which follow: diminishing, because it seeks to direct interpretation, limiting the response of the reader. The poems, on the other hand, although they constantly raise issues of interpretation and response, allow, as has been discussed, room for indeterminacy and ambiguity. This is what Lamb now tries to demonstrate, in a highly-charged defence of his own city readings, which, while it combats the diminishing strictures of the 'Preface', acts as a continuation and exploration of Wordsworthian themes.

Lamb's Wordsworthian attachments

Lamb begins his celebration of the urban by tackling Wordsworth's idea of 'local attachments':

> Separate from the pleasure of your company, I dont mu[ch] care if I never see a mountain in my life. – I have passed all my days in London, until I have formed as many and intense local attachments, as any of you **Mountaineers** can have done with dead nature. (Marrs, I: 267)

'I don't much care if I never see a mountain' – a blunt rebuttal of the idea put forward in the 'Preface' that the passions of men need to be 'incorporated with the beautiful and permanent forms of nature'. Throughout Wordsworth's work the mountain is characterised as a moral force, which, as in *The Prelude* (1805), shapes the soul through its 'influence habitual to the mind' (VII: 721–5; *Prelude* 1805, I: 211). It is a 'steady form', a 'pure grandeur', which acts as a contrast to the 'extraordinary incident' and 'frantic novels' of the city condemned in the 'Preface'. Lamb's 'dead nature', however, argues that nature's significance is entirely dependent on the beholder. That bold 'you **Mountaineers**', grounding the intensity of the Wordsworths, might seem to predict Francis Jeffrey's disparaging definition of the 'Lakers', first hinted at in his 1802 review of Southey's 'Thalaba' – which, in condemning the 'homeliness' of this 'sect', also takes a swipe at the 'sweetness of Lambe' – and expanded upon in subsequent reviews, such as his notorious 1814 abuse of *The Excursion*, which targets the 'natural drawl of the Lakers' and their rustic pretensions.[6] But Lamb is not belittling Wordsworthian attachment to mountains; rather, he is challenging the idea that such objects have an innate value, or that they should be read in the same way by all. For Lamb, it is city scenes which, 'by influence habitual to the mind', exert the same shaping power:

> The Lighted shops of the Strand and Fleet Street, the innumerable trades, tradesmen and customers, coaches, waggons, play houses, all the bustle and wickedness round about Covent Garden, the very women of the Town, the Watchmen, drunken scenes, rattles; – life awake, if you awake, at all hours of the night, the impossibility of being dull in Fleet Street, the crowds, the very dirt & mud, the Sun shining upon houses and pavements, the print shops, the **old Book** stalls, parsons cheap'ning books, coffee houses, steams of soups from kitchens, the pantomimes, London itself, a pantomime and a masquerade, all these things work themselves into my mind and feed me without a power of satiating me. The wonder of these sights impells me into night-walks about her crowded streets, and I often shed tears in the motley Strand from fullness of joy at so much **Life** – . [...] what must I have been doing all my life, not to have lent great portions of my heart with usury to such scenes? – (Marrs, I: 267)

This spontaneous, continuous poem in prose, full of energy which at times threatens to overwhelm the sentence structure, acts as an immediate response to the opening sentence of the 'Preface', when Wordsworth speaks of using 'a selection of the real language of men in a state of vivid sensation'. This is that 'vivid sensation' instantly arrested in words – a startling antidote to Wordsworth's restrictive anxiety.

Lamb asks for Wordsworth's imaginative involvement in return. Just as he had been 'dragged along' by the 'Ancient Mariner', so he carries off the Wordsworths for a walk through London as night comes on, guiding them down the illuminated Strand, through the 'bustle and wickedness', into the reaches of darkness guarded by the Watchmen.[7] Then suddenly, with that abrupt pause, the letter-reader awakes, to find the 'Sun shining upon houses and pavements', in a parody of pastoral vision. London is revealed as a 'pantomime', a place of pure show, gleefully exploiting the subjectivity of words and forms. This will be echoed in the theatrical vision of London in *The Prelude* – Wordsworth's, however, is an uneasy relationship with the pantomime excess, the dizzying conflicting languages of the city.[8] Unsettled by the barrage of words from all sides – the 'symbols, blazoned names,' the 'letters huge', the 'files of ballads', the 'Advertisements, of giant-size' which he sees in the London streets – he strives to keep his poetic identity intact, eventually retreating to 'some Show-man's Platform' above the mob to give an overview of the scene (VII: 659; *Prelude* 1805, I: 209). Lamb, on the other hand, enjoys the sensation of losing himself in the illusion, surrendering to the emotion of the crowd.

Yet Lamb continues to demonstrate his sympathy with Wordsworth's ideas of memory and creativity. The city scenes 'work themselves into my mind and feed me', paralleling Wordsworth's celebrations of the nourishing, 'fructifying' virtue of certain memories. Similarly, Lamb's 'intense local attachments' feed his creative development, as he creates his own landscape of personal symbolism in the midst of London:

> My attachments are all local, purely local – . I have no passion (or have had none since I was in love, and then it was the spurious engendering of poetry & books) to groves and vallies. – The rooms where I was born, the furniture which has been before my eyes all my life, a book case which has followed me about, (like a faithful dog, only exceeding him in knowledge) wherever I have moved – old chairs, old tables, streets, squares, where I have sunned myself, my old school, – these are my mistresses – have I not enough, without your mountains? – I do not envy you. I should pity you, did I not know, that the Mind will make friends of any thing. Your sun & moon and skys and hills & lakes affect me no more, or scarcely come to me in more venerable characters, than as a gilded room with tapestry and tapers, where I might live with handsome visible objects. – I consider the clouds above me but as a **roof** beautifully painted, but unable to satisfy the mind. (Marrs, I: 267–8)

As the barriers between Lamb's urban interior and the street break down, Wordsworth's rural hills and lakes become surreally enclosed within 'a gilded room', symbolising the way in which they constrain Lamb's own imagination. In demonstrating how associations and affections shape the consciousness of the individual, this vision of London actually enacts Lamb's criticism of the 'Preface', whilst simultaneously putting into practice ideas explored in *Lyrical Ballads*. Lamb's conversion of the landscape into a room startlingly reverses Wordsworth's evocation of the 'forms of beauty' of 'Tintern Abbey' inside 'lonely rooms, and mid the din/Of towns and cities' (ll. 26–7; *LyB*, 117), or his declaration in 'Written in Germany, on one of the coldest days of the Century' that Dorothy's love in their 'desolate' lodgings makes him 'as blest and as glad [...] As if green summer grass were the floor of my room,/And woodbines were hanging above' (ll. 33–5, *LyB*, 226). Yet, simultaneously, it continues and extends the argument for the power of personal sympathies and affections made in both poems.

Another, later, continuation of these self-created rooms might be seen in Leigh Hunt's prison cell. We have already seen how, following Lamb, Hunt used old poets and 'Old National Merrymakings' in a radical context, to create an idea of a wider sympathetic community, transcending boundaries of genre and time. Imprisoned in 1813 for his remarks about the Prince Regent in *The Examiner*, Hunt continued defiantly to celebrate the power of individual interpretation and imagination, persisting in editing the paper from jail, and transforming his cell into a flowery retreat, a recreation of Eden which even included an apple tree:

> I papered the walls with a trellis of roses; I had the ceiling covered with clouds and sky; the barred windows I screened with Venetian blinds; and when my bookcases were set up with their busts, and flowers and a pianoforte made their appearance, perhaps there was not a handsomer room on that side the water.[9]

'There was no other such room,' said Lamb, 'except in a fairy tale', and the Lambs were both frequent visitors.[10] Hunt's cell, an untouchable *hortus conclusus* of the mind inside prison walls, helps open up the wider political implications of Lamb's 1801 'painted **roof**'. Both rooms represent a fight for imaginative liberty, emphasising the power of the mind to transcend physical surroundings. Both are illuminated from within by the power of personal association and sympathy – the 'home-born Feeling' – investing the private domestic ideal with political force, and showing how an alternative radical legacy stretches from the 1790s into the second generation of Romantic writers. In their conflation of categories – interior/exterior; private/public; rural/urban – Lamb and Hunt also trouble our own critical categorisations of Romanticism. Roe suggests that Hunt allows us to trace 'an alternative Romantic temperament drawn to human community and domestic gatherings'.[11] Lamb's writing of the 1790s allows us to see not only the importance of this alternative narrative, but just how closely connected it is with the meditative Romanticism represented by Wordsworth's responses to the rural scene, since both approaches, as we have seen, are shaped by an attempt to determine and express the power of personal feeling and association.

Lamb's writing also challenges generic categories and hierarchies. Just as he transposes the power of Wordsworth's rural associations onto the urban, so too he transforms Wordsworth's poetry into prose, loosely mimicking the cadences of blank verse poems in *Lyrical Ballads*, such as 'The Brothers', or 'Poems on the Naming of Places':

> old chairs, old tables, streets, squares, where I have sunned myself, my old school, – these are my mistresses – have I not enough, without your mountains?

The first phrase of this passage, made complete in itself by those dashes, favourite devices of Lamb, can be read as a rhythmic piece of blank verse, loosely based upon iambic meter. The harmony of that internal rhyme, chairs/squares, acts to unify the series of nouns, linked by their 's' and 't' sounds; these aural similarities also help the reader to accept the progression from the domestic interior to the urban exterior, and reinforces the connection Lamb is making between these familiar spaces. The sense of a line of verse is emphasised by the caesura provided by the comma after 'squares', which marks the development of the idea, as Lamb goes on to link it to his own experience. The close association between the quotidian objects and the individual is made explicit by the assonance between the first and second phrases: chairs/squares/where, and by the repeated 's' sound of 'sunned myself'. Finally, the return to the idea of specific places, 'my old school', acts both to complete the sentence, by repetition of that leitmotif 'old', and to suggest, by means of the parenthesis, that the city encloses the individual, the writer. This careful evocation of the writer nourished and sustained by the urban landscape, with all its affectionate associations, continues the ideas put forward in *Lyrical Ballads* 1800, and puts into practice Wordsworth's insistence in the 'Preface' that there is no essential difference between poetry and prose: 'their affections are kindred and almost identical [...] the same human blood circulates through the veins of them both' (*LyB*, 749–50). This prose vision of the city assures Wordsworth that he will continue to have a 'second life' in the sympathetic – although different – reading of others.

The voice of the 'Londoner'

This different reading was not, however, greeted sympathetically by Wordsworth. A 'turmoil' of response greeted Lamb's 1801 letter – 'Cumberland and Westmorland,' Lamb joked to Manning, 'have already declared a state of war.'; 'my *Arse tickles red* from the northern castigation' (Marrs, I: 272; 276). Although Wordsworth had pleaded an 'insurmountable aversion from Letter writing' to excuse not having responded to *John Woodvil*, 'I received almost instantaneously a long letter of four sweating pages from my **reluctant Letterwriter**, the purport of which was, that he [...] "was compelled to wish that my range of **Sensibility** was more extended"' (Marrs, I: 272). 'Four long pages, equally sweaty, and more tedious,' arrived from Coleridge, suggesting that the fault must 'lie "in me & not in them"' (Marrs, I: 273). Alternative readings are a sign of a fault in the reader – that description of the letters 'sweating' with indignation vividly evokes the anxieties provoked by these issues of readership and interpretation, fears which Lamb, now removed from Coleridge's collaborative circle, could now view with more detachment. He wryly concludes that he will send them 'a very merry Letter' (Marrs, I: 273).

Although the 'very merry Letter' does not survive, the fact that the difference of opinion did not develop into a quarrel, as it had done with Coleridge several years earlier, suggests how Lamb had by now grown adept at using reading and writing as a tool of healing and reconciliation. Yet it also points to the way in which Lamb had begun to use humour as a defensive construct. Expressing his intention to write a 'very merry Letter' conceals any emotion at being chastised as an unfit reader by Wordsworth and Coleridge, and the complete rebuttal of his sympathetic, albeit provocative, readings. Lamb's humorous pose, like his puns and his antiquarianism, is a means of dissimulation which, like his urban reading model, forcefully counters Wordsworth's attempts to control the response of his reader, and 'incorporate it into a manifestation of the ego's personal control'.[12] We see its fuller manifestation as he begins to develop his prose writing into a form he was to make his own – the familiar essay.

The January 1801 letter directly feeds into his first published experiment with the genre – 'The Londoner', which appeared in the *Morning Post* on 1 February 1802, a commission enabled by Coleridge. Prompted, then, by the encouragement of a friend, the essay incorporates material which had originally been written to friends. 'Every man, while the *passion* is upon him, is for a time at least addicted to groves and meadows, and purling streams,' the anonymous essayist claims, in a close echo of the letter to Wordsworth, before launching into a declaration of his own city allegiances, including a description of him weeping in the 'crowded Strand', endlessly sympathising with the 'shifting scenes of a skilful Pantomime' presented by London – 'what have I been doing all my life, if I have not lent out my heart with usury to such scenes?'.[13] Lamb's love of London, too, forms part of a familial allegiance, since it is shared – perhaps inspired – by Mary, whose own joyful lively letters to Sarah Stoddart slightly later are fuelled by a similarly energetic, urban vision, with their descriptions of 'bustling down Fleet-Market-in-all-its-glory of a saturday night, admiring the stale peas and co'lly-flowers and cheap'ning small bits of mutton and veal for our sunday's dinner's' (Marrs, II: 90). Phrases from Charles' letters to Manning and Robert Lloyd are also incorporated, as in a description of the essayist's 'passion for crowds', his love of 'a mob of happy faces crouding up at the pit door of Drury-Lane Theatre', which 'give me ten thousand finer pleasures, than I ever received from all the flocks of *silly sheep*, that have whitened the plains of *Arcadia* or *Epsom Downs*'.[14] As with the much earlier sonnet to Siddons, which domesticated the power of the theatre, this experience questions stock responses of sensibility. The sonnet enclosed Siddons' performance within a homely story-telling scene: here, moved by the eager theatre-going 'mob', the essay similarly redirects the response of feeling, using pastoral sentiment to illuminate the urban crowd. The potential threat of the 'mob' is deflated – moreover, it becomes a viable literary subject. The 'commonest incidents of a town life' can encourage morality and sympathy, claims the essay, just as the

> *Foresters* of *Arden* in a beautiful country
>   Found tongues in trees, books in the running brooks,
>   Sermons in stones, and good in everything

This is a sly nod both to the 'impulse from a vernal wood' celebrated in 'The Tables Turned' (l. 21; *LyB*, 109) and to the recreation of Arden in *John Woodvil*, as yet still unpublished, showing how the essay forms part of an ongoing dialogue with a community of writers.

Yet while these allusions would have carried particular resonance for certain friends, the essay also seeks to befriend the reader, as in its closing promise: 'Reader, in the course of my peregrinations about the great city, it is hard, if I have not picked up matter, which may serve to amuse thee, as it has done me, a winter evening long. When next we meet, I purpose opening my budget – Till when, farewell'.

Again, we are back in the scene of convivial, friendly amusement – a winter's evening spent in mutual conversation, as in the 'Salutation' days, or the 'long Winter's night' of family story-telling evoked in the sonnet to Siddons. The 'budget' perhaps recalls the best-selling children's book by Aikin and Barbauld, *Evenings at Home, or the Juvenile Budget Opened* (1792). Emphasising the diffusion of knowledge within a framework of affection – reminiscent of the Aikin family's experiences of Dissenting Academy education – the book takes as its premise the image of the Fairborne family, who own a box filled with fables, stories, and dialogues: 'It was [...] one of the evening amusements of the family to *rummage the budget*, as their phrase was', and read aloud the different stories.[15] Despite the essay's glaring difference from Aikin's and Barbauld's educational homilies, it shares their Unitarian faith in the central importance of domestic, intimate conversation. Lamb's essay, however, while it attempts to construct an affectionate bond with the reader, simultaneously emphasises the subjectivity and waywardness of personal feeling – that closing image of reader and essayist united on a 'winter evening' is, crucially, set against the indeterminacy evoked 'by the smoke of London, [...] the medium most familiar to my vision'. The writer should not try to dictate the responses of the reader – the process Lamb had earlier termed 'put[ting] a sign post up to shew **where you are to feel**' (Marrs, I: 265). The essay thus both invites, and questions, the personal response.

This same double movement informs the essays of Elia in the *London Magazine*, the eventual outlet for the ideas first explored here. Despite his promise to the reader, he seems not to have published any more essays in the *Morning Post*, confining himself to topical jokes, squibs, and short pieces. He wrote several pieces in 1811 for the Hunts' paper *The Reflector* including 'On the Inconveniences Resulting from Being Hanged', 'On the Genius and Character of Hogarth', and 'On [...] the Plays of Shakespeare, considered with reference to their fitness for Stage-Representation'; in 1813, he also contributed to their paper *The Examiner*, and, to a lesser extent, to John Scott's *The Champion* from 1814. However, it was not until Scott's next paper, the *London Magazine*, that Lamb began to exploit the possibilities of the essay genre.

He had previously experimented with pseudonyms such as 'Edax' and 'Pensilis' – now he settled into the voice of Elia to produce his best-known work. While they address contemporary topics, political and cultural, the essays also continue the debates and the ideals of the 1790s – but as Lamb's writing from that period has sunk from view, these echoes have become obscured.

'The greatest egotist of all': some Elian sympathies

The first of the Elia essays, 'The South-Sea House' – originally published in the *London Magazine* (August 1820) as 'Recollections of the South Sea House' – offers a nice example of these refractions. It opens with a direct, intimate appeal to the reader:

> Reader, in thy passage from the Bank – where thou hast been receiving thy half-yearly dividends (supposing thou art a lean annuitant like myself) – to the Flower Pot, to secure a place for Dalston, or Shacklewell, or some other thy suburban retreat northerly, – didst thou never observe a melancholy looking, handsome, brick and stone edifice, to the left – where Threadneedle-street abuts upon Bishopsgate? I dare say thou hast often admired its magnificent portals ever gaping wide, and disclosing to view a grave court, with cloisters, and pillars, with few or no traces of goers-in or comers-out – a desolation something like Balclutha's. (Lucas, II: 1)[1]

'Balcluthas' carries a footnote: Lamb adds at the foot of the page, 'I passed by the walls of Balclutha, and they were desolate. – OSSIAN. (Lucas, II: 1). The 'South-Sea House', in decline since the 'Bubble' of speculation burst in 1720, is carefully placed in a specific locality – 'where Threadneedle-street abuts upon Bishopsgate' – yet opens onto a larger mythical landscape of desolation, Ossianic and Wordsworthian.

This deserted 'house of trade', a still, silent spot 'in the very heart of stirring and living commerce', is also a version of the ruined cottages and uninhabited houses of the 1790s. With its 'gaping' portals, its 'grave court', it could be a place of sorrow like the 'desert' which giddily opens up in 'The Old Familiar Faces'. Instead it is transformed into a place of community and shared memory. Like Wordsworth's ruined cottage, its fragmentation and decay is carefully documented – it is 'worm-eaten', 'tarnished', overrun by dust, dirt, and moths – yet it has a dignity and peace similar to that invested by Wordsworth in those 'four naked walls' (MS D: 31; *RC*, 45):

> Peace to the manes of the BUBBLE! Silence and destitution are upon thy walls, proud house, for a memorial! (Lucas, II: 2)

Like the ruined cottage, this deserted house is peopled with personal memories and associations, which Elia – like Armytage the Pedlar – invites the reader to recover and share. A community of clerks is evoked, who seem to partake 'of the genius of the place', their similarly outmoded characteristics lovingly detailed – from unfashionable 'maccaroni' hair to 'gone by' wit – so that they seem organically connected to this urban workplace. Just as the Dalesmen of 'The Brothers' enjoy a 'second life' through the memories and story-telling of their community, Elia recreates the workers of the 'South-Sea House'. Whereas the Dalesmen, however, are defined through their tough physical labour in the landscape, the clerks spend most of their time escaping their work, creating stories about themselves to dignify their situation – like Thomas Tame, whose noble ancestry is 'a piece of defensive armour' against his present status (Lucas, II: 5). Elia is fascinated by the power of personal associations in shaping environment, transforming a workplace into a landscape of remembered affection. Similarly, he meditates on the place of personal attachment – both in terms of its role in binding societies together, and in terms of specific, local 'place'. Re-reading Wordsworth, Elia maps personal affection onto an urban landscape as he remembers clerks such as Evans, who himself is distinguished by his desire to commemorate 'old and new London – the site of old theatres, churches, streets gone to decay' (Lucas, II: 4). Similarly, he celebrates 'Henry Man, the wit, the polished man of letters, the *author*, of the South-Sea House' (Lucas, II: 6).[16] Elia rescues his two forgotten volumes 'from a stall in Barbican, not three days ago' and finds him 'terse, fresh, epigrammatic, as alive' (Lucas, II: 7). Man, an author in the city, who lives again on a Barbican stall, is also, the essay implies, an author *of* the city, since in the essay London is defined purely in relation to the 'South-Sea House', whose particular characteristics are used to suggest a much larger scene. Sympathising with the particular can lead, through a Hartleian train of association, to wider understanding – to a suggestion, if not actually a realisation, of the ideal.

This is embodied in the very form of the 'familiar' essay – intimate, informal, spontaneous, 'unlicked, incondite things' (Lucas, II: 171). Uttara Natarajan has shown how the genre continues and extends the drive towards the 'real language of men' (*LyB*, 741) explored in *Lyrical Ballads* and Coleridge's conversation poems. She argues that in harnessing the rhythms and pauses of spoken speech to describe sensations and subjects deliberately drawn from the ordinary, the familiar essay represents a symbiosis of the experiential and the ideal, 'in which conversation (the everyday, the experiential) becomes the vehicle of philosophy (the abstract, the ideal)'.[17] I discussed in Chapter 4 the ways in which 'This Lime-tree Bower' attempted to access a sense of something '*one & indivisible*' (Griggs, I: 349), through its intensity of focus on particular details – weeds, leaves, a creaking rook. Coleridge's little bower, illuminated by this larger ideal, was, as we have seen, a literary successor to the ways in which small communities – the Pantisocratic commune; the 'Salutation' group – had tried to use personal friendship and affection to evoke universal benevolence. The Elia essays are imbued with Lamb's recognition of the shortcomings of such attempts – yet, like *Rosamund Gray* or *John Woodvil*, they continue to assert the importance of the ideal of benevolent community, albeit one which may be realised only imaginatively, through sympathetic recollection or reading. It is just such a community which can be glimpsed, fleetingly, between the portals of the 'South-Sea House' on the way to the 'Flower Pot' tavern, a larger ideal which opens out at a very particular city junction, between 'Threadneedle-street [and] Bishopsgate'.

As in *Rosamund Gray* and *John Woodvil*, Elia enacts this community by encouraging an active connection between reader and text – his first word, after all, is 'Reader'. Instead of Wordsworthian anxiety about the reader as separate and judgemental – 'look[ing] coldly upon my arguments' (*LyB*, 742) – this Elian reader is instead immediately, intimately involved, their response invited by the shaping of the first sentence as a question. The reader is closely identified with the essayist – both are 'lean annuitant[s]' who walk the same city streets, and mutually observe the landmark of the South-Sea House. Allusion and quotation – such as the reference to Ossian – further this connection, as do the personal references to Lamb's life which are woven into the essays. It is these 'living autobiographical touches' which, as Gerald Monsman has shown, mark the difference between Elia and earlier essay personae such as Steele's 'Isaac Bickerstaffe'.[18] For instance, Lamb had actually worked at the South-Sea House in 1791–2 – rather than, as the essay claims, 'forty years back' – and had personally known the clerks he mentions, some of whom were still alive.[19] 'Elia', moreover, was a name shamelessly borrowed – or as Lamb would later put it, 'usurped' – from a contemporary at the South-Sea House, Felix Ellia.[20] The *London Magazine* version of the essay, reinforcing the distinction between the two characters, even includes a sly footnote reference to 'Mr Lamb', the 'present tenant' of rooms which had belonged to the old accountant of the South-Sea House: 'Mr. Lamb,' the footnote claims, 'has the character of a right courteous and communicative collector' who will show Elia his rare pictures.[21]

This is part of a familiar Elian pattern, where essays frequently include personal references, portraits of friends – a very recognisable Dyer and Coleridge appear in the first essays – and fragments from personal letters, such as 'Distant Correspondents' (March 1822), subtitled 'in a letter to B. F. Esq. at Sydney, New South Wales' (his friend Barron Field, a reluctant Australian emigrant). The identity of Elia himself is teasingly suggested, but never asserted, as in the second essay, 'Oxford in the Vacation'. After his depiction of clerks in the 'South-Sea House', he imagines the reader asking whether he too is 'one of the self-same college – a votary of the desk'? 'Well,' he answers, 'I do agnize something of the sort' (Lucas, II: 8). It is hard not to read in that use of 'agnize' for 'acknowledge' an irrepressible Elian pun on Lamb's own name, common in his circle of friends – as shown by an 1800 letter from Coleridge to Godwin, telling him that 'The Agnus Dei & the Virgin Mary desire their kind respects to *you*, you sad Atheist – !' (Griggs, I: 580).

So Elia is Lamb – but he is also a 'fellow clerk of mine at the South Sea House' (Lucas, *Letters*, II: 302). Felix Ellia himself had (largely unsuccessful) literary ambitions, publishing his first novel, *Theopha*, in 1798, the same year as *Rosamund Gray*: 'Elia himself added the function of an author to that of a scrivener' (Lucas, *Letters*, II: 302). This double persona shapes the character of the essayist, who is described as writing his essays on the 'parings of a counting-house' – its waste foolscap – and allowing his pen to escape the 'cart-rucks of figures and cyphers' into the 'flowery carpet-ground of a midnight dissertation' (Lucas, II: 9). There are shades, there, of Lamb's miserable city poet in 'Composed at Midnight', discussed in Chapter 5 – but now the midnight writer is enjoying a new freedom and playfulness. This is a form of resistance against economic and environmental circumstance, since the trappings of the 'counting-house' are used to subvert the world of work. All the clerks in 'The South-Sea House', including its writer, are employing 'complex mechanisms of sublimation' to escape their clerk-hood, so that the essay becomes 'a study in alienation overcome by eccentric defenses'.[22] Elia's nostalgia and evasiveness can thus be seen as a 'readable code' of resistance to conventional cultural and economic standards, which lies behind his apparent apolitical stance.[23]

Elia is also, of course, 'a lie', a playful tease, whose apparently highly personal, subjective persona actually allows Lamb to push at the limits of personal feeling. While Elia incorporates very personal details of Lamb's life and letters, he also lays claim to several other identities – including those of Ellia and Coleridge – to break down the barriers of the individual. The essays thus register a double movement of self-recognition and self-surrender – Lamb is both finding and losing himself in the text. He is continuing the debate about personal feeling and authorial egotism begun as far back as *Poems* 1796, with its prefatory worries about 'querulous egotism' which might 'reduce the feelings of others to an identity with our own' (*Poems* 1796, viii). Lamb's own 'Preface' to *The Last Essays of Elia* (1833) makes the link clear, as he defends the writings of Elia:

> Egotistical they have been pronounced by some who did not know, that what he tells us, as of himself, was often true only (historically) of another; as in a former Essay (to save many instances) – where under the *first person* (his favourite figure) he shadows forth the forlorn estate of a country-boy placed at a London school, far from his friends and connections – in direct opposition to his own early history. If it be egotism to imply and twine with his own identity the griefs and affections of another – making himself many, or reducing many unto himself – then is the skilful novelist, who all along brings in his hero, or heroine, speaking of themselves, the greatest egotist of all. (Lucas, II: 171)

As Park has pointed out in his brilliant analysis of Lamb's role as critic, the 'specific and personal emphasis' of the Elia essays has resulted in a neglect of their 'aesthetic implications'.[24] He singles out 'Imperfect Sympathies' as an important exploration of 'the imaginative perception of the artist': its personal and circumstantial detail, he argues, opens into questions which lie at the centre of Romantic creative identity. It famously evokes two sorts of temperament, one represented by systematic, plain, 'clock-work' or 'Caledonian' thought: the other characterised by 'surmises, guesses, misgivings, half-intuitions, semi-consciousnesses, partial illuminations, dim instincts, embryo conceptions', and alert, always, to the 'falterings of self-suspicion' (Lucas, II: 67–9). This uncertainty is Elia's natural mode, and it pervades his essays: the 'eventide' duskiness of the South-Sea House, with its dusty maps 'dim as dreams' (Lucas, II: 2), for instance, is the physical manifestation of the 'twilight of dubiety' evoked in 'Imperfect Sympathies' (Lucas, II: 69). It reflects not only Lamb's negotiations with authorial egotism but also how he attempts to challenge the expectations and prejudices of the reader. For if 'Imperfect Sympathies' is about the imaginative identity of the Romantic artist, it is also about the imaginative sympathy of the Romantic reader.

Conversationally, sociably, Elia leads the reader of 'Imperfect Sympathies' into a complicit smile as he inveighs against the Caledonian temperament: 'I have been trying all my life to like Scotchmen, and am obliged to desist from the experiment in despair' (Lucas, II: 67–8). But as the prejudices become steadily darker and the jokes more savage the hapless reader is left scrabbling for an escape clause. If we have relinquished the moral high ground to smile at Lamb's Scotchmen, can we detach ourselves from his evocation of 'centuries of injury, contempt, and hate [...] cloaked revenge, dissimulation, and hate' (Lucas, II: 70) in his description of anti-Semitism? The essay invites us first to reveal and then to confront our own prejudices: it is a plea for sympathy premised on human imperfection, meant not to confirm our prejudicial instincts, but to awaken our own 'falterings of self-suspicion'. Like Elia, the reader too is challenged to 'imply and twine with his own identity the griefs and affections of another', and to re-read from another perspective. It is one of Lamb's deep-seated belief and connects with his criticism of Wordsworth, reported by Crabb Robinson: 'Wordsworth, he thought, is narrow and confined in his views....He does not, like Shakespeare, become everything he pleases, but forces the reader to submit to his individual feelings'.[25]

Lamb criticises Wordsworth's 'narrow and confined' tendencies the more harshly because he recognised at other moments the power of Wordsworthian indeterminacy – the desire to 'abate the pride of the calculating *understanding*', as Lamb puts it in his mangled review of *The Excursion* (Lucas, I: 194) – which might allow room for re-reading, for imaginative sympathy.

A very similar frustration is evident in Keats' complaints about the 'wordsworthian or egotistical sublime', which he sets against the power of the writer who can immerse himself in his subject, who 'has no Identity'.[26] Indeed, Lamb's repeated explorations of 'surmises, guesses, misgivings' have long been linked to Keats' more famous formulation of '*Negative Capability*, that is when man is capable of being in uncertainties, Mysteries, doubts, without any irritable reaching after fact & reason'.[27] The full story of the connections between Lamb and Keats – linked both through Leigh Hunt, and through Keats' interest in Hazlitt – remains to be explored. The appearance of Lamb's collected *Works* in

1818, published by Charles and James Ollier with their close links to the Cockney school, meant that his early writing – including his sonnets of the 1790s, *Rosamund Gray* and *John Woodvil* – was circulating through the Hunt, Keats, and Shelley circle in their most productive creative period. Its true influence on the 'second generation' of Romantic writers has probably not been fully appreciated yet, but may be glimpsed in, say, Mary Shelley's use of 'The Old Familiar Faces' in *Frankenstein*, or her echo of *John Woodvil* in *The Last Man* (1826). Percy Shelley, receiving it in a parcel from the Olliers in Italy in 1819, exclaimed to Leigh Hunt: 'What a lovely thing is his Rosamund Gray, how much knowledge of the sweetest & the deepest part of our nature [is] in it!'[28]

Moreover, a copy of Lamb's earlier work, *Specimens of English Dramatic Poets, Who Lived about the Time of Shakspeare*, counted as one of Keats' treasured possessions, given to him by his friend Benjamin Bailey, and annotated by both men. One of Keats' most enthusiastic comments comes next to Lamb's footnote comparing Heywood to Shakespeare: 'Shakespeare makes us believe, while we are among his lovely creations, that they are nothing but what we are familiar with, as in dreams new things seem old: but we awake and sigh for the difference'. (*Specimens*, 112)

Keats underlines the comment, and adds his own: 'This is the most acute deep sighted and spiritual piece of criticism ever penned'.[29] Both men, as Helen Haworth has pointed out, 'have similar views of the aesthetic experience, that its beauty is not a surprise, but comfortingly familiar'.[30] Lamb had been developing this aesthetic of the familiar – an experience linked to the homely, the local, the personal – since the mid-1790s and poems such as the original 'Effusion XII'. Keats' enthusiastic annotation shows its appeal for others and hints at its wider influence. The community of authors created through Lamb's extracts in the *Specimens* is extended by the annotations of Bailey and Keats, and given a further aspect when in August 1820 Keats inscribed his copy to Fanny Brawne. Lamb's writing becomes part of another's readings of friendship: a sociability which is both textual and emotional.

Lamb's collection of extracts in *Specimens* parallels his use of antique language, quotation and allusion. Like Keats' playful allusiveness, that 'sense of brotherhood' with other poets noticed by Ricks, it simultaneously allows him security and disguise, a way of putting forward his own allegiances while eluding charges of egotism.[31] In Lamb's case, this may also be traced to his changing views on friendship, looking back to the way in which he had, as early as 1798, been troubled by the way in which 'there must always be, something of **self** in friendship'

(Marrs, I: 134). The use of quotations and extracts seen in *Specimens*, or the allusive, imitative, ironic voice of Elia, allow a way around this – the freedom both to express Lamb's own local and personal allegiances, and escape the confines of the self. This is a means of celebrating the 'home-born Feeling' which, while it steers away from the 'disinterest' which had so troubled Lamb about Godwin's work in the 1790s, also manages to evade a conservative, limiting insistence on one's own tribe or 'little platoon'.[32]

Wordsworth's readings of Lamb

This process of re-reading and re-formulation could also be mutual, as Lamb's challenges encouraged others to re-evaluate their personal associations and ideals. Reading his hidden presence in 'Reflections on Having Left a Place of Retirement' or 'This Lime-tree Bower' allows us to refigure these well-known poems and place them in the context of a larger revisionary dialogue. Similarly, Lamb can also be glimpsed in the background of 'Composed upon Westminster Bridge, Sept. 3, 1803' – literally, because William and Dorothy stayed with the Lambs in 1802, when the poem was composed, and more loosely, in terms of Wordsworth's (temporarily) refigured attitude to the city.[33] Despite Wordsworth's 'sweating' refutation of Lamb's criticism of *Lyrical Ballads*, this poem registers the force of the important and original readings of city experience offered in that 1801 letter. We might even see a delayed echo of Lamb's plea for the emotive power of London – his description of the 'impossibility of being dull' in Fleet Street, and of being moved to 'tears in the motley Strand' (Lucas, I: 267) – in Wordsworth's grand opening:

> Dull would he be of soul who could pass by
> A sight so touching in it's majesty.
> (ll. 2–3; *Poems* 1807, 147)

And although the poem's list of city sights differs from Lamb's invocation of crowded streets, shops, crowds, and play-houses – 'the Sun shining upon houses and pavements' – it is illuminated by the same wonder, the same freshness of vision. Its sixth line might, indeed, carry a friendly allusion to the Lambs' personal associations with the Middle and Inner Temple, the sheltered gardens in the heart of the city:

> Ships, towers, domes, theatres, and temples lie
> Open unto the fields, and to the sky;

All bright and glittering in the smokeless air.
Never did sun more beautifully steep
In his first splendor valley, rock, or hill.
(ll. 6–10; *Poems* 1807, 147)

Wordsworth transforms the city into a rural vision, projecting the 'valley, rock, or hill' onto the urban scene just as Lamb had transformed Wordsworth's mountains into a gilded room. Moreover, the city appears as benign, and its closing image of its 'mighty heart' reinforces this sense of an organic, sympathetic, living entity. It differs markedly from the more obvious readings of the 'vanity and parade' of city life (*Poems* 1807, 413) in the other London poems of 1802 – a reason, perhaps, why Wordsworth fudges the date of its composition as 1803 and separates it from the other London poems in *Poems* 1807. Something different is happening in this evocation of the city, where, for an instant, a humanised vision of London is offered, not deliberately separated from the rural, but 'open unto the fields'. This brief moment of openness and exchange between urban and rural registers a moment of writerly exchange – of reading friendship – as Wordsworth briefly sympathises with Lamb's urban viewpoint, and sees London transfigured.[34]

Lamb's afterlives

I want to end not with a conclusion, but with a suggestion – that we continue to explore our own responses to Charles and Mary Lamb. Much remains to be uncovered. We still await an updating of Lucas' authoritative 1912 edition of their works, for instance. Much rich work could be done on their sociable evening gatherings, those conversations which are recreated in Haydon's or in Hazlitt's excited reminiscences, and which demonstrate Lamb's role as mediator between 'first' and 'second' generation Romantics, his fluid transition between 'Laker' and 'Cockney'. Although I have shown his presence at the heart of the *Lyrical Ballads* years, he was also labelled a 'Cockney scribbler' by *Blackwoods* (November 1820), and this second identity still needs to be fully explored. As I have suggested, there are fascinating overlaps between Lamb's formulation of a sociable reading and writing model, and those of Leigh Hunt and Keats. His pre-Elian journalism – his contributions to *The Reflector, The Examiner,* and *The Champion* – similarly deserves to be examined in detail.

The same is also true of Mary Lamb. In the bicentenary years of her first publications – *Tales from Shakespear* (1807) and *Mrs. Leicester's*

School (1808) – it is time fully to reconsider her nuanced and complex authorial strategies.[35] Although chronology has meant that her writing has largely had to be excluded from this study, her presence is vitally important in the formation of Charles' creative identity – demonstrated by his constant evocation of sisterly affection in *Rosamund Gray* and *John Woodvil* – and I hope that I have suggested her role as inspirer and facilitator of her brother's work, rather than, as some critics have argued, the 'cross' the Christ-like Charles was burdened with.[36]

More generally, I hope that this study has highlighted an alternative narrative of Romanticism. Lamb's sociable textual community attempts to break down rigid definitions and canonical boundaries. His writing of the 1790s therefore not only casts a different light on writers such as Coleridge and Wordsworth, but also brings some lesser-known authors into view – such as Charles Lloyd, or George Dyer. Lamb's inclusive, immersive, friendly attitude towards reading vividly contrasts with the pressing authorial anxiety felt by Wordsworth and Coleridge, and while his meditations on the place of personal feeling incorporate aspects of their thinking in the 1790s, they also continue traditions of sensibility he had encountered in Rousseau, Mackenzie and Bowles. As I suggested in my first chapter, Lamb's appeal to feeling, although eagerly answered by Victorian readers, has proved problematic for twentieth-century critics. It has meant that some of Lamb's more surprising parallels with later writers have been obscured, and I want to close with two speculative examples of the way in which we might read the legacy of his evasive yet highly personal style.

The love of indeterminacy evident in the 1801 letter with which we began this chapter, for instance, as Lamb revels in the concept of losing one's identity both through reading and through 'night-walks' about the 'crowded streets', might be read not only in Romantic terms, but also in the light of preoccupations which have been identified as modern. We might even set Lamb's 'mind that loves to be at home in **Crowds**' (Marrs, I: 277) alongside later nineteenth-century and modernist figurations of the *flâneur*. The joy of *flânerie* is linked to feeling a movement of self-loss and self-discovery, feeling 'at home' in the constantly moving swell of the city crowd: 'Pour le parfait flâneur, pour l'observateur passionné, c'est une immense jouissance que d'élire domicile dans le nombre, dans l'ondoyant dans le mouvement, dans le fugitif et l'infini'.[37]

The figure of the *flâneur* is linked to what Baudelaire identifies as the condition of modernity, characterised as 'le transitoire, le fugitif, le contingent' – something at odds with fixed forms, whether social or literary.[38] The *flâneur* loves the crowd because it allows a mobile identity, subverting established social categories. Yet, like Lamb weeping on his night-walks, the *flâneur* also feels *for* the crowd: as Walter Benjamin comments, 'Empathy is the nature of the intoxication to which the *flâneur* abandons himself in the crowd'.[39] It is both a surrender and a recovery of identity, since alongside this sense of abandonment comes a recognition of the city as a place of feeling and attachment, perhaps even a dwelling-place. For Lamb, the furniture of his rooms becomes interchangeable with the furniture of the city, as in the 1801 letter, where his book case, translated into 'a faithful dog', follows his movements around London (Marrs, I: 267). Similarly, Benjamin notes that for the *flâneur*, nameplates and advertisements are as good as oil-paintings, 'the fire walls are their desks, the newspaper kiosk their library'. Like Lamb evoking his little room in the heart of London, the city becomes both 'a landscape that opens up to him and a parlour that encloses him'.[40]

Lamb's pleasurable loss of identity in the city also functions as an analogy for a different sort of reading practice. 'When I am not walking, I am reading' (Lucas, II: 195), he claims; he is moved 'to shed tears' both by poems such as 'To A Sexton' and by the crowded Strand, and his feeling of being 'impelled' into walking the city streets mirrors his compulsive reading of 'The Ancient Mariner', which 'dragged me along' (Marrs, I: 266). This immersive reading practice finds echoes in Modernist approaches to the reader – Lamb's loss of self-determination in walking and reading, for instance, is strongly paralleled by Woolf, herself a reader of Lamb. Her essay, 'Street-Haunting: A London Adventure', is introduced by Elian comic understatement, as she speaks of going out to buy a pencil: 'as if under cover of this excuse we could indulge safely in the greatest pleasure of town life in winter – rambling the streets of London [...] The evening hour, too, gives us the irresponsibility which darkness and lamplight bestow. We are no longer quite ourselves'.[41]

Woolf is describing the same kind of experience which frightens Wordsworth in his London encounters, as he looks at the blind beggar in *The Prelude*, for example, and feels his identity threatened. But for Woolf, this loss of the self has become a valuable experience, opening limitless interpretative possibilities both for writer and reader.[42]

During the course of her street-hauntings, Woolf enters a bookshop, and begins to think about the way in which second-hand books, those 'wild books, homeless books', give the reader a glimpse of the endless, various narratives in the world: 'The number of books in the world is infinite, and one is forced to glimpse and nod and move on after a moment of talk, a flash of understanding, as, in the street outside, one catches a word in passing and from a chance phrase fabricates a lifetime'.[43]

This recalls Lamb's love of searching among 'the **old** **Book** stalls', and his fascination with the actual processes of reading and book-buying within the city, which is determined by chance. On the one hand, this kind of reading opens up creative response because it allows a glimpse of the infinite, its fragmentary nature allowing imaginative involvement. On the other, the fact that the 'number of books in the world is infinite' is deeply threatening to a writer, thinking about the ways in which he or she will be interpreted and remembered. For both Woolf and Lamb, however, *flânerie* is a form of sympathetic participation which, through immersion in the lives of others, the temporary shedding of their writerly identities, allows them to escape these fears.

Reading these chance finds, or walking the streets, one can 'give oneself the illusion that one is not tethered to a single mind, but can put on briefly for a few minutes the bodies and minds of others...'.[44] Similarly, searching among the old book stalls, one can lose a sense of literary boundaries and the canon – these are places where, as Deidre Lynch has put it, 'the literary heritage has been splintered and reordered by chance'.[45] It is a deeply appropriate image to inform our thinking about Lamb's place in relation to these later writers. The question is not whether we can find direct sources for Baudelaire and Woolf in Lamb – although both certainly knew his works.[46] Rather, it is about how the parallels between these different representations of personal feeling in the contested environment of the city allow us to glimpse a larger narrative which runs in hidden channels between the sensibility of the eighteenth century and the modern urban perspective. These different readings of the city are also linked to different *ways* of reading – an emphasis both on emotional, individual response to the text, and on 'chance' encounters with different, non-canonical works.

Lamb's interest in the 'home-born Feeling' of the personal attachment, so deeply rooted in the ideals of the 1790s, can be suggestively mapped onto a much wider literary and social scene. The 'little smoky room' in the 'Salutation' with which we began Chapter 1 might then – just as Lamb had initially hoped – open into wider meanings.

Notes

Introduction: Placing Lamb

1. For the poem, see Graeme Stones and John Strachan, *Parodies of the Romantic Age*, 5 vols (London, 1999), I: 269–85; for more details on Gillray, see Richard T. Godfrey and Mark Hallett, *James Gillray: The Art of Caricature* (London, 2001).
2. For a full discussion, see Winifred F. Courtney, 'Lamb, Gillray and the Ghost of Edmund Burke', *CLB* 12 (1975), 77–82.
3. Edmund Spenser, Book I: canto i, stanza 20, *The Faerie Queene*, ed. A. C. Hamilton, 2nd edn. rev. eds, Hiroshi Yamashita and Toshiyuki Suzuki (Harlow, 2007), 36.
4. C. C. Southey, ed., *The Life and Correspondence of the Late Robert Southey*, 6 vols (London, 1849), I: 345.
5. Thomas Noon Talfourd, ed., *The Works of Charles Lamb*, 2nd edn, 2 vols (London, 1850), I: 72. Cited by Burton R. Pollin, 'Charles Lamb and Charles Lloyd as Jacobins and Anti-Jacobins', *SiR* (1973), 633–47 (633), who gives a full account of how Lamb has been viewed as apolitical.
6. E. V. Lucas, *The Life of Charles Lamb*, 2 vols (London, 1921), I: 165.
7. See Denys Thompson, 'Our Debt to Lamb', in *Determinations*, ed. F. R. Leavis (London, 1934), 199–217 (205), and Cyril Connolly, *Enemies of Promise*, rev. edn. (Harmondsworth, 1961), 23. Thompson's complaint, to which I will return in Chapter 1, also encompasses readers of Lamb.
8. Joseph E. Riehl, *That Dangerous Figure: Charles Lamb and the Critics* (Columbia, SC, 1998), 93.
9. See also Jane Aaron, 'Charles and Mary Lamb: The Critical Heritage', *CLB* 59 (1987), 73–85.
10. Courtney's work includes a full description of Lamb's work in the *Albion*, and culminates in her strong, politically informed biography, which covers Lamb's life to 1802. See 'New Lamb Texts from the *Albion*', *CLB* 3 (1977), 6–9, and *Young Charles Lamb, 1775–1802* (London, 1982).
11. Jane Aaron, *A Double Singleness: Gender and the Writings of Charles and Mary Lamb* (Oxford, 1991), 6.
12. For an intriguing recent reading of Mary Lamb, see Adriana Craciun, *Fatal Women of Romanticism* (Cambridge, 2002); she has also been the subject of two recent biographies, by Kathy Watson, *The Devil Kissed Her: The Story of Mary Lamb* (London, 2004), and Susan Tyler Hitchcock, *Mad Mary Lamb: Lunacy and Murder in Literary London* (New York, 2005). Lamb's relationship with the *London Magazine* has been re-examined by Mark Parker, *Literary Magazines and British Romanticism* (Cambridge, 2000), and Gerald Monsman, *Charles Lamb as the* London Magazine's 'Elia' (Lewiston, 2003).
13. Karen Fang, 'Empire, Coleridge, and Charles Lamb's Consumer Imagination', *SEL* 43.4 (2003), 815–43.
14. Denise Gigante, *Taste: A Literary History* (New Haven, 2005), 90.
15. Judith Plotz, *Romanticism and the Vocation of Childhood* (New York, 2001), 87–128. Plotz's striking account, however, does have some parallels with

those earlier critics: she presents a duplicitous, at times 'willful, tendentious' Lamb, who (as in Thompson's account) shies away from engagement with real childhood suffering.
16. Anya Taylor, *Bacchus in Romantic England: Writers and Drink, 1780–1830* (New York, 1999).
17. Mary Wedd, 'Dialects of Humour: Lamb and Wordsworth', *CLB* 19 (1977), 46–54 (46).
18. Alison Hickey has very interestingly tackled the importance of Lamb's interlinked readings and friendships in this decade, and offers a fine account of the ways in which his relationship with Coleridge shaped his collaborations with Mary. See Hickey, 'Double Bonds: Charles Lamb's Romantic Collaborations', *ELH* 63.3 (1996), 735–71.
19. Joseph Nicholes, 'Politics by Indirection: Charles Lamb's Seventeenth-Century Renegade, John Woodvil', *WC* 19 (1988), 49–55.
20. Even the sociable underpinnings of Haydon's iconic image of solitude have recently been exposed by Christopher Rovee, in 'Solitude and Sociability: Wordsworth on Helvellyn', *Literature Compass* 1 (1), 2004: doi:10.1111/j.1741-4113.2004.00091.x.
21. Gillian Russell and Clara Tuite, *Romantic Sociability: Social Networks and Literary Culture in Britain, 1770–1840* (Cambridge, 2002), 4.
22. See Nicholas Roe, *Wordsworth and Coleridge: The Radical Years* (Oxford, 1988); *John Keats and the Culture of Dissent* (Oxford, 1997); and *The Politics of Nature: William Wordsworth and Some Contemporaries*, 2nd edn (Basingstoke, 2002). Excellent work has recently been done in uncovering the friendships of the Godwin and Wollstonecraft circle, and patterns of religious affiliation amongst Unitarians such as Anna Letitia Barbauld and John Aikin. Mark Philp and Pamela Clemit, for instance, have untangled the networks of Godwin's acquaintance in their editions of *The Political and Philosophical Writings of Godwin*, 7 vols (London, 1993). Work such as Daniel E. White's fine study *Early Romanticism and Religious Dissent* (Cambridge, 2006)) demonstrates growing scholarly interest in the sociability of the Dissenting circles of the 1790s.
23. Roe, *Politics of Nature*, 27.
24. See Jeffrey N. Cox, *Poetry and Politics in the Cockney School: Keats, Shelley, Hunt and Their Circle* (Cambridge, 1998), 87.
25. See, for instance, Julie A. Carlson, 'Hazlitt and the Sociability of Theatre', 145–65, and Deidre Shauna Lynch, 'Counter Publics: Shopping and Women's Sociability', 211–36, in *Romantic Sociability*, ed. Russell and Tuite.
26. Russell and Tuite, *Romantic Sociability*, 19.
27. See Lucy Newlyn, *Reading, Writing, and Romanticism: The Anxiety of Reception* (Oxford, 2000).
28. Harold Bloom, *A Map of Misreading* (Oxford, 1980), 19.
29. Lucy Newlyn, *Coleridge, Wordsworth, and the Language of Allusion*, 2nd edn (Oxford, 2001), xiii.
30. Ibid., xvi.
31. Paul D. Sheats, *The Making of Wordsworth's Poetry, 1785–1798* (Cambridge, MA, 1973), 163; Thomas McFarland, *Romanticism and the Forms of Ruin: Wordsworth, Coleridge, and Modalities of Fragmentation* (Princeton, 1981), 79; Paul Magnuson, *Coleridge and Wordsworth: A Lyrical Dialogue* (Princeton, 1988), x. In addition, there are a number of studies which deal with the Wordsworth-Coleridge

relationship in detail. An essay by John Beer brilliantly discusses the 'productive' aspects of the friendship, focussing on their fluid, fluent use of 'unstable' water imagery – rivers, streams and brooks – as a way into their thinking about ongoing questions of fluency and stasis, unity and diversity, individuality and mutuality. In some ways my close focus on the room or bower image has been informed by Beer's stimulating account, since it too is a nicely ambiguous emblem, both real and metaphorical. The place it occupies in the thoughts of the friends also shows it to be a way of approaching questions of influence, of mutual reading and writing. See John Beer, 'Coleridge and Wordsworth: Influence and Confluence', in *New Approaches to Coleridge*, ed. Donald Sultana (London, 1981), 192–211. For more discussion of the literary interplay – sometimes possessive, sometimes generous – between Wordsworth and Coleridge see Gene W. Ruoff, *Wordsworth and Coleridge: The Making of the Major Lyrics, 1802–1804* (London, 1989). The focus has been broadened by the nuanced psycho-biographical account of Richard E. Matlak, *The Poetry of Relationship: The Wordsworths and Coleridge, 1797–1800* (Basingstoke, 1997), which restores Dorothy to the dialogue. Similarly, John Worthen's *The Gang: Coleridge, the Hutchinsons and Wordsworths in 1802* (New Haven, 2001) opened the conversation to others.
32. The term 'symbiosis' is from McFarland, *Romanticism and the Forms of Ruin*, 56–103.
33. Christopher Ricks, *Allusion to the Poets* (Oxford, 2002), 147, 90.
34. Ricks, *Allusion to the Poets*, 159.
35. Leigh Hunt, 'Preface', *Foliage; Or, Poems Original and Translated* (London, 1818), 11.
36. Benjamin Robert Haydon, *The Diary of Benjamin Robert Haydon*. ed. by Willard Bissell Pope, 5 vols (Cambridge, MA, 1960), II: 173–6 (176). Although, admittedly, this sociability has its savage side, as a drunken Lamb 'roared out, Diddle iddle don' to mock the 'mild namby pamby opinions' of another guest John Kingston, Wordsworth's superior as a commissioner of stamps (175).

1 *Frendotatoi meta frendous*: Constructing Friendship in the 1790s

1. Joseph Cottle, *Reminiscences of S. T. Coleridge and R. Southey 1847* (Highgate, repr. 1970), 150–1.
2. First draft of 'This Lime-tree Bower' in letter to Robert Southey, 17 July 1797 (Griggs, I: 335–6).
3. I have followed Marrs's scrupulous rendering of the varieties of the Lambs' hands, where large writing is rendered in boldface and large underscored writing in boldface italic. Misspellings have not been corrected.
4. Edmund Burke, *Reflections on the Revolution in France* (London, 1790), 68–9.
5. E. P. Thompson, 'A Compendium of Cliché: The Poet as Essayist,' in *The Romantics: England in a Revolutionary Age* (New York, 1997), 143–55; Jerome Christensen, '"Like a Guilty Thing Surprised": Deconstruction, Coleridge, and the Apostasy of Criticism', *Critical Inquiry* 12 (1986), 769–87; Charles Mahoney, 'The Multeity of Coleridgean Apostasy', in *Irony and Clerisy*, ed., Deborah Elise White, *Romantic*

218 Notes

  Circles Praxis Series (1999) <http://www.rc.umd.edu/praxis/irony/>. (Electronic source, University of Maryland.
6. Christensen, 'Guilty Thing', 772. See also Jerome Christensen, 'Once an Apostate Always an Apostate', *SiR* 21 (1982), 461–4.
7. James K. Chandler, *Wordsworth's Second Nature: A Study of the Poetry and Politics* (Chicago, 1984).
8. This is not to suggest that Godwin did not also have an interest in friendly affections and their connection with social structures; after all, the 'true philosopher' described in *Political Justice* must have witnessed and understood the feelings when 'the soul pours out its inmost self into the bosom of an equal and a friend' (*PJ*, 211).
9. Nigel Leask, *The Politics of Imagination in Coleridge's Critical Thought* (Basingstoke, 1988), 15.
10. See Leask's argument that Wordsworth and Coleridge write within 'a Unitarianism which verged on radical deism,' drawing on 'the ideas of the English 'Commonwealthmen' of the seventeenth century' (*The Politics of Imagination*, 10–11). Nicholas Roe has similarly drawn attention to the connections between Unitarianism and Dissent in both *Wordsworth and Coleridge: The Radical Years*, and *The Politics of Nature*. See also the important earlier work of Kelvin Everest, *Coleridge's Secret Ministry: The Context of the Conversation Poems, 1795–1798* (Brighton, 1979).
11. Everest, *Coleridge's Secret Ministry*, 10.
12. David Fairer, 'Baby Language and Revolution: The Early Poetry of Charles Lloyd and Charles Lamb', *CLB* 74 (1991), 33–52 (35).
13. I, addressed to Erskine, appeared on 1 December; II, to Burke, on 9 December; III, to Priestley, on 11 December; IV, to Fayette, on 15 December; V, to Kosciusko, on 16 December; VI, to Pitt, on 23 December; VII, to Bowles, on 26 December; VIII, to Siddons, on 29 December; IX, to Godwin, on 10 January 1795; X, to Southey, on 14 January 1795; XI, to Sheridan, on 29 January 1795.
14. See descriptions of the celebratory processions in the *Morning Chronicle*, 22 December 1794. For details of the arrests and trials see John Barrell and Jon Mee, eds, *Trials for Treason and Sedition, 1792–1794*, 8 vols (London, 2006), I: xxvii–xxxix.
15. *Morning Chronicle*, 9 December 1794.
16. *Gentleman's Magazine*, December 1834 and May 1838, quoted in Everest, *Coleridge's Secret Ministry*, 18.
17. Edmund Burke, *A Letter from the Right Honourable Edmund Burke to a Noble Lord* (London, 1796), 69–71.
18. *Morning Chronicle*, 10 January 1795.
19. Roe, *The Politics of Nature*, 26.
20. *Lectures 1795*, lxvii. Extending this, Nicola Trott has shown how 'the zeal in promoting an "Answer to Godwin" seen in the 1795 *Lectures* extends more widely, and more diversely, than has been recognized,' tracing a response which stretches from 'Religious Musings' through *Edmund Oliver* to *The Recluse*. See 'The Coleridge Circle and The "Answer to Godwin"', *RES* 41 (1990), 212–29.
21. See reference to Lamb's aunt Sarah, a 'fine *old Christian*', 'finding the door of the chapel in Essex-street open one day – it was in the infancy of that heresy' in 'My Relations', Lucas, II: 81.
22. *Morning Chronicle*, 11 December 1794.

23. Similarly, Coleridge refers to the maddened 'blind multitude' responsible for the riots in his 'Religious Musings', the closing poem of the 1796 volume. He also alludes to the 'Birmingham Riots' in his *Moral and Political Lecture*, in the introduction to *Conciones ad Populum* (*Lectures* 1795, 10, 38) and in the 'Essay on Fasts' (*Watchman*, 53).
24. The crowd assembled outside the Birmingham Hotel, however, were reported to have shouted 'No popery', suggesting a general confusion of religious and political affiliation; houses and property destroyed included those of liberal Anglicans, Congregationalists and Baptists as well as three Unitarian meeting houses. See R. B. Rose, 'The Priestley Riots of 1791', *Past and Present* (1960), 68–88.
25. James Epstein, ' "Equality and No King": Sociability and Sedition: The Case of John Frost', in *Romantic Sociability*, ed. Russell and Tuite, 43–61 (47).
26. For a detailed exploration of the distinction between public and private in the context of the coffee-house, and, more generally, of the Habermasian 'public sphere', see John Barrell, 'Coffee-House Politicians', *Journal of British Studies*, 43 (2004), 206–32.
27. John Binns, *Recollections of the Life of John Binns* (Philadelphia, 1854), 44, cited in Epstein, 'Equality and No King', 45.
28. Though the term 'homosexuality' is of later date, for discussion of anxieties concerning sodomy and the sodomitical identity in the period see Michael McKeon, *The Secret History of Domesticity: Public, Private, and the Division of Knowledge* (Baltimore, MD, 2005), 774–5 n.10. For a more general discussion of sexual anxiety in the 1790s, see Katherine Binhammer, 'The Sex Panic of the 1790s', *Journal of the History of Sexuality*, 6 (1996), 409–35. A good discussion of concepts of manliness and effeminacy is offered by G. J. Barker-Benfield, *The Culture of Sensibility: Sex and Society in Eighteenth-Century Britain* (Chicago, 1992), 104–153.
29. For an excellent discussion see Claudia Johnson, *Equivocal Beings: Politics, Gender, and Sentimentality in the 1790s: Wollstonecraft, Radcliffe, Burney, Austen* (Chicago, 1995), 9.
30. For a detailed discussion of the importance of manliness to Coleridge's concepts of authority, and his negotiation with Burke, see Tim Fulford, *Romanticism and Masculinity: Gender, Politics and Poetics in the Writings of Burke, Coleridge, Cobbett, Wordsworth, De Quincey and Hazlitt* (Basingstoke, 1999), chapter 3.
31. *Morning Chronicle*, 27 December 1794. It is unclear who the author of these verses might have been. On 29 December Coleridge asked Southey, 'I am not, I presume, to attribute some verses addressed to S. T. C. in the M. Chronicle to you – To whom? –' (Griggs, I: 146).
32. Christopher Flint, *Family Fictions: Narrative and Domestic Relations in Britain, 1688–1798* (Stanford, CA, 1998), 251.
33. Lawrence Stone, *The Family, Sex and Marriage in England 1500–1800* (New York, 1977).
34. Peter Laslett, *The World We Have Lost* (New York, 1965).
35. McKeon, *Secret History of Domesticity*, 161.
36. Ruth Perry, *Novel Relations: The Transformation of Kinship in English Literature and Culture 1748–1818* (Cambridge, 2004), 4.
37. Naomi Tadmor, *Family and Friends in Eighteenth-Century England: Household, Kinship, and Patronage* (Cambridge, 2000).

38. Gurion Taussig, *Coleridge and the Idea of Friendship, 1789–1804* (Newark and London, 2002), 16.
39. Mary A. Favret, *Romantic Correspondence: Women, Politics and the Fiction of Letters* (Cambridge, 1993), 28.
40. Penelope J. Corfield and Chris Evans, *Youth and Revolution in the 1790s: Letters of William Pattisson, Thomas Amyot and Henry Crabb Robinson* (Stroud, 1996), 115.
41. Ibid. 130.
42. Ibid. 126. See also Pattison's reference to the 'Dens of Hart Street', a place of brothels and taverns, and, more respectably, to 'the pleasures of conversation' over tea, on 99, 170.
43. Ibid. 95.
44. Ibid. 126.
45. Ibid. 130.
46. Taussig, *Coleridge and the Idea of Friendship*, 17.
47. Courtney, *Young Charles Lamb, 1775–1802* (London, 1982), 91.
48. The phrase comes from William Shenstone's letter lamenting the death of his friend William Somervile, whose drinking he also comments on: 'I loved him for nothing so much as his flocci-nauci-nihili-pili-fication of money'. Shenstone, *The Works in Verse and Prose*, vol. III (Edinburgh, 1770) 47. Lamb may have been attracted to the gossipy *Letters* because of their frequent emphasis on the importance of Shenstone's friendships and shared reading (especially with the writer Richard Graves, author of *The Spiritual Quixote* (1773)).
49. Tim Fulford, *Coleridge's Figurative Language* (Basingstoke, 1991), 4.
50. Enclosed in letter to Southey, 1 September 1794; Griggs, I: 100.
51. Leask, 'Pantisocracy and the Politics of the 'Preface' to *Lyrical Ballads*', in *Reflections of Revolution: Images of Romanticism* ed. by Alison Yarrington and Kelvin Everest (London, 1993), 39–58 (39).
52. See also Maurice W. Kelley, 'Thomas Cooper and Pantisocracy', *MLN* 45 (1930), 218–20.
53. William Frend, *Peace and Union Recommended to the Associated Bodies of Republicans and Anti-Republicans* (St. Ives, 1793).
54. Frend, *An Account of the Proceedings in the University of Cambridge against William Frend for Publishing a Pamphlet Intitled, Peace and Union & C.* (Cambridge, 1793).
55. Roe, *Wordsworth and Coleridge: The Radical Years*, 95.
56. Burke, *Reflections*, 49.
57. Ibid. 48. Burke's defence of the patriarchal family is discussed in detail by Eileen Hunt Botting, *Family Feuds: Wollstonecraft, Burke, and Rousseau on the Transformation of the Family* (Albany, NY, 2006), who places it alongside the theories of Rousseau and Wollstonecraft, suggesting how, despite their differences, they shared a belief in the family as the foundation of the state, morally and socially. See also McKeon, *Secret History of Domesticity*, 355–6.
58. Burke, *Reflections*, 112.
59. Ibid. 105, 106.
60. Thomas Paine, *Rights of Man: Being an Answer to Mr. Burke's Attack on the French Revolution* (London, 1791), 21. The implications of the 'textual battle' between Burke and Paine are discussed by John C. Whale, 'Literal and Symbolic Representations: Burke, Paine and the French Revolution',

History of European Ideas, 16 (1993), 343–9. Whale points out the limits of Paine's literalism and traces the power of Burke's symbolism through Romanticism.
61. Paine, *Rights of Man,* 69.
62. Ibid. 70.
63. Ibid. 18, 52.
64. Marilyn Butler, 'Godwin, Burke, and *Caleb Williams', Essays in Criticism,* XXXII (1982), 237–57 (244).
65. George Burnett to Nicholas Lightfoot, 22 October 1796, MS Eng. Lett. c.453, fol. 198r, Bodleian Library. Quoted by Roe, *Politics of Nature,* 157, and Taussig, *Coleridge and the Idea of Friendship,* 126. Thanks to Dr. Taussig for discussing this with me.
66. Burke, *Reflections,* 286.
67. The poem was extensively revised over the next three years, appearing in different versions in the 1796, 1797 and 1803 editions of *Poems on Various Subjects.*
68. Aaron, *A Double Singleness,* 135.
69. Note the 'Preface' to Joshua Toulmin, *The Immutability of God, and the Trials of Christ's Ministry; Represented in Two Sermons, Preached at Essex Chapel, in the Strand, March 30, and April 6, 1794* (London, 1794). Toulmin emphasises that, 'The second was delivered before the great and excellent Dr. Priestley, on the day preceding his leaving the capital of this kingdom to go a voluntary exile into America.'
70. Thomas Belsham, *Memoirs of the Late Reverend Theophilus Lindsey* (London, 1812), 305.
71. Theophilus Lindsey, *A Sermon Preached at the Opening of the Chapel in Essex-House, Essex-Street, on Sunday, April 17, 1774* (London, 1774), 14.
72. John Disney, *A Defence of Public or Social Worship. A Sermon, Preached in the Unitarian Chapel, in Essex-Street, London; on Sunday, 4 December 1791* (London, 1792), 13.
73. For example, Toulmin emphasises the 'Love and Friendship of Christ' in *The Practical Efficacy of the Unitarian Doctrine Considered* (London, 1796).
74. Joseph Priestley, *An Answer to Mr. Paine's Age of Reason [...] With a Preface by Theophilus Lindsey* (London, 1795), xviii.
75. The Priestley work to which Lamb refers is by Richard Price and Priestley, *A Free Discussion of the Doctrines of Materialism and Philosophical Necessity, in a Correspondence between Dr. Price and Dr. Priestley,* ed. J. Priestley (London, 1778).
76. Taussig, '"Lavish Promises": Coleridge, Charles Lamb, and Charles Lloyd, 1794–1798', *Romanticism,* 6.1 (2000), 78–97 (78).
77. There is a wide range of secondary literature placing sensibility in the context of eighteenth-century thought. Particularly relevant to this section is R. S. White's *Natural Rights and the Birth of Romanticism in the 1790s* (Basingstoke, 2005), a thorough and excellent new reading of the ways in which the ideas, literature and politics of the 1790s draw on a long 'tradition of sentimental benevolence', positioned in relation to Hobbes, Locke, Hutcheson and Smith as well as writers such as Oliver Goldsmith, Henry Mackenzie, and Robert Merry. A lively account of sensibility's debt to Newton and Locke is given by Jerome J. McGann, *The Poetics of Sensibility: A Revolution in Literary Style* (Oxford, 1996). An overview of the relationship between Locke,

Shaftesbury, Hume and Smith has also been given by Chris Jones, *Radical Sensibility: Literature and Ideas in the 1790s* (London, 1993), 1–58, and covered by Janet M. Todd, *Sensibility: An Introduction* (London, 1986) 23–8, and Adela Pinch, 'Sensibility', in *Romanticism: An Oxford Guide*, ed., Nicholas Roe (Oxford, 2005), 49–60. For a detailed and subtle exploration of specific engagement between Romantic writers and eighteenth century thought see Tim Milnes, *Knowledge and Indifference in English Romantic Prose* (Cambridge, 2003).

78. See Isabel Rivers, *Reason, Grace, and Sentiment: A Study of the Language of Religion and Ethics in England, 1660–1780*, 2 vols. Vol. 2: *Shaftesbury to Hume* (Cambridge, 1991).
79. Anthony Ashley Cooper, Third Earl of Shaftesbury, *Characteristics of Men, Manners, Opinions, Times*, ed., Lawrence E. Klein, Cambridge Texts in the History of Philosophy (Cambridge, 1999), 202. For a good discussion of the 'ambiguity of sympathy in Shaftesbury's account' as he separates this polite 'Company' from society at large, see John Mullan, *Sentiment and Sociability: The Language of Feeling in the Eighteenth Century* (Oxford, 1988), 29.
80. T. A. Roberts, *The Concept of Benevolence: Aspects of Eighteenth-Century Moral Philosophy* (London, 1973), 2–26.
81. Hutcheson did attempt to address the nature of self-love, but firmly distinguished it from his concept of benevolence as a natural affection: the two could *sometimes* be interlinked, but benevolence did not stem from self-love. Discussed by Roberts, *Concept of Benevolence*, 15–17.
82. Bernard Mandeville, *The Fable of the Bees: Or, Private Vices, Publick* [sic] *Benefits. With an Essay on Charity and Charity-Schools. And a Search into the Nature of Society*, 3rd edn (London, 1724), 427–8.
83. Rivers has meticulously shown how Shaftesbury's thinking was taken in different directions through the eighteenth century, whether that was through an attempt to Christianise his thinking, as with Bishop Butler, or through the scepticism of Hume. Rivers, *Reason, Grace, and Sentiment, 1660–1780, Vol 2*.
84. David Hume, *A Treatise of Human Nature: A Critical Edition*, ed., David Fate Norton and Mary J. Norton, 2 vols (Oxford, 2007), I: 164–5. Again, Milnes's study, *Knowledge and Indifference*, covers the Romantic response to Hume in detail.
85. Hume, *Treatise of Human Nature*, I: 175. See Mullan, *Sentiment and Sociability: The Language of Feeling in the Eighteenth Century*, 39.
86. 'My Own Life', David Hume and J. C. A. Gaskin, *Principal Writings on Religion Including Dialogues Concerning Natural Religion; and, the Natural History of Religion* (Oxford, 1998), 9.
87. See James Chandler, 'The Emergence of Sentimental Probability', in *The Age of Cultural Revolutions: Britain and France, 1750–1820*, ed., Colin Jones and Dror Wahrman (Berkeley, 2002), 137–70 (138).
88. The difference has been widely discussed. McGann sees a clear distinction: 'sensibility emphasises the mind in the body, sentimentality the body in the mind' (McGann, *Poetics of Sensibility*, 7). Todd suggests that 'sentiment' is dependent upon 'moral reflection' and thought, and 'sensibility' is 'an innate sensitiveness or susceptibility', but points out the terms' interchangeability (Todd, *Sensibility*, 9). Chandler opts simply for the term 'sentimental', arguing that this term with its 'decidedly modern origins' of around 1740 is better suited to a discussion of an eighteenth-century movement (Chandler, 'The Emergence of Sentimental Probability', 139). I, however,

use the term 'sensibility' in discussion of Coleridge and Lamb's own writing, since it is this term which appears in their own work.
89. Chandler, 'The Emergence of Sentimental Probability', 138.
90. The force of this belief in natural benevolence is discussed by R. S. White, *Natural Rights*, especially chapter 2, and R. F. Brissenden, *Virtue in Distress* (London and Basingstoke, 1974), 22–55.
91. Barker-Benfield, *The Culture of Sensibility*, 216.
92. Henry Fielding, *The History of Tom Jones, a Foundling*, 4 vols (London, 1749), I: 138. See Barker-Benfield's discussion of this passage, *The Culture of Sensibility*, 254.
93. Henry Mackenzie, *The Man of Feeling* (London, 1771), 96–7.
94. Stones and Strachan, *Parodies of the Romantic Age*, I: 273.
95. Ibid.
96. Chris Jones makes this point in *Radical Sensibility*, 8; see also R. S. White, *Natural Rights*, 77–84. Gregory Dart has expanded the idea to show the pervasive influence of Rousseau's confessional language of the heart in Romanticism in his *Rousseau, Robespierre and English Romanticism* (Cambridge, 1999), 11–13. Dart argues that, mediated through Robespierre, Rousseauvian radicalism can be traced through the rhetoric strategies, particularly the autobiographical and confessional voices, of Godwin, Wollstonecraft, Malthus, Wordsworth, and Hazlitt. Indeed, Godwin began a translation of Rousseau's *Confessions* in December 1789 for George Robinson, working on it again in 1792, 1801 and 1804, but it was never completed. See Pamela Clemit, 'Self Analysis as Social Critique: The Autobiographical Writings of Godwin and Rousseau', *Romanticism*, 11: 2 (2005), 161–80, for a discussion of Rousseau's influence on Godwin. Thanks to Dr. David O'Shaughnessy for his discussion of this point.
97. Edmund Burke, *A Letter from Mr. Burke, to a Member of the National Assembly* (London, 1791), 37
98. Ibid, 37. 'Elegy on finding a young THRUSH in the Street, who escaped from the Writer's Hand, as she was bringing him home, and, falling down the Area of a House, could not be found', Helen Maria Williams, *Julia, a Novel; Interspersed with Some Poetical Pieces*, 2 vols (London, 1790), II: 27.
99. Mary Wollstonecraft, *A Vindication of the Rights of Men, a Letter to E. Burke Occasioned by His Reflections on the Revolution in France*, 2nd edn (London, 1790), 6.
100. Paine, *Rights of Man*, 26.
101. See Jones, *Radical Sensibility*, 15.
102. For a detailed discussion, see Richard C. Allen, 'Charles Lloyd, Coleridge, and *Edmund Oliver*', *SiR* 35 (1996), 245–94.
103. David Hartley, *Observations on Man, His Frame, His Duty and His Expectations*, 3 vols (1749; London, 1791), II: 285–6.
104. Hartley, *Observations*, II: 287.
105. As recounted in a letter by C. V. Le Grice, published by Richard Madden, 'The Old Familiar Faces: An Essay in the Light of Some Recently Discovered Documents of Charles Valentine LeGrice Referring to Lamb, Coleridge and Wordsworth', *CLB* (1974), 113–21 (118).
106. George Dyer, *A Dissertation on the Theory and Practice of Benevolence* (London, 1795).

107. Dyer, *An Inquiry into the Nature of Subscription to the Thirty-Nine Articles* (London, 1790), 6.
108. Dyer, *A Dissertation on Benevolence*, 'Preface'. For the full poem see William Lisle Bowles, *Sonnets, with Other Poems*, 3rd edn (Bath, 1794), 49–55.
109. Dyer, *Dissertation*, 25.
110. R. Brimley Johnson, *Christ's Hospital, Recollections of Lamb, Coleridge, and Leigh Hunt* (London, 1896), xii.
111. 'On CHRIST'S HOSPITAL and the Character of the CHRIST'S HOSPITAL BOYS', published in the *Gentleman's Magazine*, June 1813, and reprinted in Lamb's *Works* (1818) under the title, 'Recollections of Christ's Hospital', Lucas, I: 141.
112. See, for example, J. E. Morpurgo ed., *The Autobiography of Leigh Hunt* (London, 1948).
113. Hunt, *Autobiography*, 83. As Sarah Moss has shown, the school hierarchies echoed those of eighteenth and nineteenth-century ships, in keeping with the school's strong naval connection. Sarah Moss, ' "The Bounds of His Great Empire": The "Ancient Mariner" and Coleridge at Christ's Hospital', *Romanticism*, 8.1 (2002), 49–61.
114. See James Treadwell, 'Impersonation and Autobiography in Lamb's Christ's Hospital Essays', *SiR*, 37.4 (1998), 499–521.
115. Indeed, Allen, who went up to Balliol after Christ's Hospital, was responsible for introducing Southey to his school-friend Coleridge. For an account of Allen's role as a catalyst for the Pantisocratic scheme see Lynda Pratt and David Denison, 'The Language of the Southey-Coleridge Circle', *Language Sciences*, 22 (2000), 401–22.
116. Joshua Toulmin, 'An Essay on the Grounds of Love to Christ', appendix to Toulmin, *The Practical Efficacy of the Unitarian Doctrine Considered*.
117. Alexander Pope, *An Essay on Man*. ed., Maynard Mack, *The Twickenham Edition of the Poems of Alexander Pope*, III: i (London, 1950), 163–4.
118. In what Carl Woodring sees as a dissociation between Bowles and the doctrine of universal brotherhood, the 'Brother' of line four is changed to a 'mourner' in the 1796 version. See Woodring, *Politics in the Poetry of Coleridge* (Madison, 1961) 106–7. This anxiety about how emotions might be directed fits in with more general questions concerning the self-indulgence of sensibility, such as Burke's condemnation of Rousseau as a 'hard-hearted father, of fine general feelings'. Burke, *Letter to a Member of the National Assembly*, 37.
119. *Morning Chronicle*, 14 December 1795.
120. Adela Pinch, *Strange Fits of Passion: Epistemologies of Emotion, Hume to Austen* (Stanford, CA, 1996), 11.
121. McGann, *Poetics of Sensibility*, 4. He points out that cultural studies and feminist criticism have drawn attention to such forgotten writing, but has a tendency to 'evade' aesthetic questions (5), a lack which critics such as Pinch have since attempted to rectify.
122. Chandler, 'The Emergence of Sentimental Probability', 138; McGann, *Poetics of Sensibility*, 4.
123. Chandler, 'The Emergence of Sentimental Probability', 139.

124. See, for example, Nanora Sweet and Julie Melnyk, eds, *Felicia Hemans: Reimagining Poetry in the Nineteenth Century* (New York, 2001). Readings of Smith have emphasised her subtle re-readings and successful marketing of the mode of sensibility, especially Sarah MacKenzie Zimmerman, *Romanticism, Lyricism, and History* (New York, 1999). For a cogent overview of the connections between Romantic and Victorian uses of sensibility and sentimentality, see 'Rethinking Victorian Sentimentality,' ed., Nicola Bown, *19: Interdisciplinary Studies in the Long Nineteenth Century*, 4 (2007), <http://www.19.bbk.ac.uk/issue4>.
125. Nicola Bown, 'Introduction' (5), and Emma Mason, 'Feeling Dickensian feeling' (16), in 'Rethinking Victorian Sentimentality,' ed. Bown, *19*, 4 (2007).
126. Augustine Birrell, *Obiter Dicta* (London, 1884), 102–3; Algernon Charles Swinburne, *Miscellanies* (London, 1886), 195.
127. Alfred Ainger, *Charles Lamb* (London, 1882), 119.
128. *The Examiner*, 21 and 28 March 1819, 187–9; 204–6 (206).
129. Letter to W. B. Donne, 14 March 1878. Riehl, *That Dangerous Figure: Charles Lamb and the Critics*, 52.
130. Thomas Carlyle, *Reminiscences*, ed., James Anthony Froude, 2 vols (London, 1881), 65.
131. Thompson, 'Our Debt to Lamb', 205. See Riehl, *That Dangerous Figure: Charles Lamb and the Critics*, 99–100.
132. Riehl, *That Dangerous Figure: Charles Lamb and the Critics*, 100.
133. McGann, *Poetics of Sensibility*, 8.
134. Mason, 'Feeling Dickensian feeling', 16.
135. Thomas Holcroft, *The Adventures of Hugh Trevor* (London, 1794), 28.
136. Anonymous, *An Asylum for Fugitive Pieces, in Prose and Verse*, 2nd edn, 3 vols (London, 1795), III: 58.
137. John Taylor, *Verses on Various Occasions* (London, 1795), 53.
138. Charles Valentine Le Grice, *The Tineum. Containing Estianomy, or the Art of Stirring a Fire: The Icead, a Mock-Heroic Poem: An Imitation of Horace* (Cambridge, 1794), 45. Le Grice, described by Lamb as an 'equivocal wag', was a direct contemporary of Coleridge at Christ's Hospital, and senior Grecian. Coleridge overtly dismissed Le Grice's book as a jumble of 'quaint stupidity', but the suggestion that he may have read and been following Le Grice's literary career is supported by the inclusion of a notebook entry drawn from the same page of the *British Critic*, May 1795, as a review of *The Tineum*; the same issue also carried a brief notice of Coleridge's *Fall of Robespierre*. See *Notebooks*, I: 48.
139. 'Sonnet, to Mrs. Siddons', *Poems, by Helen Maria Williams* (London, 1786), 179–80.
140. McGann, *Poetics of Sensibility*, 140.
141. First published in the *European Magazine*, March 1787 (XI: 202). *Early Poems*, 396.
142. *Morning Chronicle*, 29 December 1794. Published with some minor changes (the 'Warlock hags' become simply 'those hags', for instance) in *Poems* 1796 and *Poems* 1797, attributed in both instances to Lamb. However, by the 1803 edition of *Poems on Various Subjects*, where Lamb's work does not appear at all, this poem is attributed solely to Coleridge.

226 Notes

143. William Lisle Bowles, *Fourteen Sonnets, Elegiac and Descriptive. Written During a Tour* (Bath, 1789), 9.
144. Williams, *Poems*, 179–80.
145. Roy Park, 'Lamb, Shakespeare, and the Stage', *Shakespeare Quarterly* 33 (1982), 164–77 (164).
146. James Beattie, *The Minstrel; or, the Progress of Genius. A Poem. Book the First.* (London, 1771), 24.
147. Lamb goes on, famously, to criticise 'the cursed Barbauld crew', and their educational books for children – such as Barbauld's *Early Lessons for Children* (1778). Yet Lamb himself, as we shall see, was deeply influenced by the same Unitarian tenets promoted by Barbauld. His reaction may in fact be one of literary rivalry, given that he and Mary were just about to publish their own children's books with Godwin.
148. 'On Christ's Hospital, and the Character of the Christ's Hospital Boys', Lucas, I:165. Other books read and circulated there included what Lamb described as 'classics of our own...*Peter Wilkins* – *The adventures of the Hon. Captain Robert Boyle* – *The Fortunate Blue Coat Boy* – and the like.' ('Christ's Hospital Five and Thirty Years Ago'; Lucas, II: 21) See Reggie Watters, '"We Had Classics of Our Own": Charles Lamb's Schoolboy Reading', *CLB* 104 (1998), 114–28. Another pupil, almost a contemporary of Lamb, remembered how greatly prized stories such as 'Jack the Giant Killer' and 'Valentine and Orson' were, contributing to 'wild and romantic notions among the boys'. See George Wickham, *Recollections of a Blue-Coat Boy, or, a View of Christ's Hospital* (London, 1829), 27.
149. See Pinch's discussion of Wordsworth's sonnet in *Strange Fits of Passion*, 81.
150. Aaron, *A Double Singleness*. See especially chapters 1 and 5.
151. Aaron, *A Double Singleness*, 94–5.
152. Clare's appropriation of the Byronic identity, which began in Matthew Allen's High Beech asylum in Epping and continued during his time at Northampton General Asylum, has similarly been seen as a response to his literary and social disenfranchisement; cornered by his own categorisation as a 'peasant poet' and his loss of status in the literary market-place, he adopts a disruptive and deliberately misogynistic voice in 'Don Juan'. See Jason N. Goldsmith, 'The Promiscuity of Print: John Clare's "Don Juan" And the Culture of Romantic Celebrity', *SEL* 46 (2006), 803–32.

2 Rewritings of Friendship, 1796–1797

1. 'Sonnet VIII. To the River Itchin, near Winton', Bowles, *Fourteen Sonnets*, 9.
2. 2 Samuel 12: 3, *King James Version*. Thanks to Stephen Bernard for his comments on this.
3. See Hickey's excellent discussion of this exchange in 'Double Bonds: Charles Lamb's Romantic Collaborations', 740–1.
4. Several critics have identified sympathetically with Lamb; Blunden, for example, praising the 'quiet significance' of Lamb's sonnets, in contrast to Coleridge's 'loud' rewritings, and casting Coleridge as 'mentor and almost tormentor' (Edmund Blunden, *Charles Lamb and His Poetic Contemporaries* (Cambridge, 1937), 46–7). However, some have taken a

staunchly pro-Coleridgean line, see, for example, B. J. Sokol, 'Coleridge on Charles Lamb's Poetic Craftsmanship', *English Studies*, 71 (1990), 29–34.
5. Duncan Wu, 'Unpublished Drafts of Sonnets by Lamb and Favell', *CLB* 75 (1991), 98–101.
6. See Lucy Newlyn's excellent discussion of this in *Reading, Writing, and Romanticism: The Anxiety of Reception* (Oxford, 2000), 49–85.
7. Rachel Crawford, *Poetry, Enclosure, and the Vernacular Landscape, 1700–1830* (Cambridge, 2002), 226.
8. In the case of 'Effusion XII', the original version of the poem has generally been taken to be the version which appears in the 1797 edition of *Poems*. However, Rosenbaum and White list, and reproduce, an imperfect manuscript version of the poem in Lamb's hand, dated 1796, which is probably the original. *Index of English Literary Manuscripts*, vol. 4. 1800–1900, pt. 2. Hardy – Lamb, ed., Barbara Rosenbaum and Pamela White (London, 1982) pl. 9b, 688. The MS, watermarked 1795, is in the Victoria University Library, Toronto. See note 25 below).
9. The bottom of the manuscript is torn away, so the last line of the sonnet has been supplied from the versions in the 1797 edition of *Poems* and Lamb's 1818 *Works*. The 1797 version incorporates some aspects of Coleridge's reworking, retaining, for instance, 'o'er-shadowing' in line 2, whereas the 1818 version follows the 1796 text more closely.
10. The Rugby manuscript copy (Rugby MS, 43/f 18r. Facsimile in British Library RP179A) is almost identical to this version, and bears no marks of revision; Coleridge's alterations are therefore complete before transcription.
11. Crawford, *Poetry, Enclosure, and the Vernacular Landscape*, 227.
12. Spenser, Book II: canto xii, *The Faerie Queene*, ed. Hamilton, 279.
13. See his letters to Cottle, by turns requesting supplies for his house – 'a pair of slippers; a cheese toaster; two large tin spoons' (Griggs, I: 160) – and defensively promising the arrival of his poems, 'The Printer may depend on copy by to-morrow' (Griggs, I: 173). For more details on the move to Clevedon see Cottle, *Reminiscences*, 40–2.
14. See Everest, *Coleridge's Secret Ministry*, 69–96.
15. Burke, *Reflections*, 69.
16. Everest, *Coleridge's Secret Ministry*, 41.
17. Rugby MS, 61/f 26r.
18. For more on the Eolian harp as symbol, see Paul Cheshire, 'The Eolian Harp', *Coleridge Bulletin*, 17 (2001), 1–26.
19. See McGann, *Poetics of Sensibility*, 20.
20. Everest, *Coleridge's Secret Ministry*; Leask, *Politics of Imagination*; White, *Early Romanticism and Religious Dissent*.
21. Leask, *Politics of Imagination*, 12, 13.
22. Lynda Pratt, 'Interaction, Reorientation, and Discontent', *N&Q* 47 (245) (2000), 314–21 (318).
23. White, *Early Romanticism and Religious Dissent*, 148.
24. Jon Mee, *Romanticism, Enthusiasm, and Regulation: Poetics and the Policing of Culture in the Romantic Period* (Oxford, 2003), 160.
25. The Coleridge Collection, Part III: The Coleridge Circle, S MS F4.5., Victoria University Library, Toronto. The last lines are added from the version included as 'Sonnet II' in *Poems* 1797, 218.

26. The 'friend' was Fulwood Smerdon, Coleridge's father's successor as vicar of Ottery, about whom Coleridge had previously been less than complimentary; as Mays points out, the poem is prompted as much by 'partial self-identification as by former friendship' (Mays, I: i, 149).
27. E. S. Shaffer, 'The Hermeneutic Community: Coleridge and Schleiermacher', in *The Coleridge Connection: Essays for Thomas McFarland*, eds, Richard Gravil and Molly Lefebure (Basingstoke, 1990), 200–29 (205).
28. Ibid., 220. See Norman Fruman's *Coleridge, The Damaged Archangel* (London, 1972) for a vehement argument in opposition.
29. Newlyn, *Reading, Writing, and Romanticism*, 51; Fulford, *Coleridge's Figurative Language*, 2, 5.
30. Lamb's comments foreshadow recent analyses of Coleridge's compulsive revisionary practice as indicative of his 'conscious but doomed search for autonomy, for a stable "will" or "self"'. See, for instance, Zachary Leader, *Revision and Romantic Authorship* (Oxford, 1996), 135, or Seamus Perry's comments on Lamb's 'profound knowledge of his friend's philosophical compulsions', in Perry, *Coleridge and the Uses of Division* (Oxford, 1999), 172–3.
31. Mary Jacobus, *Romanticism, Writing and Sexual Difference: Essays on the Prelude* (Oxford, 1989), 147.
32. Described by Rosenbaum, *Index of Literary Manuscripts*, 145, British Library facsimile RP395; now in the Robert H. Taylor collection, Princeton. See my article '"Sweet is Thy Sunny Hair": an unpublished poem by Charles Lamb', *CLB* 127 (2004), 54–6, for further discussion of the dating of this poem.
33. For an interesting discussion of the novel's form, see Nicola J. Watson, *Revolution and the Form of the British Novel, 1790–1825: Intercepted Letters, Interrupted Seductions* (Oxford, 1994), 25.
34. Lamb's subversion of the myth of solitary inspiration embodied by Coleridge's Chatterton is furthered by his own participation in another publication of 1796, *Original Letters, & c, of Sir John Falstaff and His Friends*. Although it was published under the name of James White, Lamb's friend from Christ's Hospital, Lamb certainly had a hand in the book, and promoted it energetically amongst his friends. The playful book parodies contemporary forgers such as Chatterton and William Henry Ireland, author of the hoax Shakespeare play *Vortigern* (1796), to whom it is dedicated. It similarly urges a sociable, friendly approach to reading and writing. See David Chandler, 'Lamb, Falstaff's Letters, and Landor's Citation and Examination of William Shakespeare', *CLB* 131 (2005), 76–85, for a discussion of its afterlife. See also Chandler's '"There Never Was His Like!": A Biography of James White (1775–1820),' *CLB* 128 (2004), 78–95.
35. In July 1796, 'We were two pretty babes, the youngest she'; in December 1796, 'To the Poet Cowper'; in January 1797, 'To Sara and her Samuel'; in March 1797, 'To a Young Lady'; in October 1797, 'Sonnet to a Friend', and 'To a Friend'; in December 1797, 'The Lord of Life shakes off his drowsihed'.
36. Geoffrey Carnall, 'The Monthly Magazine', *RES* 5 (1954), 158–64 (158).
37. See Marilyn Butler, 'Culture's Medium: The Role of the Review', in *Cambridge Companion to British Romanticism*, ed, Stuart Curran (Cambridge, 1993), 120–76 (126).
38. Lindsey, *A Sermon Preached at the Opening of the Chapel in Essex-House, Essex-Street, on Sunday, April 17, 1774*, 14.

39. First published in the *Monthly Magazine*, 7 (April 1799) 231–2. Reprinted in *The Poems of Anna Letitia Barbauld*, eds, William McCarthy and Elizabeth Kraft (Athens, Georgia, 1994), 132–3, from the MS – I have followed their version.
40. See also Lisa Vargo, 'The Case of Anna Letitia Barbauld's "to Mr C[olerid]ge"', *CLB* 102 (1998), 55–63.

3 The 'Day of Horrors'

1. Demonstrated by the lack of apprenticeship records for her assistant, who was probably a workhouse girl, not an independent worker bound over by her parents. See Aaron, *A Double Singleness*, 68, and Leslie Joan Friedman, *Mary Lamb: Sister, Seamstress, Murderer, Writer*, PhD thesis (Stanford, CA, 1976), 143.
2. Thomas Noon Talfourd, *Memoirs of Charles Lamb* ed., Percy Fitzgerald (London, 1892), 22.
3. William Bent, *Eight Meteorological Journals 1793–1804* (London, 1804), 20.
4. *Morning Chronicle*, 26 September, 1796; cited by Marrs, I: 45.
5. Ibid.
6. Nigel Walker, *Crime and Insanity in England, the Historical Perspective* (Edinburgh, 1968). Cases abound in the 1780s and 1790s of acquittal due to temporary mental illness: once a jury had brought in a verdict of 'lunacy' or 'madness', offenders were either sent to a secure hospital such as the Bethlem Royal Hospital ('Bedlam' or 'Bethlem'), or, if their families could offer sufficient protection, they could be cared for at home. Accounts of Mary's treatment in madhouses may be found in Aaron, *A Double Singleness*, 97–103, and Hitchcock, *Mad Mary Lamb*.
7. Mary's illness has, retrospectively, been diagnosed as manic depression, or bi-polar disorder, by critics such as Mary Blanchard Balle, 'Mary Lamb: Her Mental Health Issues', *CLB* 93 (1996), 2–11, who gives a full account of Mary's capacity for self-harm and harm to others during certain very clearly defined episodes of mania. However, such retrospective diagnoses have been challenged by Craciun in *Fatal Women of Romanticism*, who complains that narratives of the matricide 'cushion the impact of the violence by inserting mental illness, insanity, madness as the true agent of the deed' (35). However, Craciun's insistence on the 'unhelpfulness' of reading Mary Lamb's violence in medical terms overlooks the way in which the writing identity of both Mary and Charles is shaped by their consciousness of her illness, and their resourceful ways of coping with its episodic returns as an inescapable part of their lives. Her implicitly critical comments that Mary 'was repeatedly removed from their home' (26) obscure the immense, mutual effort it took to reconstruct and sustain a sense of 'home' for the Lambs post-1796. Moreover, while her argument that Mary's actions actively resist a persistent myth of 'women's natural nonviolence and benevolence' is a welcome re-reading of later critical viewpoints, Charles' own concept of benevolence had never been premised on a specifically feminine ideal, but, rather, on a Unitarian and Hartleian-inflected attention to the homely as model for social relations – which he struggled to reconstruct in the wake of

the matricide. See also Bonnie Woodbery, 'The Mad Body as the Text of Culture in the Writings of Mary Lamb', *SEL* 39 (1999), 659–74.
8. Craciun, *Fatal Women of Romanticism*, 27–46.
9. Reeve Parker, *Coleridge's Meditative Art* (Ithaca, NY, 1975), 30.
10. This text is from the first manuscript version of the poem, sent to Southey on 17 July 1797 (Griggs, I: 334–6), reprinted in Mays, II: i, 480–7.
11. As Parker also points out, a pun on Lamb's name may also be at work here (*Meditative Art*, 39). Cf. Coleridge's letter to John Rickman, 14 March 1804, 'I will be with you by a quarter before 7 infallibly; and the Virgin Mary with the uncrucified Lamb will come with me' (Griggs, II: 1090).
12. Priestley, *The Doctrine of Philosophical Necessity* (London, 1777), vii.
13. Aaron, *A Double Singleness*, 136.
14. Jane Stabler, 'Space for Speculation: Coleridge, Barbauld, and the Poetics of Priestley', *Samuel Taylor Coleridge and the Sciences of Life*, ed., Nicholas Roe (Oxford, 2001), 175–206 (175, 184).
15. 'To Mr. S. T. Coleridge', l. 34; McCarthy and Kraft, *Poems of Barbauld*, 132–3.
16. Letter of 10 May 1796; first printed by Warren E. Gibbs, 'An Unpublished Letter from John Thelwall to Samuel Taylor Coleridge', *Modern Language Review* 25 (1930), 85–90.
17. Thelwall, *The Tribune, a periodical publication, consisting chiefly of the political lectures of J. Thelwall. Taken in short-hand by W. Ramsey, and revised by the lecturer*, 3 vols (London, 1795), I: 19.
18. Lamb's scepticism about this ideal emerges in his doubtful response to these agricultural schemes – 'Is it a farm you have got? & what does your worship know about farming?' (Marrs, I: 87) – and his repeated attempts (which will be discussed further in the final chapter) to break down the link between nature and the ideal: 'Remember, you are not in Arcadia when you are in the west of England, and they may catch infection from the world without visiting the metropolis' (Marrs, I: 58).
19. NYPL Berg Collection, Copy 6, Mays, I: ii, 1281.
20. Walter Jackson Bate, *Coleridge* (London, 1969), 49.
21. Bate's idea is picked up by numerous critics, including Eugene Stelzig, who writes that both Coleridge and Wordsworth rely on the 'rhetorical co-opting or subordination of a person addressed in a poem to fit the poet's psychic needs or to reify his self-image' ('Coleridge in *The Prelude*: Wordsworth's Fiction of Alterity', *WC* 18: 1 (1987), 23–7 (25)).
22. The connection is made by John Beer, in his edition of *Poems, Samuel Taylor Coleridge* (London, 1993), 96.
23. Newlyn, *Reading, Writing and Romanticism*, 74.
24. Lucas, *Charles Lamb and the Lloyds* (London, 1898), 14.
25. 'Dedicatory Sonnet: Ad Amicos'; 'Song', in *Poems on Various Subjects* (Carlisle, 1795), 3 ; 36.
26. Lucas, *Charles Lamb and the Lloyds*, 20.
27. Charles Lloyd, Sonnet 12, 'To Coleridge', MS Ashley 1005, fol. 13r, British Library. First transcribed by Taussig, 'Lavish Promises', 81.
28. Sonnet 13, 'To The Same', Charles Lloyd, notebook, MS Ashley 1005, fol. 14r.
29. For a subtle and sympathetic account of Lloyd's stay in Nether Stowey see Taussig, *Coleridge and the Idea of Friendship*, 214–46.

30. See also letter to Coleridge, 10 December 1796: 'Your packets, posterior to the date of my misfortunes, commencing with that valuable consolatory epistle, are every day accumulating – they are sacred things with me' (Marrs, I: 78).
31. Fairer, 'Texts in Conversation: Coleridge's "Sonnets from Various Authors"', in *Re-Constructing the Book: Literary Texts in Transmission*, ed., Maureen Bell (Aldershot, 2003), 71–83 (81).
32. See letter to Josiah Wade, 16 March 1797, detailing Lloyd's fits and delirium (Griggs, I: 316).

4 'Cold, Cold, Cold': Loneliness and Reproach

1. 'We have both a distinct remembrance of his arrival – he did not keep to the high road, but leapt over a gate and bounded down the pathless field, by which he cut off an angle' (Mary Wordsworth to Sara Coleridge, 7 November 1845, *LY* 719) For a recent sympathetic evocation of this scene, see Adam Sisman, *The Friendship: Wordsworth and Coleridge* (London, 2006).
2. Wu, 'Lyrical Ballads (1798): The Beddoes Copy', *The Library: The Transactions of the Bibliographical Society*, 15 (1993), 332–5.
3. Damian Walford Davies, *Presences That Disturb: Models of Romantic Identity in the Literature and Culture of the 1790s* (Cardiff, 1999). Appendix 3, 296.
4. Lamb mentions in a letter to Coleridge of 6 August 1800 that he is longing to 'read W.'s tragedy, of which I have heard so much and seen so little – only what I saw at Stowey' (Marrs, I: 220); in a letter of 26 August, again to Coleridge, he renews the request: 'I should be very glad of it just now, for I have got Manning with me and should like to read it *with him*' (Marrs, I: 234).
5. Emile Legouis, *The Early Life of William Wordsworth 1770–1798*, 2nd edn, trans. J. W. Matthews, ed., Nicholas Roe (1895; London, 1988), 362.
6. See, for instance, the account of Lamb's stay offered by Juliet Barker, *Wordsworth: a Life* (London, 2000), 185.
7. Wu, *Wordsworth's Reading 1770–1799* (Cambridge, 1993), 101.
8. Jacobus, *Tradition and Experiment in Wordsworth's Lyrical Ballads (1798)* (Oxford, 1976), 33.
9. Compare his speech to Rivers, III. ii. 83–91, *Borderers* 188, where he speaks of 'wise men' in what appears to be a parody of Godwinian views about action and retreat.
10. Chandler, *Wordsworth's Second Nature*, 140.
11. The parallels between the closing moral of 'Lines left upon a Seat in a Yew-tree' and Coleridge's writing have long been noted. It is quite possible that Coleridge had some part in the final lines, particularly, as Jonathan Wordsworth shows, in its use of the term 'imagination'. See J. Wordsworth, *The Music of Humanity* (London, 1969), 206n.
12. For the connections between 'To Sara and her Samuel' and 'This Lime-tree Bower' see Grevel Lindop, 'Lamb, Hazlitt and De Quincey', in *The Coleridge Connection*, eds, Gravil and Lefebure, 111–32 (112–18).
13. Revisions made to 'The Eolian Harp' in 1817 (Mays, I: i, 233).
14. Everest, *Coleridge's Secret Ministry*, 250.
15. *Journals of Dorothy Wordsworth*, ed., Ernest de Selincourt, 2 vols (Basingstoke, 1941), I: 8.

16. Mays, *Works*, I: i, 351.
17. The confusion over the mood of the verb has been discussed by Michael Simpson, 'Coleridge's Swinging Moods and the Revision of "This Lime-tree Bower my Prison"', *Style* 33.1 (1999), 21–42 (27). Thanks to Dr. Simpson for discussing this with me.
18. Also pointed out by Everest, *Coleridge's Secret Ministry*, 254.
19. Perry, *Coleridge and the Uses of Division*, 151. Indeed, The phrase 'a living thing/Which *acts* upon the mind' disappears from post-1828 editions, suggesting Coleridge's own doubts about both Berkeley, and the poem's negotiations with materialism.
20. Thelwall, *Poems, Chiefly Written in Retirement* (Hereford, 1801), 129.
21. Roe, 'Coleridge and John Thelwall: The Road to Nether Stowey', *The Coleridge Connection*, eds, Gravil and Lefebure, 60–80 (76); Thelwall, *Poems in Retirement*, xxxiv. See also Mrs. Sandford's quotation of a letter from Poole to Mrs. St. Albyn, probably drafted in collaboration with Coleridge and Wordsworth, publicly distancing themselves from Thelwall. Margaret E. Sandford, *Thomas Poole and his Friends*, 2 vols (London, 1888), I: 242.
22. Thelwall, *Poems in Retirement*, 156; Walford Davies, *Presences That Disturb*, 228–32.
23. See the notebook entry of 1806 relating to 'Albert and Maria' (Coburn, *Notebooks* II: 2928); this, in the context of an argument over chastity, appears to cast Southey as the unreliable witness, the unfaithful brother. Coburn also points out that the first poem to be published by Coleridge in the *Morning Post*, 7 December 1797, was signed 'Albert'.
24. Reeve Parker, '*Osorio's* Dark Employments: Tricking out Coleridgean Tragedy', *SiR* 33 (1994), 119–60 (142).
25. *Monthly Visitor* 2 (1797), 180.
26. Lloyd's notebook poems, containing versions of sonnets written and revised during his stay at Nether Stowey, show still clearer parallels with Coleridge's parodies. See MS Ashley 1005, British Library, and Taussig's analysis in *Coleridge and the Idea of Friendship*, 236–7.
27. Taussig, *Coleridge and the Idea of Friendship*, 103.
28. Furthermore, the attack on 'simplicity', and Coleridge's use of the words 'simple' and 'plaintively' look back to Southey's poem 'Hannah, A Plaintive Tale', which contains the phrase 'It was a very plain and simple tale'. See David V. Erdman, 'Coleridge as Nehemiah Higginbottom', *MLN* 73 (1958), 569–80; and Newlyn, 'Parodic Allusion: Coleridge and the "Nehemiah Higginbottom" Sonnets, 1797', *CLB* 56 (1986), 253–9.
29. 'The Soldier's Wife', *Anti-Jacobin* VI, in Stones and Strachan, *Parodies of the Romantic Age*, I: 53.
30. Graeme Stones, 'The Ragged-Trousered Philanthropist', *CLB* 100 (1997), 122–32 (132).
31. Newlyn, 'Parodic Allusion', 258.
32. See Erdman, 'Coleridge as Nehemiah Higginbottom', 578.

5 *Blank Verse* and Fears in Solitude

1. Magnuson, *Reading Public Romanticism* (Princeton, 1998), 67; 70.
2. *Analytical Review* 27 (1798), rev. of *Blank Verse*, 522.

3. Fairer, 'Baby Language', 47.
4. For a discussion of the importance of this poem, see Lucy Newlyn, 'Lamb, Lloyd, London: A Perspective on Book Seven of the Prelude', *CLB* 47–8 (1984), 169–85.
5. MS Ashley 1005, British Library.
6. Kelly Grovier, 'An Allusion to Charles and Mary Lamb in Wordsworth's "A Slumber Did My Spirit Seal"', *N&Q* 51 (249) (2004), 152.
7. Mary Shelley, *Frankenstein or The Modern Prometheus*, ed., M. K. Joseph (London, 1969), 45.
8. David Higgins, *Frankenstein: Character Studies* (London, 2008). Thanks to Dr. Higgins for his generous discussion of this with me.
9. David Chandler, 'A Study of Lamb's "Living without God in the World"', *CLB* 99 (1997), 86–101. See Lloyd, *Lines Suggested by the Fast, Appointed on Wednesday, February 27, 1799* (Birmingham, 1799), 3.
10. Roe, *The Politics of Nature*, 78–83.
11. Priestley, *Letters to a Philosophical Unbeliever* (Bath, 1780). This also connects with the popular conflation between Unitarianism and Deism, which angered Joseph Toulmin. See his July 1797 sermon *The Injustice of classing Unitarians with Deists and Infidels* (London, 1797).
12. John Cornwell, *Coleridge: Poet and Revolutionary, 1772–1804* (London, 1973), 219; *Notebooks*, III: 4006n. See also Bate, *Coleridge*, 88, and Richard Holmes, *Coleridge: Early Visions* (London, 1989), 142.
13. Griggs, I: 86; *Lectures 1795*, 46.
14. Philip Cox, 'Introduction', *Edmund Oliver* (1798; London, 2005), xii.
15. *A Letter to the Anti-Jacobin Reviewers* (Birmingham, 1799). This also drags Charles Lamb into the argument, claiming that he is 'far from being a democrat', since his 'real and painful duties, duties of high personal self-denial' (32) preclude an engagement with politics – a prefiguration of many later critical arguments. Lamb, however, remained silent about Lloyd's public defence, and his own treatment of 'Anti-Jacobinism', his essay in the *Albion*, differs significantly from Lloyd's, as we will see in chapter eight.
16. *Morning Post*, 9 January 1798, reprinted and slightly revised from *The Watchman*, no 3. See *Essays on His Times*, ed., David V. Erdman, 3 vols (Princeton, 1978) I: 11–12.

6 A Text of Friendship: *Rosamund Gray*

1. G. Kim Blank, *Wordsworth and Feeling: The Poetry of an Adult Child* (Madison, 1995), 105. For an extended and subtle reading of the key importance of grief in Wordsworth's poetic development see Wu, *Wordsworth: An Inner Life* (Oxford, 2002).
2. Jonathan Wordsworth, 'Introduction', *A Tale of Rosamund Gray and Old Blind Margaret, 1798* (Woodstock, 1991) has discussed the 'purely Wordsworthian' nature of Lamb's symbol, although this, perhaps, too easily assumes the prior importance of Wordsworth.
3. Magnuson, *Coleridge and Wordsworth: A Lyrical Dialogue*, 97; Theresa M. Kelley, 'Revolution, Friendship, and Romantic Poetics: The Case of Wordsworth and Coleridge', *MLQ* 50: 2 (1989), 173–82 (176).

4. Richard Bourke, *Romantic Discourse and Political Modernity: Wordsworth, the Intellectual and Cultural Critique* (London, 1993), 2.
5. Stephen Gill, *William Wordsworth, a Life* (Oxford, 1989), 161.
6. Coleridge, *Aids to Reflection*, ed., Beer, Bollingen Collected Coleridge Series (Princeton, 1993), 59.
7. Gary Kelly, *English Fiction of the Romantic Period, 1789–1830* (London, 1989), 68.
8. 'Ode to a Nightingale', *The Poetical Works of John Keats*, ed., H. W. Garrod, 2nd edn (Oxford, 1958), 259. Compare Hazlitt's reference to her as symbol of affection in 'On Poetry in General' (Howe, V: 16); Wordsworth's 'Solitary Reaper' (1807), and Scott's *Guy Mannering* (1815) where it becomes associated with Sampson's loyalty. There is another, inverted, echo of the Ruth story in *The Borderers*, when Rivers tells Mortimer, sinisterly, that wherever he goes, 'I still will be your friend, will cleave to you', III. v. 1499; *Borderers*, 210.
9. Kelly, *English Fiction of the Romantic Period*, 68.
10. There have been two major editions of the poems: Jonathan Wordsworth's *Music of Humanity*, which uses the 1799 version of *The Ruined Cottage* as a base, and also prints material about the Pedlar. However, James Butler's Cornell edition contains two parallel versions of *The Ruined Cottage*, MS B (1798) and MS D (1799) as well as versions of *The Pedlar*, and I refer to Butler's MS B and MS D.
11. Evan Radcliffe makes the argument that *The Ruined Cottage* 'may be profitably interpreted in terms of Wordsworth's defensiveness about his pastoral retirement, and defines the special, restricted sense in which the poet is truly a dreaming man' in Radcliffe, ' "In Dreams Begins Responsibility": Wordsworth's Ruined Cottage Story', *SiR* 23 (1984), 101–19 (101).
12. Ibid.
13. *Table Talk*, ed., Carl Woodring, Bollingen Collected Coleridge Series, 2 vols (Princeton, 1990), I: 273.
14. D. D. Devlin, *Wordsworth and the Poetry of Epitaphs* (London, 1980), 110.
15. Ibid.
16. Chandler, *Wordsworth's Second Nature*, 138
17. Ibid. 144–55.
18. For McFarland this is 'nothing less than a politics of survival'; in *Romantic Cruxes: The English Essayists and the Spirit of the Age* (Oxford, 1987) he discusses what he terms Lamb's 'whimsy' as an 'intricate system of defence', and emphasises the anger and despair which lie behind his humour (25–52).

7 Sympathy, Allusion, and Experiment in *John Woodvil*

1. The play is not divided into scenes, nor are its lines numbered in any edition, so I give page references to the first edition (1802); the play is reproduced in Lamb's *Works* 1818, and in Lucas, IV: 149–98.
2. Anya Taylor's specific, subtle readings show the importance of this aspect of Lamb, with particular reference to *John Woodvil*. See *Bacchus in Romantic England*, 61–92.
3. Arthur Symons, *The Romantic Movement in English Poetry* (London, 1909), 164.
4. The idea of being 'marked' or branded recurs in *Mr H* –, where the 'cursed name' of the protagonist makes his erstwhile admirers flee from him, like a

man 'discovered to have marks of the plague' (Lucas, IV: 228–9). Similarly, 'Pensilis', author of 'On the Inconveniences Resulting from Being Hanged', who has been hanged and cut down, is described as 'branded with a stain', and bemoans 'that fatal mark' which points him out to others (Lucas, I: 65). See Monsman, *Confessions of a Prosaic Dreamer: Charles Lamb's Art of Autobiography* (Durham, NC, 1984), 23–5, and Aaron, '"We Are in a Manner Marked": Images of Damnation in Charles Lamb's Writings', *CLB* 33 (1981), 1–10.
5. F. V. Morley, *Lamb before Elia* (London, 1932), 198.
6. This meaning is, incidentally, picked up by Mary Shelley in *The Last Man* (1826), when Lionel uses the line to describe Perdita's love for Raymond, her 'dear heart's confessor'.
7. Aaron, *A Double Singleness*, 160.
8. In fact the quotation is from Southey's poem 'Rosamund to Henry', published in his collaborative volume with Lovel, *Poems, containing 'The Retrospect'* (Bath, 1795).
9. See 'Blakesmoor in H—shire', Lucas, II: 174–8.
10. Thomas Noon Talfourd, *Final Memorials of Charles Lamb: Consisting Chiefly of His Letters Not before Published, with Sketches of Some of His Companions*, 2 vols (London, 1848), II: 228.
11. *The Midsummer Cushion*, in *John Clare: Poems of the Middle Period, 1822–1837*, IV, eds, Eric Robinson, David Powell, and P. M. S. Dawson (Oxford, 1998), 205. The poem was later published in the *British Magazine*, 1830.
12. Mina Gorji, 'Clare and Community: The "Old Poets" and the London Magazine', in *John Clare: New Approaches*, eds, John Goodridge and Simon Kovesi (Helpston, 2000), 47–63.
13. The phrase is from *Troilus and Cressida* (III: iii. 176).
14. John Coates, "'Damn the Age! I Will Write for Antiquity': Lamb's Style as Implied Moral Comment", *CLB* 47–8 (1984), 147–58 (154).
15. The centenary of the Glorious Revolution was celebrated by members of the London Revolutionary Society, such as the Unitarian minister, Price, who saw it as an egalitarian move. The meetings of the society were refuted by Burke in the opening of *Reflections*: similarly, pamphlets such as *The Anti-Levelling Songster* (1793) vilified republican reformers and Dissenters alike, as being begotten 'Upon Oliver's whore, / Who has been long dead and rotten'. See also Joseph Nicholes, 'Politics by Indirection: Charles Lamb's Seventeenth-Century Renegade, John Woodvil', *WC* 19 (1988), 49–55. Lamb's allusion to Cibber's play *The Non-Juror* may also have carried a political charge: see Dudley H. Miles, 'The Political Satire of "The Non-Juror"', *Modern Philology*, 13:5 (1915), 281–304.
16. *British Critic*, 19 (June 1802), 646–7. The reviewer also singles out for particular criticism Lamb's 'very puerile prose', in a way reminiscent of the earlier condemnation, by the *Anti-Jacobin*, of the 'baby language' of Lamb and Lloyd.
17. See Lucas, II: 255–6.
18. As Nicholes notes, Lamb may also have been thinking about Lloyd's very public rejection of 'Jacobin' opinions in his *Letter to the Anti-Jacobin Reviewers* (Nicholes, 'Politics by Indirection', 50–1).
19. Roe, *Keats and the Culture of Dissent*, 151–3. See also Hunt's essays on 'Christmas and Other Old National Merrymakings Considered, with Reference to the Nature of the Age, and to the Desireableness of their

Revival', *Examiner* 21 and 28 December 1817 and 4 January 1818, cited by Roe, 151. Moreover, there are frequent mentions of *John Woodvil* in the pages of the *London*, such as Charles Abraham Elton's 'Epistle to Elia' (August 1821), which uses Woodvil's reference to the 'grape's uncheck'd virtue' to create an allusive tribute to Lamb. His essays, suggest Elton, create not only a sense of present friendship, evocative of drinking and laughing around the hearth, but also a sociability which will extend beyond the grave, to allow Elia heavenly friendship with Ulysses and Shakespeare.

20. For this attribution we are greatly indebted to Courtney, 'New Lamb Texts from the Albion', *CLB* 3 (1977), 6–9 (reprinted in *Young Charles Lamb*, 343–6). I have been unable to trace the copy she saw in Bath Municipal Library, which seems to be the only sighting of an 1801 run of this paper so far.
21. Indeed, Southey reports an uncomfortable reference to the cartoon souring the first meeting between Godwin and Lamb. Whilst they were at dinner together with the Coleridges Lamb 'got warmed with whatever was on the table, became disputatious, and said things to Godwin which made him quietly say, 'Pray, Mr. Lamb, are you toad or frog?' (*The Life and Correspondence of Robert Southey*, ed., C. C. Southey, 537). However, the next day Coleridge found them breakfasting together, and their friendship quickly grew deeper, with Lamb writing the prologue for Godwin's unsuccessful play *Antonio* (1800).
22. Lamb might well also have been thinking of the way in which he himself had judged Godwin only a year or so before.
23. *Prospectus of a Daily Evening Newspaper, to Be Called the Albion, and Evening Advertiser* (London, 1799).

8 The Urban Romantic: Lamb's landscapes of Affection

1. Wu, 'Lamb's Reading of 'Lyrical Ballads', 1800', *CLB* 92 (1995), 224–5.
2. John Stoddart, 'Wordsworth's Lyrical Ballads. Two Vols', *British Critic* 17 (February 1801), 125–31, reprinted in Donald Reiman, *The Romantics Reviewed: Contemporary Reviews of British Romantic Writers (Part A: The Lake Poets)* 2 vols (New York and London: Garland, 1972), I: 133.
3. Margaret Oliphant, *The Literary History of England in the End of the Eighteenth and Beginning of the Nineteenth Century*, 3 vols (London, 1882), I: 257.
4. Walter Pater, *Appreciations, with an Essay on Style* (London, 1913), 39–64.
5. Mark Jones, *The 'Lucy Poems': A Case Study in Literary Knowledge* (Toronto, 1995), 239; xiii.
6. Francis Jeffrey, review of 'Thalaba', *Edinburgh Review*, I: 63–83; review of *The Excursion*, *Edinburgh Review*, XXIV: 1. See Peter A. Cook, 'Chronology of the "Lake School" Argument: Some Revisions', *RES* 28 (1977), 175–81.
7. We may recall that it was Lamb who guided the Wordsworths through London in September 1802; he writes to Coleridge, apparently with some pride, 'I was their guide to Barthelmy fair!'; 8 September 1802 (Marrs, II: 66).
8. For some discussions of Wordsworth's relationship with theatrical aspects of the city see Jacobus, *Romanticism, Writing and Sexual Difference*, 113; William Chapman Sharps, *Unreal Cities* (Baltimore, 1990), 19; Julian Wolfreys, *Writing London* (Basingstoke, 1998), 124.

9. Hunt, *Autobiography*, 243.
10. Ibid., 243. See also Hunt's poem 'To Charles Lamb', which celebrates the sociability of Charles and Mary's prison visits to the Hunts, and the community created around the fire-side 'sipping together' and talking of 'all sorts of writers': Spenser, Chapman – 'whose Homer's a fine rough old wine' – Marvel and Richardson (*Foliage*, cviii–cxiv).
11. Nicholas Roe, *Fiery Heart: The First Life of Leigh Hunt* (London: Pimlico, 2005), 209.
12. Aaron, *A Double Singleness*, 145.
13. This text is from the *Morning Post* for 1 February 1802. The piece was reprinted in *Works* 1818, and this is reproduced in Lucas, I: 46–7. Elsewhere, I have used Lucas's edition for references to the *Essays of Elia* and the *Last Essays of Elia*, unless noting a specific difference in the *London Magazine* version.
14. Cf. Lamb's letter to Robert Lloyd, 7 February 1801 (Lucas, I: 271).
15. John Aikin and Anna Letitia Barbauld, *Evenings at Home; Or the Juvenile Budget Opened*, 6 vols (London, 1792–6). Lamb would later condemn the educational literature of the 'cursed Barbauld Crew' (Marrs 2: 81–2) – yet, as I have shown elsewhere, his and Mary's writing for children is indebted to her work. See 'Wild tales' from Shakespeare: Readings of Charles and Mary Lamb' *Shakespeare*, 2.2 (2006), 152–67.
16. Henry Man or Mann (1747–99) published a volume of essays, *The Trifler*, in 1770, followed by a novel and a dramatic satire. He was deputy secretary at the South Sea House during Lamb's brief employment there. The volumes to which Lamb refers were his collected works, published, with a 'Memoir', in 1802.
17. Uttara Natarajan, 'Hazlitt, Lamb, and the Philosophy of Familiarity', *CLB* 124 (2003), 110–18 (113).
18. Monsman, *Charles Lamb as the* London Magazine's *'Elia'*, 21.
19. David Chandler, 'Charles Lamb and the South Sea House', *N&Q* 51 (249) (2004), 139–43.
20. David Chandler's expert literary detective work has uncovered forgotten biographical details of Felix Ellia (or sometimes Elia), which reveal the importance of this 'colourful, eccentric, memorable character' to the construction of Lamb's essayist persona, and shows that his assumption of the name began as a literary hoax, before Ellia died in September 1820. See 'Elia, the Real': The Original of Lamb's *Nom De Plume*', *RES* 58 (2007), 669–683.
21. *London Magazine* (August 1820), 144. I am also indebted to Monsman, *Charles Lamb as the* London Magazine's *Elia*, 31–56.
22. Parker, *Literary Magazines and British Romanticism*, 44. This argument has also been explored by McFarland, *Romantic Cruxes*, 25–52; Monsman, *Charles Lamb as the* London Magazine's *Elia*, 31–55; and Aaron, *A Double Singleness*, 51–96.
23. Parker's analysis of 'the political context of the *Elia* essays' sees Lamb's contributions to the *London* as defined by John Scott's Burkean-Coleridgean allegiances. However, what Scott saw as the consolations of displacement should be set against Lamb's continuing belief in the power of the personal attachment, which, because rooted in the radical Unitarian culture of the 1790s, is not entirely Burkean – what can be read as escape on one level can

also be read as engagement on another. See Parker, *Literary Magazines and British Romanticism*, 30–59.
24. Park, *Lamb as Critic*, 10.
25. *Henry Crabb Robinson on Books and their Writers*, ed., Edith J. Morley, 3 vols (London, 1938) I: 17.
26. *The Letters of John Keats: 1814–1821*, ed., Hyder E. Rollins, 2 vols (Cambridge, MA, 1958) I: 387.
27. Ibid. I: 193. See Park, *Lamb as Critic*, 10–12; Natarajan, 'Hazlitt, Lamb, and the Philosophy of Familiarity', 117; Robert Frank, *Don't Call Me Gentle Charles: An Essay on Lamb's 'Essays of Elia'* (Corvallis, Oregon, 1976), 10.
28. *The Letters of Percy Bysshe Shelley*, ed., Frederick L. Jones, 2 vols (Oxford, 1964), II: 111–12. Shelley's high opinion of Lamb was not, however, reciprocated.
29. Helen E. Haworth, 'Keats's Copy of Lamb's *Specimens of English Dramatic Poetry*', *Bulletin of the New York Public Library*, 74 (1970), 419–27 (422).
30. Ibid.
31. Ricks, *Allusion to the Poets*, 159.
32. Burke, *Reflections on the Revolution in France*, 68–9. See discussion of Lamb's perspective on Burke and Godwin in chapter one.
33. For more discussion of the critical questions raised by the poem, see Paul H. Fry, 'The Diligence of Desire: Critics on and around Westminster Bridge', *WC*, 23: 3 (1992), 162–4.
34. A further suggestion of the way in which Lamb's remonstrances might have carried far into Wordsworth's sensibilities comes in the revisions made to 'Poor Susan' in the 1815 edition of *Lyrical Ballads*. The last stanza, which addressed Susan as a 'Poor Outcast!', was cancelled, pleasing Lamb, since 'it threw a kind of dubiety upon Susan's moral conduct. Susan is a servant maid. [...] to term her a poor outcast seems as much to say that poor Susan was no better than she should be, which I trust was not what you meant to express' (Marrs, III: 147). Wordsworth's change (made before Lamb's comments) reflects a delayed response to Lamb's earlier support of the liminal and marginal in the city, and allows a more indeterminate, open-ended reading of the poem and its subjects. See David Simpson, 'What Bothered Charles Lamb About Poor Susan?' *SEL* (1986), 589–612, and P. J. Manning, 'Placing "Poor Susan": Wordsworth and the New Historicism', *SiR* 25 (1986), 351–69. Elsewhere, as John Ades has pointed out, Wordsworth's habitual pattern was to complain, and then 'make the change as Lamb suggested', John I. Ades, 'Friendly Persuasion: Lamb as Critic of Wordsworth', *WC* (1977), 18–24.
35. Continuing the work done by, for instance, Wedd, 'Mary Lamb', *CLB* 102 (1998), 42–54 and Craciun, Watson and Hitchcock.
36. McFarland, *Romantic Cruxes*, 50.
37. 'For the perfect idler, for the passionate observer it becomes an immense source of enjoyment to establish his dwelling in the throng, in the ebb and flow, the bustle, the fleeting and the infinite'. See Charles Baudelaire, 'Peintre de la vie moderne', first published 1863, repr. *Baudelaire: Selected Writings on Art and Artists*, trans. P. E. Charvet (Cambridge, 1972), 399. For a discussion of Baudelaire's modernity see Mary Gluck, 'Reimagining the Flâneur: The Hero of the Novel in Lukács, Bakhtin, and Girard',

Modernism/Modernity 13 (2006), 1–18. McFarland has also made the connection between the prose poetry of Baudelaire and Lamb, in *Romantic Cruxes*, 49.
38. 'Modernity is the transient, the fleeting, the contingent; it is one half of art, the other being the eternal and the immovable'. Ibid., 403.
39. Walter Benjamin, *Charles Baudelaire: A Lyric Poet in the Era of High Capitalism*, trans. Harry Zohn (London, 1973), 55.
40. Walter Benjamin, 'The Return of the *Flâneur*', rev. of *Spazieren in Berlin*, by Franz Hessel, *Die Literarische Welt* (October 1929), repr. in *Selected Writings, Volume 2, 1927–1934*, trans. Rodney Livingstone and others, eds, Michael W. Jennings, Howard Eiland, and Gary Smith (Cambridge, MA, 1999), 263–4.
41. 'Street Haunting: A London Adventure', *The Death of the Moth and other Essays* (1942) (London, 1945), 19 .
42. Rachel Bowlby has offered a particularly interesting reading of Woolf's construction of a female flâneur to push back the boundaries of her writing identity. See Rachel Bowlby, *Still Crazy after All These Years: Women, Writing, and Psychoanalysis* (London, 1992), 5–33.
43. 'Street Haunting', *The Death of the Moth*, 25–6.
44. Ibid., 28.
45. Deidre Lynch, '"Wedded to Books": Bibliomania and the Romantic Essayists', in *Romantic Libraries*, ed., Ina Ferris, *Romantic Circles Praxis Series* (2004) <http://www.rc.umd.edu/praxis/libraries/lynch/lynch.html>.
46. Baudelaire knew Lamb through De Quincey; Woolf frequently commented on his letters and essays. Moreover, there are numerous subtle links between Lamb and Modernist writers, a reminder of how his essays saturated late nineteenth and early twentieth-century education and culture. Pointing to the 'lambdad's tale' of *Finnegans Wake* (1939), for instance, Anne Marie Flanagan has discussed Lamb as a literary father for Joyce, not only through the *Tales from Shakespear* and the *Adventures of Ulysses*, but also through the evasiveness and uncertainty of the Elian voice. See Flanagan, 'Charles Lamb: The unforeseen precursor in *Finnegans Wake*', *In-between*, 12 (2003), 159–73.

Bibliography

Only works cited in the endnotes are listed here: see the List of Abbreviations at the front of the book for works cited in the text.

Primary works

1. Manuscripts cited

British Library.
MS Ashley 1005: Volume of poems by Charles Lloyd with annotations by Samuel Taylor Coleridge, 1795–1800.
Rugby MS, Harry Ransom Humanities Research Center, University of Texas, Austin, facsimile in British Library RP179A: Volume of poems by Coleridge.

Firestone Library, Princeton University.
Robert H. Taylor collection, Lamb Case, Record ID: 73345: Lamb poem, 'Sweet is thy sunny hair'

Victoria University Library, Toronto.
The Coleridge Collection, Part III: The Coleridge Circle, S MS F4.5.: Lamb poem, 'Methinks how dainty sweet it were'

2. Printed sources cited

Aikin, John and Anna Letitia Barbauld, *Evenings at Home; or the Juvenile Budget Opened*, 6 vols (London, 1792–6).
Anonymous, *An Asylum for Fugitive Pieces, in Prose and Verse*, 2nd edn. 3 vols (London, 1795).
Barbauld, Anna Letitia, *The Poems of Anna Letitia Barbauld*, eds, William McCarthy and Elizabeth Kraft (Athens, Georgia, 1994).
Baudelaire, Charles, *Baudelaire: Selected Writings on Art and Artists*, trans. P. E. Charvet (Cambridge, 1972).
Beattie, James, *The Minstrel; or, the Progress of Genius. A Poem. Book the First* (London, 1771).
Belsham, Thomas, *Memoirs of the Late Reverend Theophilus Lindsey* (London, 1812).
Bent, William, *Eight Meteorological Journals 1793–1804* (London, 1804).
Bowles, William Lisle, *Fourteen Sonnets, Elegiac and Descriptive. Written During a Tour* (Bath, 1789).
—— *Sonnets, with Other Poems*, 3rd edn (Bath, 1794).
Burke, Edmund, *Reflections on the Revolution in France* (London, 1790).

—— *A Letter from Mr. Burke, to a Member of the National Assembly; in Answer to Some Objections to His Book on French Affairs* (London, 1791).

—— *A Letter from the Right Honourable Edmund Burke to a Noble Lord, on the Attacks Made Upon Him and His Pension, in the House of Lords, by the Duke of Bedford and the Earl of Lauderdale, Early in the Present Sessions of Parliament.* 1st edn (London, 1796).

Clare, John, *John Clare: Poems of the Middle Period, 1822–1837 V*, eds, Eric Robinson, David Powell, and P. M. S. Dawson (Oxford, 1998).

Coleridge, Samuel Taylor, *Essays on His Times*, ed., David V. Erdman, Bollingen Collected Coleridge Series 3, 3 vols (Princeton, 1978).

—— *Table Talk*, ed., Carl Woodring, Bollingen Collected Coleridge Series 12, 2 vols (Princeton, 1990).

—— *Aids to Reflection*, ed., John Beer, Bollingen Collected Coleridge Series 9 (Princeton, 1993).

Corfield, Penelope J. and Chris Evans, *Youth and Revolution in the 1790s: Letters of William Pattisson, Thomas Amyot and Henry Crabb Robinson* (Stroud, 1996).

Cottle, Joseph, *Reminiscences of S. T. Coleridge and R. Southey 1847* (Highgate, 1970).

Disney, John, *A Defence of Public or Social Worship. A Sermon, Preached in the Unitarian Chapel, in Essex-Street, London; on Sunday, Dec. 4, 1791* (London, 1792).

Dyer, George, *An Inquiry into the Nature of Subscription to the Thirty-Nine Articles* (London, 1790).

—— *A Dissertation on the Theory and Practice of Benevolence* (London, 1795).

Fielding, Henry, *The History of Tom Jones, a Foundling*, 4 vols (London, 1749).

Frend, William, *Peace and Union Recommended to the Associated Bodies of Republicans and Anti-Republicans* (St. Ives, 1793).

—— *An Account of the Proceedings in the University of Cambridge against William Frend for Publishing a Pamphlet Intitled, Peace and Union &C* (Cambridge, 1793).

Frost, John, *The Trial of John Frost, for Seditious Words. Taken in Short Hand by W. Ramsey* (London, 1794).

Godwin, William, *An Enquiry Concerning Political Justice* (1793), vol. 3 in *Political and Philosophical Writings of William Godwin*, ed., Mark Philp, 5 vols (London, 1993).

Hartley, David, *Observations on Man, His Frame, His Duty and His Expectations.* 3 vols (1749; London, 1791).

Hays, Mary, *Memoirs of Emma Courtney*, ed., Eleanor Ty (Oxford, 1996).

Hazlitt, William, *The Complete Works of William Hazlitt*, ed., P. P. Howe, 21 vols (London, 1930–4).

Holcroft, Thomas, *The Adventures of Hugh Trevor* (London, 1794).

Hume, David, *Principal Writings on Religion Including Dialogues Concerning Natural Religion; and, the Natural History of Religion*, ed., J. C. A. Gaskin (Oxford, 1998).

—— *A Treatise of Human Nature: A Critical Edition*, eds, David Fate Norton and Mary J. Norton, 2 vols (Oxford, 2007).

Hunt, Leigh, *The Autobiography of Leigh Hunt*, ed., J. E. Morpurgo (London, 1948).

Keats, John, *The Poetical Works of John Keats*, ed., H. W. Garrod, 2nd edn (Oxford, 1958).

—— *The Letters of John Keats: 1814–1821*, ed., Hyder E. Rollins, 2 vols (Cambridge, MA, 1958).

Le Grice, Charles Valentine, *The Tineum. Containing Estianomy, or the Art of Stirring a Fire: The Icead, a Mock-Heroic Poem: An Imitation of Horace* (Cambridge, 1794).

242 Bibliography

Lindsey, Theophilus, *A Sermon Preached at the Opening of the Chapel in Essex-House, Essex-Street, on Sunday, April 17, 1774* (London, 1774).
Lloyd, Charles, *Poems on Various Subjects* (Carlisle, 1795).
—— *A Letter to the Anti-Jacobin Reviewers* (Birmingham, 1799).
—— *Lines suggested by the fast, appointed on Wednesday, February 27, 1799* (Birmingham, 1799).
Mackenzie, Henry, *The Man of Feeling* (London, 1771).
Mandeville, Bernard, *The Fable of the Bees: Or, Private Vices, Publick* [sic] *Benefits. With an Essay on Charity and Charity-Schools. And a Search into the Nature of Society*, 3rd edn (London, 1724).
Paine, Thomas, *Rights of Man: Being an Answer to Mr. Burke's Attack on the French Revolution* (London, 1791).
Pope, Alexander, *An Essay on Man*. ed., Maynard Mack, *The Twickenham Edition of the Poems of Alexander Pope* III: i (London, 1950).
Price, Richard, *A Discourse on the Love of Our Country, Delivered on Nov. 4, 1789, at the Meeting-House in the Old Jewry, to the Society for Commemorating the Revolution in Great Britain* (London, 1789).
—— and Priestley, *A Free Discussion of the Doctrines of Materialism and Philosophical Necessity, in a Correspondence between Dr. Price and Dr. Priestley*, ed., J. Priestley (London, 1778).
Priestley, Joseph, *The Doctrine of Philosophical Necessity* (London, 1777).
—— *Letters to a Philosophical Unbeliever* (Bath, 1780).
—— *An Answer to Mr. Paine's Age of Reason, a Continuation of Letters to the Philosophers and Politicians of France, on the Subject of Religion; and of the Letters to a Philosophical Unbeliever. With a Preface by Theophilus Lindsey* (London, 1795).
Prospectus of a daily evening newspaper, to be called The Albion, and Evening Advertiser (London, 1799).
Robinson, Henry Crabb, *Henry Crabb Robinson on Books and their Writers*, ed., Edith J. Morley, 3 vols (London, 1938).
Shaftesbury, Anthony Ashley Cooper, Third Earl of, *Characteristics of Men, Manners, Opinions, Times*, ed., Lawrence E. Klein, Cambridge Texts in the History of Philosophy (Cambridge, 1999).
Shelley, Mary, *Frankenstein or The Modern Prometheus*, ed., M. K. Joseph (London, 1969).
Shelley, Percy, *The Letters of Percy Bysshe Shelley*, ed., Frederick L. Jones, 2 vols (Oxford, 1964).
Shenstone, William, *The Works in Verse and Prose, of William Shenstone, Esq; Containing Letters to Particular Friends, from the Year 1739 to 1763*, Vol. III (Edinburgh, 1770).
Southey, C. C., ed., *The Life and Correspondence of Robert Southey* (London, 1849).
Taylor, John, *Verses on Various Occasions* (London, 1795).
Thelwall, John, *Poems, Chiefly Written in Retirement* (Hereford, 1801).
—— *The Tribune, a Periodical Publication, Consisting Chiefly of the Political Lectures of J. Thelwall. Taken in Short-Hand by W. Ramsey, and Revised by the Lecturer*, 3 vols (London, 1795).
Toulmin, Joshua, *The Immutability of God, and the Trials of Christ's Ministry; Represented in Two Sermons, Preached at Essex Chapel, in the Strand, March 30, and April 6, 1794* (London, 1794).

—— *The Practical Efficacy of the Unitarian Doctrine Considered* (London, 1796).
—— *The Injustice of Classing Unitarians with Deists and Infidels* (London, 1797).
White, James, *Original Letters, &c, of Sir John Falstaff and His Friends* (London, 1796).
Wickham, George, *Recollections of a Blue-Coat Boy, or, a View of Christ's Hospital* (London, 1829).
Williams, Helen Maria, *Poems, by Helen Maria Williams. In Two Volumes* (London, 1786).
—— *Julia, a Novel; Interspersed with Some Poetical Pieces*, 2 vols (London, 1790).
Wollstonecraft, Mary, *A Vindication of the Rights of Men, a Letter to E. Burke Occasioned by His Reflections on the Revolution in France*, 2nd edn (London, 1790).
Woolf, Virginia, *The Death of the Moth and Other Essays* (London, 1945).
Wordsworth, Dorothy, *Journals of Dorothy Wordsworth*, ed., Ernest de Selincourt, 2 vols (Basingstoke, 1941).

Secondary works

Aaron, Jane, '"We Are in a Manner Marked": Images of Damnation in Charles Lamb's Writings', *CLB* 33 (1981), 1–10.
—— 'Charles and Mary Lamb: The Critical Heritage', *CLB* 59 (1987), 73–85.
—— *A Double Singleness: Gender and the Writings of Charles and Mary Lamb* (Oxford, 1991).
Ades, John I., 'Friendly Persuasion: Lamb as Critic of Wordsworth', *WC* (1977), 18–24.
Ainger, Alfred, *Charles Lamb* (London, 1882).
Allen, Richard C., 'Charles Lloyd, Coleridge, and *Edmund Oliver*', *SiR* 35 (1996), 245–94.
Balle, Mary Blanchard, 'Mary Lamb: Her Mental Health Issues', *CLB* 93 (1996), 2–11.
Barker, Juliet, *Wordsworth: a Life* (London, 2000).
Barker-Benfield, G. J., *The Culture of Sensibility: Sex and Society in Eighteenth-Century Britain* (Chicago, 1992).
Barrell, John, 'Coffee-House Politicians', *Journal of British Studies* 43 (2004), 206–32.
—— and Jon Mee, eds, *Trials for Treason and Sedition, 1792–1794*, 8 vols (London, 2006–7).
Bate, Walter Jackson, *Coleridge* (London, 1969).
Beer, John, 'Coleridge and Wordsworth: Influence and Confluence', *New Approaches to Coleridge*, ed., Donald Sultana (London, 1981), 192–211.
—— ed., *Poems, Samuel Taylor Coleridge* (London, 1993).
Benjamin, Walter, *Charles Baudelaire: A Lyric Poet in the Era of High Capitalism*, trans. Harry Zohn (London, 1973).
—— *Selected Writings, Volume 2, 1927–1934*, trans. Rodney Livingstone and others, eds, Michael W. Jennings, Howard Eiland, and Gary Smith (Cambridge, MA, 1999).
Binhammer, Katherine, 'The Sex Panic of the 1790s', *Journal of the History of Sexuality* 6 (1996), 409–35.

Birrell, Augustine, *Obiter Dicta* (London, 1884).
Blank, G. Kim, *Wordsworth and Feeling: The Poetry of an Adult Child* (Madison, 1995).
Bloom, Harold, *A Map of Misreading* (Oxford, 1980).
Blunden, Edmund, *Charles Lamb and His Poetic Contemporaries* (Cambridge, 1937).
Botting, Eileen Hunt, *Family Feuds: Wollstonecraft, Burke, and Rousseau on the Transformation of the Family* (Albany, NY, 2006).
Bourke, Richard, *Romantic Discourse and Political Modernity: Wordsworth, the Intellectual and Cultural Critique* (London, 1993).
Bowlby, Rachel, *Still Crazy after All These Years: Women, Writing, and Psychoanalysis* (London, 1992).
Bown, Nicola, ed., 'Rethinking Victorian Sentimentality', *19: Interdisciplinary Studies in the Long Nineteenth Century* 4 (2007), <http://www.19.bbk.ac.uk/issue4>.
Brissenden, R. F., *Virtue in Distress* (London and Basingstoke, 1974).
Butler, Marilyn, 'Godwin, Burke, and *Caleb Williams*', *Essays in Criticism* XXXII (1982), 237–57.
—— 'Culture's Medium: The Role of the Review', in *Cambridge Companion to British Romanticism*, ed., Stuart Curran (Cambridge, 1993), 120–76.
Carlyle, Thomas, *Reminiscences*, ed., James Anthony Froude, 2 vols (London, 1881).
Carnall, Geoffrey, 'The Monthly Magazine', *RES* 5 (1954), 158–64.
Chandler, David, 'A Study of Lamb's "Living without God in the World"', *CLB* 99 (1997), 86–101.
—— '"There Never Was His like!": A Biography of James White (1775–1820)', *CLB* 128 (2004), 78–95.
—— 'Charles Lamb and the South Sea House', *N&Q* 51 (249) (2004), 139–43.
—— 'Lamb, Falstaff's Letters, and Landor's Citation and Examination of William Shakespeare', *CLB* 131 (2005), 76–85.
—— '"Elia, the Real": The Original of Lamb's *Nom De Plume*', *RES* 58 (2007), 669–683.
Chandler, James K., *Wordsworth's Second Nature: A Study of the Poetry and Politics* (Chicago, 1984).
—— 'The Emergence of Sentimental Probability', in *The Age of Cultural Revolutions: Britain and France, 1750–1820*, eds, Colin Jones and Dror Wahrman (Berkeley, 2002), 137–70.
Cheshire, Paul, 'The Eolian Harp', *Coleridge Bulletin* 17 (2001), 1–26.
Christensen, Jerome, *Coleridge's Blessed Machine of Language* (Ithaca, NY, 1981).
—— 'Once an Apostate Always an Apostate', *SiR* 21 (1982), 461–4.
—— '"Like a Guilty Thing Surprised": Deconstruction, Coleridge, and the Apostasy of Criticism', *Critical Inquiry* 12 (1986), 769–87.
Clemit, Pamela, 'Self Analysis as Social Critique: The Autobiographical Writings of Godwin and Rousseau', *Romanticism* 11: 2 (2005), 161–80.
Coates, John, '"Damn the Age! I Will Write for Antiquity": Lamb's Style as Implied Moral Comment', *CLB* 47: 8 (1984), 147–58.
Connolly, Cyril, *Enemies of Promise*, rev. edn (Harmondsworth, 1961).
Cook, Peter A., 'Chronology of the "Lake School" Argument: Some Revisions', *RES* 28 (1977), 175–181.

Cornwell, John, *Coleridge: Poet and Revolutionary, 1772–1804* (London, 1973).
Winifred F. Courtney, 'Lamb, Gillray and the Ghost of Edmund Burke', *CLB* 12 (1975), 77–82.
—— 'New Lamb Texts from the *Albion*', *CLB* 3 (1977), 6–9.
Cox, Jeffrey N., *Poetry and Politics in the Cockney School: Keats, Shelley, Hunt and Their Circle* (Cambridge, 1998).
Cox, Philip, ed., and 'Introduction', *Edmund Oliver* (1798; London, 2005).
Craciun, Adriana, *Fatal Women of Romanticism* (Cambridge, 2002).
Crawford, Rachel, *Poetry, Enclosure, and the Vernacular Landscape, 1700–1830* (Cambridge, 2002).
Dart, Gregory, *Rousseau, Robespierre and English Romanticism* (Cambridge, 1999).
Davies, Damian Walford, *Presences That Disturb: Models of Romantic Identity in the Literature and Culture of the 1790s* (Cardiff, 1999).
Denison, David, and Lynda Pratt, 'The Language of the Southey-Coleridge Circle', *Language Sciences* 22 (2000), 401–22.
Devlin, D. D., *Wordsworth and the Poetry of Epitaphs* (London, 1980).
Epstein, James, '"Equality and No King": Sociability and Sedition: The Case of John Frost', in *Romantic Sociability*, eds, Russell and Tuite, 43–61.
Erdman, David V., 'Coleridge as Nehemiah Higginbottom', *MLN* 73 (1958), 569–80.
Everest, Kelvin, *Coleridge's Secret Ministry: The Context of the Conversation Poems, 1795–1798* (Brighton, 1979).
Fairer, David, 'Baby Language and Revolution: The Early Poetry of Charles Lloyd and Charles Lamb', *CLB* 74 (1991), 33–52.
—— 'Texts in Conversation: Coleridge's "Sonnets from Various Authors"', in *Re-Constructing the Book: Literary Texts in Transmission*, ed., Maureen Bell (Aldershot, 2003), 71–83.
Fang, Karen, 'Empire, Coleridge, and Charles Lamb's Consumer Imagination', *SEL* 43.4 (2003), 815–43.
Favret, Mary A., *Romantic Correspondence: Women, Politics and the Fiction of Letters* (Cambridge, 1993).
Flanagan, Anne Marie 'Charles Lamb: the Unforeseen Precursor in *Finnegans Wake*', *In-between* 12 (2003), 159–73.
Flint, Christopher, *Family Fictions: Narrative and Domestic Relations in Britain, 1688–1798* (Stanford, CA, 1998).
Frank, Robert, *Don't Call Me Gentle Charles: An Essay on Lamb's 'Essays of Elia'* (Corvallis, Oregon, 1976).
Friedman, Leslie Joan, *Mary Lamb: Sister, Seamstress, Murderer, Writer*, PhD thesis (Stanford, CA, 1976).
Fruman, Norman, *Coleridge, The Damaged Archangel* (London, 1972).
Fry, Paul H., 'The Diligence of Desire: Critics on and around Westminster Bridge', *WC* 23: 3 (1992), 162–4.
Fulford, Tim, *Coleridge's Figurative Language* (Basingstoke, 1991).
—— *Romanticism and Masculinity: Gender, Politics and Poetics in the Writings of Burke, Coleridge, Cobbett, Wordsworth, De Quincey and Hazlitt* (Basingstoke, 1999).
Gibbs, Warren E., 'An Unpublished Letter from John Thelwall to Samuel Taylor Coleridge', *Modern Language Review* 25 (1930), 85–90.
Gigante, Denise, *Taste: A Literary History* (New Haven, 2005).
Gill, Stephen, *William Wordsworth, a Life* (Oxford, 1989).

Gluck, Mary, 'Reimagining the Flâneur: The Hero of the Novel in Lukács, Bakhtin, and Girard', *Modernism/Modernity* 13 (2006), 1–18.
Godfrey, Richard T. and Mark Hallett, *James Gillray: The Art of Caricature* (London, 2001).
Goldsmith, Jason N., 'The Promiscuity of Print: John Clare's "Don Juan" And the Culture of Romantic Celebrity', *SEL* 46 (2006), 803–32.
Gorji, Mina, 'Clare and Community: The "Old Poets" and the *London Magazine*', in *John Clare: New Approaches*, eds, John Goodridge and Simon Kovesi (Helpston, 2000), 47–63.
Gravil, Richard, and Molly Lefebure, eds, *The Coleridge Connection: Essays for Thomas McFarland* (Basingstoke, 1990).
Grovier, Kelly, 'An Allusion to Charles and Mary Lamb in Wordsworth's "A Slumber Did My Spirit Seal"', *N & Q* 51 (249) (2004), 152.
Haworth, Helen E., 'Keats's Copy of Lamb's *Specimens of English Dramatic Poetry*', *Bulletin of the New York Public Library*, 74 (1970), 419–27.
Haydon, Benjamin Robert, *The Diary of Benjamin Robert Haydon*, ed., Willard Bissell Pope, 5 vols (Cambridge, MA, 1960).
Hickey, Alison, 'Double Bonds: Charles Lamb's Romantic Collaborations', *ELH* 63: 3 (1996), 735–71.
Higgins, David, *Frankenstein: Character Studies* (London, 2008).
Hitchcock, Susan Tyler, *Mad Mary Lamb: Lunacy and Murder in Literary London* (New York, 2005).
Holmes, Richard, *Coleridge: Early Visions* (London, 1989).
Hunt, Leigh, 'Preface', *Foliage; Or, Poems Original and Translated* (London, 1818).
Jacobus, Mary, *Tradition and Experiment in Wordsworth's Lyrical Ballads (1798)* (Oxford, 1976).
—— *Romanticism, Writing and Sexual Difference: Essays on The Prelude* (Oxford, 1989).
James, Felicity, 'Sweet is thy sunny hair: an unpublished poem by Charles Lamb', *CLB* 127 (2004), 54–6.
—— ' "Wild Tales" from Shakespeare: Readings of Charles and Mary Lamb', *Shakespeare* 2.2 (2006), 152–67.
Johnson, Claudia, *Equivocal Beings: Politics, Gender, and Sentimentality in the 1790s: Wollstonecraft, Radcliffe, Burney, Austen* (Chicago, 1995).
Johnson, R. Brimley, ed., *Christ's Hospital, Recollections of Lamb, Coleridge, and Leigh Hunt* (London, 1896).
Jones, Chris, *Radical Sensibility: Literature and Ideas in the 1790s* (London, 1993).
Jones, Mark, *The 'Lucy Poems': A Case Study in Literary Knowledge* (Toronto, 1995).
Kelley, Maurice W., 'Thomas Cooper and Pantisocracy', *MLN* 45 (1930), 218–20.
Kelley, Theresa M., 'Revolution, Friendship, and Romantic Poetics: The Case of Wordsworth and Coleridge', *MLQ* 50: 2 (1989), 173–82.
Kelly, Gary, *English Fiction of the Romantic Period, 1789–1830* (London, 1989).
Laslett, Peter, *The World We Have Lost* (New York, 1965).
Leader, Zachary, *Revision and Romantic Authorship* (Oxford, 1996).
Leask, Nigel, *The Politics of Imagination in Coleridge's Critical Thought* (Basingstoke, 1988).
—— 'Pantisocracy and the Politics of the "Preface" to *Lyrical Ballads*', in *Reflections of Revolution: Images of Romanticism*, eds, Alison Yarrington and Kelvin Everest (London, 1993).

Legouis, Emile, *The Early Life of William Wordsworth 1770–1798*, 2nd edn, trans. J. W. Matthews, ed., Nicholas Roe (1895; London, 1988).

Lindop, Grevel, 'Lamb, Hazlitt and De Quincey', in *The Coleridge Connection*, eds, Gravil and Lefebure, 111–32.

Lucas, E. V., *Charles Lamb and the Lloyds* (London, 1898).

—— *The Life of Charles Lamb*, 2 vols (London, 1921).

Lynch, Deidre, ' "Wedded to Books": Bibliomania and the Romantic Essayists', in *Romantic Libraries*, ed., Ina Ferris, *Romantic Circles Praxis Series* (2004) <http://www.rc.umd.edu/praxis/libraries/lynch/lynch.html>.

Madden, Richard, 'The Old Familiar Faces: An Essay in the Light of Some Recently Discovered Documents of Charles Valentine LeGrice Referring to Lamb, Coleridge and Wordsworth', *CLB* 6 (1974), 113–21.

Magnuson, Paul, *Coleridge and Wordsworth: A Lyrical Dialogue* (Princeton, 1988).

—— *Reading Public Romanticism* (Princeton, 1998).

Mahoney, Charles, 'The Multeity of Coleridgean Apostasy', in *Irony and Clerisy*, ed., Deborah Elise White, *Romantic Circles Praxis Series* (1999) <http://www.rc.umd.edu/praxis/irony/>.

Manning, P. J., 'Placing "Poor Susan": Wordsworth and the New Historicism', *SiR* 25 (1986), 351–69.

Mason, Emma, 'Feeling Dickensian Feeling', in 'Rethinking Victorian Sentimentality', ed. Nicola Bown, *19: Interdisciplinary Studies in the Long Nineteenth Century*, 4 (2007), <http://www.19.bbk.ac.uk/issue4>.

Matlak, Richard E., *The Poetry of Relationship: The Wordsworths and Coleridge, 1797–1800* (Basingstoke, 1997).

McFarland, Thomas, *Romanticism and the Forms of Ruin: Wordsworth, Coleridge, and Modalities of Fragmentation* (Princeton, 1981).

—— *Romantic Cruxes: The English Essayists and the Spirit of the Age* (Oxford, 1987).

McGann, Jerome J., *The Poetics of Sensibility: A Revolution in Literary Style* (Oxford, 1996).

McKeon, Michael, *The Secret History of Domesticity: Public, Private, and the Division of Knowledge* (Baltimore, 2005).

Mee, Jon, *Romanticism, Enthusiasm, and Regulation: Poetics and the Policing of Culture in the Romantic Period* (Oxford, 2003).

Miles, Dudley H., 'The Political Satire of "The Non-Juror" ', *Modern Philology* 13: 5 (1915), 281–304.

Milnes, Tim, *Knowledge and Indifference in English Romantic Prose* (Cambridge, 2003).

Monsman, Gerald Cornelius, *Confessions of a Prosaic Dreamer: Charles Lamb's Art of Autobiography* (Durham, NC, 1984).

—— *Charles Lamb as the* London Magazine's *'Elia'* (Lewiston, 2003).

Morley, F. V., *Lamb before Elia* (London, 1932).

Moss, Sarah, ' "The Bounds of His Great Empire": The "Ancient Mariner" and Coleridge at Christ's Hospital', *Romanticism* 8.1 (2002), 49–61.

Mullan, John, *Sentiment and Sociability: The Language of Feeling in the Eighteenth Century* (Oxford, 1988).

Natarajan, Uttara, 'Hazlitt, Lamb, and the Philosophy of Familiarity', *CLB* 124 (2003), 110–18.

Newlyn, Lucy, 'Lamb, Lloyd, London: A Perspective on Book Seven of the Prelude', *CLB* 47: 8 (1984), 169–85.

Newlyn, Lucy, 'Parodic Allusion: Coleridge and the "Nehemiah Higginbottom" Sonnets, 1797', *CLB* 56 (1986), 253-9.
—— *Reading, Writing, and Romanticism: The Anxiety of Reception* (Oxford, 2000).
—— *Coleridge, Wordsworth, and the Language of Allusion*, 2nd edn (Oxford, 2001).
Nicholes, Joseph, 'Politics by Indirection: Charles Lamb's Seventeenth-Century Renegade, John Woodvil', *WC* 19 (1988), 49-55.
Oliphant, Margaret, *The Literary History of England in the End of the Eighteenth and Beginning of the Nineteenth Century*, 3 vols (London, 1882).
Park, Roy, ed., *Lamb as Critic* (London, 1980).
—— 'Lamb, Shakespeare, and the Stage', *Shakespeare Quarterly* 33 (1982), 164-77.
Parker, Mark, *Literary Magazines and British Romanticism* (Cambridge, 2000).
Parker, Reeve, *Coleridge's Meditative Art* (Ithaca, NY, 1975).
—— '*Osorio's* Dark Employments: Tricking out Coleridgean Tragedy', *SiR* 33 (1994), 119-60.
Pater, Walter, *Appreciations, with an Essay on Style* (London, 1913).
Perry, Ruth, *Novel Relations: The Transformation of Kinship in English Literature and Culture 1748-1818* (Cambridge, 2004).
Perry, Seamus, *Coleridge and the Uses of Division* (Oxford, 1999).
Pinch, Adela, *Strange Fits of Passion: Epistemologies of Emotion, Hume to Austen* (Stanford, CA, 1996).
—— 'Sensibility', in *Romanticism: An Oxford Guide*, ed., Nicholas Roe (Oxford, 2005), 49-60.
Plotz, Judith, *Romanticism and the Vocation of Childhood* (New York, 2001).
Pollin, Burton R., 'Charles Lamb and Charles Lloyd as Jacobins and Anti-Jacobins', *SiR* (1973), 633-47.
Pratt, Lynda, 'Interaction, Reorientation, and Discontent', *Notes and Queries,* 47 (245) (2000), 314-21.
Radcliffe, Evan, '"In Dreams Begins Responsibility": Wordsworth's Ruined Cottage Story', *SiR* 23 (1984), 101-19.
Reiman, Donald *The Romantics Reviewed: Contemporary Reviews of British Romantic Writers (Part A: The Lake Poets)* 2 vols (New York and London, 1972).
Ricks, Christopher, *Allusion to the Poets* (Oxford, 2002).
Riehl, Joseph E., *That Dangerous Figure: Charles Lamb and the Critics* (Columbia, SC., 1998).
Rivers, Isabel, *Reason, Grace, and Sentiment: A Study of the Language of Religion and Ethics in England, 1660-1780*, 2 vols, *Vol. 2: Shaftesbury to Hume* (Cambridge, 1991).
Roberts, T. A., *The Concept of Benevolence: Aspects of Eighteenth-Century Moral Philosophy* (London, 1973).
Roe, Nicholas, 'Coleridge and John Thelwall: The Road to Nether Stowey', in *The Coleridge Connection*, eds, Gravil and Lefebure (Basingstoke, 1990), 60-80.
—— *Wordsworth and Coleridge: The Radical Years* (Oxford, 1988).
—— *John Keats and the Culture of Dissent* (Oxford, 1997).
—— *The Politics of Nature: William Wordsworth and Some Contemporaries*, 2nd edn (Basingstoke, 2002).
—— *Fiery Heart: The First Life of Leigh Hunt* (London, 2005).
Rose, R. B., 'The Priestley Riots of 1791', *Past and Present* (1960), 68-88.

Rosenbaum, Barbara, and Pamela White, eds, *Index of English Literary Manuscripts*, vol. 4. 1800–1900, pt. 2. Hardy – Lamb (London, 1982).
Rovee, Christopher, 'Solitude and Sociability: Wordsworth on Helvellyn', *Literature Compass* 1: 1, 2004: doi:10.1111/j.1741-4113.2004.00091.x.
Ruoff, Gene W., *Wordsworth and Coleridge: The Making of the Major Lyrics, 1802–1804* (London, 1989).
Russell, Gillian, and Clara Tuite, eds, *Romantic Sociability: Social Networks and Literary Culture in Britain, 1770–1840* (Cambridge, 2002).
Sandford, Margaret E., *Thomas Poole and his Friends*, 2 vols (London, 1888).
Shaffer, E. S. 'The Hermeneutic Community: Coleridge and Schleiermacher', in *The Coleridge Connection*, eds, Gravil and Lefebure, 200–29.
Sharps, William Chapman, *Unreal Cities* (Baltimore, 1990).
Sheats, Paul D., *The Making of Wordsworth's Poetry, 1785–1798* (Cambridge, MA, 1973).
Simpson, David, 'What Bothered Charles Lamb About Poor Susan?', *SEL* (1986), 589–612.
Simpson, Michael, 'Coleridge's Swinging Moods and the Revision of "This Lime-tree Bower my Prison"', *Style* 33.1 (1999), 21–42.
Sisman, Adam, *The Friendship: Wordsworth and Coleridge* (London, 2006).
Sokol, B. J., 'Coleridge on Charles Lamb's Poetic Craftsmanship', *English Studies* 71 (1990), 29–34.
Stabler, Jane, 'Space for Speculation: Coleridge, Barbauld, and the Poetics of Priestley', *Samuel Taylor Coleridge and the Sciences of Life*, ed., Nicholas Roe (Oxford, 2001), 175–206.
Stelzig, Eugene, 'Coleridge in *The Prelude*: Wordsworth's Fiction of Alterity', *WC* 18: 1 (1987), 23–7.
Stone, Lawrence, *The Family, Sex and Marriage in England 1500–1800* (New York, 1977).
Stones, Graeme, 'The Ragged-Trousered Philanthropist', *CLB* 100 (1997), 122–32.
—— and John Strachan, *Parodies of the Romantic Age*, 5 vols (London, 1999).
Sweet, Nanora, and Julie Melnyk, eds, *Felicia Hemans: Reimagining Poetry in the Nineteenth Century* (New York, 2001)
Swinburne, Algernon Charles, *Miscellanies* (London, 1886).
Symons, Arthur, *The Romantic Movement in English Poetry* (London, 1909).
Tadmor, Naomi, *Family and Friends in Eighteenth-Century England: Household, Kinship, and Patronage* (Cambridge, 2000).
Talfourd, Thomas Noon, *Final Memorials of Charles Lamb: Consisting Chiefly of His Letters Not before Published, with Sketches of Some of His Companions*, 2 vols (London, 1848).
—— *Memoirs of Charles Lamb*, ed., Percy Fitzgerald (London, 1892).
Taussig, Gurion, '"Lavish Promises": Coleridge, Charles Lamb, and Charles Lloyd, 1794–1798', *Romanticism* 6.1 (2000), 78–97.
—— *Coleridge and the Idea of Friendship, 1789–1804* (Newark and London, 2002).
Taylor, Anya, *Bacchus in Romantic England, Writers and Drink, 1780–1830* (New York, 1999).
Thompson, Denys, 'Our Debt to Lamb', in *Determinations*, ed., F. R. Leavis (London, 1934), 199–217.

Thompson, E. P., 'A Compendium of Cliché: The Poet as Essayist', in *The Romantics: England in a Revolutionary Age* (New York, 1997), 143–55.
Todd, Janet M., *Sensibility: An Introduction* (London, 1986).
Treadwell, James, 'Impersonation and Autobiography in Lamb's Christ's Hospital Essays', *SiR* 37.4 (1998), 499–521.
Trott, Nicola, 'The Coleridge Circle and The "Answer to Godwin"', *RES* 41 (1990), 212–29.
Vargo, Lisa, 'The Case of Anna Letitia Barbauld's "To Mr C[olerid]ge"', *CLB* 102 (1998), 55–63.
Walker, Nigel, *Crime and Insanity in England, the Historical Perspective* (Edinburgh, 1968).
Watson, Kathy, *The Devil Kissed Her: The Story of Mary Lamb* (London, 2004).
Watson, Nicola J., *Revolution and the Form of the British Novel, 1790–1825: Intercepted Letters, Interrupted Seductions* (Oxford, 1994).
Watters, Reggie, '"We Had Classics of Our Own": Charles Lamb's Schoolboy Reading', *CLB* 104 (1998), 114–28.
Wedd, Mary, 'Dialects of Humour: Lamb and Wordsworth', *CLB* 19 (1977), 46–54.
—— 'Mary Lamb', *CLB* 102 (1998), 42–54.
Whale, John C., 'Literal and Symbolic Representations: Burke, Paine and the French Revolution', *History of European Ideas* 16 (1993), 343–49.
White, Daniel E., *Early Romanticism and Religious Dissent* (Cambridge, 2006).
White, R. S., *Natural Rights and the Birth of Romanticism in the 1790s* (Basingstoke, 2005).
Wolfreys, Julian, *Writing London* (Basingstoke, 1998).
Woodbery, Bonnie, 'The Mad Body as the Text of Culture in the Writings of Mary Lamb', *SEL* 39 (1999), 659–74.
Woodring, Carl, *Politics in the Poetry of Coleridge* (Madison, 1961).
Wordsworth, Jonathan, *The Music of Humanity* (London, 1969).
—— ed., and 'Introduction', *A Tale of Rosamund Gray and Old Blind Margaret, 1798* (Woodstock, 1991).
Worthen, John, *The Gang: Coleridge, the Hutchinsons and Wordsworths in 1802* (New Haven, 2001).
Wu, Duncan, '*Lyrical Ballads* (1798): The Beddoes Copy', *The Library: The Transactions of the Bibliographical Society* 15 (1993), 332–35.
—— *Wordsworth's Reading 1770–1799* (Cambridge, 1993).
—— 'Lamb's Reading of *Lyrical Ballads*, 1800', *CLB* 92 (1995), 224–5.
—— *Wordsworth: An Inner Life* (Oxford, 2002).
Zimmerman, Sarah MacKenzie, *Romanticism, Lyricism, and History* (New York, 1999).

Index

Aaron, Jane, 2, 53–4, 88, 174
Addison, Joseph, 2
Aikin, John, 75, 76, 216n
  Evenings at Home, or the Juvenile Budget Opened (with Barbauld), 202
The Albion, and Evening Advertiser, 146, 179–81, 183
Alfoxden, 102, 104, 155
Allen, Matthew, 226n
Allen, Robert, 13, 14, 42
allusion
  Burke's use of, 7
  Clare's use of, 178
  Coleridge's use of, 7, 64
  as form of sociability, 6–8, 28
  Keats' use of, 7
  Lamb's use of, 8, 28, 52, 58, 72, 111: in *Essays of Elia*, 175, 205, 210; in *John Woodvil*, 168, 172–5, 177; in *Rosamund Gray*, 147, 149, 152, 163–6; in *Specimens*, 209–10; in 'What is Jacobinism?', 182–3
  parodic, 117–18
  as reproof, 111–12
Amyot, Thomas, 5, 26
Analytical Review, 125
The Annual Anthology, 86, 107, 134
The Anti-Jacobin, 1–3, 4, 38, 39, 117, 119, 120, 124, 135, 138, 179–80, 181
anti-Semitism, 208
anxiety, 36, 64–74, 104, 118, 123, 134
  about definition of family, 25
  about friendship, 146–7
  about national events, 183
  about self and society, 36
  authorial, 6, 57, 69, 70, 104, 160, 195–7, 205, 212
  Lamb's, 88, 104, 189
  reading, 69
Arnold, Matthew, 190

Association for Preserving Liberty and Property against Republicans and Levellers, 22
associationism, 15, 39–41, 43, 57
  see also Hartley, David
atheism, 20, 91, 97, 135, 167, 206

Bage, Robert, 155
Bailey, Benjamin, 209
Bampfylde, John, 'To Evening', 99
Barbauld, Anna Letitia, 75, 76, 78, 90, 91, 216n
  'To Mr S. T. Coleridge', 78–9, 90
  see also Aikin, John
Barker-Benfield, G. J., 37
Bate, Walter Jackson, 95
Baudelaire, Charles, 188, 212, 214
Baxter, Richard, 89, 150
  'The Saint's Everlasting Rest', 86, 87
Beattie, James, *The Minstrel*, 51
Beaumont, Francis, 168, 174, 175
Beddoes, Thomas, 'Domiciliary Verses', 101
Beer, John, 217n
bells, 173
Belsham, Thomas, 133
benevolence
  Christ's Hospital and, 24, 41–2
  Coleridge and, 42–5, 56–7, 67, 85, 92, 99, 107, 112, 120, 123, 137
  Dyer on, 41
  Godwin and, 137, 164
  Hartley on, 39–40
  Lamb on, 15–16, 24, 85, 121, 147, 164, 182, 205
  Lloyd on, 96, 121, 123, 127–8, 137
  Mary Lamb and, 229n
  and particular friendship, 147
  problems of, 35–7
  Shaftesbury and Hutcheson on, 35–7
  universal, 15–16, 205
  Wordsworth and, 104, 157

251

benevolence – *continued*
  see also home-born feeling;
    sensibility; sociability;
    sympathy; Unitarianism
Benjamin, Walter, 213
Berkeley, George, 108
Bethlem Royal Hospital, 229n
Blackwood's Magazine, 211
Blakesware, 176
Bloom, Harold, 6
  The Anxiety of Influence, 7
Bonney, John Augustus, 5
bower
  dangers of, 70, 72–3, 78
  embowered poet, 62–70, 93–4,
    104–12, 156–7
  as space of friendship, 14–15,
    62–70, 93, 94, 185, 205
  urban, 198
Bowles, William
  Coleridge and, 174
  Coleridge's sonnet on, 15, 16, 22–4,
    51, 147, 435
  Lamb and, 212
  and *Poems* (1796), 56, 69–70
  WORKS: *Fourteen Sonnets*, 57, 173;
    'On Mr. Howard's Account of
    Lazarettos', 41; 'To a Friend',
    98; 'To the River Itchin', 49, 57
Bown, Nicola, 45
Brawne, Fanny, 209
The British Critic, 179, 188
Brooks, Henry, 99
brotherly kindness, 89
Browne, Sir Thomas, *Religio Medici*, 187
Brydges, Egerton, 'When eddying
  Leaves begun in whirls to fly', 99
Bunyan, John, 150
  Pilgrim's Progress, 78
Burke, Edmund, 26, 50
  Coleridge's sonnet on, 15, 18–19, 24
  conservatism, 4, 17, 64, 186
  Paine on, 31
  patriotism, 120
  on Rousseau, 38, 244n
  use of allusion, 7
  Wordsworth and, 17, 104
  WORKS: *Letter to a Noble Lord*, 1, 19;
    *Reflections on the Revolution in
    France*, 16, 17, 21, 23, 30, 39

Burnett, George, 27, 32
Burton, Robert, *The Anatomy of
  Melancholy*, 176–7, 187
Butler, Bishop Joseph, 222n
Butler, Marilyn, 31, 228n

Calne, Wiltshire, 173
Cambridge, 19, 29–30, 186, 187
Cambridge Intelligencer, 19
Carlyle, Thomas, 46
The Champion, 202, 211
Chandler, David, 134–5, 228n, 237n
Chandler, James, 17, 37, 45, 105, 163
Chatterton, Thomas
  Coleridgean identification with,
    74–5
  invited to join Pantisocratic
    scheme, 28, 56
choice, relationships of, 27–8, 31
Christensen, Jerome, 17
Christ's Hospital, 13, 14, 24, 27, 41–2,
  44, 51, 54, 75, 149
Cibber, Colley, *The Non-Juror*, as
  source for *John Woodvil*, 168
city-based writing, 5–6, 126, 131,
  185–8, 196–200, 204, 210–16
Clare, John, 54, 168, 177–9
  'Don Juan', 226n
  'Robin Hood and the Gamekeeper',
    180
  'To Charles Lamb', 178
Clarke, Charles Cowden, 55
Clevedon, Somerset, 44, 64, 65, 66
Coates, John, 179
Coleridge, Berkeley, 189–90
Coleridge, David Hartley, 92, 102,
  122, 132, 183
Coleridge, George, 92–3, 94–6
Coleridge, Samuel Taylor
  breaks off with Lloyd, 139–40
  childhood appropriated by
    Lamb, 173
  as 'confessor' for Lamb, 38, 171–2
  and death of son Berkeley, 189–90
  and *Edmund Oliver*, 138, 139–40
  and *Essays of Elia*, 206, 207
  friendship with Wordsworth, 7, 17,
    71, 91, 101–3, 105–11, 115, 136
  in Gillray cartoon, 1
  Lamb's version of his poems, 4, 53

Coleridge, Samuel Taylor – *continued*
  letters on Mary Lamb, 8
  marriage to Sara Fricker, 27, 55, 64
  moves to Clevedon, 64, 66
  at Nether Stowey, 92–100
  political views, *see* politics, Coleridge and
  praise of Wordsworth, 110
  quarrel with Lamb, 139–40
  'religious' letter to Lamb, 86–8
  renewal of friendship with Lamb, 166
  revision of Lamb's sonnets, 56–62, 63–4, 67–9, 91, 99, 133–4
  at Salutation tavern, 13–15, 18, 20, 31
  Thelwall's criticism of, 91
  Unitarianism, *see* Unitarianism, Coleridge and
  WORKS: 'Address to a Young Jack-Ass, and its *Tether'd* Mother, In Familiar Verse', 28; *Biographia Literaria*, 44, 114; *The Borderers*, 4, 8, 103, 104, 113, 127, 134, 136, 137, 159, 164; 'Christabel', 146; *Conciones ad Populum*, 39, 66, 123; *Dactylics*, 1, 117; 'Effusion XV: Pale Roamer thro' the Night!', 56; 'Effusion XVI: To an Old Man in the Snow' (with Favell), 42, 56, 98, 98–9, 112; 'Effusion XXII: To a Friend together with an unfinished poem', 59, 131–2; 'Effusion XXXV, composed August 20th 1795, at Clevedon, Somersetshire', 65; 'Eminent Characters', sonnets to, 18–24, 43–5, 47, 49, 51, 53, 56; 'The Eolian Harp', 62, 65–9, 71; *The Fall of Robespierre*, 225n; 'Fears in Solitude', 120, 121, 122, 140–1; 'The Foster Mother's Tale', 126–7; 'Frost at Midnight', 67, 94, 120–3, 130–1, 136, 138, 140–1, 182, 183, 193; 'In the Manner of Spenser', 70; *Lectures on Revealed Religion*, 87; 'Lines on a Friend', 70, 73; 'Monody on the Death of Chatterton', 28–9, 55–6, 74–5, 78; 'Nehemiah Higginbottom' sonnets, 7, 114–19, 124, 125, 164; 'On a Ruined House in a Romantic Country', 118–19; *Osorio*, 4, 8, 103, 113, 126, 131, 134, 136, 164, 173; *The Piccolimini* (translation), 176; *Poems on Various Subjects* (1796), 9, 14, 22, 43, 44, 50, 55–71, 76, 78, 99, 112; *Poems on Various Subjects* (1797), 65, 86, 91–3, 103, 112, 115–19; 'Preface' to *Poems* 1796, 55, 56–9, 61, 62; 'Reflections on Entering into Active Life', 66–7, 77–8; 'Reflections on Having Left a Place of Retirement', 62, 65–9, 71, 94, 95, 104, 122, 156–7, 210; 'Religious Musings', 32–3, 78, 86, 91, 97, 217n; *Remorse*, 113–14; 'The Rime of the Ancient Mariner', 76, 160, 194, 196, 213; 'Songs of the Pixies', 69–70, 73, 94; *Sonnets from Various Authors* (ed.), 98–9, 112; 'This Lime-tree Bower my Prison', 8, 14, 85, 86, 88, 94, 103, 105–11, 121, 130–2, 136, 140, 162, 186, 188, 205, 210; 'To an Old Man in the Snow', *see Effusion XVI: To an Old Man in the Snow*; 'To the Author of "The Robbers"', 98; 'To the Nightingale', 131; 'To the Rev. George Coleridge', 92–3, 94–6, 114, 124; 'To the Rev. W.J.H., While Teaching a Young Lady Some Song-tunes on his Flute', 56; 'To the River Otter', 98; 'Wanderings of Cain', 160; *The Watchman*, 19, 43, 66, 75, 140
  see also Lamb, Charles, WORKS; Wordsworth, William, WORKS
Congreve, William, 177
Connolly, Cyril, 2
Cottle, Joseph, 55, 64, 115
  Reminiscences, 14

Courtney, Winifred F., 2, 27, 181, 215n, 236n
Cowper, William, 76–7
    The Task, 173
Cox, Jeffrey N., 5, 7
Cox, Philip, 137–8
Craciun, Adriana, 229n
Crawford, Rachel, 62
creativity
    Barbauld reassures Coleridge over, 78
    in the city, 197
    at Clevedon, 64
    differing views between Coleridge and Lamb, 68–9
    in the 'Lime-tree Bower', 107
    shared in the 'Salutation and Cat', 13, 98

Darwin, Erasmus, 100
Davies, Damian Walford, 110, 232n
dedications, 4, 91–2, 93, 95, 112, 123, 126, 137, 149, 172
Devlin, D. D., 162
Dilly Brothers, 22–3
Disney, John, 33
Dissenters, 15, 19, 21, 23, 24, 26, 29–30, 33, 41, 66, 75, 76, 163, 179, 202
    intellectual life and networks, 26, 75–9, 202, 216n
    and *John Woodvil*, 179
    persecution, 21, 29
    see also Unitarianism
Dyer, George, 5, 13, 14, 29, 41–2, 187, 206, 212
    Dissertation on Benevolence, 41, 51
    Inquiry into the Nature of Subscription, 41

East India House, London, 13, 27, 54, 83
egotism
    authorial, 57–8, 61, 91–2, 114, 140, 207, 208, 209
    in friendship, 147–8
Ellia, Felix, 205–6, 207
    Theopha, 206
Enquirer, 1

epic, Lamb encourages Coleridge to write, 71–2
Epstein, James, 22
eroticism, 64, 69–70, 73, 178
    see also reading, as sensual seduction
Erskine, Thomas, 18, 22, 23, 56
Essex Street Chapel, London, 20, 29, 33, 76, 218n
Everest, Kelvin, 17, 30, 67, 107
The Examiner, 46, 198, 202, 211

Fairer, David, 18, 98, 125, 137
fairy tales, 51–2
    see also story-telling
family
    absolution through, 168, 169
    and benevolence, 159
    Burke's views of, 16, 30
    of Christ, 68
    Coleridge and, 1, 27–30, 92–3, 102, 120–1, 186
    community of, 66
    debated in 1790s, 16, 25, 31, 37
    disruption of, 84, 85, 124, 128, 145, 148, 150, 167, 170
    familial affection, 17, 23, 90, 91–4, 121, 125, 171, 176, 182, 189, 201
    Godwin's views of, 16, 31–2, 159–60
    Lamb and, 13, 42, 53, 83–5, 91–2, 102, 125, 147–8, 152–5, 159, 168–73, 182
    loyalties, 152–5
    of mankind, 16
    narratives, 169–73
    Paine's views of, 31
    and Pantisocracy, 27–30, 30–31
    and reading, 50, 53, 102
    as society, 102
    traditions, 191
    and Unitarianism, 17, 32, 41
    Wordsworth and, 159–60, 191
    see also friendship; reading
Fang, Karen, 3
Favell, Samuel, 13, 14, 27, 29, 42, 55–6
    see also Coleridge, Samuel Taylor, WORKS

Favret, Mary, 26
Fayette, Gilbert de La, 22, 23
femininity, 61-2, 64, 73
Fenwick, John, 181
Field, Barron, 206
Fielding, Henry
  Jonathan Wild, 37
  Tom Jones, 37
Fisher House, Islington, 84
FitzGerald, Edward, 46
flâneur, 212-13, 228n
Fleet Street, London, 196, 210
Fletcher, John, 168, 174, 175
Flint, Christopher, 25
Flower, Benjamin, 19, 48
Fox, Charles James, 1, 21
Frend, William, 29-30
Fricker, Edith (later Southey), 27
Fricker, Martha, 27
Fricker, Sara (later Coleridge), 27, 28, 55, 64, 65-6, 68, 70, 89, 101, 106
The Friend (magazine), 29, 72
friendship
  and allusion, 6-7
  and benevolence, 34-6
  betrayal of, 94, 111-19, 130-6, 139-41
  books as friends, 150
  as 'brotherly kindness', 89
  collapse of, 8, 110, 118, 123, 139-41
  and community, 5-7, 18, 26-30, 70-1, 110, 146
  as concept in the 1790s, 25-6, 30-6, 137, 139
  definitions of, 25, 26
  false, 94, 112, 114, 116, 124, 164-5, 170, 171
  as idolatry, 88, 171, 172
  and kinship, 25
  and 'manliness', 14, 23-4, 26, 32, 44, 53
  as model for reform, 5, 7, 40-1
  'particular', 35, 135, 147
  politicisation of, 18
  and pride, 167
  reading and, *see* reading, and friendship
  and religion, 33-4, 40, 42-3, 86, 89-90
  and sensibility, 34-9, 43-5
  of sentiment, 164
  as social ideal, 3, 5, 7-8, 14-18, 26-7, 141, 170-1, 205
  sympathetic, 36, 165, 170
  see also bower; Pantisocracy; Salutation, as ideal sociable space; Unitarianism
Fulford, Tim, 28, 219n

Gifford, William, 85
Gigante, Denise, 3
Gillray, James, 1-3, 21, 38, 119, 120, 215n
Girondins, 29
Godwin, William
  atheism, 20, 135
  and benevolence, 137, 164
  Coleridge and, 13, 17, 126, 127, 206
  Coleridge's sonnet on, 19-20
  disinterest, 158, 186, 210
  egotism, 134
  and Fenwick, 181
  in Gillray cartoon, 1
  and *John Woodvil*, 175
  novels of, 155
  rationalism, 128
  and *Rosamund Gray*, 149, 170
  theories, 26, 104, 105, 135, 159
  WORKS: *Antonio*, 236n; *An Enquiry Concerning Political Justice*, 15-16, 20, 31-2, 54, 96, 97, 125, 135, 137, 154; *Faulkener*, 179; *Lectures on Revealed Religion*, 20; *St Leon*, 193
Gorji, Mina, 178
Goslar, 148, 160, 189
Gothic novel, 25
Gravel Pit, Hackney, 33
Graves, Richard, 220n
grief and mourning
  Bowles on, 57
  Coleridge and, 189-90
  Lamb on, 8, 58, 104-5, 129, 130, 148-9, 153, 161-2, 166, 171, 172, 189
  Thelwall and, 111
  Wordsworth and, 129, 145, 148-9, 156-8, 161-3, 189-90

Grovier, Kelly, 129
guilt, sense of, 68, 73, 85, 95, 113–15, 127, 134, 167, 168, 169–70

Hardy, Thomas, 18, 41
Hartley, David, 39–40, 57, 96, 98, 123, 137, 177, 204
 Observations on Man, 40
Haworth, Helen, 209
Haydon, Benjamin Robert, 4, 8–9, 211
 diary, 9
Hays, Mary, 75
Hazlitt, William, 4, 9, 16–17, 72, 163, 175, 180, 208, 211
 'My First Acquaintance with Poets', 14
hermeneutic community, 70–1
Heywood, Thomas, 209
Higgins, David, 129
High Beech asylum, Epping, 226n
Hobbes, Thomas, 35, 36, 37, 147, 221n
Hodgson, William, 22
Holcroft, Thomas, 1, 13, 26
 The Adventures of Hugh Trevor, 47
 Anna St. Ives, 96
Home, John, *Douglas*, 54
'home-born feeling'
 and 'bower', 93, 105–7
 celebrated in *Essays of Elia*, 210
 Coleridge and, 15, 35, 39, 40–1, 65–7, 93, 105–7, 117, 141
 continuation, 163, 180, 186, 187, 214
 Lamb and, 71, 84, 85, 92, 103, 106, 121, 128–30, 134, 152, 185
 and Leigh Hunt's imprisonment, 198
 and literature of sensibility, 152
 Lloyd and, 117
 in *Poems* (1796), 44–5
 philosophical basis, 35, 39–40
 in *Rosamund Gray*, 152, 163
 in *Specimens of Dramatic Poets*, 209–10
 in urban writing of Lamb, 187
 see also benevolence; Salutation and Cat tavern, London
homosexuality, 23, 219n
Howard, John, 67

Hoxton asylum, London, 53–4, 84, 177
Hume, David, 47, 222n
 A Treatise of Human Nature, 36
 Enquiry Concerning Human Understanding, 36
 Enquiry Concerning the Principles of Morals, 36
humility, 87, 88, 90, 104, 109
Hunt, James Henry Leigh, 5, 42, 46, 55, 180, 198–9, 202, 208–9, 211
 'Robin Hood: To a Friend', 180
Hunt, John, 202
Hutcheson, Francis, 35, 221n
Hutchinson, Mary, 155
hypocrisy, 86

'immortal dinner', 8–9
Inchbald, Elizabeth, 155
indeterminacy in the writings of Wordsworth and Lamb, 188, 190, 193, 195, 202, 208, 212
indolence, 69–70, 72–3, 78, 94, 157
indulgence, 37, 64, 66, 152
 see also self-indulgence
insanity, 53–4, 77, 84, 229n
intertextuality, 71, 149, 163
Ireland, William Henry, *Vortigern*, 228n

Jacobinism, 180–4
Jacobus, Mary, 72, 105
Jeffrey, Francis, 196
Jesus Christ, 42–3, 67, 68, 86, 87, 88, 123
Jesus College, Cambridge, 29–30
Johnson, Joseph, 33, 75, 76, 120
Jones, Mark, 190
Jonson, Ben, 175
Joyce, James, *Finnegans Wake*, 239n

Keats, John, 5, 7, 55, 153, 180, 208–9, 211
 annotating Lamb, 209
 and negative capability, 208
 'Robin Hood: To a Friend', 180
Kelly, Gary, 152
Kemble, John, 178
Keppel, Lord, 19
Kingston, John, 217n

kinship, 25
see also family
Kosciusko, Tadeusz, 22, 50, 56

Lake District, 186
Lamb unmoved by, 186, 197–8
Lamb, Charles
  on books and book-buying, 98, 150, 178, 194, 196, 196–9, 214
  breaks off with Coleridge, 139, 147
  children, imagery of, 3
  at Christ's Hospital, 13, 42, 51, 149, 173
  and Coleridge's revisions, 56–69, *see also* Coleridge, Samuel Taylor, revision of Lamb's sonnets
  comments on Coleridge's 'Preface' to *Poems* (1796), 58, 59
  critical views of, 2–3, 46–7, 211–12
  and drink, 168–9, 170, 217n
  as Edax, 3, 203
  as Elia, 3, 13, 28, 151, 168, 173, 174, 178, 181–2, 203–8, 210, 213
  as essayist, 200–10
  forgeries, 176–7, 228n
  in Hoxton asylum, 53–4
  humour, 167, 168–9, 179–80, 200
  letters to Coleridge, 9, 14, 33, 34, 38, 53, 55, 71, 83–4, 87–8, 150, 153, 170, 172, 200
  letters to friends, 6, 9, 15
  letters to Robert Lloyd, 146–8
  letters to Southey, 168, 175
  letters to Wordsworth, 9, 188–201
  and *London Magazine*, 3
  love of London, 187, 195–8, 201, 210, 212–13
  on *Lyrical Ballads*, 188–201, 210
  medleys, 176–7
  on nature, 187, 195–8
  at Nether Stowey, 101–3
  parodied by Coleridge, 115–19
  as Pensilis, 203, 235n
  political views, *see* politics, Lamb and
  on prejudice, 208
  on problems of friendship, 147–8, *see also* friendship
  punctuation, 151–2, 199
  puns, 6, 30, 58, 206
  as reader, 168, *see also* on books and book-buying
  on reading newspapers, 181–4, 194
  relationships: with Ann Simmons, 54, 149; with Charles Lloyd, 98–100, 121–3, 128, 137, 139–41; with Coleridge, 13–14, 28, 32–4, 40, 51–2, 58, 71–2, 75, 86–8, 89–91, 101–3, 111–13, 114–19, 130–4, 136, 171–4, 176–7; with Mary Lamb, 52–3, 83–5, 91–2, 129, 152–4, 176–7, 185, 212; with Wordsworth, 5, 71, 91, 102–3, 103–5, 111, 129, 135, 136, 139, 145–6, 148–9, 149–51, 155–63, 175, 179, 182–4, 186, 188–90, 193–5, 195–200, 201, 203
  religious opinions, *see* Unitarianism, Lamb and
  reproaches Coleridge, 111–13, 130–6
  rewriting Wordsworth, 195–200, 201, 203–4, 208, 210–11
  and Shakespeare, 50, 168, 174, 202, 208, 209
  shared faith with Coleridge, 16, 20, 32, 102, 182
  transforms verse into prose, 199–200
  as Unitarian, *see* Unitarianism, Lamb and
  and the urban, 6, 131, 174, 183–4, 185–204, *see also* love of London
  use of antique style, 168, 179
  'very merry letter' to Wordsworth and Coleridge, 200
  on Wordsworth, 208
  WORKS: *Blank Verse* (with Lloyd), 1–2, 7, 8, 18, 86, 101, 111, 121, 123–34, 139; 'Christ's Hospital Five and Thirty Years ago', 173; 'Composed at Midnight', 130–4, 206; *Confessions of a Drunkard*, 169; 'Curious Fragments', 176–7, 180;

Lamb, Charles – *continued*
'Detached Thoughts on Books and Reading', 73, 181–2, 194; 'Distant Correspondents', 206; 'Dream Children', 54; 'Effusions', 54; 'Effusion VII: As when a child', 60; 'Effusion XI: Was it some sweet device/delight of faery land', 58, 61; 'Effusion XII: 'Methinks, how dainty sweet it were, reclin'd', 56, 58, 62–5, 67–9, 72–3, 78, 93, 122, 133, 209; 'Effusion XIII: 'Written at Midnight, by the Sea-Side, after a voyage', 58, 59–60; *Essays of Elia*, 175, 178, 181–2, 202–8; 'Imperfect Sympathies', 182, 207–8; *John Woodvil*, 3, 8, 52, 85, 146, 167–80, 182, 189, 200, 201, 205, 209, 212; 'Lines Addressed, from London, to SARA and S.T.C. at Bristol, in the Summer of 1796', 77, 117, *see also* 'To Sara and her Samuel' (earlier title); 'Living without God in the World', 86, 134–7, 138, 147, 148, 164, 166, 170, 172; 'The Londoner', 201–2; 'The Old Familiar Faces', 85, 121, 129–30, 149, 160, 163, 165–6, 171, 203, 209; 'The Old Margate Hoy', 175; 'On the Genius and Character of Hogarth', 202; 'On the Inconveniences Resulting from Being Hanged', 202, 235n; 'On [...] the Plays of Shakespeare', 50, 202; 'Preface' to *The Last Essays of Elia*, 207; *Rosamund Gray*, 8, 52, 74, 130, 145–66, 168, 172, 173, 174, 184, 189, 190, 205, 206, 209, 212; 'The Sabbath Bells', 173; sonnet on Mrs Siddons (with Coleridge), 15, 47–53, 59, 68, 126–7, 201, 202; 'Sonnet to a Friend', 117; 'The South-Sea House', 203–4, 205, 206; *Specimens of English Dramatic Poets, Who Lived about the Time of Shakspeare*, 85, 209–10; 'Sweet is thy sunny hair', 73–4, 151; 'Theses quaedam Theologicae' (with Lloyd), 139–40, 170; 'To a Friend', 117; 'To My Sister', 52–3; 'To the Poet Cowper, on his recovery from an indisposition', 76–7; 'To Sara and her Samuel', 74–5, 77–8, 102, 106, 117; 'To Sir James Mackintosh', 179–80; 'What is Jacobinism?', 180–4; *Works* (1818), 55, 60, 61, 64, 150, 208–9; 'Written on Christmas Day 1797', 129; 'Written on the day of my aunt's funeral', 128

Lamb, Charles, and Lamb, Mary
Mrs Leicester's School, 54, 84, 191, 211–12
Tales from Shakespeare, 50, 211

Lamb, Elizabeth, 83–5, 91, 92, 128, 153–4, 166

Lamb, John (father), 13, 83, 84, 185

Lamb, John (son), 83, 85, 153

Lamb, Mary, 2, 3, 27, 52–3, 117, 172, 211–12
dedication to, 91–2
'Elizabeth Villiers', 191
'Helen', 176
illness, 129, 130, 132, 150, 153, 166, 177, 185, 189, 229n
letters, 201
matricide, 8, 83–5, 86, 91, 92, 145, 169
recent criticism concerning, 229n
'The Sailor Uncle', 191
see also Lamb, Charles, and Lamb, Mary

Laslett, Peter, 25
Leask, Nigel, 17, 29, 67
Leavis, F. R., 46
Legouis, Emile, 103
Le Grice, Charles Valentine, 13, 19, 40, 42, 223n
'On Seeing Mrs Siddons the First Time, and then in the character of Isabella', 47–8, 49, 52
The Tineum, 225n

Le Grice, Samuel, 13, 27, 42
Lindsey, Theophilus, 5, 20–1, 33–4, 76, 96
Little Queen Street, Holborn, 83
Llandaff, Bishop of, 120
Lloyd, Charles
  at Ambleside, 186
  Coleridge and, 96–100, 111, 139–40, 164
  and Gillray cartoon, 1, 2, 4
  and *Monthly Magazine*, 76
  neglected by Coleridge, 111
  at Nether Stowey, 92, 94, 96–8, 102–3
  parodied by Coleridge, 115–19
  and *Poems* (1797), 93
  relationships with Coleridge and Lamb, 7, 96–100, 115, 212
  WORKS: 'Address to Wealth', 120; 'The Dead Friend', 125; *Edmund Oliver*, 111, 136–9, 165; 'Lines on passing a place of former residence', 121; *Lines Suggested by the Fast*, 134; 'London, a poem', 126; 'Nature's Simplicity', 149; *Poems on the Death of Priscilla Farmer*, 98; *Poems on Various Subjects*, 96, 149; 'To Coleridge' (manuscript sonnet), 97, 118; 'To Friendship', 117; 'To a Sister', 124–6, 182; 'Turn not thy dim eyes to the stormy sea', 126–7; 'Written at Burton in Hampshire', 124
  see also Lamb, Charles; Wordsworth, William
Lloyd, Charles senior, 94, 99
Lloyd, Robert, 96, 146–8, 171, 201
Locke, John, 221n
  Essay Concerning Human Understanding, 35
London, 5, 187, 195–8, 204, 210–11, 212–13
London Corresponding Society, 17, 18, 22
London Magazine, 3, 9, 151, 178, 202, 203, 205–6
London Revolutionary Society, 235n

loneliness, 4–5, 11, 61, 64–9, 98, 104, 106, 110–14, 121–30, 156–66, 160, 178
Longman, 188
Losh, James, 104
Lovell, Robert and Mary (née Fricker), 27
Lucas, E. V., 2, 211
'lunacy', 84
  see also insanity
Lynch, Deidre, 214

Mackenzie, Henry, 24, 212, 221n
  Julia de Roubigné, 74, 151–2, 166
  The Man of Feeling, 37, 74
Mackintosh, Sir James, 179–80
Magnuson, Paul, 120, 141, 146
Mahoney, Charles, 17
Man, Henry, 204
Manchineel (poison tree), 111–12, 114
Mandeville, Bernard, 36
manliness and masculinity
  Coleridge on, 45, 53, 219n
  and friendship, 14, 23, 26, 32, 44, 53
  Lamb and, 174
  and sensibility, 23–4, 45
Manning, Thomas, 169, 170, 185, 186, 187, 188, 189, 200, 201
Marie Antoinette, Queen, 30
marriage, 25, 27
Marrs, Edwin W., 28, 217n
Mason, Emma, 45, 47
Massinger, Philip, *A Very Woman*, 92
Mays, J. C. C., 22
McFarland, Thomas, 90, 234n, 239n
McGann, Jerome, 45, 47, 48, 221n, 222n, 224n
McKeon, Michael, 25
Mee, Jon, 67
Merlin, Joseph (of Oxford Street), 62
Merry, Robert, 221n
Milton, John, 77, 95
  Samson Agonistes, 135
Mitre Court Buildings, London, 185
Monsman, Gerald Cornelius, 205
Monthly Magazine, 1, 4, 66, 75–8, 104, 114, 117, 128, 180
Monthly Visitor, 115
Morgan family, 173

Morley, F. V., 171
Morning Chronicle, 13, 18, 41, 44, 50, 84
  see also Coleridge, Samuel Taylor, WORKS, 'Eminent Characters', sonnets to
Morning Post, 140, 186, 201, 202
Mullan, John, 36, 222n

narrator
  as means of merging identity, 137–8, 158, 164, 173, 182, 205–6
  solitary and isolated, 130–3, 145, 150
  Wordsworthian, 156–7, 192
Natarajan, Uttara, 204–5
nature, 4, 65, 94, 131, 148, 183, 184, 187, 193, 195–8
  and sympathetic response, 184
necessarianism, 86, 87, 128
negative capability, 208
  see also Keats, John
Nether Stowey, Somerset, 8, 14–15, 44, 55, 92–4, 102–3, 116, 118, 123, 137, 138, 155, 186
Newbery, John, 51
New Criticism, 46–7
Newlyn, Lucy, 6, 95, 118, 233n
'New Morality', 1, 38, 120, 135, 180
newspapers, 181–4, 194
Nicholes, Joseph, 3, 179, 235n
Northampton General Asylum, 226n

Oliphant, Margaret, 190
Ollier, Charles and James, 209
Omnipresence, Lamb's distrust of Coleridge's reference to, 90
Ossian, 203, 205
Ottery St. Mary, 69, 173, 228n

Paine, Thomas, 17, 20, 33, 39
  Rights of Man, 31
Pantisocracy
  and *Blank Verse*, 123, 124
  Chatterton invited to join, 28–9, 55–6
  choice of Susquehannah, 29, 33–4
  collapse of, 44, 55, 64, 141, 146
  'common identity', 138
  Edmund Oliver and, 138
  ideals and aims, 7, 27–30, 32–5, 41–2, 58, 64, 128, 205
  indiscriminate invitations to join in, 28–9
  influence of, 71, 92, 110
  Lamb and, 27, 33–4, 42, 146
  and relationships of choice, 27–8, 30, 31
  Rosamund Gray and, 165
  Southey and, 34
Paris, Terror, 18
Park, Roy, 50, 207
Parker, Mark, 215n, 237n
Parker, Reeve, 87, 114
parody, 115–19
Pater, Walter, 190
Pattison, William, 26
Perry, James, 18
Perry, Ruth, 25
Perry, Seamus, 90, 108
Phillips, Richard, 75
Pigott, Charles, 22
Pinch, Adela, 45, 224n, 226n
Plotz, Judith, 3
politics, 1, 15, 21–31, 39, 41, 56, 137, 155, 198–9, 203
  Coleridge and, 16–17, 21, 43, 64–7, 76, 120, 140–1
  Lamb and, 1–4, 5, 17–18, 138, 179–83, 206
  Wordsworth and, 16–18, 146, 163
  see also radicalism
Pollin, Burton, 2
Poole, Thomas, 14, 51, 92, 93, 99, 102, 112, 123
Pope, Alexander, *Essay on Man*, 43
Price, Richard, 33
  Discourse on the love of our country, 21
pride, 96, 104, 133, 134–6, 140, 147, 167–71
Priestley, Joseph, 3, 5, 15, 16, 20–2, 24, 29, 32–4, 40, 56, 86, 90, 96
  Letters to a Philosophical Unbeliever, 135

Quakers, 96, 133, 171, 187
Quarles, Francis, 150
Quarterly, 85

quotation
  Elian use of, 205, 209–10
  from Elizabethan literature, 168, 174
  general use of, 4, 6, 52, 71–2, 152, 168, 174, 205, 209–10
  from personal letters, 152–4
  see also allusion; Shakespeare, William

Racedown, 101, 104
radicalism, 16–19
  and *Blank Verse*, 123–4
  Coleridge and, 129–30, 141
  and *Edmund Oliver*, 138–9
  and *Fears in Solitude* collection, 120–3, 141
  friendship and, 4–5, 16, 21–2, 24, 26
  Hunt and, 198
  Lamb and, 180–4, 198
  and manliness, 23
  Monthly Magazine and, 75
  and *Poems* (1796), 56
  and reading, 179–80
  and retirement, 67
  and sensibility, 18, 22–4, 37–9
  societies connected to, 26
  and Unitarianism, 29–30
  Wordsworth and, 146, 157, 163
rationalism, 128
reading
  and anxiety, 6, 57–8, 67, 69, 70
  with feeling, 45–6, 49–51, 57–8, 73, 151–3, 178, 188, 194, 208
  and friendship, 4, 56–8, 70–1, 74–9, 129–30, 150, 164, 166, 168, 174, 210–12, 214
  of newspapers, 181–4, 194
  as sensual seduction, 70, 72–3, 178
  as social good, 182–4
Reeves, John, 22
The Reflector, 202, 211
remorse, 70, 113–14, 167
Reynolds, John Hamilton, 180
Richardson, Samuel, *Pamela*, 73
Ricks, Christopher, 7, 209
Riehl, Joseph E., 46
Robinson, Henry Crabb, 5, 26, 208

Roe, Nicholas, 5, 17, 20, 30, 41, 110, 135, 180, 199
Romanticism, 4–5, 8–9, 45, 199, 208, 212
'rose-leaf beds', 66–8, 93, 157
Rousseau, Jean-Jacques, 38–9, 212, 220n, 223n, 224n
  Confessions, 38
Russell, Gillian, 5, 6, 7

Salt, Samuel, 13, 83
Salutation and Cat tavern, London
  and Coleridge's 'bower', 65, 93
  as 'foul stye', 20
  as ideal sociable space, 13–15, 24, 55, 62, 129, 134, 202
  ideals of, 56, 85, 92, 105–6, 183, 187
  and manly friendship, 23–4, 165
  and Pantisocracy, 27
  remembered by Lamb, 14, 23, 34, 40–1, 98, 102, 165
  sonnet on Mrs Siddons composed in, 47
  and Unitarianism, 32
Savory, Hester, 187
Schiller, Friedrich, *Wallenstein*, 176
Schleiermacher, Friedrich, 71
Scott, John, 202, 237n
sedition, 22
self-contradiction, 114, 146
  Lamb's engagement with Wordsworth's, 188, 193–5
self-indulgence, fears of, 44, 65, 69, 70
sensibility
  affective, 45–6
  battles over in the 1790s, 37–9, 41–5
  and benevolence, 34–9, 42–5
  Coleridge and, 22–4, 43–5, 53, 65–6, 70, 115–16
  critical readings of, 45–7, 221–3n
  Dyer on, 41
  Lamb and, 46–7, 52–4, 62, 68–9, 74, 86, 91, 149–52, 174, 201, 212
  literature of, 15, 47, 74, 85, 151–2, 152
  and manliness, 14, 23–4, 26
  and *Monthly Magazine*, 76–7

sensibility – *continued*
  Poems (1796) and, 56–7
  and radicalism, 18, 23–4, 37–9
  and self-indulgence, 37, 62, 66
  and Williams' sonnet to Siddons, 48
  Wordsworth questioning, 104
sentimentality, 25, 222n
'sentimental probability', 45
sexuality, *see* eroticism
Shaffer, E. S., 70–1
Shaftesbury, Anthony Ashley Cooper, third earl of, 35, 37, 38, 222n
Shakespeare, William, 168, 174, 179, 208, 209
  As You Like It (quoted), 201
  Elia in heavenly company with, 236n
  forged, 228
  Hamlet, 50, 172
  King Lear, 112–13
  Lamb on, 50, 179, 208, 209
  Macbeth, 50, 136
  Othello, 113, 172
  used in friendship, 172
  used as reproach, 112–13
Shelley, Mary
  Frankenstein, 129, 209
  The Last Man, 129, 235n
Shelley, Percy Bysshe, reading *Rosamund Gray*, 209
Shenstone, William, *Letters to Particular Friends*, 28
Shepherd, William, 76
Sheridan, Richard Brinsley, 21, 50, 56
Siddons, Sarah, 15, 47–53, 59, 60, 68, 126, 201, 202
Sidney, Philip, 77
Simmons, Ann, 54, 149
simplicity, 2, 23, 90, 91, 93, 114, 116–17
Smerdon, Fulwood, 228n
Smith, Adam, 45, 221n
  Theory of Moral Sentiments, 36–7
Smith, Charlotte, 147
  Elegiac Sonnets, 53
sociability, 5–6, 8–9
  and allusion, 6–8
  and Clare, 178
  deceptive forms of, 170

  ideal of, 55
  Lamb and, 8, 128, 141, 180
  literature of, 74
  and manliness, 23, 26
  narrative of, 9
  reading and, 73, 168, 183
  and Romanticism, 4–5, 8–9
  and sedition, 21–2
  textual, 168
  and Unitarianism, 33, 93
  urban, 5–6
  see also friendship; reading; Salutation and Cat tavern, London
Southampton Buildings, London, 185
Southey, Herbert, 156
Southey, Robert
  accused of 'Apostasy', 44
  The Annual Anthology (ed.), 86, 107, 134
  Coleridge and, 15, 20, 27–30, 34, 39, 41, 108, 110, 113–15, 137
  Coleridge explains the 'home-born Feeling' to, 35
  Coleridge parodies, 114
  Coleridge's sonnet to, 44
  desire to 'secede' from society, 66–7
  and *Edmund Oliver*, 111
  as 'false' friend, 44, 114, 137
  and Gillray cartoon, 1, 2
  and Godwin, 20
  'Hannah, A Plaintive Tale', 232n
  and *John Woodvil*, 168, 174
  Lamb and, 20, 150, 156, 168, 175, 182
  Lloyd and, 111, 123
  marriage, 27
  and *Monthly Magazine*, 76
  and *Osorio*, 113–14
  and Pantisocracy, 27–30, 34, 35, 44, 94, 123
  and *Poems* (1796), 55
  on *Rosamund Gray*, 156
  'The Soldier's Wife', 117
  'Thalaba', 196
  and 'This Lime-tree Bower', 107–8, 110
Spenser, Edmund, 1, 64, 77
Stabler, Jane, 90

Steele, Richard, 205
Sterne, Laurence, 45, 193
　Tristram Shandy, 25
Stoddart, John, 188, 189
Stoddart, Sarah, 201
Stone, Lawrence, 25
Stones, Graeme, 117
story-telling, 49, 68–9, 126, 156, 165
　see also narrator
Strand, London, 196, 197, 210, 213
Stuart, Daniel, 186
Swift, Jonathan, 1
　Gulliver's Travels, 194
Swinburne, A. C., 46
Symons, Arthur, 169
sympathy
　Burke and, 19
　Coleridge's negotiations with, 22–4, 42, 57–8, 95, 99, 106, 121–2
　Coleridge's parody of, 116–19
　and grief, 129
　Hartley and, 40
　Hume and, 36
　Lamb and, 58, 71–4, 85, 117, 119, 134, 150–66, 182–4, 193–4, 208
　Lloyd and, 117, 119, 124–7
　and reading, 166, 183, 194, 208
　revolutionary, 122
　and Romanticism, 45
　and sensibility, 36
　Smith (Adam) and, 36
　sympathetic identification, 47, 85, 126, 133–4
　sympathetic response, 17, 47, 58–62, 71, 72, 75, 76, 84, 95, 116, 184
　Wordsworth and, 104–5
　see also friendship; 'home-born feeling'

Tadmor, Naomi, 25
Talfourd, Thomas Noon, 2, 177
Taussig, Gurion, 25, 26, 34, 137
Taylor, Anya, 3
Taylor, Jeremy, 187
Taylor, John, 47, 49
Test Acts, 21
Thackeray, William Makepeace, 46

Thelwall, John, 5, 18, 20, 22, 41, 67, 76, 88–9, 90–1, 93, 97, 99, 102, 103, 108, 110–11
　'Effusion VII: on STELLA's leaving me, to Visit some Friends, at Hereford', 21
　Essay, on the Principles of Animal Vitality, 20
　'Lines written at Bridgewater', 110
　Poems, Chiefly Written in Retirement, 110
　Poems Written in Close Confinement in the Tower, 41
Thelwall, Maria, 111
Thelwall, Stella, 89, 103
Theo-Philanthropic sect, 1
Thompson, Denys, 2, 46–7
Thompson, E. P., 17
Thompson, Marmaduke, 149
Tooke, John Horne, 18, 21, 41
Toulmin, Joshua, 33
Treason Trials, 18, 26, 50
Tribune, 91
Tuite, Clara, 5, 6

Unitarianism
　and afterlife, 132
　and Belsham, 133
　Coleridge and, 16, 20–1, 29, 39, 43, 47, 66–7, 86–90, 91, 99
　and communicativeness, 57, 75, 202
　Crabb Robinson and, 26
　Frend and, 29–30
　and friendship/sociability, 15, 16, 26, 30–4, 42–3, 93, 134
　and humility, 109
　Lamb and, 3–4, 16, 20, 32–4, 42, 86–91, 102, 132–4, 135, 147, 181, 182
　Lloyd and, 96
　and *Monthly Magazine*, 75
　and persecution, 21, 29
　and sociability, 167, 202
　social position and practices, 21, 33–4, 75–6, 202, 216n
　see also Dissenters; Priestley, Joseph; radicalism

vanity, 8, 86, 92, 133, 154
Voss, Johann Heinrich, *Luise*, 89

Wakefield, Gilbert, 76, 120
Walker, Nigel, 84
Walton, Izaak, 150
The Watchman, 19, 43, 66, 75, 140
Wedd, Mary, 3
Whig Reform groups, 17
White, Daniel, 67
White, James, 14, 228n
Williams, Helen Maria, 48–9
  Julia, 39
  sonnet to Mrs Siddons, 48
  Wordsworth's sonnet to, 48–9
Wither, George, 150
Wollstonecraft, Mary, 75, 126, 220n
  Vindication of the Rights of Men, 39
  Wrongs of Woman, 1
Woolf, Virginia, 188, 213–14
  'Street-Haunting: A London Adventure', 213
Wordsworth, Dorothy, 102, 130, 139, 148, 155, 189, 192, 198, 210
  journal, 107–8
Wordsworth, William
  at Alfoxden, 102–3, 155
  and 'Ancient Mariner', 76
  and *Blank Verse*, 124–30
  critical views on, 4, 5, 6, 7, 16–18, 45, 101
  criticised by Lamb and Keats, 208
  exemplifying solitary bard, 4
  at Grasmere, 186
  and Helen Maria Williams, 48–9
  Lamb and, 5, 71, 91, 102–3, 103–5, 111, 129, 135, 136, 139, 145–6, 148–9, 149–51, 155–63, 175, 179, 182–4, 186, 188–90, 193–5, 195–200, 201, 203
  Lamb responds to 'Lines left upon a Seat', 102–5
  Lamb responds to *Lyrical Ballads* (1800), 188–90, 193–5
  Lamb's rewritings of, 195–200, 201, 203–4, 208, 210–11
  Lloyd and, 124–8, 137, 139
  and local attachment, 5, 190–3
  on mountains, 195–6
  at Nether Stowey, 100
  on poetry and prose, 199–200
  political views, *see* politics, Wordsworth and
  quoted in *Edmund Oliver*, 137
  quoted in 'Living Without God in the World', 135–6
  readings of Lamb, 210–11
  relationship with Coleridge, *see* Coleridge, Samuel Taylor, friendship with Wordsworth
  and *Rosamund Gray*, 145–6, 149, 155–63
  sends 'sweating' letter to Lamb, 200
  and 'This Lime-tree Bower', 105–8, 110
  and 'What is Jacobinism?', 182–4
  WORKS: 'Advertisement' to *Lyrical Ballads*, 179, 195; 'A slumber did my spirit seal', 129; 'The Brothers', 191, 192, 199, 204; 'Composed upon Westminster Bridge', 126, 210–11; *Essays on Epitaphs*, 162; *The Excursion*, 155, 196, 208; 'The Female Vagrant', 128–9; 'Goody Blake and Harry Gill', 113; 'I wandered lonely as a Cloud', 9; 'The Last of the Flock', 128; 'Lines left upon a seat in a Yew-tree', 8, 103–5, 113, 126–7, 134; 'Lucy poems', 129, 189–92; *Lyrical Ballads* (with Coleridge), 2, 4, 8, 101, 104, 123, 125–30, 148, 149, 160, 188–95, 199, 205, 210, 211; 'Ode. Intimations of Immortality', 146; 'Poems on the Naming of Places', 199; *Poems in Two Volumes* (1807), 211; 'Poor Susan', 238n; 'Preface' to *Lyrical Ballads*, 183, 184, 193, 195, 198, 199–200; *The Prelude* (1805), 161, 196, 197, 213; *The Ruined Cottage*, 103, 145–6, 149, 155–63, 190, 192, 203–4; 'Salisbury Plain'

Wordsworth, William – *continued*
poems, 146; 'She dwelt among th'untrodden ways', 189, 191; 'Song for the Wandering Jew', 160; 'Sonnet on Seeing Miss Helen Maria Williams Weep at a Tale of Distress', 48–9; 'Strange fits of passion have I known', 189; 'The Tables Turned', 163, 201; 'Tintern Abbey', 124–5, 125–6, 130, 160, 175, 182, 188, 192, 198; 'To a Sexton', 190–3, 213; *The Two-Part Prelude*, 130, 148–9, 189; 'We are Seven', 190–1; 'Written in Germany, on one of the coldest days of the Century', 198
see also Coleridge, Samuel Taylor; Lamb, Charles

Wu, Duncan, 188, 233n